MW00569272

Hoyden

Hoyden

a novel

ECW PRESS

Pamela Westoby

Copyright © ECW PRESS, 2002

All rights reserved. No part of this publication may be reproduced, stored in a retrieval system, or transmitted in any form by any process — electronic, mechanical, photocopying, recording, or otherwise — without the prior written permission of the copyright owners and ECW PRESS.

This is a work of fiction. The characters, incidents, and dialogues are products of the author's imagination and are not to be construed as real. Any resemblance to actual events or persons, dead or living, is purely coincidental.

NATIONAL LIBRARY OF CANADA CATALOGUING IN PUBLICATION DATA

Westoby, Pamela
Hoyden

ISBN 1-55022-504-9

I. Title.

PS8595.E74H69 2002 C813'.6 C2001-904076-8
PR9199.4.W488H69 2002

Edited by Jennifer Hale
Cover and text design by Tania Craan
Cover, interior, and author photos by Pamela Westoby
Centre cover image by Tony Stone Images
Layout by Mary Bowness

Printed by AGMV

Distributed in Canada by
General Distribution Services,
325 Humber College Blvd.,
Toronto, ON M9W 7C3

Published by ECW PRESS
2120 Queen Street East, Suite 200
Toronto, ON M4E 1E2
ecwpress.com

This book is set in AGaramond.

PRINTED AND BOUND IN CANADA

The publication of *Hoyden* has been generously supported by the Canada Council, the Ontario Arts Council, and the Government of Canada through the Book Publishing Industry Development Program. Canada

dedication

To Past — the ultimate storyteller and quintessential saucy girl.

You can tell a tale like no one else can, bending and molding the vernacular into an inventive and rich tapestry, and converting the ordinary into extraordinary. You inspire me to seek imaginative ways to paint my own parables and I can only hope to attain your command of the English language. So, thanks for mesmerizing me with fairytales as a youngster, for enriching our lives with your vignettes, and for providing such a wonderful example of creativity in expression. Most of all, thanks for being you.

Love,
Pres

acknowledgements

Jack David and Jennifer Hale Thank you for taking the time to read my initial manuscript, seeing promise in it and for believing in it enough to want to smooth out the rough edges. **Jack** Thank you for taking a risk on me and for laughing out loud at all the right spots. You gave me my start and I will forever be beholden to you. Expect my first born in a few years. Or at least expect for it to be named after you, even if it's a girl. **Jennifer** Thank you for guiding me through the editing process. As an editor and a friend you were always there to answer my bazillion questions and to quell my fears with diligence, patience, and humour — quite a feat considering what a freaky first-time writer I am. As an editor you do indeed complete me. As a friend you ain't so shabby, either. **Robert** and **Mary Westoby** Where do I start? Thank you for staying at The Regal Constellation. The planets did indeed align that night. In all seriousness, I cannot express my love and gratitude for your generosity, support, and wisdom. Thank you for always being there, for always believing in me and truly listening to me, for making me do my homework, and for always accepting collect calls. Lastly, thank you for instilling in me a love of literature, art, and history. Without you I literally would not be where I am now. **Jenny and Karen Westoby** Thank you for being the best "sibs" and for not picking on me *too* much when we were growing up. Even if you gave me stitches and taunted me about reading encyclopedias now and again, you're still the greatest sisters I could have asked for. **Michael Baldus** Thank you for being not only a great bro-in-law, but also a caring, loving husband to my sister. **Barbara Westoby** Thank you for all of your help and encouragement over the past few years (my entire life, actually, but specifically the past few years) and for sharing your love of cookies with me. You've always provided a wonderful home-away-from-home and I love you for that. **The Moreys** Thank you for opening your homes and hearts to me and for providing a much-needed Muskoka retreat. Your sense of fun, love of family and friends and constant generosity reaffirms my faith in the human race. **Amy Logan** Thank you for having the guts to become my handler/publicist extraordinaire. I've never done press before so I think you've got your hands full — your courage is to be applauded. But with your enthusiasm, vision, and expertise I know we'll have people screaming "hoyden" from deepest, darkest Peru. **Tania Craan** Thank you for all your hard work in deciphering my vision and translating the nuances of *Hoyden* into a fantastic and inventive design inside and out. The result is second to none. And thanks for choosing to use so many of my photos. I hope it means you have a great eye. **Wiesia Kolasinska** Thank you not only for ensuring that the i's were dotted and t's crossed in *Hoyden*, but also for writing my first fan letter. I'm definitely going to have it framed. Who knows, maybe it will be worth something on eBay some day and I can put my kids through college. In all seriousness, it meant a lot to have the first review beyond the inner sanctum of editor and publisher and I'll remember it always, especially because it was so glowing. **Mary Bowness** Thank you for all your type-setting magic, for making *Hoyden* come to life and for getting giddy about working on this project. **Dallas Harrison** Thank you for katching all mi mistax and for insuring that every coma waz in place. you make mi lok az if I culd actually surviv without spell-czech. **International School of Brussels, St. Joseph's Academy, and The University of Western Ontario** Thank you for providing an intellectually nourishing environment and for teaching me readin', writin', and 'rithmetic. I can honestly say that my educati on was exceptional and only now am I able to grasp how fortunate I was to attend such incredible institutions of learning. Because of you I know what I don't know. Coulda done without PE, though. **To ALL of my friends** (I don't want to name specific individuals in case I leave someone out. At any rate, you know who you are) Thank you for supporting me throughout this process, for listening to my babbling and laughing at my babbling, for buying me beer when I was broke, and for everything else that Hallmark says better than I ever could. **Henry David** Thank you for providing inspiration and grounding. Your words are my bible. **Paw-Paw** Thank you for being the best damn cat and quintessential companion. Wherever you are I hope you're happily shedding all over someone's lap. Keep on purrin', little buddy. I miss ya. **The Carpet Beetles** Thank you for helping me to keep it real. You sure know how to get a girl to clean out her closets. **Rabba** Thank you for always leaving the light on for me. And, last but not least, I want to thank my beloved **Heineken**. I definitely couldn't have done it without you.

winter

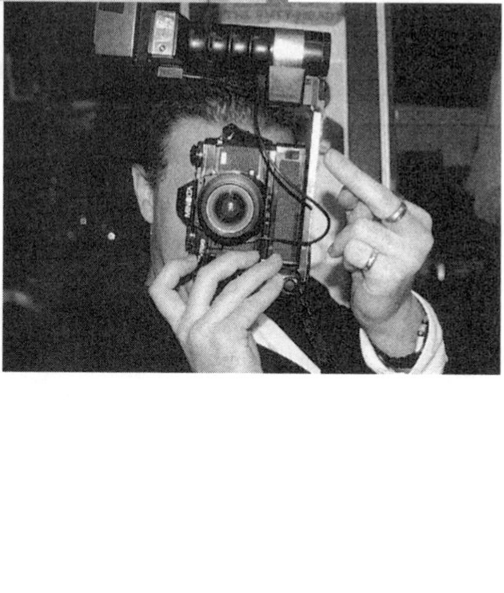

chapter one

Dawn in the city. Middle of winter. Look out window. Snow, baby, snow. Wool tights. Wool skirt. Wool sweater. Functional yet fashionable. Boots! Where are the boots? There they are. Wait. Where's the mate? God, it's dark in here. Shed some light. There it is. Pause. How did it get under the couch? No time to consider the possibilities. The inevitable has been postponed long enough. Check thermostat. Adjust another quarter inch. One last sip of coffee. One last bite of breakfast. Glance at job ad. A photojournalism job at last? Nab cv. Grab portfolio. Take the stairs. Gotta beat the masses. Glance through lobby window. Dawn sky. Speckled white. Whirlin' mounds. Winds whine. Take deep breath. Open door. Total ice-cream headache. Frozen breath. Frozen nasal hairs, and even more frozen cheeks. Cross street. Cross chest. Portfolio getting heavy. Muffled traffic whizzes by. Avoid churning salt and mush. Leisurely chats morph into harried waves and nods. The neighbourhood isn't as friendly in a blizzard. Gotta get the paper. Take off mittens. Fumble for seventy-five cents. The paper box is frozen shut. News isn't that important anyway. Too cold to walk. Indulge in transit. Rush to station. The subway's packed. The heat is overbearing. Too hot or too cold, take your pick. Unbutton coat. Take off scarf. Try not to faint. Almost lose balance on thawing ice. Try to avoid hitting guy wearing Castanza coat. One more stop. Flood gates open. Battle the way upstream. Go toward the light. Ah, fresh air. Drop a mitten. Nostril hair refreezes. Headache returns. Blonde coif windswept white. Cold air not so welcome. Mission almost complete. Credentials in arms. Fire in belly. Destination at last.

Hoyden Elevator doors open, twenty-seventh floor, please. Moving on up. Check look in mirrored walls. Try to pull ice out of hair. Doors open. Confidently stride up to desk. Raise portfolio, receive look of pity. Position's been filled. CV put on file. Better luck next year. Turn to brave the cold once again. Another day has begun.

chapter two

Abi had finally gotten off her ass and left her pad. That was one benefit of volunteering for the shelter — it forced Abi to leave the safe confines of her apartment and participate in the community. And it made her feel good helping others in need, even if they were only slightly better off than she. Seeing up close how others struggled kept her real, kept her honest, and put her own plight into perspective. Her trials were never as tough as theirs. Reaching the lobby, she noticed the super sweeping up the office. He must've been busy today, she thought, looking around at all of the holiday decorations up.

"Evening," she called, about to open the front door.

"Hi, Abi. Oh — wait a minute, I've got something for you." After rummaging around his desk, he rushed out to her, holding a little reindeer constructed out of pipe cleaners. "Just a little something my granddaughter made. Merry Christmas," he said, placing the trinket in her hand.

"That's so sweet! Merry Christmas to you as well. And be sure you thank your granddaughter for me, too. I wish I could chat, but I've got to get to the shelter," she said.

"It's going to be full tonight, what with this cold snap and all. I just don't know how you have the time to help. Bless you for it, though."

That man is too thoughtful to inhabit such a harsh landscape, she thought as she exited the building. She wondered where his kindness came from.

It was nippy now, and she buttoned up tight as she walked

down Isabella. The super was right — with these temperatures, the shelter would be full tonight. Waiting to cross Church, Abi admired the holiday cheer that had become so evident. It seemed that everyone had gotten into the act. Garish Christmas lights adorned the balconies. Fake snow was sprayed on the coffee shop window. Santas — or reasonable facsimiles thereof — reindeer, and elves were purposefully placed for all to see. The lights and decorations did cheer her. Abi adored the tackiness of it all. It was the white trash in her.

Doing the duck walk in the snow, she found it all so paradoxical. Here she was heading to a mission, a place where people didn't have a pot to piss in, let alone a mantel to decorate. Where was all the true Christmas cheer? Watching the last-minute shoppers scuttle past, Abi was nearly bowled over by their rush to consume. Whatever happened to goodwill toward man? Man, it's all about showin' me the money. And she wondered why she had become so disenchanted with the world.

As she made her way up Church, Abigail couldn't help but consider her own position. She had been in Toronto for almost six full months. When she arrived in June of '98, she figured that she would have Hogtown by the tail: she was going to get a job in journalism — either writing or photography — find a fab apartment, and establish herself as a true adult. She thought that she had her shit together and that it was only a matter of time before her humble plans came to fruition. At first she had let the rejection roll off her back, convinced that this was only part of paying her dues, adamant that she was going to make it. The rebuffs had been relentless, however, and she was on the verge of quitting. Maybe it just wasn't in the cards for her. She was sick of dusting herself off.

Reaching the church, Abi saw that a lineup for dinner had already formed. Smokers huddled closely together, and families huddled even closer. She entered through the service entrance and was greeted by Sam, the mission's coordinator.

"Howdy, Abi. How are you doin' tonight? Looks like it'll be a busy one. First cold snap we've had all year."

"It certainly is," Abi responded, hanging her coat up behind the door.

The program was held in the bowels of the church, away from those churchgoers who could possibly be offended by the inhabitants. God forbid anyone should be interrupted or disturbed by their presence. The program made do with the accommodations they had, though, and the spartan room always took on a pleasant, warm atmosphere when it was their night. The smell of stew, the children's games on the low table near the television, and the dinner chatter that ensued came together and made the place seem inviting.

The kitchen was a flurry of activity as preparations for dinner were being made. Soup was simmering, potatoes were being cut, tables were being laid in the small Sunday School-cum-dining room. A sign above the kitchen service portal proclaimed the rules of the shelter: no drugs, no alcohol, no smoking, no sex. Lights out by eleven. Lights on by six. The rules were more than lip service, and while the majority abided by them some did attempt to circumvent them. They were always shown the door. This was, after all, a place of worship.

"So what's the movie tonight?" Abi asked, grabbing a basket of rolls to take out to the dining room.

"Two if by Sea," Sam sang from the stove.

Abi was on the social committee, her sole purpose to keep people company. Here the homeless and downtrodden were never referred to as homeless or downtrodden; they were respectfully considered guests. Putting together puzzles, playing cards, lending an ear, or, more often than not, sitting and watching a PG flick, Abi had realized that she was there for the same reasons that the guests were. Indeed, many actually had a home to go to, they simply craved human interaction, someone to listen to and to confide in. A warm meal prepared by another never hurt, either. And Abi was seeking the same comforts.

They were all characters in one way or another. Some barely spoke, others nattered incessantly. For the most part, Abi felt safe here, but she was aware that the level of excitement largely depended on who had taken their meds that day. Generally it was quiet, though, and Abi never considered any of them to be truly harmful. Pulling up a chair, she waved to Gus in the corner. It made her smile how much her presence meant to them, and it was one of the reasons she kept on returning. Not only did she feel safe and welcome, but she also felt valued by them, and that made it all worthwhile.

Gus was one of her favourites. An older man who had fallen on rough times, Gus always had something sunny to say, some positive words of encouragement. He was just one of those people who screamed integrity, who was just honest to the core. Gus had just had a few too many bad breaks, that's all. Abi wished desperately that she could do more for him, but she knew she wasn't much better off than he was.

Dinner having been served, the patrons began milling about and staking their claims in front of the small television in the corner. Show time.

"Guess we should put the flick on. The natives are getting restless," Abi noted, placing a tray of dirty dishes on the kitchen counter.

"Yup. Time to get the show on the road," Sam concurred.

Grabbing the video, Abi made her way through the guests toward the VCR. There's certainly a crowd tonight, she thought, gazing back at Sam, who was chatting with a few stragglers who were almost too late for a hot plate.

A couple of kids, obviously siblings, were battling over a beat-up bear. "Come on, kids. Play nice," their mother wearily instructed, the fatigue and desperation blatant in her deep circles and furrowed brow.

"Okay, everyone. Tonight, for your viewing pleasure, we present *Two if by Sea*," Abi cheerily addressed the gathering. Grabbing the remote, Abi headed to the back and pressed "play." The credits beginning to roll, Abi dimmed the lights and found a spot at one of the back tables.

Abi was just getting into the flick when she noticed Gus making his way over to her. "Hey you," she smiled, conscious to keep her voice low.

"How are you doin'?" Gus asked, settling down in the chair next to her.

"Not bad. Not bad at all," she responded, munching a handful of popcorn. Man, I've got to learn not to talk with my mouth full. "Not much new to report," she continued. "Anything new with you?" she asked, wiping her mouth.

"Yup. Got a job today," Gus replied, sitting up proudly.

"That's fantastic! Where?" Abi could barely contain her excitement. She was pleased as punch for him. If anyone deserved a decent break, it was Gus. A few people, annoyed that their cinematic experience had been interrupted, whipped around and shushed Abi with the look of death. "Oops. Sorry," she mouthed sheepishly. Contented, the grumpies turned back to the TV and to the real drama. "So where'd you get a job?" Abi asked in a hushed tone and leaning in toward him.

"Place called The Trough," Gus replied.

"The Trough?" Abi exclaimed in surprise. What a tiny world. "I used to go there all the time when I was a student!"

"Yup. It's certainly a Toronto institution. Friend told me that they needed a busboy and hooked me up with the owner. Figured, hell, I used to own a bar, so bussing couldn't be that hard." He was the most humble man she knew.

"So when do you start?" Abi asked, grabbing some more popcorn.

"Tomorrow. I mean, it's not much, but it's something. At least I have a place to be now," Gus answered, sipping his pop and smiling. "And some regular coin."

"Well, congratulations," Abi proclaimed as quietly as she could. "Here's to brighter days," she said, raising her plastic cup in a toast.

"To brighter days," Gus concurred, gently tapping her glass in agreement.

Good for Gus, she thought. The winds of change are blowin' now.

The night before had gone well, and Abi had been momentarily uplifted by the experience. She had begun thinking about detailing the lives and experiences of the people she encountered at the program, of giving a face to the silent, working poor. People like Gus deserved to have their stories told, deserved to have people know that they weren't lazy junkies. It was so great that Gus had got a gig. Now if only she could find one.

Standing under the shower nozzle, all of the warm fuzzies flowed off her and were replaced by anxiety and despair. Reality was setting in. Time to exfoliate. Sponging herself from head to toe, Abi tried to relax, but she knew that it wouldn't do a bit of good. Her mood had already cemented itself for the day. Shrug it off, girl, shrug it off. Abi turned off the shower and stepped out onto the cool tile floor, shivering in the cool morning air. I really ought to get a bath mat, she thought. Wrapping the towel about her, she took a deep breath and sighed the sigh of the unemployed.

Reaching for the decrepit-looking blow dryer, Abi couldn't wait to feel its electrically charged zephyr. Switch on. Nothing. Switch off. Switch on. Nothing. What the. . . ? Jiggle the cord. Nada. Pulling a Fonzie, Abi slammed the damn thing down on the counter. Switch on. It didn't even fart. Oh, well, dry hair is overrated anyway, she thought. Thankful for her fashionably short coif, Abi moved on to the makeup phase. At least she had control over that. Two minutes later, she was done, save for her damp lid. Conjuring up some resolve, Abi tried her Miss America smile, but it didn't take. She looked and felt like a two-bit whore trying to be Heidi. But it was show time whether she was ready or not.

8 a.m. Sighing, Abi sat down to set the agenda for the day. Staring at the blank inserts in her daytimer, she couldn't help but feel useless and undirected. Man, I need a place to be in the mornings. It would sure be nice for someone else to call the shots and to have some structure for once. Flipping to that day's date, she didn't even know why she had one of the damn things. When in doubt, make up stuff. Let's see. Groceries. Laundry. Clean litter box. Scribbling the make-work errands, she began to feel a bit better. It all comes down to focus, she thought. Build it and they will come. Besides, her time as a famous journalist would eventually come. She hoped. Standing up, Abi reached and grabbed her coat, zapping herself. Damn static. Time to hit the road and start makin' some noise.

Opening the door to the apartment building, Abi shuddered. It was freezing. A layer of thick ice had formed across the driveway, and Abi gingerly shuffled toward the safety of the city's salt-laden sidewalk. Heat exchangers on the roofs of neighbouring buildings spewed out heat, forcing billowing steam clouds high into the arctic air. Her hair, not quite dry in places, began to solidify into small, downy chunks. Moving quickly down Isabella toward Rabba, Abi prayed she didn't look like a freak. And to think they had only nine more weeks to endure. At least the days were getting longer now.

The glass doors swooshed open, warm air flowing over her bulked-out body. Abi darted to the back of the store toward the magical money machine. Shoving her bank card into the slot, Abi prayed that she hadn't indulged in too much magic. Crossing her fingers, Abi punched in her PIN and held her breath. Please have one more twenty. Please.

Waiting for her numbers to come up, Abi picked up one of the transaction receipts from the top of the machine. She loved looking at the balances of strangers. Hmm. $2,147.14. Nice balance, buddy. Too bad it wasn't hers. Her own savings were drying up fast, and if she didn't do something pronto she'd find herself on the other side of the program. When the FOAD letters and bills had begun piling up, Del had suggested temping. Temping? Surely that's beneath me, she had thought initially. It just seemed so desperate and, well, *clerical*. A pseudo-wannabe-photojournalist answering phones and opening mail? It would be admitting defeat, which was difficult for a Leo like Abigail. Swallowing her pride was generally not on her daily agenda, so originally she scoffed at the idea and patiently waited for the cherry job at a national paper. But deep down she knew that Del was right. Besides, temping (a.k.a. prostituting) would keep her in the city and would expose her to a whole host of industries and contacts. And she could hawkishly take advantage of internal job postings once she was on the inside of some nondescript office. And, who knows, maybe it would lead to a permanent position somewhere. Tilting at windmills and drawing on a meagre savings account could sustain her for only so long.

Whirring to life, the magical money machine spat out four crisp five-dollar bills. Thank you, God. Taking her own receipt, Abi frowned knowing that it would be the bearer of bad news. Staring at her bank balance, she quickly recognized what necessity dictated: she'd have to sign herself over to indentured servitude. Abigail would have to make the call.

Hurrying back to the apartment, paper and bananas in hand, she wondered how straightforward the process of signing on with a temp agency would prove to be. Couldn't be all that involved. Entering the apartment, she set down her paper and breakfast and began her quest with the Good Book. Opening up the yellow pages, she found a slew of establishments peddling their human wares, offering them up like so much carrion. It was depressing in a white-collar sort of way. Propping the book up on her desk, Abigail closed her eyes and tossed a dart at her destiny. ACME Placement. She picked up the phone and grudgingly made the call. A perky woman by the name of Betty answered pleasantly, inquiring how she could direct her call. Almost stuttering, Abi didn't know how to begin.

"Hi. I'm interested in joining your agency," she managed.

"That's great. What kind of experience do you have, uh. . . ."

"Abigail," Abi completed. She hoped she didn't sound rude.

"Abigail. Do you have much administrative experience?"

That was a stumper. She should have considered that before she phoned. Bad Girl Scout, bad.

"Um, yes. A fair amount. I helped to set up the office at the store I used to work for," she responded, praying that it would suffice. Lord knew she had taken about enough rejection recently.

"That sounds fine," Betty said reassuringly. "You'll have to come in for an interview and take some tests. The whole process should take less than two hours," she politely explained.

Two hours? What the hell are they testing for? The CIA? Christ. And an interview. She *loathed* interviews. They were so demeaning. And her résumé was so pathetic. She really ought to embellish it.

"Sounds great. What time should I come in?" Abi crossed her fingers that there wouldn't be an opening until tomorrow.

"Well, if you'd like, you could come in a half hour. I think Sandra's available to test and interview you."

Great. Now she was going to have to either lie or give up on rewriting her résumé. Be responsible. Reach out and touch your creditors.

"Certainly. I'll be there in a half hour," Abi said.

"I look forward to meeting you, Abigail. See you soon."

A half hour. I'd better get motoring. Setting down her beloved coffee, she scooted to the bedroom. She didn't think she even had something appropriate to wear. What a pathetic selection of smart-casual. Man, I'll have to go shopping. Or call Mom. Perusing her wardrobe, she reviewed her responses and gathered momentum. Suddenly she was gripped with anxiety. She hoped that she had come off as professional and affable. Ah, screw it. If it's meant to be, it's meant to be. "At least I'm a little actress," she laughed to herself. She was a commitmentphobe. "This bites. I hope I don't get sucked into something très horrible, kitty," she said, glancing down at Paw. Paw was thoroughly ensconced on her only black blazer. "No, Paw, no. Shoo. Not today, not this morning," Abi screamed, snatching the jacket right out from under him. And she didn't even have one of those sticky roller things. Duct tape. Magic duct tape. That'll work.

Abi ran to the kitchen in her gitch and grabbed it from the utensil drawer. Stick, pull, stick, pull. Why isn't the damn cat bald? Pulling as much of the cat hair off as possible, Abi swore he knew when it counted. "Damn cat," she muttered. Abi continued her lesson in futility, making her way back to the bedroom.

Now the really tough part came. Light sweater or blouse? Skirt or pants? With the clock ticking, Abi grabbed her only black pants, her only suitable blouse, her recently defurred blazer and went for it. Checking herself in the mirror, she didn't look half bad. Not exactly polished but passable. Oh, to have an image consultant, she mused. Crap. The only bag that she had to match had definitely seen better days. Abi was so annoyed. She should have invested in that cute black purse instead of the Nike cross-trainers. Man, I'm sick of life being either/or.

Pawing through her front closet and coming up empty-handed, Abi resigned herself to the fact that the offending bag would have to do. Abi bent back down to pat Paw, who had come to check out the action in the hall. Some day, baby, some day I'll be able to afford both the pumps *and* the purse.

The office was small and bland, identified only by a tiny plastic sign stating ACME next to the frosted-glass door. Critically Abi looked around. Dropped ceiling and fluorescent lighting. Taupes and neutral tones. Particleboard shelves covered in rosy-hued laminate and fake brass lamps lent the reception area a doctor's office feel. Beige metal cabinets housed the lives of the hundreds who had preceded Abi in their own pursuit of the bourgeois dream. Approaching the vacant desk, Abi leaned over and rang the bell that sat patiently silent behind a neatly printed "Please Ring" sign. Holding her breath, Abi tried not to look too hesitant or nervous. *Please let me have made the right decision.*

A perfectly groomed head popped out from behind the wall. "Hi! You must be Abigail," the woman said a little too perkily, especially considering the hour of the day. "Please have a seat. I'll be right with you." The head ducked back behind the wall before Abi had even considered what she was going to say.

Decaf, baby, decaf. Alone once again, Abi silently scoffed at the cheap, stackable chairs. Who the hell "decorated" this place? Some people just don't have any flair. Okay. One. Little wobbly. Two. Unidentifiable stain. Probably liquid paper, but you never know. Three. Guess this one will suffice, Abi thought, selecting the middle chair. Setting down her beat-up bag, Abi searched for something, anything, to peruse. Great. No magazines. No *Globe and Mail.* Christ, not even a *Sun.* Don't they want an educated workforce? Abi reached into her bag and began reapplying her lipstick. What to do, what to do, what to do?

Waiting for the redhead to return, Abi figured she'd make use of the downtime and practised her interview responses for the umpteenth time. Check, check. Testing one, two, three.

Q. What related job experiences do you have?
A. [Easy.] I am a people person; each of the [joe] jobs I've held has pertained to customer service, either internal or external. Whatever position one holds, one must be able to deal with their coworkers and clients and be able to manage conflict effectively. [Blah, blah, blah.]

Q. Give an example of where you've gone above and beyond the call of duty.
A. [Less easy.] Um, ah, having a background in journalism, I'm accustomed to doing whatever it takes to meet a deadline, to get the story, or to get the shot. One time this entailed working in the darkroom until 4 a.m. to get a student election story out for the morning paper. [Um, pretty damn bland. Anyone can pull an all-nighter.] When I worked in retail, I traipsed all over my store selecting items for a paraplegic. [That will show my Good Samaritan side better.] In my hospitality days, I specially prepared a room — turning on mood lights, setting the Jacuzzi, arranging the flowers, adjusting the thermostat — for a regular guest. [Man, they're all so humdrum. May as well play this one by ear.]

Q. What are your greatest strengths?
A. [This is easy peasy.] I'm a perfectionist and very detail-oriented. I strive to do the best job I can at all times. For me, doing the best job I can is paramount, and I'll never leave a job half-done. [Needs a bit of work, but I can wing it okay. Just rifle through my repertoire of work ethic BS.]

Q. Weaknesses?
A. [See above, man. They totally expect it.] Sometimes I hold myself back by focusing on the details and not rushing a job.

Q. How do you feel studying liberal arts will help you in an administrative role?
A. [Duh.] Being a student of history has helped me to hone my skills as a researcher, writer, and analyst. [Just focus on the communication aspect and it'll be fine. Oh, and don't forget to bring up how it teaches the art of interpretation shit.]

Hmm. Hopefully she'd do okay. She just had to remember to throw in the requisite phrases and terms like "proactive, efficiently, hone, administer, and multitask." And anytime she could utilize "manage" would be a bonus. Manage expectations, manage time, manage clients, and manage duties. Manage this. What a load of crap. It's all so cheesy. Not accustomed to scrutiny or playing the game, Abi began to squirm in her seat, wiping her palms on her poly pants and rethinking the sagacity of her decision. Maybe she wasn't cut out for this after all.

Voices from behind the wall broke Abi out of her self-induced trance. "Oh, no. That's okay. I can test her," chirped a soprano.

The woman bounced around the wall and, approaching Abi, thrust her hand out to greet her. Reagan red nails. Nice touch.

"Hi Abigail. I'm Betty, the woman you spoke with earlier. Sorry to have kept you waiting. Why don't we go in here, and we can begin the interviewing process." Betty indicated the small, undecorated privacy room adjoining the lobby.

"That's okay. It's not like I have anywhere I need to be," Abi joked, trying to ease her own nerves. Crap. That sounded bitter. Mental note — be all sunshine and roses from here on in. Still on journalistic alert, Abi began straining to hear what was occurring behind the scenes and quickly determined that this was a testosterone-free zone. Do you have to have tits to work here or something?

"Did you want coffee or tea?" Betty offered.

"Oh, no, thank you. I think I'm caffeined out for the day," Abi smiled, sitting down at the tiny round table.

"All righty, then. Why don't we get started?" Betty smiled back. Abi nodded obediently and slid the only copy of her cv across the table. The starter pistol fired, and they were off.

Standing at the reception desk, Abi was beaming. She had been put through the paces on typing, Word, Excel, Power Point — programs she'd never used — but she was confident they had been impressed. She couldn't wait to find out how she had scored. It was like participating in some sort of cool psych experiment or something.

Betty rounded the corner, holding Abi's test results and also beaming. Grins are a good sign. "Well, Abi. You did fantastic. Your words per minute are on target, and your scores for the programs are exceptionally high. I can't believe you've never used Power Point before — you scored a ninety percent on it alone," Betty exclaimed, flipping through the results.

Cool. At least I know I've got a future in corporate slide presentations.

"I know. I couldn't believe how easily I took to it," Abi confessed modestly.

"Welcome aboard, Abi. I'm certain you'll be a fantastic attribute to ACME Placement," Betty announced, holding out her hand and welcoming Abi to the fold.

Phew. It is over and done with. She was now a temporary worker.

Waiting for the elevator, Abi discreetly checked her watch. Hmm. Two hours of dodging bullets. It certainly hadn't seemed that long. Abi exited the innocuous building grinning, exhausted yet triumphant. Totally painless. Strutting south on Bay to Bloor, Abi was pleased. She had navigated the seemingly relentless questions and tests beautifully, not even grazing one sandbar. And she had charmed Betty. She had run the gauntlet, and her future as a temp was now secure. The sun was now shining, and the cold appeared to have abated. Pleased with herself, Abi felt like commemorating the occasion, she just didn't know how. With thirty-seven dollars in the bank, she didn't have a lot of choice. Ah. Who needs to buy when the street scene is free?

Taking a right on Bloor, Abi decided to take the long way home to celebrate, her confidence and energy having been renewed by the entire ACME experience.

Pausing in front of Escada, Abi beamed at the ladies who lunched. Suddenly everything seemed to be within her grasp. She felt stellar about the whole situation. What had taken her so long to do this? What had she been so afraid of? Despite first impressions, ACME, especially Betty, was fantastic. It's going to be like having your own interview coach. Shoving her hands deep into her pockets to ward off the chill, Abi knew she had made the right decision. What a difference a risk makes.

"Hey, hey! Guess what I did today?" Abi taunted, knowing that Del would cream her pants once she heard the news. "I signed up with ACME Placement."

"Omigodthazgreeat! I'm so proud of you!" Del squealed.

"And it wasn't even that hard. Just went in, did my testing, and now I'm good to go," Abi explained, still glowing with pride.

"See? I told you there was nothing to be afraid of. And now you'll have regular money coming in, you'll be getting experience, and, who knows, maybe it'll even lead to a permanent position somewhere," Del gushed like a proud parent.

Now, now. Don't get ahead of yourself there. "One step at a time, babe," Abi reined her in. "Hopefully I'll start tomorrow, but I guess we'll have to see."

"Good. I'm going to take you out to celebrate. I'm so happy you finally listened to my advice," Del cried, now even more giddy than Abi.

"I know, I know," Abi conceded. Del had had a point. "Sounds good about going out, too. If I get a gig tomorrow, it'll probably be in the Core, so did you want to meet up somewhere down there?" She felt so cool saying "Core."

"Perfect. Why don't we meet at The Duchess at 5:30? You'll definitely be off by then," Del instructed.

"5:30 at The Duchess. I gotta be bright eyed and bushy tailed for tomorrow, so I should scoot, scoot. See you tomorrow," Abi said, anxious to get off the phone before her bubble burst. Sitting back on her dingy divan, Abi felt empowered. ACME. The Core. The Duchess. She was now officially part of the Working City.

chapter three

Slightly weirded out, Abi rose early, somewhat prepared for a day's work. 7:45 a.m. Plenty o' time. Betty had said to call in at about 9 or 9:15 for her placement. Showering, Abi tried to mentally gear up for what the day might hold. She had a new agenda, and it was strange to think that she was now somewhat beholden to someone else. Deciding to shave her legs, Abi half hoped she'd have an assignment and half hoped she wouldn't. A is for Apprehension. Being a creature of habit, she needed that buffer to assimilate to her new routine of actually working for The Man. After all, this was going to be her life for at least the next couple of months, and it was important to have the time to absorb her new reality. Completing her legs without a nick, Abi turned off the water and stepped out of the shower. Putting on her robe and looking about her tired, tiny bathroom, Abi shrugged. A is also for Affordability. Time to put my money where my mouth is. Time to play adult.

Pulling on the same outfit she had worn to the agency, Abi began boosting herself up. It was kind of nice to know that she might make some dough today. Maybe now she could afford some more film.

Applying her mascara, it dawned on her that none of the johns knew her and that the chances of ever seeing them again were slim to none. What a little treat for a little thespian. She could be whoever she wanted to be and portray any aspect of her personality she chose to portray. This temping thang could actually be fun, she thought as she continued to put on her face.

Confidence renewed, Abi floated out of the bathroom and

picked up the phone to make her first call to the agency.

Nervously dialling the number, Abi was giddy with expectation. She really felt like a call girl being dispatched on her first run. One ring. Two rings. Three rings. Abi looked at the clock on the VCR. 8:30 a.m. They should be open by now. Four rings — "Good morning, ACME Placement," a voice smiled through the receiver. Phew. Someone is there working to make or break my career.

"Hi there. It's Abigail Somerhaze. I was just wondering if any assignments have been called in yet," Abi said, her voice quivering slightly. Please God, now that I've made the decision, don't let me down now.

"Hi Abi, it's Betty. You're calling early. That's wonderful. I wish all our girls did that. Actually I just got a call from Generic Financial. They need someone to cover their reception for the day. Do you know the Nortel phone system?"

Uh, oh. "Um, I'm not certain. The assignment sounds good, though," Abi said, glossing over her inadequacies. Fake it till you make it, baby.

"That's okay about the phones. You're a bright girl, you'll be able to handle it," Betty encouraged. "The address is One First Canadian Place, 15th Floor. I think you know where that is. When you arrive, ask for Cecilia, and she'll set you up. She's expecting you in about an hour. Give me a call if you have any questions; otherwise, good luck and congratulations on your first ACME placement!"

"Thanks, Betty. I'll let you know how it goes," Abi replied, jotting the address and details on a handy Post-it. And I hope it'll be good news, she thought to herself.

The morning rush hour had hit without fail, and the subway was packed. Is this Tokyo or Toronto? Pissed at the lack of personal space, Abi tried to console herself. At least it was warm in there, and she was on her way to her first paycheque. Abi was riding the rails with the rest of the schmucks, resenting the fact that she couldn't walk. If she had to do this every day, she'd be as big as a cow in no time. Still, can't be late when it's your first day. Christ, every day is going to be my first day. This was her first assignment, and it was weird — unnerving and empowering at the same time. Abi was gripping the pole overhead and trying to maintain her balance and her composure. The train was jerking ahead, and her sweaty palms began to slip along the railing. Why don't they make these things for short people? Abi bumped into the suit next to her. The train slid to a stop, the doors opening to release a few of the hounds. A seat now sat invitingly open, and Abi rushed to commandeer it. Survival of the fittest, man.

Straightening her pants, Abi thought of the day ahead. It was a half hour before show time. Time to get into The Zone. She had two clear choices: she could view this as a totally temporary stint and not invest any energy or pride in it — you're there for the day, so why bother? — or she could maximize her one-day gig and try to parlay it into something larger — you're there for the day, so you may as well do your level best. Abigail decided to settle on the latter, preferring to go in, be perky, fill that void, and go home with a sense of accomplishment and pride. The last thing she wanted to do was jeopardize what could be a fantastic anthropological experiment or taint her chances for a more lucrative position in the future. Gotta give action to get action.

The train jolted, propelling Abi slightly forward. Must be a driver in training. Almost giddy with satisfaction, Abi didn't even care that she had almost spilled coffee across her lap. Roll, baby, roll. All right, we have some philosophical action happening. Now all we require is a suitable moniker. God, I'm such a label fucker. Temp Extraordinaire? No, way too fromage. Picture of Proletariat Perfection? Nah, too bitter. Super Temp. That's the stuff. Abi slackened her death grip on the railing beside her, smiling broadly with satisfaction. Another Abigail philosophy was born. She leaned back and, unlike the rest of the commuters, enjoyed the remainder of the ride.

Emerging from The Path via an escalator, Abi looked about her and, like a mockingbird, was instantly impressed by the glistening granite and glass. She had heard about First Canadian Place from Del but had never seen it for herself. So this is the Corridors of Power. With its sweeping high ceilings, young and old suits, and marvellously expensive shops, it was definitely something to write home about. Dad would love this, Abi thought, almost tripping as she reached the end of the escalator. Okay, pretend like *that* didn't happen.

Abi noticed the elevators and beelined for them, trying desperately to look as if she belonged. Reaching the call button, she glanced down at the Post-it. Generic Financial, 15th Floor. Fuck. These elevators only go to even-numbered floors. What nimrod thought of that? It was way too early for logistical thinking. Scuttling across to the next bank of elevators, Abi pushed the up button. She was beginning to perspire. Why do they have to crank the heat in these places? Sensing her crossover to anxiety and crustiness, Abi began checking herself. Super Temp, baby, Super Temp. The elevator arrived, and, deferring to the well-heeled, Abi squeezed on last. The doors closing, Abi used the two-minute ride to the sky to observe her fellow passengers. Not a one was showing cosmetically enhanced dental work. Christ, it can't be all that bad. One woman, who looked as if she had stepped out of a Holt's display, kept checking her watch. Cool your jets, chiquita, only sixty more seconds to go. The man next to her was a coronary waiting to burst, his neck bulging out of his collar. Loosen up, Jose, you'll be able to put your Golden Boys through UCC *and* Richard Ivey. Checking their progression, Abi felt herself becoming more agitated. Shit, it's catching. Eleven. Twelve. Thirteen. Phew, at last. The doors opened, and Abi disembarked from the Vator of the Venerated and stepped into Super Temp. Generic Financial, here I come.

Confidently striding toward the expansive reception desk, Abi put her pageant smile on and raised her chin proudly. A middle-aged woman sat dwarfed by the desk, trying to unravel the mystery of the phone system. "Hello. I'm Abigail Somerhaze. I'm here to see Cecilia," Abi spouted assuredly.

Looking up from the confusing panel of lights and buttons, the woman smiled with a look of relief. "Is she expecting you?"

Nah. I just like to go around asking for women named Cecilia. "Yes, she is," Abi replied.

"Have a seat and I'll call her for you. Would you like a cup of coffee?"

Say, are they always this kind to lowly day workers? "No, thank you," Abi said, lifting her Donut Hut cup. "I've already indulged." Abi took a seat on the sofa, admiring what purported to be real art on the wall. Nice joint. Not bad for my first gig. Certainly not bad for an office.

Another woman of the same generation as the first came trotting out from behind reception, accompanied by the frenzied phone woman. "Abigail! So nice to see you. Thank you for arriving so promptly as well. I'm Cecilia, and this is Sandra, although I believe you two have already met," Cecilia bellowed.

Whoa, kick it down a notch, babe.

"I'm so sorry I didn't introduce myself earlier. I didn't realize you are with the agency. I thought you were Cecilia's 9 a.m.," Sandra added.

Abi stood up, thrusting her hand forcefully out to meet Cecilia's. "Nice to meet you, too. Where would you like me to start?" Hmm. Guess that sounded all right. "I trust this will be my home for the day," Abi quipped, smiling broadly and indicating the cherry desk.

"It most certainly is," Cecilia replied. "I sure hope you're familiar with the phone system, because Sandra and I haven't been able to make heads or tails of it."

What the hell, it's a phone system — how hard can it be to master? "I haven't had too much exposure to this one," yeah, like none, "but I'm sure I can figure it out," Abi stated.

Cecilia and Sandra retreated into the back office, leaving Abi to her own devices. Stupendous. It was sink or swim time. Abi sat down and commenced her eight hours of waiting for the phone to ring.

10:59 a.m. Tick, tick, tick. The old-fashioned pseudo-digital clock rolled over. 11 a.m. Shifting in her seat, Abi didn't know how much longer she could hold on. Christ, she had to pee. That coffee had dripped right through her. Picking up the receiver, Abi was about to dial Cecilia's extension when Sandra reappeared from the back.

"Hi, I'm here to relieve you for your break," she declared unceremoniously.

There is a god. "Oh, thank you. One thing, where are the washrooms?" Abi said, a detectable note of desperation in her voice.

"Oops. Guess we forgot to mention that."

Yup, you did.

"It's back toward the kitchen. Let me know if you need to go again, and you can transfer the phones to me. Oh, and you get ten minutes in the morning, ten in the afternoon, and an hour for lunch. So has it been busy for you?"

Depends on your definition of "busy." "No. Just one call so far," Abi responded politely but shuffled her feet impatiently.

"Great, hopefully I won't muddle up again. See you in ten," Sandra said, giggling, as Abi raced toward the back. She hoped she had enough time to relieve herself *and* go for a smoke.

3:45 p.m. Only five phone calls all day. No other employees had even introduced themselves to her. Just queer, quick glances from those who belonged. Nothing to see here, folks. She wanted something, *anything*, to do. This was positively mind-numbing. Answering her prayers, the heavy frosted door swung open, and a suit sauntered in.

"Hello. You're not Tiffany."

Ah. The power of observation. "No, unfortunately Tiffany is ill today. My name's Abigail. I'm here from the agency," Abi said, standing up and grinning her best shit-eating grin.

"I'm Ned, the vice president of operations here at Generic," Ned said, puffing up proudly. Pink-cheeked and more than slightly bloated, good ol' Ned looked like a trussed-up pig. Placing a manila envelope on the high part of the desk, Ned looked paternally down at Abigail. "This needs to be couriered overnight. Do you know how to do that?"

No, asshole. I've studied physics at university, but I doubt that I could handle that. "Certainly," Abi responded sweetly, taking the envelope off the counter.

"Good. I knew you seemed bright enough," Ned said, turning to continue on to his little corner office.

Abi returned to her seat, yanking out a FedEx slip angrily. What does he take me for? A simpleton? Patriarchal dickwad. Completing the form, Abi counted the minutes until her daily sentence was complete. Only an hour and seven minutes left to withstand. Abi sat back and dove into the crossword. Again.

"Hello there, Abi. It's five o'clock. Did you need me to sign your slip?"

Rousing herself from a boredom-induced stupor, Abi nodded

and handed Cecilia her time slip. Five o'clock. Quittin' time. She felt as if she should be slipping out a window and down a brontosaurus's neck. Peeking over her bifocals, Cecilia dutifully signed the sheet and slid it back over the counter to Abi.

"Thank you again. It was a pleasure having you here at Generic. I'll be sure to request you again," she smiled at Abi.

What makes you think I'd want to come back? Abi thought. "It was a pleasure for me as well. Thank you for having me." God, I sound like such a conformist schmuck. Picking up her bag and coat, Abi waltzed back out the doors of Generic for what she knew would be the last time. Waiting for the elevator, Abi adopted a relaxed stance. She strangely felt as if she now belonged in the hallowed halls nestled between King and Adelaide. She could now truthfully declare that she had completed a stint at a financial institution. She was no longer a Bay Street virgin.

Reaching the entrance to the hallowed Duchess, Abi was giddy. Not only would there be a buffet of eligibles at this hour, but The Duchess would also be the perfect portal for an inside look. It would be like observing gazelles from the safe confines of a Range Rover. Full of moxy, Abi was confident that she could now walk the walk, talk the talk, and get the skinny on the power brokers.

Between Moby and Gwen blaring from the stereo, the cacophony of shoptalk, and the rich tableaux of ties, Abi could barely keep up with the stimuli. Rounding the corner of Golden Tee and smiling coquettishly at the young tiger of a driver, Abi was in anthropological heaven. Quenching her thirst here would certainly complete her initiation. Espying a gaggle of middle management downing Jaeger, Abi made a silent vow that she wouldn't imbibe to the point of diluting or blurring the experience. Then again, a couple of brewskies might just enhance the situation. It was Thursday, after all. Now where is that bar?

Utilizing her inner divining rod, Abi hung a left at the stairs into the loungier part of The Duchess. Bingo. Barely visible through the pinstripes, the mahogany watering hole was dead ahead, and Abi beelined for it, scanning the crowd for Del. Bingo again. Del was holding court by the bar, three gents panting patiently by her side. Legs invitingly crossed at her delicate ankles, Del had flirtatiously removed the top to her sassy suit, revealing her aerobicized biceps. She looked the bomb as always. She was giggling as her courtiers crooned, her chestnut hair glowing under the low light. Sauntering up to Del the Diva, Abi suddenly felt very shabby. The mix-and-match pantsuit from Winners suddenly seemed not to suffice. Some day, some day, Abi sighed, trying to appear confident once again. Besides, like my best friend will give a fuck what I'm wearing.

"Hey! How's it going, working girl?" Del called, raising a half-empty glass of Creemore with her American-manicured hands. "Come sit down," she ordered, patting the seat beside her. "I've been saving this spot for you for ages. Oh. And these darling men are Fred and Joe. Fred and Joe, meet Abi. They work at the station with me. Fred is my fantabulous producer, and Joe is one of our key grips. Abi is a freelance writer who is currently on contract at a financial institution down in the Core," Del crowed, squeezing Abi's less toned arm.

Exchanging vise grips, Abi was stunned. "On contract? In the Core? Man, do you ever know how to spin. Guess there's a reason why you're on TV and I'm not," Abi quipped discreetly in Del's ear, her pageant smile plastered across her face.

"It's all in the way you hold yourself, babe," Del replied with a wink.

Giving Fred and Joe a quick once over, Abi was pleased and relieved that Del had portrayed her that way, and she made a mental note to remember the spiel. They were both very doable, and any knowledge that she was just temping might short-circuit any potential. Unless, of course, they were into saving Cinderella. The night could prove very interesting indeed.

Setting her bag down on the floor and perching daintily on the stool, Abi turned and tried to flag one of the wenches. The bar was packed, and everyone seemed to be desperate for a drink. "Hi there," Abi began to call over the stereo. The woman with whom Abi *thought* she had made eye contact leaned over and served the chap right next to her. Christ, do my breasts make me invisible?

"Did you want me to get you something?" Monsieur X queried. "They're just a little biased here."

"Yeah, I noticed," Abi chuckled. "That'd be great. Heineken, please." Phew. Offering a fiver to the chivalrous gent, Abi tried to cop a better look in the dim lighting. Hmm. Too bad he's got a band. Still, at least now she wouldn't have to wait until last call for a measly beer.

"Don't worry about it. It's on me," Married Mr. X said kindly, handing her the beer.

"Uh, thanks," Abi responded. Wow. This place is rich in more ways than one. The last time some guy bought her a drink, he puked Purple Jesus all over her toga.

"So he was pretty cute," Del observed.

"And pretty married," Abi retorted, drawing heavily on her smoke.

"Fuck. Aren't they all, honey," Del stated resignedly. "Still, you got a free drink outta the deal." She raised her glass to Abi's. "Cutie at four o'clock. And he's comin' our way."

Abi glanced over at Fred and Joe. Phew. They were engrossed in their own spectatorship. Settling back onto the stool, Abi grinned at Del. Mystery Hottie was heading toward them, his exact course as yet undecided. Jostling through the crowd now encircling Abi and Del, he stopped dead in front of Del. Fuck.

Don't they always.

"Excuse me, but don't I know you from somewhere?" Mystery Hottie asked, obviously undressing Del with his baby blues.

"Probably," Del responded haughtily. "I'm a host on the Convenient Shopping Channel," she continued confidently, arching one eyebrow and striking one of her demo dolly poses. Total deadpan.

Man, she can be such a feline.

"Oh, uh, I thought I recognized you," Mystery Hottie stuttered.

"Yeah, I get that a lot," Del cooed, raising an expectant eyebrow. Well, how do ya respond to that? Mystery Hottie, looking more than a little befuddled, quickly turned his back and disappeared into the sea. Swivelling back to Abi with a don't-worry-there's-more-where-that-came-from kinda look, Del was completely nonplussed. She sure did know how to take care of herself.

Beers bandying about them, Abi and Del were in their element. "Here's to you and your first day of work," Del declared, raising her glass and gesturing to Fred and Joe to partake in her toast.

Abi grinned, revelling in her friend's encouragement. Del had been her best friend since university, and, like it or not, they were the toxic twins. Despite the inevitable hangover, Abi was grateful for Del for bringing her out of her shell and providing a foray into parts unknown. She sure did know how to spice up their lives.

"So how was your first day?" Del asked, swallowing the last of her Creemore.

"Pretty damn dull, actually," Abi replied.

"I know, I know. I hated temping when I first started," Del consoled. "But then I realized that I had a choice. I could either stare at the walls and bore myself to tears, or I could use the time to study and to map out my five-year plan. Progress always wins, my friend."

"Was there ever a time that you didn't have it together?" Abi wondered, laughing.

"Don't worry, sweetie, you'll get there, too. It just takes time. Remember, I've been in the city a lot longer than you have."

True enough, true enough. "Yeah, I know. I keep reminding myself of that. I was thinking I've got to start bringing a notepad and reading material to work," Abi said.

"Speaking of which, I've got something for you," Del cried. Reaching into her briefcase, Del pulled out a copy of *What Colour Is Your Parachute?* "This helped me so much in figuring out where I wanted to go with my life. I swear I wouldn't have made it in broadcasting without it," she continued convincingly, holding her Good Book and handing it over to Abi.

Christ, is she Miss Self-Improvement or what?

Sensing Abi's trepidation, Del continued her sell. "I know you're not into these things, but give it a read, if only to placate me." She looked Abi straight in the eye maternally. "It'll help, I swear."

Chuckling, Abi checked her defences. Their differences aside, Del did have her best interests at heart, after all. "Okay, okay. I'll give it a read. But only for you, man," Abi laughed. "Tomorrow. Now's the time for drinking in the scene," Abi joked, putting the book in her bag.

chapter four

Flipping through her daytimer, Abi was incredulous. Three weeks had already eased by, and Abi was amazed at how quickly she had acclimatized to her new groove. It was as if she had never been unemployed at all. A typical day now meant rising early, showering, dressing, and pretending like she had a regular job to go to. Make coffee, eat breakfast, watch the morning news, and wait for the agency to call. If 9 a.m. rolled around and she hadn't been dispatched, she took the proactive approach and called them. It was rare that the phone didn't ring, though. Her Super Temp work ethic had quickly worked its magic, and Abigail had become one of ACME's most sought after "girls." It had gotten to the point that her reputation almost guaranteed her a full week's work, she bragged to her friends and her parents. It was fab for everyone — they loved her, and she used them.

The gig was usually at a downtown investment firm or mutual fund company. Sometimes, if she was really lucky, she was placed at a hopping ad agency, chock full of young, eligible hotties. Those were the days that she came home with a sense of accomplishment, feeling that she had been rewarded for all the slogging she had been doing. Assignment in hand, it was check the wardrobe, pack the light lunch, and head out the door. The work was easy — stuffing envelopes, copying and collating, sometimes just sitting at a very quiet reception desk. She almost preferred those assignments. They allowed her time to observe, reflect, and collect vignettes. The best part was she always got her two breaks, a lunch, and always left at 5 p.m. on the dot. No worries, no stress to take home.

When the agency didn't call, Abi revelled in pseudo-unemployed slackerdom, enjoying the best of both worlds. She spent quality time with friends and always had a smile on her face and something intelligent to say. She had never been so up on current events, had never had so much time to think and observe. She had never been so alive. There was something so invigorating, stimulating, about being a casual participant in an office. No politics, no commitment beyond eight hours, no pressure. Something different every day. And she said when, and she said how much. She was in control. For the first time in years, she was confident, witty, and loving life. She was a beatnik with a bank account.

Temping provided her with fantastic opportunities to investigate companies and industries and to indulge herself and her amateur thespian endeavours. Being a social and now a professional chameleon, Abi had pleasantly discovered that, when nobody knew or cared who you were, you could be whoever you wanted to be. Relentlessly plunked in a variety of corporate cultures, Abi had become adept at moulding herself according to any situation, blending in for better observation. Sometimes she would quietly scrutinize. Other times she would fuck with them, betraying their faux friendship and pretending that she was something that she was not. She would never lie, of course. She was way too honest for that, but she would selectively omit details. Forgetting to mention that she had attended one of the best universities in Canada on an academic scholarship, for instance. Or not disclosing her true age when taken for a twenty-year-old. It was fun. It was a gas to play the young bimbette in the face of self-absorbed execs. And the best part was that they never knew she was making fun of them.

On the downside, one of the aspects of temping that truly

haunted her was the fact that she had never been paid to think. Not yet, anyway. And in that she was well behind her peers. While they toiled over analysts' reports and edited copy, making judgement calls and demonstrating knowledge, she was faxing and couriering. Not exactly highbrow. Abi couldn't help but wonder if this was all that she was meant to do. Throughout her entire "career," she had always engaged in menial tasks that required little or no brainpower. She was mortified by what she did for a living and shied away from talking shop with friends. What would she contribute that would be of any interest or relevance? It wasn't like she was attempting to eradicate world poverty or unravel the latest retrovirus.

Yet another disadvantage was less cerebral, creating more practical implications and hindrances. Despite having worked solidly for a few weeks, Abi was still barely eking out an existence. She had enough to cover her immediate bills, but she rarely had enough to spare at the end of the month to indulge herself or her passions, and she never had enough to tuck even a dime away for a rainy day. Having been surrounded by a financially successful peerage, Abi had begun to contemplate securing a permanent position, if even for ten to twelve months. The drones seemed to be content enough, so how much could it hurt? She had mentioned to ACME that she was looking for something more long term, and they said they'd let her know if anything came up. If only she could find a gig that would indulge her need for time, one that would allow her to interview, research, write, and do photos. Still, it wasn't all bad. She was making enough to get by, and, if she played her cards right, she should be able to catch a suitable fish and sock away some cashola yet. Time to move to the next level.

The stainless doors slid open, showcasing the floor-to-ceiling view of Lake Ontario from the pinnacle of T.O. It's show time. Abi sauntered over to the maple reception desk, trying to appear cool and confident. Trying to appear as if she fit in. Looking about the foyer, she knew this place meant business. Thank God Del had lent her some accoutrements. What was ACME thinking, sending her on a job interview to such a classy joint? "Yup, I would fit in here," she snickered. Standing prima ballerina erect and gracefully placing Del's satchel on the counter, Abi rang the little metal bell and awaited her fate. As if summoned by the queen, a hazel-headed PYT hurriedly appeared from the back room and approached the desk.

"Yes?" La Petite Noisette inquired with an arched, overwaxed brow.

Hmm. Perfunctory, aren't we? I'll see your eyebrow and raise you a smirk, you minx. "Hi. My name is Abigail Somerhaze, and I'm here for an interview with Josephine," Abi calmly explained.

Glancing down at the all-important appointment log, Noisette reddened and picked up the phone. "Josephine, your 9 a.m. is here," Noisette stated, barely finishing her sentence before placing the receiver back in the cradle. "She'll be right with you. Please have a seat in the waiting area," she instructed, marmishly gesturing to the moss green leather sofa near the entrance.

Man, this gal is just Miss Congeniality, isn't she? "Certainly," Abi replied obediently, suppressing the urge to bite her thumb at the woman. Left to her own devices, Abi began to check out the digs. Copies of the *Globe and Mail* and *National Post* lay on the maple end table, lit discreetly by a barrister's lamp. The walls, painted a pale, soothing green, were adorned by tranquil watercolours and gentle oils. A picture-perfect floral arrangement stood on the opposite end table, set off by the pot light above. It was way too quiet in there. It was worse than her gynaecologist's office. It was so *law*. The lack of stimuli raising her anxiety level up a notch, Abi began to gently wag her foot. Grabbing her daytimer from her briefcase, Abi pretended to occupy herself. Where were her judge, jury, and executioner?

Click, click, click. Sliding her empty daytimer back into Del's case, Abi looked up in the direction of the tiny, confident footsteps to see a woman, this time a walnut, approaching her. Saved by the stilettos. Beginning to rise, Abi held out her hand to meet Josephine.

"Hi Abigail. I'm Josephine. Why don't we take you into the boardroom," Josephine smiled in a soothing, matronly manner.

Do these people ever get excited? "Certainly," Abi replied, following Josephine the Exuberant into the adjoining conference room and taking the opportunity to assess the situation. Pin-straight hair, pin-straight suit, nude hose, and standard-issue heels. Not exactly what you would call an easy-going broad. Mental note — do not mention love of Hunter S. Thompson in interview.

Josephine turned on the lights to reveal a cherry-panelled Old Boy's Club-style room, replete with antique bar, brass appointments, and requisite speakerphone in the middle of the massive cherry table. "I'm sure that the agency fully explained our requirements," Josephine began.

Uh. Well. Actually they didn't.

"So this interview will be fairly brief," she continued, sitting down at one end of the table and indicating the chair opposite. Submissively following her silent order, Abi was all ears. "I see from your CV that you studied history. That's fairly typical of those who work in law offices, but did you happen to take any legal courses at all?"

Ah. That would be a negatory. "No, um, unfortunately I did not. But only due to the fact that so few electives fit into my schedule," Abi replied, already feeling sheepish.

"So what do you think you would gain from working in a law firm? What are your current career aspirations?"

Okay, I suppose freelance writer ain't gonna fly here. "Well, I've been debating going back to school for law, and this would provide the perfect exposure to the world of law, if even on a very cursory level." Josephine's beady blue eyes lit up. Good response, Abi, good response.

"Oh, really? The agency didn't mention that. What type of law are you considering pursuing? Corporate law?"

Bad response, Abi, bad response. "Um. Well, I haven't focused in on one exact area, so I'm open to it all at this point," Abi mumbled, trying not to look too much like an ass.

"That's fine," Josephine responded, looking slightly disappointed. "How are your research skills?"

Now this one's easy. "Actually my research skills are excellent. Studying history allowed me to hone my skills as both a researcher and a writer, and I'm quite meticulous about it," Abi boasted. Point one.

"Fine, then. Now I notice that you don't have much in the way of computer experience. Are you familiar with Excel and Access?"

Deduct point one. "Um, no, I'm not that familiar, but I'm a very quick study and a self-starter, so I hope that's not going to be a problem." Cool. Regain point one for throwing in "self-starter." They love that shit.

"Well, that may provide a bit of an obstacle. The majority of the work that you would be doing here is on computer. I also notice that most of your experience is media-related. What skill set do you think you would bring to a law firm?"

Good question, lady. That one wasn't in her script. "Well, the way I see it, my skills as a researcher and writer can be applied universally. Also, I'm very detail-oriented and deadline-driven, and I've got an incredible work ethic, or so I'm told," Abi stated, sitting proud as a peacock. Way to think on your feet, babe. Point two for "detail-oriented."

"As with most firms, the hours are often long and overtime, mostly on evenings and weekends, is all but required. Would this be a problem for you?"

Hmm. There goes the concept of writing in my free time. "Ah. Well, sure it's fine," Abi stuttered, looking down at her shoes and barely concealing the fact that it obviously wasn't fine.

Josephine set her number two down and folded her hands across her notebook. "Well, I suppose that's it, then. We've got a few more candidates to interview, and I'll let the agency know in a day or two," she curtly declared.

What? Did I fart or something? "Thank you so much for meeting with me, Josephine," Abi managed, gathering her belongings and rising to follow Josephine out of the room. Josephine, smiling politely in response, quickly ushered Abi out into the elevator lobby.

Exiting the firm, Abi knew she hadn't even come close to getting the job. She hadn't even offered her business card like Betty said she probably would. Her response to the overtime question had been the kiss of death. Through the glass doors, Abi made eye contact with Noisette, who was smirking knowingly at her. Even she could tell that Abi had failed miserably in her first professional interview. Pushing the elevator button, Abi was relieved that the interrogation was over. It was too creepy quiet there anyway. Interview number one down, God knows how many left to endure. Now on to the debriefing with Betty.

Abi slumped back on the couch, clicking on Regis and Kathie Lee. Cool, I haven't missed the trivia question. Relaxed, she was pleased with herself. Today she had decided to play a little hookie. No johns, no interviews. Just her and the day. Thank God I didn't get the gig at the firm. Picking up her map of Toronto, she considered what the field trip of the day would be. Hmm. The Conservatory at Allen Gardens. Poverty and beauty. Not a bad combination at all. A toonie and a dream. Gathering her camera bag and wallet, Abi realized that she hadn't had knots in her neck for weeks now. Of course, she had to watch how much she shot today — her bank balance dictated strict rationing of film — but the important thing was that she was out journeying, observing, and capturing her world on celluloid again. What a wonderful world it was, and she felt as if it belonged to her. Or at least Allen Gardens did for the day.

The park, covered in a dusting of snow and ice, was almost completely vacant. Timidly opening the door and wandering into the glass conservatory, Abi was amazed. She couldn't believe that she had never ventured there before. The joint was a frost-encrusted gem, a modest jewel plunked directly in the middle of the dilapidated Core. Not a soul was in sight, and the silence was bliss. Is this downtown's best-kept secret or what? Velvety greens arched overhead, straining toward the weak winter sunlight above, covered in condensation. A tiny yellow butterfly flittered down toward a fuchsia bud, ready for its noonday meal. Perching on a bench, Abi sighed contentedly. She could definitely live in the tropics. Caressed by the heat and humidity, Abi began removing her mittens and unzipping her jacket, gazing about at the turn-of-the-century architecture. Thin metal spires and glass panes latticed and bowed gracefully, creating a delicate umbrella overhead and thwarting the inclement elements outside. Ferns and flowers flourished and spired in all directions, drinking in the gentle mist. The tranquil sound of water lapping from one of the fountains relaxed Abi further. Ah, solitude. Now *this* is Walden.

Closing her eyes, Abi tried to imagine the gardens in their heyday. Visions of Gilded Age lovers strolling about came to her mind, and Abi revelled in the romance of it all. Women, genteelly adorned with parasols and nosegays, risquély raised their skirts above their ankles, blushing coyly. The gentlemen, discreetly noting the invitation, held out an arm. Using their canes as pointers, the men proudly displayed their knowledge of horticulture while the women listened in awe, enraptured by their beaux and marvelling at the exotic beauty. It would've been a local attraction, bringing the foreign flora to the Victorian masses. A marvel of modernity in the middle of the metropolis.

Stomp, stomp, stomp. The sound of footsteps on the cold, hard concrete snapped Abi back to reality, and she turned to see a homeless man heading into the rear greenhouse. So much for solitude. "Thoreau he ain't," Abi quipped to herself, focusing on a shot of a large blossom. Today's challenge is nature photography, Abi reminded herself, and not a lesson in history. Moving down the path toward the rear, Abi found herself stopping every other foot to shoot. The place was positively rife with photo ops. It felt good to shoot something new. Practically racing from plant to plant, Abi was shooting everything in sight. Fuck her celluloid rationing. There was too much eye candy to be had there. Abi was ecstatic, not only because of the subject matter, but also because she had uncovered the gem all by her lonesome. Now this was an urban adventure. Disregarding winter outside, Abi quickly lost herself among the potted plants and cascading boughs. This morning she was on a safari.

Having depleted the flora and fauna of the park, Abi decided to be really spontaneous and venture out of her 'hood. Where to go, where to go? Traipsing down Jarvis to King, she felt like such a rebel. Time to ride the rails, man. Reaching King and hopping on the streetcar, she began her magic Rocket Ride. Observing the changing streetscapes, Abi was elated. Man, I should do this more often. Who knew there was a whole city out there? Clattering down King, the streetcar skittered past the dark façade that dominated the block. It was The Trough. It had certainly stood the test of time. It had stood proudly on its corner for more than three-quarters of a century, frequented by hookers and financiers alike, albeit during different decades. It had seen it all. In its modest, early days, it was simply a neighbourhood pub, owned by a single man. As his family and his profits grew, The Trough blossomed, cresting the '20s, surviving the '30s, and decimating the '40s. Even when Toronto was Good, it had been a fashionable place to see and be seen. Joints peppered around it had come and gone, but The Trough had steadfastly remained. Abi grinned, recalling The Trough not as an establishment of grandeur but rather as a holding pen for the club adjacent, a joint that had been kind to drunken minors. The club, which Abi could no longer name, had long since changed hands, looks, and clientele, but The Trough had remained tried and true. The seasons had weathered it, and it looked a bit battered in the winter light, but it was undoubtedly a permanent fixture. What a blast from the past. The trolley trundled by, and Abi continued her journey westward to Roncesvalles.

Rumbling along King past the Core and slicing through the garment and entertainment districts, the trolley travelled toward the residential reaches of the city, slowly snaking down the narrowing street and through the ever-thickening traffic. Massive, old warehouses lined both sides of the street, replacing the glistening new skyscrapers of The Street and rising four and five stories above ground level. The Corridors of Power had become the Foundries of Fashion. Runners dragged racks of rags to sample sales, budding young designers nipped into funky fabric stores, models scampered on go-sees, and yuppie couples scrutinized rock-bottom lofts. It was a whole new ball game here.

Several blocks past Bathurst, the landscape morphed once

again, the ominous brick buildings having transformed into working-class homes and small businesses. Zipping past storefront upon storefront, Abi was excited and stimulated by the sights and sounds of the community. It was like an entirely new city, honest, hard working, and full of integrity. Despite the snow and slush, bins cascaded from consignment shops, bookstores, and vintage joints, creating a tactile tapestry of shoes, books, and clothing. Pedestrians bustled about, carrying their afternoon shopping and partaking in the bounty of the avenue. Blue-haired ladies ventured out of salons, and yummy mummies wandered into their luncheon destinations. Abi decided to get off the streetcar and hoof it the rest of the way home. Antique shops, cafés, dollar stores. It was all at her feet. Smiling, Abi relished the normalcy of it all. Her tummy beginning to rumble, Abi removed her mitt and glanced at her watch. Hmm. 2 p.m. Well past lunchtime. Pulling out her map, Abi located her coordinates and realized how close she was to Kensington Market. She could walk there on her way home instead of TTCing it the whole way. Mmm. Fresh produce. Leaning over and taking her wallet out of her knapsack, Abi frowned. Ten bucks. Definitely not enough to splurge on a delectable dinner. Guess it's brown rice for supper again. Slightly dejected, Abi rang the bell and prepared to disembark for her return home. "Thank you," she called to the driver, smiling and hopping off the tram.

Crossing King to catch the eastbound, Abi was content. Life was pretty good, she had to admit. Sure, she may not be able to blow dough on exotic cheeses and out-of-season veggies, but at least she was creative. And, hey, she figured when she got to the shelter tonight she'd be reminded why those things weren't so important.

chapter five

The music was pulsing, and the suits were dancing. Ah. Saturday night at The Courthouse. What a treat. Sweaty, successful, and, above all, Beautiful People inhabited every square inch of space and writhed to the beat of the "alternative" rock. After knocking back some liquid courage, most of the young professionals were reeking of desperation. They were seeking a merger of a different kind. Doubles, anyone? Triples, even? Like a dense and decadent gateau, Abi found the scene to be at once appealing and nauseating.

She tried to move to the bar, but it was futile. Old boys in training had commandeered every square inch to indulge themselves in Jaegermeister, tequila, and old fraternity shenanigans. Their ties hanging slovenly from their chubby necks, they had shed the appearance of golden boy on the up and up in favour of rake on the slippery, mucho-lubricated slope. They were practising to be sponges. So this is how they blow their expensively tuned brain cells. Wine, women, and song. Original, guys, original.

Frustrated, Abi jockeyed closer and more forcefully toward the watering hole. She was revolted. If they didn't start serving faster, there'd be a stampede. Or at least there should be a stampede.

"Excuse me," she shouted over the bass.

A body turned to face the offending sound. "Well, helloo there," the suit said. Had he been sober, the ass wouldn't have been that bad-looking, attractive almost, but the beer goggles framing his face did nothing to flatter his mediocre appearance. Abi waited for the pickup. One, two, three, four. . . . "Can I interest you in a shot?"

the gentleman offered, holding out a shot glass and spilling half the contents down the front of his Hugo blazer. Five seconds. Not a bad record at all. Had his charm not been so saturated, it would have been flattering.

"No thanks. Heineken only for this damsel," she replied, suppressing the urge to laugh at him.

The ass moved out of the way, indicating a path to the bar. "At your service, madam."

Madam? Hey, buddy, that's your problem right there. If you really want to get lucky, don't call women "madam." "Thank you," Abi mouthed, having given up on competing with the DJ. Somewhat satisfied now that she was at the bar, Abi wedged herself between two brats, one female and one male, and attempted to make herself as compact as possible. Receiving a jolt from behind, it obviously wasn't compact enough. And Del wondered why Abi loathed crowds.

Feeling the jolt a second time, Abi decided to find out who was chomping at the bit. The face behind her was beaming in the dim lighting. It was Eddy, an old frat buddy of one of her ex's. Great. What a stupendous blast from the past. "Eddy! Fancy meeting you here," Abi very fakely cried. She really had to work on her delivery. Thankfully the music was too loud for tonality to transcend.

"Howdy! Long time no see. I didn't know you were in T.O. How long have you been here?" Eddy asked, trying to edge surreptitiously closer to the bar.

Once a user, always a user. "Oh, a few months. What are you up to now?" Abi eyed the bartender, refusing to be usurped by Eddy's advantageous position. The attentive servers were still consumed by thirsty throngs at the other end of the bar.

"I'm a trader at Nesbitt now. How about you?"

Crap. The cross-examination. I really ought to have thought

out my current line of questioning. "I'm a freelance writer," she responded. Cognizant that this would wind up getting back to Mr. X, Abi was trying to sound as confident and professional as possible.

"That's awesome. Where have I seen your work?"

D'oh. More cross-examination. Abi looked down into her empty bottle and shrugged casually. "Um, nowhere, *yet.* I'm still pounding the pavement, though I haven't given up hope yet." Abi couldn't wait until she had a better answer for that. Que sera. At least she looked good.

"Well, what kind of work do you focus on?" Eddy smiled encouragingly.

"Mostly nonfiction. Documentary photojournalism stuff." Abi looked nervously over at the bar. The wenches were gradually moving closer.

"Say, that sounds great. I'd love to hear more about it. What's your e-mail address?" Eddy asked.

"I don't have e-mail yet," Abi shyly stated.

"No e-mail? How can you live without e-mail?" Eddy said, dumbfounded.

What a twat. "Very easily. I just don't see the need for it at present. It only perpetuates the disconnect between man and his community and decreases the value of interpersonal interaction," Abi responded defensively. (She'd rehearsed that one.) Why do people always have to react that way when I say that?

"What can I get you?" a voice boomed from the other side of the bar.

Saved by the bartender. "Um. A Heineken. Bottle," Abi quickly requested, looking at Eddy to see what she could get him at the same time.

"Same for me," he said.

The bartender trotted off to retrieve their order. Watching the server gingerly sprint and lunge toward the fridge, Abi was amazed with the speed and endurance required for the position. Thank God they're too swift for us to resume our conversation, she thought. The bartender returned and, snapping off the caps, gave them the damage.

"That'll be $9.50," he said.

Time to face the music. Abi was relieved that she had a bill for once. Eddy didn't have to know that it was her last twenty bucks. As she pulled the wallet from her purse, Eddy placed his hand over hers.

"Let me get this one," Eddy said.

God, I must have poverty written across my forehead. Thank you, Trader Boy. Abi picked up a bottle and handed it to Eddy. "Thanks. I owe you one," she yelled over the music. She just hoped that she wouldn't have to owe him tonight.

"My pleasure. Here's my card. We should get together sometime."

Abi took his card, glanced at it, and smiled back at him. "I'd give you mine, but they don't give out your freelance cards until you've 'made it,'" she joked, making little quotation marks with her fingers. "I should go find my friend. Thanks again for the drink. I'll call you sometime." She leaned over and gave Eddy a fashionably quick embrace, then shuffled out of formation, giving Eddy a coquettish little wave good-bye. Time to track down Del. But first, pee break. She headed for the washroom line.

"Have you been waiting long?" Abi inquired of the beautifully accessorized blonde ahead of her. Is that a real Kate Spade? The blonde looked down her narrow Barbie nose, obviously not knowing what to make of such an intrusion. Nice rhinoplasty.

"No. Just a couple of minutes," she responded slowly and tentatively.

"Good. My name's Abi. What's yours?" And the games begin.

"Mitsie," she said definitively.

"Mitsie. That's a nice name. Is that your given name or just a nickname?" God, I love fucking with these people.

"My real name," Mitsie responded, too stoned to feel Abi's barb.

Don't worry doll, we're laughing near you, not at you. "So, Mitsie. What do you do for a living?" Abi quickly put her money on event planner or image consultant.

"I'm in IR. What do you do?" Poor Mitsie's back, straightened from a tragic yet mild case of scoliosis, was up against the wall.

Hmm. IR. Studying Mitsie's very blue and very glazed eyes, Abi was surprised. Mitsie didn't look swift enough for IR. Then again, fathers do have a tendency to pull strings for their darling daughters.

Recognizing how what you did was who you were in this city, she had decided to conduct a little covert experiment and have fun with the dinkerrati. At cocktail parties, she'd say one of two things: either she'd say that she was an artist, which garnered a very positive, intrigued reaction and prompted questions from the butterflies, or she'd bluntly state that she was unemployed, which did not go over as well. A horrified look would cross over the butterflies' faces, as if she had just told them that she had run over one of their dogs in the parking lot. Feet shuffled, silence ensued, and, like moths that had just been zapped, they bolted on to the next bulb. Very amusing indeed.

"I'm unemployed," Abi stated. Check.

"You don't have a job? You poor thing. What do you do all day?" Mitsie stood up as erect as she could in her condition, utterly aghast. "I would be bored to tears. Positively bored to tears," she continued, completely unaware that her tone was drenched in a sickly sweet concoction of sympathy and condescension. The bathroom door opened, and two X-rays tumbled out, a little too full of holiday cheer. As if sensing a Level Four, Mitsie lurched at the door, taking the opportunity to disengage herself from Abi, the pathetic, underachieving waif.

Abi leaned back, triumphant. Her guinea pig had reacted just as she had hypothesized. Posit and they will conform.

As if heeding a silent call, Del appeared just as Abi was making her way back through the crowd, drunk but still looking fabulous. Does this woman *ever* look bad?

"So, what do you think? This place is happenin', eh?" Del screeched over the cacophony.

"It's amazing. Kinda expensive, though, eh?" Abi responded, trying to sound enthusiastic but feeling awkward among the upwardly mobile. Running into Eddy had certainly left her feeling a little shaken, not stirred. Looking about at the fashionista fillies and caddish colts, Abi wasn't so sure she belonged. Glancing down at her vintage jacket and pants, she suddenly sensed she had made a bad fashion decision. What had seemed funky and fun at home now seemed worn and wayward at the club.

"Don't worry, sweetie. I've got it covered," Del reassured maternally, cognizant of Abi's precarious financial status. "Next time you can treat me." Sensing Abi's drop in self-esteem, Del steered them toward a quieter corner for a pep talk. "Look. I know it's hard starting out in the city — no one has a good time of it their first year of working here. But bear with it. Everything will turn around, you'll see. Soon you'll be buying new clothes, going out for dinner, courting some young buck, and all of this will seem like a bad dream," Del yelled over the music.

"I know, I know. It's just that I feel so out of synch with it all. I mean, I don't know anything about business. I don't know anything about advertising. I don't know anything about computers. I don't even have e-mail, for God's sake. All I know is writing and photography, and these people don't seem to appreciate or understand that too much." Abi's voice began to quiver. Whoever said there's courage in a bottle certainly got it wrong. "I feel like I'm from Mars or something," she continued, taking a big gulp of her beer.

"Look," Del began, placing her hands on Abi's shoulders and looking her squarely in the eye. "You'll be fine. You'll learn about business. You'll pick up what you need to know about computers. Just take some courses like I did. Play around on your computer at home. Apply yourself and be patient. Rome wasn't built in a day, you know that."

"Sure, that's dandy if you've got the cash for courses," Abi countered, setting her empty bottle on the amp and feeling a little annoyed and envious. Del always had a plan, a focus, a raison d'être.

"Now, now. Don't be such a naysayer. Okay. So you can't afford the right classes right now. That'll come soon enough. Hell, once you get a full-time job, they may be willing to pay for them. But in the meantime, there's a ton that you can teach yourself. There's the Reference Library. There's always the Internet. You just have to seek out the resources, that's all. I taught myself Spanish that way, you know, which helped me get my job at the station. Speaking of which, have you read *What Colour Is Your Parachute?* yet?"

Busted. "Um, no. It's just that I've had so much to do recently. What with the temping, my writing and photo, volunteering. . . ." Abi trailed off, hoping Del wouldn't rake her over too much.

"Tsk, tsk, Abi. You really have to focus and prioritize more," Del admonished. "I've got a great book on time management, too."

Nice segue. Abi stared at her empty beer, trying not to look pissed. Del just doesn't get it.

Feeling even more junior than before their chat, Abi tried to buck up as she followed Del to the bar. That was a poopy conversation. She hated it when their differences were so apparent, when their approaches to life and passion were laid bare. Still, Abi knew that Del's intent hadn't been malicious. Del was trying to help in the only way she knew how.

"Oh, look! There's Eddy!" Del cried, waving at Eddy as he approached the duo at the bar and handing Abi her beer.

"I know. I've already chatted with him," Abi cried back.

"Hi, gals. How are we doing now? Oh, I see you've found another person to fund your habit," he said, ribbing Abi. "Lucky duck to have such generous pals," Eddy smiled, pointing at Del paying the bill.

Pardonez moi?

"Now, now. Remember what it was like when you were just starting out in the Core," Del answered protectively.

Crap. La jeu son fait. This is *so* getting back to my ex.

"Working in the Core? I thought you were freelancing?" Eddy said, looking taken aback and confused.

"Freelancing?" Del queried, shooting Abi a puzzled look. "You haven't freelanced in ages."

Fuck. Nicely done, Benedict Arnold. "Um. Well, I'm actually temping in the Core right now," Abi explained, completely mortified that her cover had been blown. "I guess you could say I'm freelancing in a sense." So much for faking it till you make it.

"Oh. I see. Um, well, I guess you gotta eat somehow," Eddy responded, trying not to show his disappointment. "Well, listen gals. I gotta get back to my friends. Good luck with work and hopefully I'll see you around," he called, turning his back and disappearing into oblivion.

Abi wanted to kill Del. How could she have betrayed me like that? Especially after the damn rah-rah-rah she just gave me. For someone who's supposed to be quick on her feet, she's a little slow on the take. Abi turned to Del, about to chew her out. "Thanks so much," Abi seethed.

Del put her hand on Abi's shoulder, looking as embarrassed as Abi felt. "I am so sorry. I didn't know," Del implored, looking suddenly like a shamed doe in the spotlight.

Seeing Del's honest look of apology, Abi decided to let it drop. Del hadn't meant any harm. "That's okay. It was dumb of me to say, anyway. Next time just play along, though," Abi said, accepting her apology but relishing the fact that Del had actually slipped up. "Fuck it. Let's drink to honesty," Abi said, raising her glass and trying to laugh it off. She was just going to have to learn to play the game better.

4:30 a.m. Her room was dark and cold. Abi cuddled up next to Paw, who was purring away on the pillow beside her. Trying to combat the bed spins, Abi was haunted by what Del had said. Maybe she was right. Maybe I do have to grow up sometime. God knows my parents have been hounding me for ages to settle down. Abi had never been one to toe the party line, to abide by the rules. She simply didn't understand how she could compromise her being for a stupid paycheque. A wave of nausea hit her, and she beelined for the bathroom and aimed for the toilet bowl.

Peeking out from under her eye cover, Abi instantly knew by the grade of light that it was way late. Rolling onto her stomach to check her alarm clock, Abi was filled with toxins and trepidation. 9:00 a.m. Falling back to sleep can be such a blessing and a curse. On the upside, her I've-definitely-got-a-tumour headache had been quelled to a mere throbbing of the temples. Abi delicately sat up, testing to see if she could cope with an erect position. As if she didn't feel poor enough, Abi caught sight of her wallet, which had somehow made its way out of her handbag and onto the floor. Fuck, I blew so much dough last night. The sight of her empty billfold and visions of the evening's shenanigans left her feeling drained and much, much poorer than she actually was. What on earth had possessed her to think that she could live as Del did? Abigail had always considered herself to be a member of the impoverished nobility. Classy yet flat broke. She had breeding, certainly. Just not a liquid bank account. More importantly, Abi had her pride. She was decent, honest, and making her own way. So what if she couldn't afford Gucci or Prada? At least she wasn't compromising herself in the pursuit of a Kate Spade handbag.

Unfortunately, it was becoming increasingly difficult to maintain this façade, and it had come to the point where Abigail hated the political and materialistic sides of the city. She felt as if her values were being challenged and rocked to the core daily. It was never who you were and what you stood for but what you did and what you wore. Never what you brought to a relationship but what you could take. It was never the fibre of your being that was scrutinized but rather the cashmere threads of your Armani jacket that were duly noted. Toronto was always benchmarking where you stood within the gang. It was reading the paper to glean a quick quip to be tested at a cocktail party. It was corresponding with people because they could get you that promotion or get you onto that committee. Toronto was so utilitarian in that regard, and Abi was growing increasingly cynical as a result. Mental note — live *vicariously* through Del next time.

Paw, desperate after a full hour with an empty food dish, crawled on top of her stomach. He always knew the right buttons to push. Or at least the right parts of the anatomy. Getting out of bed, Abi groaned and gave the famished feline the most loving pat she could muster. God, just let me get to the bathroom.

Conjuring up just enough energy, she shuffled to the bathroom and checked her look in the mirror. Jesus, I look old. Brushing her teeth, Abi tried to wish her hangover away. She glanced at the shower and thought the better of it.

Slowly she moved into the kitchen and yanked open the fridge. Peering into the cavernous white interior, she quickly thought the better of breakfast. What to do, what to do? What to do to exorcise this headache? Foggily recalling that she hadn't even touched yesterday's paper, Abi slid over to the couch, not even bothering to lift her feet. Perusing the paper was definitely doable. Maybe.

Hmm. Business or pleasure first? Pleasure. Reaching for the paper, Abi smiled contentedly for the first time that morning. There was something about reading the Saturday *Globe* on Sunday morning that always cracked her up. Opening the paper, Abigail was stunned. Her trusted friend, her morning sunshine, had succumbed to society's wishes and had employed the use of a so-called gossip columnist. Et tu, venerated publication, et tu? Yet another fallen comrade. Abi felt betrayed. She had applied to the *Globe* countless times, and countless times she had been rejected. No matter what writing she submitted, what photographs she hocked, what job she applied for, it always came back to the same issue — not enough experience. Abigail took a sip of her room-temp water and slumped back, incensed. Clearly the only credentials this woman had to be a journalist at a premier national paper were that she had the correct pedigree, she knew lots of beautiful people, and she could afford to see and be seen at the toniest of Toronto's restaurants. Kudos for her. Abigail was pissed beyond belief that someone such as her, an aspiring photojournalist, was slogging away as a temp and experiencing rejection left, right, and centre by various publications while Ms. Shit waltzed into Abigail's idea of a dream job just because she had the right papers, the right connections, the right genes. Abi surveyed her dilapidated couch, ancient computer, and worn area rug. "Time to fight fire with fire," she murmured.

Booting up her trusty 486, she translated negative into positive and began to write her own version of Ms. Shit's column. That's it. Write the column, submit it to the *Globe*, they'll discover what talent I have and hire me on the spot, and the rest will be journalistic history. Easy peasy.

Challenge to Ms. Shit

Someone bagged quite the windfall last week. To the chagrin of casino-patronizing, bingo-playing blue-hairs, someone walked into a store near **Fenway Park**, unloaded some pocket change, and walked out a millionaire. Just waltzed up to the cashier and, at the last minute, decided "Yeah. What the hell, I'll take one of those tickets." Now he's laughing all the way to the bank. But what odds did he defy? Will he retire and squander his fortune or share the wealth and better himself? Is he single?

More importantly, why didn't one of us win? Despite the fact that none of us had been able to purchase a ticket, we ignored the important tenet "You can't win if you don't play" and debated furiously over this obvious injustice. An exercise in juvenile soul-searching and sheer consumerism, we attempted to answer the question "What would I do if I won?"

This was the dire discourse that was tabled up at **702 Isabella**, otherwise known as my apartment, last Friday night. A tidy junior one-bedroom with a decorative edge, my eclectic mix of particle-board bookcases, chairs salvaged from the garbage, and casual couch-cum-cat scratching post served as the supreme sanctum for our dialogue. **Frank, Hunter, Janine**, and I had adjourned from our nine-to-five jobs to discuss the matter and to fill an otherwise humdrum evening. Sardonic yet salubrious, it was our typical Friday-night fête. "I'd have a huge party, invite all of my friends, and have a bonfire stoked with **Ben Franklins**," quipped Frank, with the savoir-faire of a thoroughbred. It must have been the previously owned shirt from **Goodwill** that gave him the chutzpah to speak with such confidence, because Frank wasn't normally that eloquent or concise. "What friends?" retorted Janine, herself resplendent in a body-conscious **Charo**-esque number from **Winners**. Slouching back in a green ski sweater liberated from my dad's closet, I casually drank in the scene and began to strategize for the evening's events. The conversation was quickly dissolving into hopeless rhetoric and tiresome tirades. Something had to be done to salvage the evening. On the premise of refreshing everyone's Pilsners, I retired to my kitchen to calculate our next move.

The difficulty of orchestrating a Friday night filled with fun, frolic, and folly is immense. Let's face it, there are so many invitations proffered up to normal folks like Frank, Hunter, Janine, and me that the options are overwhelming, and, above all else, the hostess with the mostest has got to keep their interest. I was at a loss. Fluttering about my guests like a little **Anna Pavlovna**, I had to find a topic that would keep the conversation fresh and furious but civil and welcoming at the same time. A common denominator was necessary, and dinner was the perfect solution. I returned to the living room, armed with pop and the knowledge that the evening might well be saved. Doling out the drinks, I straightened up and, with authority in my voice, asked, "What did you guys want to do for dinner?" There, it was out. Phew. Didn't know I had the guts.

Unfortunately, I had been naïve in thinking that this issue would bring an even keel to the group dynamics. A complete miscalculation, this simple question bred an entirely new conundrum, and debate was rampant once again. Fresh rifts erupted, and allies were sought. It was a no-holds-barred fight to the death. Pizza or Chinese? The nutritional and financial merits of each were dissected, calculated, and compared. The group once again descended into pandemonium, and we squared off into our respective epicurean corners, clutching our partners-in-arms tightly. After much debate and mud-slinging, pizza finally won out. Then it was thin-crust or deep-pan? Meat lovers or Hawaiian? **Domino's** or **Pizza Pizza**? The quarrelling simply wouldn't end. I was close to slitting my wrists, but I decided that quitters never win. With much courage, I made the unilateral decision, disregarded all opposition and recalcitrant egos, and boldly said, "Large, thin crust, pepperoni, with extra cheese. Hand me the phone." I picked up my sleek, neutral-toned **Princess Bell** telephone and placed the all-important phone call. The group stared up at me, incredulous and envious at my ability to take the reins and actually make a decision.

Thereafter, the evening adopted a more joyful and gregarious tenor. Dialogue swiftly turned away from agendas and leaned toward art and politics. Should ***90210*** be resurrected? Did **Jennifer Grey** have more than just the tip of her upturned nose snipped off?

I could tantalize you with the remainder of the evening's events, but I am afraid that they may appear to be too high-brow and pretentious on paper. After all, enriching you with the salacious details of our blessed existence would serve no purpose except shameless self-promotion and to make you feel inferior and repressed, envious even. And who needs that? As you peruse this, remember that things in your pedestrian lives could be worse — you could be a society columnist.

Abigail Somerhaze

Abi pushed back from her computer, reviewing her masterpiece like a mural. That'll learn 'em. She knew she'd never hear back, but what the hell? It was worth a try. "Hell, maybe it'll even get me out of this dive," she said aloud, dreaming of being discovered.

Rejuvenated, Abi rose from her desk to finally rinse the previous night's antics away. Surveying her living room, she began picking up the empty cigarette packages, beer bottles, and unmentionables that were littered about. I really ought to learn how to tidy up when I party. Tossing her garbage into a plastic shopping bag and tying it off, Abi trotted out into the hallway and into the garbage chute room. Hmm. Vas is das?

Memo to Residents

Please refrain from disposing of used syringes down the garbage chute as such items pose a definite health hazard to both residents and building management when discarded in such a manner. Pursuant to this, please utilize the proper receptacles for the disposal of syringes and other medical equipment.

Building Management

Opening the metal hatch and ceremoniously depositing her bag into it, Abi had to chuckle. Yeah. Like they're all using them syringes for medicinal purposes, man. Definitely a new first for her.

As she re-entered her pad, Paw trotted over to greet her, rubbing himself up against her leg. Christ, she had forgotten to feed him. Time to really start her day. Abi set down her paper and poured enough food in his dish to satisfy a herd of cats. That should tide him over for now, she thought. Or at least for the next four hours. Running to the dish on the floor, Paw was acting as if he had never seen food before. Damn selfish cats. They're always thinkin' of themselves. Now if she could only get rid of her hangover as easily.

Abi hit the shower, figuring that maybe the coffee shop would do the trick. Caffeine is your friend.

The sun was glistening off the ice and snow, casting a cool aura onto Yonge. Abi pushed her sunglasses farther up her button nose, attempting to curtail the luminescence. Could it be any brighter? Her head was pounding, and shards of light were stabbing her brain, reminding her how late it actually was. Christ. I really ought to exercise better judgement. Squinting down the street, Abi noticed a couple of 51's finest parked outside Rabba. "Good, maybe they've busted those punks' asses," she mumbled to herself. Painfully inching forward, Abi caught sight of something else glinting in the sunlight. Is it? Nah. Can't be. Putting her myopia to the test, Abi squinted harder, trying to make out what was draped across the intersection of Yonge and Isabella. It was. Festive canary yellow strips were delicately suspended across the street like some sick Cinqo de Mayo soirée gone wrong. Adrenaline pumping her hangover away, Abi hustled toward the scene. Man, I don't have my Canon. Que sera. She couldn't afford film anyway.

Squad cars and cops were crawling all over. Sidling up to the police line, Abi tried to gain the best vantage point. Hmm. No body bags. No chalk lines. No shell casings strewn across the avenue. What the hell happened? Abi noticed some fellow rubberneckers standing outside the neighbourhood pub and moved toward them. They look like they know what time it is.

"So, um, what happened here?" Abi casually asked.

"Shooting. Killed a bouncer and nearly killed another kid," the man said, pointing to the entrance of the after-hours club. She knew it. The throngs of kids and pushers outside Rabba had been steadily growing since the fall, pissing Abi off to no end. Damn ravers had begun to impede her path to the morning paper, and she resented them for it. And her friends were trying to convince her that she was too uppity about the raves. That she was getting too old.

"When did it happen?" Abi thought back to a few short hours before when she herself had been swaggering home.

"4:30 or something."

Christ, that was close. She had staggered into Rabba at about 4 a.m. to replenish her cigarette stash. Someone up there must like me. Abi made a mental sign of the cross and continued to survey the spectacle. While the investigators were busily investigating, the detectives hurriedly detecting, and the newsmen documenting, it was clear that Abi had missed all of the action. Nothing much to see here, folks. Shrugging, Abi supposed she'd have to wait to get the full story at six. Crap. And she couldn't even pop into Rabba to pick up more milk. There's always tomorrow.

Ah. There's nothing like a homicide to start your day. Taking a deep, cleansing breath, Abi continued on to Donut Hut. Maybe someone there will know what the hell happened. "Because every time is donut time," Abi smiled to herself. She loved her pseudo-office. Donut Hut was one of the first places where Abigail had established herself as a regular. It provided the perfect bird's-eye view of Yonge, and it was where her real work took place. It had its share of kooks and ravers and proffered up enough material for social commentary that would impress Studs Terkel. Thankfully this morning had not let her down.

Abi yanked the door open, a cloud of blue smoke billowing out into the crisp air. Clumps of people crowded the cheap, Formica tables dotted around the shop, plumes of smoke ascending to the stained ceiling tiles above. The joint will never change.

Approaching the counter, Abi scanned the room for Tim, a regular whom she had recently struck up a conversation with. He was definitely quirky, keeping detailed records of the various crimes that occurred in the city. The statistics, gleaned from various sources ranging from the *Sun* to regular jaunts to the Reference Library, were neatly tabulated in a spiral-bound notebook that Tim carried with him everywhere. If anyone would know, Tim would. "Double-double, please," Abi requested, keeping her eyes trained on Tim's usual spot, which was empty.

Paying for her coffee, Abi moved to her own preferred seating by the front window. Hmm. Maybe he just slept in. Or maybe he actually got up at a reasonable hour. Testing her chair to ensure that she hadn't gotten stuck with a bum one, Abi sat down, satisfied. Pulling out her own spiral-bound notebook and pen, Abi hunkered down and tried to focus on her journal.

The kids were still sitting there, yakking away, and flapping their jaws about nothing at all. Glow sticks, pacifiers, matchbooks, and H_2O bottles littered the table. Impractical, cutesy Le Crapeau handbags were slung over the painted metal chairs. The girls were mere caricatures of themselves, lipstick long bitten off, and mascara crying for some remover. The boys stroked their downy facial hair and flexed their puny muscles under their microfleece vests, wallets chained safely to their belt loops. Being typical teenagers, they were annoying as hell. As it was only 10:30 a.m. on a Sunday, the kids must have been coming down from a rave, possibly the one on Isabella. What else would they be doing there at that hour? Hmm. Maybe they know something about the murder. For a split second, Abi was grateful for their presence. Slurping and usurping, Abi did what she did best — casually observe. They were all decked out in platforms, tiny tees, and baggy jeans. Inspecting her own duds, Abi wondered how they had the cash and she didn't. Then again, they were at the age where form was favoured over function. And cash from your part-time job at the mall went a helluva lot further when you were living at Ma and Pa's abode. Abi pushed back her chair, hauled on her smoke, and silently scoffed the scoff of the damned. At least she knew the value of a buck.

Pretending to scribble in her notebook, Abi couldn't help but feel old and bitter in the face of their exuberance. Since arriving in the city, Abi had become increasingly territorial; her tolerance for the giddy mallrats and looped-out ravers was waning. Daily her maternal approval was descending like their Hilfigers; her anger was rising with their microminis. Where the hell are their parents, for God's sake? Maybe she was too disparaging and judgemental. Or maybe it was just that she knew she could never look that good in a halter. Whatever it was, Abi wished that they would get out of her 'hood, praying that the little shits would get grounded for once. Maybe then she could enjoy her morning cup of sugary goodness in peace.

Straining to properly eavesdrop, Abi couldn't help but note how oddly out of place the kids looked in the morning sun. They were sucking on their candy pacifiers and cigarettes, most of them not a day over fifteen. Did they not know they were ruining their baby teeth? Sugar is a silent killer, you know. The gaggle, which was never the same but always the same, looked a little worse for wear. Judging from their shrill conversation, they were in good spirits nonetheless. A chronic insomniac, Abi was trying to remember what it was like to stay up all night and be ecstatic about it. Must be the Special K. She knew their adventures would be recounted countless times in the corridors and bathrooms of their high school the next day. Who made out with whom, who got sick, who got grounded because of their escapades. All the shenanigans gave them bragging rights. They were too cool for school. Usually Abi was somewhat amused by their prattering, but not this morning. She wanted the skinny on the homicide, and they weren't dishing it out. Now she'd really have to wait with the rest of the world to find out. So much for having the inside scoop.

Ensconcing herself in her journal, Abi tried to block the kids out. Leave, dammit, leave.

"Can I hitch a ride with one of you guys?" Bimbette Number One coquettishly inquired.

"Me, too," Bimbette Number Two chimed.

Suddenly remembering what it was like to be their age, Abi had to laugh. It was all just hormones and harmless fun.

"Sure, dolls. Anything for my ladies," Tony Testosterone replied as manly as possible.

A flurry of activity ensued, and Abi discreetly observed them, pretending to continue jotting notes in her journal. Chairs shuffled, coats were donned, bags were zipped, and the gaggle tumbled out the door, leaving a silent void in their wake. No music, no childish chatter, no vibe. Just coffee and donuts. Looking about the empty shop, Abi didn't find the joint so interesting now. Kind of blah and boring, as if all the guests had just vacated a party. "Careful what you wish for," Abi mumbled to herself, shoving her journal in her bag. Tossing her backpack over her shoulder, Abi followed suit and headed out into the wintry day.

chapter six

Surrounded by cherry wood, leather, and brass taps, Abi was snug as a bug at the bar. She loved this place. Smack in the middle of Yorkville, it was the perfect balance between casual sports bar and upscale eatery. Studying the nautical photos adorning the panelled walls and the well-heeled clientele dressing the bistro-style tables, Abi couldn't think of a better place to have a quiet Sunday repast. Especially if someone else was paying. Still, it was all so bittersweet. It was indeed a free meal but also a last supper with Justin.

Playing with a pack of matches, Abi fought the tears that had begun to surface. She couldn't believe that he was actually leaving. Gently shaking her head, it seemed like yesterday that she had timidly set foot in the student paper office and Justin had interviewed her for her first journalistic position. Sensing that she was more than a little wet behind the ears, he had gladly tutored her for hours au gratis and taught her all he knew. Reflecting back, the deluge abated, and Abi smiled. Those were definitely the good ol' days. Smoking, drinking, developing. All that mattered was making the deadline and praying for a page 1. So much had changed, yet so much had remained the same. Having morphed into a management consultant, Justin had settled into responsible adulthood well, much better than Abi had. Despite their differences in fortune, their relationship had stood the test of time. He was still the same old Justin, mentoring her and guiding her through the lofty pursuits of her twenties just as he had done at the paper. He just did it in pinstripes as opposed to jeans. Letting out a sigh, Abi began to feel a bit better about his impending departure. If their friendship could survive the transition from swilling beer and downing shots to sipping wine and shucking oysters, it could transcend a few thousand miles.

The door opened abruptly, and Abi turned to see Justin approaching her. "Hey, hey," Abi called, rushing over and hugging Justin. "How are you doin'?" she chirped, giving him another squeeze. It was so great to see an old friend.

"Fine, fine," Justin responded, grinning broadly at her exuberance. "I think I'm finally all packed up for the move to San Jose. I can't believe I'm leaving next week," he added.

"I know, I know. I'm so sad to see you go, especially since we never really got a chance to hang since I moved to the city. But I'm happy for you all the same. It's a great move for you," Abi replied, sitting back down on her stool and patting the chair next to her. "I have to say that I am quite envious of you and your move. I mean, it's a chance at a fresh start, a new beginning. Christ. Then again, I'd be excited at any opportunity right now," she admitted, trying not to sound too jaded. Everyone seemed to be moving on up except her.

"It'll happen for you," Justin said, flagging down the waiter. "Just be patient. You've got a lot of talent, and it's only a matter of time before you're discovered," he continued encouragingly.

That's what she loved about Justin. He was so patient and nurturing, a true friend whom she could confide in without fear of reprisal.

"I know. It's just that it's been so tough. I mean, I had to pawn some jewellery the other day. How pitiful is that? I am such a starving artist, man," she tried to joke, her embarrassment apparent. "Don't get me wrong, it was interesting to go through the process and all. Total grist for the mill, but very humbling nevertheless," she added, reviewing the menu and avoiding Justin's eyes. God, I'm being such a downer. "And don't believe the commercials that say they pay top dollar for gold, either. Fucking cheapskates robbed me blind. I think my grandmother would be proud of the fact I traded her bracelet for toilet paper," she laughed, attempting to bring some levity to the conversation.

As the waiter took their order, cheering erupted at the rear of the bar, and Abi and Justin both turned to see what the commotion was all about. Several burly men encircled the large-screen TV, filling the small room, and focused only on the rugby game that was being played out continents away. Bottles of Fosters were strewn across the tables among souvenir Australian flags and homemade banners. A couple of the jocks broke out into a rugby cry, waving their hands about for the others to join in and baiting the New Zealanders to counter. It was all striped jerseys and testosterone.

"What would the Aussies and Kiwis do without satellite?" Justin quipped over the ruckus.

"I do not know," Abi laughed. "All I know is never date a rugby player. It's all they care about."

"I'll have to remember that," Justin chuckled.

"So I've finally realized that I've got to find a regular nine-to-five gig. I mean, if you can't beat 'em, join 'em," Abi said, trying to resume their conversation over the noise of the sports enthusiasts. "I've gone on a few interviews, and things are looking pretty good, actually. I've just got to be pragmatic and take care of the bottom line." She was trying to sound as adult and as confident as possible. "Don't get me wrong. I'm not succumbing to the suburban dream, I'm just trying to be responsible. I mean, who knows if I'm even cut out to be a photojournalist. It's time I grew up and got serious, after all." She hoped he didn't think she was a quitter. Suddenly a plate appeared before her, and Abi looked up at the waiter, grateful for the interruption. Service was certainly quick here.

"Don't worry about it," Justin reassured, grabbing the Heinz and wagging it over the fries. "It'll all turn out fine. Just remember your dreams, and you'll be okay. There's nothing wrong with having to support yourself, especially if it's in the name of making your dreams happen," he stated, now shaking the bottle of reluctant ketchup.

"You're right. Just because I work in an office doesn't mean that I've given up on my dreams. All it means is that I'm being smart about it," she said, handing Justin a knife so he could liberate the ketchup.

"That's right. And remember that it's not what you wear or where you work that matters. It's who you are. It's doing what you love. Besides, I know it's only a matter of time before you're some Pulitzer Prize-winning journalist," he continued.

He was so good to her. Who was going to talk sense into her now? Who was going to believe in her and her dreams? Feeling the waterworks welling up, Abi acted quickly and raised her glass to Justin.

"Here's to our future successes," she stated triumphantly.

"To success," Justin concurred, clinking his glass with hers.

Savouring the vino, Abi hoped she was making the right decision. Conforming wasn't going to be easy.

chapter seven

"WCBS — your winter weather survival station." "God, they're such sensationalists," Abi mumbled to herself, giving Paw a pat. Lazily rolling over and shutting off the clock radio, Abi wished she didn't have to do time this morning. She felt way too great to waste her time cavorting with strangers in some drab office. Besides, she wanted to poke around about the shooting. All she had been able to glean was that some dissed dealers had shot some bouncer. God, and I thought *I* needed anger management. Oh, to be a trophy wife. Ah. Big stretch. What a difference a sober night's sleep makes. Time to rise and shine and squeeze in some real work before the grind begins.

7 a.m. The graveyard was turning at Donut Hut. Empty tables, chairs, and cups were strewn about, and silence reigned. It was so quiet you could have heard a roach fart. Abi leaned back and lowered her lids, savouring her morning fix. Ah. The phantom palace. It was the perfect forum in which to write. The sun was sleepily deciding whether or not to make an appearance, and with the dawn the traffic was increasing. The city was waking up, and Abi adored observing it. It was one of her favourite nontoxic indulgences. Attempting to capture the moment, Abi began to scribble furiously, continuing her journal entry.

The door jangled open, and Abi glanced up, perturbed. She hated it when she lost her groove. Don't they know this is a place of business? The offending male manoeuvred over to the counter, bellowing for a quad-quad. Quad-quad? Is he nuts? That amount of sugar could morph you into the Hulk. Oh, well.

It's your diabetes waiting to spring, buddy.

Reaching for the paper, Abi wondered what enlightenment it held for her today. She flipped to the entertainment section, and a curious article caught her eye. Napster? What the hell kind of name is that? The tale was titillating. A little ol' Internet company was being walloped by one helluva suit by the RIAA and Metallica. Pulling her chair closer to the table, Abi was amused and enthralled by the vision of some pubescent punk being cornered in a panelled boardroom by a bunch of Rogaine-dousing suits and a still-limber Lars. Still, she had to agree with The Man on this one. How can the little twats get away with downloading music au gratis? That is tantamount to stealing from the chirping mouths of starving performers. Do they think recording deals and publicists grow on trees? Being a sensitive artist herself, she had to concur with the industry. But just this once. And she would never admit it to her father.

Completing the treatise, Abi looked up from her page and over at the delectables behind the counter. Hawaiians, maple-dipped, crullers. They were all so huge, so sweet, so tempting, and so calling her name. Feeling her waist and hips inconspicuously, she confirmed what she already knew — she was having a thin day. Maybe just a couple of donut holes. They can't hurt none, can they? Remembering that New Year's was only a couple of short weeks away, she thought better of it and returned to her writing. The fleeting sugar high just wasn't worth it. Sorry, taste buds, you'll just have to wait another day, she thought, a proud smile of defiance on her face. She felt powerful and sexy. She was in control. And she wasn't prepared to relinquish all that over a few innocent balls of dough and sugar. Renewing her commitment, Abi slapped her journal closed and got up to start her day.

Exiting the Donut Hut, Abigail stuffed her keys into her purse, shoved on her mitts, and with an it's-gonna-be-cold-out-there huff pushed the door open with her backside. Her day had officially begun. She had been placed in a software company, which was a refreshing change to the mutual fund companies that were becoming her usual haunts.

The air was clean and crisp, the sky crystal, and the stars were only just beginning to dim. She hoped that she wasn't overdressed or, worse, underdressed. That was one downside to temping — you never knew the atmosphere of the joint until it was too late. No dress rehearsals for this chiquita. The more positive flipside to that was that, if you looked like a jerk, chances were you'd never see these people again. Now where was she headed? Abigail pulled the strap of her purse over her head, getting it stuck on the sleeve of her coat. Fuck. Straitjacket city. Tugging violently, she was finally able to free herself. Not wanting to remove her mitts, she struggled with the zipper on the front compartment. She hated Canada. Or at least in the winter she did. Conceding to the situation, Abigail removed one mitt, unzipped the compartment, and fumbled for the Post-it with the mission details. Hubris. Who the fuck ever heard of calling a company that? Pretty ballsy. "I just hope it's legit," Abigail mumbled to herself, stuffing the paper back into the bag. A paycheque's a paycheque.

The 'hood was a ghost town. Those who were around looked pissy and self-absorbed. Scurrying along, Abigail passed the stoop of Progress Place and glanced over. At the foot of a frost-encrusted sleeping bag, three pigeons pecked haltingly at a half-eaten piece of pizza. Abi shuddered at both the plight of the homeless and the urban fare of the vermin. It was scary that they were carnivorous. The shrouded figure did not move for fear of breaking the cocoon and releasing the warm shield that had been hours in the making. Watching the people step over the figure and rush past her, Abigail hoped that she would never be that callous, that wrapped up in her pathetic life not to give a damn about her fellow man.

Motoring down Queen East to Jarvis, Abi approached the Fred Victor Centre. Some bedraggled homeless men were already stomping their feet on the corner in an attempt to ward off the cold. Winter had settled in quickly, seemingly overnight. Only a few short days before, it had been unseasonably warm and pleasant. The morning commute would get a dreadful fright this Monday morning. Even with her down jacket, tights, and heavy mitts, Abigail was chilled to the core, bracing herself every time a gust tried to whisk her back to her warm apartment. It was in this cold that Abigail realized how fortunate she truly was. She had shelter, warm food, and enough for a coffee in the morning. Sometimes. The cocooned bodies huddled in the doorways of her route were a testament to the hundreds who were not as lucky. How did they have the wherewithal to survive? Abigail herself was devastated when she couldn't afford the second bottle of wine or had to sacrifice a night on the town for some nice boots. As steadfast as she was, Abi couldn't imagine what it must take to survive on the streets.

Bypassing the men, Abi avoided eye contact, staring deadpan down the avenue. When she had first come to the city, Abigail had been startled by the poverty and plight on the city's streets. She had dropped change in the ball caps and had attempted to help where she could. She had been naïve enough to believe that every little bit helps and that she could make a difference should she choose to do so. After months of being confronted by panhandlers, junkies, sniffers, and squeegee kids, Abi now politely refused their pleas for assistance, preferring instead to play the Good Samaritan at the mission. Her parents had always given of themselves, instilling in her a strong sense of responsibility to help the less fortunate, and she refused to become one of the heartless prancing and dancing around the vulnerable in their furs and fleeces, their bellies bloated with Christmas cheer. Working at the program felt great, too. At least there she could see the impact on the patrons. At least there she was able to put names to the faceless. At least there she didn't have to relinquish a buck.

Her eyes glinting with adventure, Abi was relishing the scenery of her new surroundings. The neighbourhood was eclectic, to say the least. A melding of dilapidation and decadence, stray pockets of upscale dwellings butted up against abandoned tenements. The pedestrian traffic, as light as it was at that hour, reflected the dichotomy, ranging from brokers aiming for Bay to squatters shuttling to shelters. Approaching Richmond, Abi paused to study the forlorn structure nestled between the Salvation Army and Goodwill. Bricks black from years of exhaust and exhaustion and windows boarded up to avert squatters, the building retained its stately street front, a testament to a more prosperous and idyllic time. Studying the architecture, Abi's eyes came to rest on the crest. Built in 1898. The façade was incredible. They just don't make them like they used to, she thought. Admiring the squalid building, Abi noticed the silent crane hawkishly hanging over the construction site directly next to it. Noting the "Sold" sign over the doorway, Abi wondered how long before it would be reduced to rubble.

Shrugging and continuing down to Adelaide, Abi suddenly got the sneaking suspicion that she was lost. Leaving her territory, her dependable internal compass was totally off kilter. *Where the fuck is this place?* Abigail began to wonder what kind of goose chase the agency had sent her on. She looked down at her trusty Post-it, looked up at the street sign, looked across at the building numbers once again, and shrugged her shoulders. Methadone clinic on one side, $500K condos on the other. Now if that isn't a statement on society. "This must be it," she mumbled, turning her back on the anxious junkies and tentatively stepping toward the building. She took a deep breath and embarked on her latest folly. "Super Temp," she sighed, opening the front door and jamming it on the carpet. Nice entrance.

So this is it. Not bad, not bad. At least it was a departure from the usual stuffy stints she got. The sound of nails clicking on concrete and the jingling of a collar brought Abigail out of her morning fog. A dog trotted into the lobby, sniffed the garbage, and trotted directly into the boardroom. Abigail glanced at it but said nothing. The reception area was typical industrial chic, a little worse for wear but hip nonetheless. Polished concrete floors, exposed pipes, tiny task lights dangling delicately from the ceiling, curved-wood and burnished-steel appointments. The place was decked out — flat-screen monitors, printers and fax machines, Britney-like headsets. A massive bronze sign emblazoned with the company name — HUBRIS Software Corp. — was mounted prominently behind the reception desk. No mistaking where you are here. It reminded her of something out of *Metropolis.* Stark. And creepy in a way. Dark, catacomby, and womblike — rather like a termite hill.

Flipping through an *ROB*, Abigail was dying for another jolt of caffeine. "Christ, I'd give anything for a coffee about now," she muttered to herself, unravelling her scarf and folding it across her lap. Looking down at her Post-it, all she had was the name of the joint. Even Betty hadn't a clue what the gig was, except that the stint would last for a few days. All she had told Abi was that she would be providing sales support, specifically for Joshua Nesatis, the EVP of Sales. Sales support? For all Abi knew, it could be code for scrubbing the john with a toothbrush. What to do, what to do, what to do? Stuff envelopes? Photocopy? Enter endless names in an already antiquated database that no one will ever use? Ah. The glamorous, superfluous life of a temp. You just never know what the date is going to be like. Abigail sighed, depositing her scarf and mitts in her bag. "I am so glad I went to university for this." Now,

now. Not so negative. "At least I'll be making a few bucks," she quickly self-edited. Good thing, too, 'cause it is getting close to month-end. Seeing as none of her interviews had panned out, Abi was in desperate need of a financial injection.

Hmm. Still no sign of the receptionist. Yup. Hurry up and wait. Typical. Checking out the floors polished to a glassy sheen, Abi had to admit that the joint was pretty funky. As she gazed at the burnished metal reception desk, Hubris screamed image, and the vibe was answering yes. Voices were booming from the boardroom, laughter lilting from the neighbouring office, gossip transmitting down the hallway. The uniform was black pants (Armani gabardine, of course), black mock (Banana Republic, of course), black shoes (Kenneth Cole, of course), silver bracelet (Tiffany's, of course), stainless steel watch (TAG, of course), platinum ring (Cartier, of course). Abigail drank in the scene, incredulous. They looked way too young to be so blatantly prosperous. Not one individual appeared to be over the age of thirty. Sneaking a peek into the boardroom, Abigail was certain that one of the guys couldn't be a day over eighteen. "How can this place be legit when it's run by Doogie, for God's sake?" she said to herself. It was going to be a very good day for people watching.

"Hi. You must be Abigail. I'm Cassandra, but call me Cass. Josh told me to expect you." A hand appeared out of nowhere and thrust itself into Abi's palm. Startled, Abi looked up from the current issue of *Wallpaper*. A petite, funkily dressed woman stood before her, wagging her hand. "He's in a meeting right now, but he should be out in a few minutes. Did you want a cup of coffee while you wait? Cappuccino?"

With a winsome grin, Abi responded in kind. Who could turn the world on with her smile? Super Temp. Giving Cass the once over, Abi glanced down at her own cheap rayon suit and immediately felt like just that — a cheap suit. Way too conservative.

Mental note — don't wear this here again.

"Coffee'd be great. If you just point me in the right direction, I can get it myself, though." Abi immediately began to look and feel lost. Get it back, girl. Super Temp. She put down the magazine, straightened her posture, and followed Cassandra back to her desk.

There was a constant parade of people through the lobby. Cassandra was bombarded by everything from cab chits to HR questions to travel to lunch orders to gossip. She was clearly the nucleus of the joint, and she didn't miss a beat. Totally connected, totally on the ball. Abigail wondered why such a bright, obviously capable woman was sitting behind reception. Then again, she herself was no slouch and had been doing the same work for several months now. People probably had wondered the same thing about her. Abi shrugged. Everyone's got their own story, their own deal, their own agenda. And everyone's gotta eat.

"What's this?" Abi pointed to the laminated award on the wall.

"Oh, that. We won some sort of a media award last month. Kinda cheesy looking, huh? Still, exposure's exposure. Good morning, Hubris. Please hold." The dog reappeared and decided to lie down in the middle of the floor. "That's Cordy, by the way. She belongs to one of the technical writers. She shit on the floor yesterday. Really pissed me off." Abi tried not to look taken aback. Cassandra took a scant second to check her watch. Abi did the same. "Since Joshua is running behind — he's always running behind, the poor thing's cup is positively running over — I may as well let you in on what you're going to do today."

Ah. The moment of truth. Abigail held her breath, gleefully filled with expectation. "That's what I'm here for," Abi chirped cheerily.

"We've got a trade show coming up, and I need some help getting the collateral ready."

Collateral? Is she talking loans or casualties of war?

Abi wisely decided to just smile, nod, and look like she knew what Cassandra meant. Collateral. That's a new one.

Abi was following Cassandra down the corridor toward what appeared to be a full-fledged bar area. Say. They've got booze here. This will *definitely* be good people watching.

"That's the kitchen there. Help yourself to some coffee whenever you feel like it. And here's where you'll be working." The three-minute tour stopped in the photocopy room.

The copy room. The beloved home of the temp. Sizing up the massive machine, Abi knew she'd have a day of it. The bigger they are, the harder they jam.

Sensing Abigail's apprehension, Cassandra reassured her. "Don't worry, I'll show you how the hog works. It looks intimidating, but it's really a pussy. Here's a notebook if you want to take notes."

Abi was impressed. It was a funky, spiral-bound book with the Hubris logo imprinted on the cover.

"You can keep it, too, we've got hundreds of the things." Cassandra pointed to the stacks on the shelves.

Cool. A freebie. Abi grinned. She usually didn't get to keep things.

The copy tutorial went swiftly, and Abi was well on her way to copy heaven. She had only gotten a couple of paper cuts, too. At least so far. She was so thankful for having remembered her hand cream, though. Her hands were so parched that they were white and cracking. Heavy bond paper looks fabulous, but it could suck the sweat off a fat Elvis no problem.

12:30 p.m. Three solid hours. Thirty-six dollars before taxes. Not bad for a morning's white-collar work. God. I'm such a whore. Her stomach grumbling, Abi thought about lunch break, and her brow furrowed. Cassandra hadn't mentioned anything about a lunch break. Maybe this is one of those psycho places that doesn't believe in déjeuner. As per her policy, Abi never brought such issues up, fearing that she would come off as a wimpy admin. Shit. Should've asked.

As if reading her mind, Cassandra appeared around the corner. "We're going for sushi. Wanna come?"

Abi hadn't been expecting that. She had had barely enough to buy her breakfast bars for the week. It sounded expensive, and there was no way she could swing it. Luckily she was adept at not seeming like a drag.

"Actually I'm meeting a friend for lunch. Thanks for the offer, though. Speaking of which, how long is lunch?" Phew. Dodged that one. Now she just prayed that she wouldn't run into Cassandra and the gang over break.

"Oh. About an hour. Not that anyone keeps track here. See you in a bit, then." Cassandra turned and left and Abi gathered her purse and coat.

Not knowing where to go, Abi settled on a bench in the park around the corner. Luckily the snow had held off, and the cold was manageable; otherwise, she would've really been up a creek. Munching on her breakfast bar, Abigail evaluated the day thus far. Cool space, hip and affable people, easy assignment. She decided she'd give it a 7.5 so far. The only black mark against Hubris was that Joshua hadn't even bothered to pop his head in and introduce himself yet. Then again, the day was only half over, and the people were warm and fun. The place was a gas. Kinetic, in fact. Land of the Beautiful and Productive, roaming free on wireless opportunity. She definitely wouldn't mind working there. A lucrative start-up. Her dad would be so pleased. A funky environment. Her friends would be so envious. A steady paycheque. Her creditors would be so relieved. A whole lot of nuts.

She would be ecstatic. Working there would satiate everyone. Her mind reeled with the possibilities. Hubris was a place to bear in mind. Shit! It's almost half past. "That's what I get for being so wrapped up in my supposed future." Abi quickly stuffed her wrapper in her pocket and headed back through the front doors. Ah. She paused momentarily. Warmth.

Crap. The letterhead was upside down. The copy machine was spewing sheet after sheet of perfectly ruined heavy bond. "Oh, for the love of," Abi caught herself and allowed the statement to trail off into impotent oblivion, nervously looking about to see if anyone had heard her truncated tirade. Super Temp, baby, Super Temp. "Cassandra's gonna kill me," Abi muttered, pressing the Def Con "Stop" button. "Come on, work with me." The machine halted abruptly, and Abi began pulling out the offending evidence. She opened the paper drawer and, turning the blank sheets over, shut 'er up and let 'er rip again. Sixty. Fifty-nine. Fifty-eight. Fifty-seven. Fifty-six. Screw carbon monoxide, copying is the silent killer of dreams.

Leaning with her back to the machine, Abi looked around the copy-cum-supply room. Man, my cell is small. Downright dim and depressing. No window or skylight, just tiny twinkles emanating from task lights. Shelves and shelves of varying shades of heavy, fingertip-slicing bond paper, all of which had a specific, TBA purpose in life. The joint was a mess, too. Little clumps of staples, tossed away due to an imperfect fit, and evidence of the previous occupant's copying were littering the work counter. Picking up an empty box of Sharpies, Abi tossed it into the garbage, now overflowing with her mistakes. Christ, they're pigs.

Reaching for the kit template, Abi began reading the contents of what she was copying. May as well make use of my time. Hmm. Product Management Overview. Case Studies. Corporate Bios. Press Releases. Too exciting for words. What to read first?

Abi judiciously selected the overview, figuring it was best to start at the top. Borrowing lexicography from every field of study, twisting the context, and repurposing it to suit la moment. Man, this tech writing is a science. Reading more like a blurb from *Wired* than from *Business Week*, the discourse was embedded with all the hip verbage of the day. Convergence. Architecture. Leveraging. Media-rich. Repository. Robust. Scalable. Aggregating. Streaming. Channelling. Dogmatic in its tenor, the treatise purported to be digital iteration of *Field and Stream.* More traditional terminology reared its head. ROI. Enterprise. Market share. Revenue streams. Minority interest. Gotta appeal to the dollars that be. Now this was something she kind of understood. The copier completed its second run, and, setting down the content, Abi shrugged. Too bad it was out of date the second the bubble jet blasted the page.

Arriving home that evening, Abi was tired and happy. The day hadn't been exactly stellar, but it had given her hope and a sense of accomplishment. While she had been bored to tears by her assigned task, Abi had been impressed with Hubris. It was young and way more fun than she was accustomed to. Everyone had been welcoming — people had actually stopped to ask her name and to say hi, and she'd felt less like a lowly temp and more like a member of their sanctum. It was definitely a departure from the financial institutions she was accustomed to. And they had offered her an additional couple of days' work. That would secure groceries and the cable bill, at least. Reaching up into her postbox, she noticed a letter from the *Globe and Mail.* Extremely thin and innocuous looking, Abi knew exactly what it was. Great. Another rejection letter.

The street was deserted, its shops closed up tight for the night. A few blue screens flickered in the apartments above, the only signs of life in the otherwise desolate neighbourhood. What kind of scavenger hunt has Justin put me on? A lone street lamp shone weakly, revealing the sparse flakes falling to the ground and collecting at its base. Yup. Not a creature was stirring. Nervously scanning the street, Abi was beginning to get freaked. Squinting desperately in the low light, she finally caught sight of Justin standing by himself in front of what appeared to be an old furniture shop. Thank God. It's kind of creepy around here. "Oh, I can't believe it's your last night in town," Abi cried, bursting across the street and breaking the silence. Leaping into his arms, Abi gave Justin a huge bear hug.

"I know. It's so bizarre. At 9:20 a.m. I'm heading west, young girl," he laughed, holding the nondescript door open for her. The pair climbed the steep, narrow staircase to the second floor, stomping the snow off their boots and removing their cumbersome mitts and scarves.

"So what is this place again?" Abi asked, stopping in front of the makeshift ticket booth.

"It's a clown school," Justin explained.

Clown school? Who the hell goes to clown school?

"It's actually more of an improv group. Ya know, not traditional birthday party clowns or anything. Kind of like stand-up with a twist," he elaborated. Phew. No balloon animals.

"A friend told me about it. He's actually performing tonight. Don't worry, Abi. If anyone will appreciate and enjoy this, you will. It's totally not run-o'-the-mill."

A bristol board sign above the portal simply stated "Welcome to The Loft. $5 donations accepted." Five bucks? Can't be all that bad. And if it was, at least it's cheap.

"Hey, well, I like the price of admission," Abi joked.

"I got this one," Justin said, slapping down a tenner on the counter.

"Hey, thanks, big spender. Seriously, though, thanks. I'm embarrassed to say that I'm on my last fifty bucks," she quickly admitted, knowing he was saving her a pack of smokes.

Having paid the princely sum of admission, they moved into what appeared to be a living room, replete with bookcases, coffee tables, and couches. Deep reds and golden yellows covered the walls, the ambient light of several strategically placed pillar candles arched up toward the high ceilings, illuminating the original mouldings and accentuating the bohemian romance of the old structure. A pair of girls, obviously grad students, were hunkered in the corner, puffing away and discussing the performance to come. Cool. Addicts are welcome here. Plopping down onto one of the '70s-plaid sofas, Abi immediately felt at home. It was low-key and loungy and right up her alley.

"Did you want a drink?" Justin asked, indicating the impromptu bar set up in what clearly used to be the kitchen. Beer $3, Wine $4, Pop $2 the menu board neatly detailed. Cheap booze *and* improvisation. This is my kinda joint. Relaxed, eclectic, and not a highbrow fashionista in sight. No *Saturday Night* readers here.

"Sure, just a beer, please," Abi responded, picking up one of the brochures. Groups of people began filling the living room, milling about, and chatting intelligently. An energizing air of creativity and anticipation quickly infused the room. A couple, obviously performers, were excitedly putting the finishing touches on their makeup, garnering praise and admiration from their friends and family who had gathered around. It must be so cool to have such guts and support.

Justin returned with drinks in hand and settled down in the spot next to Abi. Catching the excitement, Abi couldn't help but feel upbeat. "Oh, I have to tell you about Hubris, the company I was placed at today," Abi began. "It is such a cool joint. It's a software company, and it's so young and hip. I could actually see myself working there, Justin. And Cassandra — that's the girl I worked with — said that there might even be a position opening up. I mean, it'd probably just be admin work, but isn't that great?" Abi grinned with glee.

"Hubris? No kidding. I've heard of that place — it's an awesome company," Justin said, taking a liberal sip of his beer.

"Really? Oh, this could really be the break I need. I mean a regular paycheque, a cool environment, flexible hours, and total material. It's got it all. Now I really hope they take me," she sighed.

"If they have any sense, they certainly will," Justin replied, clinking his plastic cup against hers. People around them started to get up and filter in to the performance area in the rear. "Guess it's almost show time. Come on, time to be entertained," he declared, pulling Abi to her feet and coaxing her toward the back room. "You're gonna love this."

Following Justin into the tiny theatre, Abi had to admit that she was already impressed. With its low ceilings, grade-school risers, simple backdrops, and minimal scenery, The Loft had an intelligent, gritty, underground kind of feel — just the uncontrived, homespun kind of place that she had been searching for in the city. Selecting one of the seats in the front row, Abi couldn't wait for the show to start now. This was definitely grist for the mill.

chapter eight

It was Abi's second week of photocopying and collating at Hubris, and she waltzed in like she owned the joint. There was something there that just clicked. In a way, Abi felt like she had found her stride, her home. The place was always jumping and jovial, and the scenery wasn't bad either. Everyone was young, happy, productive, and making their parents, their partners, their bosses, and themselves proud. And the tenor was staccato, not staid — just get the job at hand done. Abi felt respected there and knew that nobody was frowning on her while she completed menial tasks. Different hats were worn by different people, regardless of age, gender, or race. Hierarchy was nonexistent. Or maybe it was just that they looked too young to even define hierarchy or to have lived long enough to create it. Either way, it didn't matter to her; the first week had been enjoyable, and she was making decent coin. And this was the first time a firm had asked Abi to stay on past the first three days where she had gladly accepted the proposition. She felt like Pretty Woman.

On her way to the kitchen, a ball bounced past her, an unfamiliar dog skittering by to chase it. The company was so relaxed and at ease. Abi had spent the previous days covertly scrutinizing the various departments and discerning how they jived. The programmers were the quietest and the most down to earth. In keeping with start-up tradition, they had been remunerated well in salaries and options, yet they remained true to their brand of jeans and sweatshirts, their pizzas, their all-important regular coffee. Nothing had changed, especially not their attitudes. All that had been affected was their bank balances, for the positive, and the newfound admiration from the parentals. They were the darlings of the media, of Thanksgiving dinner, of the high school reunion. It was revenge of the nerds, and they were enjoying every moment of it.

The sales team was interesting to study, with their positioning and verticals, revenue streams, and pipelines. They were way more uptight and wound up than the rest of the gang, but maybe it was just the copious amounts of Grande Americanos they consumed. Indeed, they were more social than the programmers. They would have been the in-crowd in high school, on the varsity teams and prom committees. They were definitely kinetic Type A's and viewed themselves as the drivers of the company. The sales guys were obvious, constantly crying "Coffee's for closers" and incessantly bragging about the sale they were about to close.

Josh, her supposed temp contact, was the most intriguing subject of them all. He was mysterious and powerful in a Wizard of Oz sort of way, and Abi had been able to forensically pluck a fair profile from the details Cass had related thus far. Having the rakish repute of an ambitious driver, he had single-handedly transformed the higgledy-piggledy Hubris sales force into an efficient, competitive machine and was flourishing under the praise from the board. He travelled relentlessly to squeeze the lead and close the deal, was known to send e-mails in the wee hours of the morning and conduct meetings before breakfast. He was the embodiment of the New Old Boy's Club and now Hubris's illustrious favoured son. Rumour had it that he had his eye on the top job, and Abi had the impression that it was his if he wanted it. Envisioning a golden boy, Abi couldn't wait to meet him. An alpha male would be so much fun to study up close and personal, especially in its native environment.

Today Abi was going to zero in on Finance. She figured she'd have a rough time of it as they barely ever emerged from their corner of the office. From what she had seen of them thus far, they were straightlaced accountant types, and while they were generally pleasant they weren't exactly extroverted. Pouring herself a coffee, Abi mulled over the possibilities. They were definitely a tough nut to crack. She'd have to find some way to break rank and get the skinny on Finance. Too bad they were so damn secretive about everything. She shrugged and picked up the communal stir spoon.

"Good morning. You must be Abi — I'm Joshua. We finally get to meet."

Startled, Abi nearly spilled the milk she was about to pour into her mug. "Morning. Pleased to meet you," she managed, extending her hand out to his. Joshua. She had been working at Hubris for a full week, apparently at his behest, and he was finally making an appearance. He seemed affable enough, and Abi didn't know what Cassandra had been talking about. He was a lot better looking and, of course, substantially younger than she had imagined. A thirty-year-old EVP. Nicely done. Bet your papa's proud.

Josh squeezed past her and began pouring himself a cup. "Listen. Cassandra has been raving about you, and she's pretty hard to impress. I trust her instincts completely. We have a position open that you may be interested in. Did you want to meet with me later to discuss it? I'm free at about 3 p.m."

Abi slumped back, stunned. "Sure, that sounds great. Shall I meet you in your office?" Her heart pounded like she had just been asked out on the ultimate date.

"Sure. See you there!" Squeezing back past her, Josh waltzed into his office.

Abi opened up the dishwasher and, beginning to unload it, couldn't believe her luck. Pondering her fate, Abi busied herself with the engrossing task at hand. After months of being dispatched at the eleventh hour, she was beginning to wear out. Super Temp was fading fast. She had reached the point where she wanted to know where she was going to be the next day, the next week, the next month. More importantly, she wanted a paycheque that she could count on. And dental coverage.

Fuck. Another paper jam. She was only ten minutes and twenty copies into her day. Abi opened the front of the machine and tried to rip the offending leaf from the drawer.

"Morning. Thanks for unloading the dishwasher for me."

Abi looked up, praying that she didn't have a pissed-off look on her face. She always wore her heart on her sleeve. Super Temp. "No problem, Cassandra. I was here a bit early, so I figured I'd get going. Oh, I finally got to meet Josh. He seems nice enough, and he mentioned that a position has opened up here. I'm supposed to talk to him about it at three this aft." Abi tugged at the caught piece of paper, finally releasing it from its trap.

"Sure, he *seems* nice enough now, but wait until he bites your head off over a screwed-up catering order. Great news, though, I'd be really happy to see you stay. Although sometimes I wouldn't wish this place on my worst enemy."

Cassandra trailed off toward reception, and Abi tossed the crumpled letterhead in the garbage. Damn heavy bond. One less tree in the forest.

Abi was sitting in a Donut Hut near Hubris, sipping the coffee purchased with her last bill. Only fifteen more minutes before lunch was up. Her stomach was still growling, and Abi thought about the breakfast bar in her bag, wishing that she could eat it here but knowing that she couldn't. She could wait until she got back to the office. She'd just say that she was still hungry after lunch. A bunch of people had invited her to join them in the Hubris kitchen, but she had declined, feeling too much like an outsider to partake. Besides, she didn't want to jinx herself just yet. Finishing her coffee, Abi got up to leave. Screw it, I'll go back early. She was too hungry to wait.

Abi looked at her watch. Again. 2:35 p.m. Twenty-five more minutes before she'd know what Josh was going to offer her. Giddy, she had been distracted by the prospect all day. She hoped it was something more cerebral than an administrative role, but she certainly wasn't holding her breath. Even if it was admin-based, she knew she could work her way up and out of it soon enough. Better to get my foot in the door first, she figured. There were hundreds of others clamouring at the door, all dying for the opportunity to work at a start-up, with its promise of options and untold potential-wealth-soon-to-be-recognized-in-the-next-quarter. She should thank her lucky stars that she was even being considered for a position. Who knows, maybe she'd be one of those millionaire Girl Fridays she'd read about in *Business Week*.

It was 3 p.m. on the nose, and Abi knocked timidly on Josh's door.

"Come in," he boomed.

She gently opened the door, and Josh waved her in, mobile to his ear. Why doesn't he just use a landline? Ours is not to wonder why, Abi giggled silently. He motioned to the chair in the corner, and, like a spaniel, Abi obediently sat down. Cupping his hand over the receiver, Josh mouthed, "I'll just be a minute." She nodded understandingly. "Yup. I definitely think we should be attacking interactive. It's an incredible vertical. Yup. Yeah, I agree. Wilco. Listen, I've got a meeting right now — can we continue this later? How about I call you from the car? Okay. Talk to you then. Sorry about that," Josh stated apologetically, snapping the flip phone shut and facing Abi.

Cool. I'm officially a meeting. "No problem," Abi smiled,

shrugging her shoulders in a nonchalant manner. Her palms were sweaty, and she could feel the tick under her left eye kicking in.

Rolling his chair over toward her, Josh began to enlighten her. "We've got a position opening up for an admin assistant. Assis-tant to me, actually. It'll largely be admin-based — keeping my crazy schedule in line, travel arrangements, ensuring my database is up to date, some reception, things like that. But there's plenty of opportunities to move up here at Hubris, so please don't let the initial job description put you off. A person as capable and bright as you are has a fantastic future in this company. We need people like you."

Abi tried desperately not to look disappointed. Fuck. When am I going to be viewed as something more than admin? Still, at least he had included that "need" part. Smart and strategic.

Sensing her hesitation, Josh jumped right in for the kill, quashing any queries. "The salary starts at $31K a year, plus bonuses and, of course, options. Those should come in very handy when we IPO." He was the quintessential salesperson. Somehow he made it all sound so attractive, so delectable. "So what do you think?" Josh leaned back in his chair, cognizant of the fact he'd gotten her with the salary.

It was more than she had ever been offered before, and she'd be doing the same work she'd been doing for $10 or $12 an hour for the past few months. It didn't take her long to make the decision. "I'd be honoured to join Hubris," she uttered confidently, stunning herself with her response. Go with your gut, girl. Specious Hubris is not.

"Great. I'll have Cassandra contact the agency and get the ball rolling on your permanent contract. Who is it that you deal with again? ACME?" Abi nodded. "Of course, we don't have a desk for you yet, but I think you can probably use David's while he's away," Josh continued, holding out his hand and formally welcoming her aboard. "You'll enjoy the ride, I know you will." He pointed his finger at her, aiming with one squinted eye.

Abi smiled. Yeah, sure I will. Time for a little happy dance in the john.

Shutting the washroom door behind her, Abi was close to hyperventilating. God, I'll be getting my own business cards. Abigail was smitten with the idea of Hubris, enamoured of entering the corporate world, wistful of eventually becoming a power broker. Hubris was very tantalizing indeed. By signing on the dotted line, she would become legit. While it wasn't her dream job in journalism, it was potentially a lucrative opportunity, one that could give her the respect and acceptance that she needed. With the rudimentary hierarchy at Hubris, Abi figured that she could move up quickly and be exposed to areas of operation that she would never dream of. Deciding wholeheartedly to make a go of it, Abi exited the bathroom with renewed commitment. She had made the right decision. Photojournalism can wait. For now. Abi beelined it for reception to tell Cass the good word.

Cass was sitting at her desk, reviewing an e-mail and smiling. "Congratulations," she said, getting up to give Abi a hug. "I knew Josh would finally listen to me."

Huh? Giving her a quick squeeze, Abi stepped back, smiling but confused. "How did you know already?" Abi asked, a little weirded out by how quickly the news had spread.

"I'm basically HR, remember?" Cass replied, handing Abi some benefits forms to fill out.

"Shit, that's right." Phew. At least Cass isn't some bizarre psychic or something.

"Besides, Josh asked me to send out your announcement e-mail. Here — have a look," she said, turning the monitor to face Abi.

Abi leaned down to read it, squinting and giggling with glee.

Subject: From the Desk of Joshua Nesatis – New Addition to the Fam

```
I'd like to extend a warm welcome to
Abigail Somerhaze, who has accepted the
position of my executive assistant. With
her sparkling, energetic personality and
incredible work ethic, I know that she
will be a valuable asset to the Hubris
team. Many of you may have already met
Abi over the course of the past few days,
but in the event that you haven't please
take the time to introduce yourself to
her.
Welcome to the family, Abi!
```

This was so cool. She had actually had an e-mail announcement about her. "I should send this on to Dale. I mean, my dad," Abi cried excitedly. "Wait. No, I'm going to tell him 'in person.' I can't wait to call them and tell them the good news." Christ. I feel like I'm going to pee my pants. Who knew corporate life can be so exciting? "My parents are going to be over the moon about this. Especially my dad 'cause it's kind of like I'm following in his footsteps," she explained.

"I'm sure they're going to be very proud of you," Cass replied. "I'm just happy 'cause I finally have an injection of estrogen around here. We'll have to take you out to celebrate, of course. And soon, 'cause before you know it Hubris will have sucked you in just like it sucked me in."

"You got it, babe," Abi beamed. Getting up from Cass's chair, Abi looked around. The place was definitely slow today. Catching sight of the clock, she saw it was nearly half past four. "Hey, listen. Do you think it's okay if I pack it in early today? I'd just like to get home and tell my parents, call the agency, stuff like that," she said, a note of timidity suddenly in her voice. Some habits are just hard to break.

"Sure thing, kid. And go out and have some fun," Cass replied maternally.

"Thanks, Cass. See you tomorrow," Abi grinned. God, that sounded good. Time to head home and boast to the parentals.

Walking up Church Street, Abi was again gripped with fear. What if I've made the wrong decision? She knew Del would say that she should've held out for more money, but the offer had sounded so tempting, and she knew she would get regular raises anyway. Money couldn't be it. The atmosphere and the people were great, so that couldn't be it, either. She tried to pin down the source of her anxiety. Could it be a commitment thing? Could she be getting cold feet?

Walking into the Dominion nestled under the Merchandise Building, she mulled over the possibilities. Grabbing a basket, it hit her — it was an inferiority thang. She didn't have a clue what she was doing or, more importantly, what Hubris was doing. Abigail didn't even have a background in software. I've never even worked for a real company before, for God's sake. Her only saving grace was her ability to appear knowledgeable when she was not. She was adept at playing the part, at succumbing to the role at hand. She'd get by on wits alone, she knew she would. Grabbing her dinner potato, she felt calmer. She could flub it. Beaming as she headed to the cash, she couldn't wait to get home to tell her parents. They had been waiting so long for her to come into her own, and now she finally had. No more sheepish admissions of rejection. No more late-night phone calls crying for cash. She was golden. For now.

Nearing her digs, Abi could make out the squad car parked in front of her building. What the hell is going on now? As she moved closer, Abi just hoped that it was nothing too violent. There had already been two shootings on her street, and the violence was beginning to get tiresome. She was comforted by the fact that there was only one car, which indicated that it couldn't be anything that big. Maybe a domestic dispute or something. Abi spotted her neighbour near the railing at the entrance to the building. If anyone would know, she would. "Hey, Sandy. What's up?" Abi gestured to the cop car, trying to appear nonchalant.

"They're evicting some homeless guy from the fifth-floor stairwell. I'm sure you've seen him — young guy, scrawny, always wears a blue hooded jacket."

Abi had no clue whom she was talking about. "No. I've never seen him before. I had no idea this kind of stuff was going on."

"Oh yeah. They've evicted this guy before. Oh. Here they come now."

Along with the rest of the gang, she looked over to catch a good glimpse of the guilty party. Two boys in blue were leading him out of the elevator, and the super, obviously rattled, followed at a quick clip behind. The crowd parted to make way for the parade. Closing her jacket tightly across her chest, Abi shivered. She was struck by how young the displaced guy was, and her initial fear turned to sympathy.

"Guess there's nothing more to see here," Sandy joked and led the rest of the gang indoors.

Abi followed them but stopped in front of the super's door. He looked overwhelmed. "You okay?"

The super looked up from his incident report, the vein on his forehead still bulging from excitement. "Yeah. I suppose. I can't believe this damn place, though. Wanna drink?" The super pulled open his desk drawer and hauled out a twenty-sixer of scotch.

Who the hell is this guy? Lou Grant? "Just a finger, thanks." Abi wasn't much for scotch, but she could see he needed company.

The super poured two substantial shots into mismatched mugs and handed her one. "I tell you, if I had known this kind of shit was going to go on, I woulda never left Guelph."

Abi took a dainty sip, trying not to grimace. "Oh yeah? You're from Guelph? I didn't know that."

The super slam-dunked the shot and set himself up with another, nodding as he did so. "Yup. Wife and me came here for the money. Can't do this forever, ya know, and we were hoping to sock away some retirement savings. Now I know why they pay so much here. Goddamn hooligans and homeless. They shit in the stairwell the other day, ya know that?"

Abi's eyebrows arched. No, I did not know that.

"And my wife found syringes in the back. Good thing she didn't get pricked. Goddamn pigs."

Abi reluctantly took another polite sip and waited for the rant to continue.

"I tell you, we've got another eight months on this contract, and there's not a snowball's chance in hell that we'll renew. They can throw as much cash at me as they want to, but we're hightailing it out of here the first chance we get. My wife's heart's bad — we don't need this stress." The scotch must have taken hold; he was slowing down, and the vein on his forehead had disappeared.

Abi wanted to leave him with some advice, but she didn't know what to proffer. She was feeling the same way herself. She choked back the last of her scotch, thinking of something sagacious to relate. "Listen. All I know is that you've got to take it one day at a time. Eight months may seem like a long way off, but there is an end in sight. Focus on that end." She hoped that would suffice.

The super nodded in agreement. "Thanks for listening to an old man prattle on." He looked so helpless, and she wanted to hug him.

"No sweat. You've been so kind to me since you've been here — it's the least I can do. Next drink's on me." Abi pushed the chair back and collected her belongings. She hoped he'd make it through.

Finally entering her apartment, Abi decided not to bother with her groceries and dialled her parents' number. One ring. Two rings. Come on, pick up. Three rings. Shit. What if they're not home? Fou —

"Hello?"

"Hi, Dad."

"Hiya, honey. You just caught us heading out to a charity dinner," Dale said.

Charity dinner? Must be nice. How's about tossing some of that charity this-a-way?

"So what's up?" he asked.

"Guess what?" Abi replied, barely suppressing her excitement.

"Um. Don't know, sweetie. You're pregnant," her dad responded, chuckling.

"No. I'm not pregnant. Better. I got a job today!" Abi cried, coaxing the cat away from her lap and waiting to hear his reaction.

"Well, I'll be damned. Where at? Not McDonald's, I hope."

"Not that that would necessarily be a bad thing, Dad, but no. I got a job at Hubris, if you can believe it." Relieved, joyous laughter. Phew. Wonder what he would've done if it *had* been a gig slinging fries. Hypotheticals aside, Abi was very content. She and her father now had a connection — life in the corporate world — and she would finally be making him proud.

"That's great, honey! What's the base? How many options?

Remember, I'm expecting you to take care of your mother and me during our golden years."

Hmm. As always it was coming down to the money. "$31K to start," Abi stated, as proudly as she could.

"Not bad. Not bad at all," Dale said supportively.

"Plus options. Not many, though," Abi elaborated. "Actually could you look over my options agreement?"

"Sure, not a problem. Fax it to me in the morning, and I'll take a look at it. And remember — no one made a million in their first job, sweetie."

Gee. Thanks for the enlightenment, Dad.

"Hey, Edith! Abigail got a job!"

Holy encomium, Batman. She could barely hear her mother in the background, but she could tell that she had done right by both of them. They were finally pleased with her and for her.

"No, she just called. Don't blame me if you didn't hear the phone ring. Here, let me put you on speaker phone, sweetheart — your mother wants to hear the good news."

Jesus. You'd think I'd just won the Pulitzer or something. The phone screeched, and Abi winced, holding the receiver away from her ear. They could put a man on the moon, but they couldn't figure out how to make a speaker phone without feedback.

"Hi, sweetheart. So what's this? You got a job? Where?" her mother panted.

"At Hubris. It's only an admin position, though, Mom. And I'll have to work reception for now, so it's not like I'm running the company or anything. Yet."

"Yes, but you've gotten your foot in the door. That's what counts," her father replied with authority.

"True, but it'd be nice to get paid to actually *think*," Abi retorted. "I mean, the biggest decision I'll be making is whether to use UPS or FedEx."

"Soon enough, soon enough. Everyone's got to start somewhere. We are so proud of you, honey," her mother chimed in.

Abi smiled, pulling Paw close. Thinking is overrated anyway. God, I'm such a sycophant.

"I remember when I got my first job at No-Risk Insurance. Your mother and I had just found out that she was pregnant with you, and it was such a relief to know that I had gotten a decent job that would provide for us all. I came home, swaggered into our tiny kitchen, cracked open a beer, and let out one big 'yipee-ki-ay.' Your mother thought I was nuts. Yup, those were definitely good days," her father reminisced. And he claimed not to be sentimental.

"Oh, and I remember my first job, too," Edith laughed. "I was so proud of myself, making $250 a month working for this awful man named Ed. God, he had me doing the darndest things. Everything from preparing projection reports to writing birthday cards for his wife. Still, I thought I was the cat's pajamas," she continued, giddy with nostalgia. "Oh, and the office didn't have any air conditioning, and I remember one day being so wilted that I fell asleep while balancing the books. I thought I was going to get fired for sure. Be sure that doesn't happen to you, Abi. The last thing you want to do is lose your first job."

O ye of little faith. "Don't worry, Mom. I'm not going to lose my job. I mean, I technically haven't even started yet," Abi firmly assured them. "Besides, I could always move back home." She loved pulling that one out.

"Yeah, right. We changed the locks, remember? In all seriousness, we are so proud of you," her dad said.

"Keep doing what you're doing, because you're obviously getting it right," her mom added.

She loved her parents. Even if they were a bit sappy at times.

"Thanks, guys. At least now you know I won't be calling home for money any time soon," she laughed.

"Very funny. Talk to you on the weekend, sweetheart. Oh, and don't forget to send me that options agreement in the morning. Gotta start planning our retirement, after all."

"Ha, ha. What kind of cat food do you like? Don't worry, I'll send you the agreement tomorrow. Good night, Dad. Good night, Mom," Abi said.

"Night, sweetie," they said in unison.

Abi hung up the phone, smiling. *They didn't grill me half as bad as I thought they would. Yup. The parentals are definitely pleased.*

chapter nine

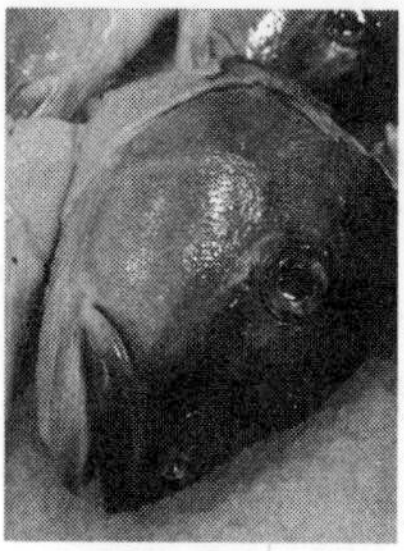

It was early yet, and the office was a ghost town. Most people having slaved late into the night prior, Abi was savouring having the joint almost to herself. It was almost as nice as the Donut Hut. *Mental note — come in as early as I can.* Abi was an official Hubris employee, and she was over the moon. Having baked chocolate chip cookies to commemorate the event, Abi strode back to the kitchen and gleefully arranged them on a plate for all to partake.

"You're here early," Cass said, walking up to Abi. "So have they given you a job description yet?"

Geez. I hadn't even thought of that. "No, not yet. I'm supposed to talk to Joshua about it today, though. Guess I'll find out then. Cookie?" Abi passed the dish over to Cass.

"Sure. Just be sure you get one from him. Believe me, I know what it's like to not have one. One thing I know for certain is that you and I are going to be sharing reception duties, at least for the time being. We can sit down later and go over how you want to break it down, okay?"

Abi nodded, trying not to look disappointed. *Great. Reception.* She had forgotten that's where they said they'd stick her. Abi picked up an errant chocolate chip and popped it into her mouth, savouring the morsel with a fleeting look of glee. *Crumbs are better than nothing.*

"Josh said something about me using David's desk, but I guess if I'm covering reception I can leave my things here for the time being."

"I think you're going to wind up sitting where Trixie, his last assistant, sat. It's back toward the kitchen and near his office. I'll find out today and get your phone set up and business cards ordered. Do you prefer Abi or Abigail?" she asked as they wandered back to the reception area.

Cassandra was amazing. She was HR, Standard Telecom girl, and travel whiz all rolled into one. At first Abi had been sceptical of Cassandra's willingness to help, but now she realized that it was simply part of her maternal nature. Sure, she put on the air of a tough Queen West chick, but Abi knew she was just a lamb in wolf's clothes. After all, Cassandra had taken her under her wing and brought her into Hubris, and Abi knew she was beholden to her for that.

The doors opened, and Cordy sauntered in, promptly followed by Josh. "Welcome, fellow Hubris employee," he said, smiling. "Has Cassandra got you all set up yet?"

Abi and Cassandra looked at each other, practically rolling their eyes over his bravado.

"We're workin' on it, Josh, don't you worry," Cassandra said.

"I'll leave it in your capable hands," he said, grabbing his Starbucks from the reception desk and continuing on to his office.

"He can be so annoying sometimes," Cassandra said. Noticing Abi's panicked look of torn allegiance, she checked herself. "I'm sorry, I shouldn't have said that. He can be a good guy. Did you want to help me unload the dishwasher? It's reeaallly fuuuunnn."

Personal crisis averted, Abi laughed. "Actually I've already done it."

Cass stood back, incredulous. "God, you're amazing. Guess I'll just grab myself a coffee, then." Cass stood up, straightened her skirt, and went to the kitchen, Cordy trailing behind her.

Abi sat back down in her spanking new chair and watched the Hubris world go by. She was still sussing the place out, taking copious mental notes. This place was great fodder, and she knew it would make a wonderfully poignant great American novel some day. Abi caught sight of her Donut Hut cup in the garbage and suddenly felt so provincial. Everyone here fell into the Starbucks camp. Sighing, she knew she had to do some serious image work if she was going to fit in. Glancing around at all the smartly dressed young 'uns, Abi knew a call to Mom was in order. Grabbing a slip of paper, Abi diligently began scribbling a list of needs. Black pants, black mock turtleneck, black socks, black shoes, black sunglasses, and perhaps even a new leather bag. And screw buying Canadian. Everyone looked like they owned shares of Gap, Banana Republic, or J Crew. Of course, the de rigueur flip phone and PDA, or Black Berry if she *really* wanted to be hip, would have to wait until at least her birthday. Folding the list and placing it in her daytimer, Abi had no idea how these guys managed it. Then she realized that they were geeks with money. In overdrive, they ruled the New World now. And they weren't even Rogaine age. It was truly sickening. The phone rang, reminding Abi why she was there. "Good Morning. Hubris," she managed without laughing. It was going to be a great day.

The kitchen was a hive when the drones converged. Toast browning. Microwave zapping. Kettle boiling. Knives chopping. Voices nattering. Everyone appeared to have felt peckish all at once. Sitting down with her Power Bar, Abi was just happy that she actually had a warm place to eat. For a week now, she had been relegated to park benches and seats in the Path, consuming her lunch as quickly and inconspicuously as possible among the lunch-hour shoppers and pedestrians. She had always been permitted to use the staff room, but being a day worker she had always been intimidated to do so. Lunch hour was far too personal a time for intrusions by an offending foreign presence. Sitting on the barstool, Abi grinned. She now had a home.

"There you are," Cass said, entering the kitchen area, coat in hand. "I've been looking for you."

Uh, oh. What have I done wrong? "Oh, uh. Yeah, I was just sitting down for a quick lunch — is that okay?" Abi shyly explained, fearing reprisal.

"Of course it is," Cass replied, a look of surprise on her face. Abi was just too deferential. "You have to eat, you know. Which is why I was looking for you. I was thinking we could go for a celebratory lunch."

Lunch? Out? Abi looked down at her breakfast bar, mentally calculating how much she had in the bank. What to do, what to do?

"Don't worry, it's on Hubris," Cass quickly added, recognizing the look of poverty and humility in Abi's eyes.

Phew. She could come up with only so many excuses for not accompanying people out for a noonday repast before they would start to think she was a snob or a social moron. "Hey, if it's on Hubris, I'm there," Abi quipped, adopting a more relieved and relaxed mien.

"Good. How's sushi?"

Hmm. Sounds a little exotic and expensive for lunch but okay. "Just as long as I don't have to eat anything that moves," Abi laughed, rising from her stool and following Cass down the hall. And they said there is no such thing as a free lunch.

A gentle bell chimed them in, and Abi glanced around, immediately feeling a bit awkward and encumbered for the cool, Zen minimalism of the restaurant's environs. Simple, low tables cloaked in white tablecloths lined the outer walls, methodically placed at regular intervals. A small water fountain sat in the corner, trickling slowly into the carp pond below and quietly attempting to restore their chi and tranquillity. A couple of suits sat at the sushi bar, silently consuming their California rolls and sashimi, adhering to the hushed code of conduct.

"Are you sure this is okay? It looks pretty expensive," Abi wondered, mindful not to break the silence.

"Of course," Cass replied, more loudly. The suits looked up, lacquered chop sticks in midair. Sorry to have disturbed you, man. Removing her gloves and coat, Cass moved to one of the tables in the back. "Besides, I've got the Hubris corporate card," she smiled, plunking down across from Abi.

A hostess stealthily slipped up next to them, placing two simply printed menus in front of each of them. Reviewing one of them, Abi had no clue what to order. Wonder if they have tuna melts.

Two small glasses of water appeared in front of them. "Welcome, Cass," the woman said in a beautifully soft voice.

"Thank you, Aoi," Cass said, slightly nodding her head. "She's so sweet," she remarked, watching Aoi disappear into the back. "Well, congratulations, Abi." Cass raised one of the glasses, not even glancing at her menu.

Guess she's practised in ordering raw fish. Picking up the other glass, Abi couldn't help but feel a little self-conscious. She wasn't accustomed to being congratulated, and she certainly wasn't used to being taken out for lunch. "Thanks, Cass. This is all so overwhelming, though," she admitted, softly clinking her glass against Cass's.

"Don't worry," Cass chided. "You'll do fantastic at Hubris. I know you will." Famous last words. "Besides, I can't believe how well you've settled in so far. And Josh loves you already. That's the toughest test."

The waitress returned, a small order book in hand. Crap. The moment of truth. "Oh, ah. I'm not sure yet," Abi said, flustered and attempting to decipher the menu. Must not look like an ass. "Um. What's good here, Cass?" she asked, trying to save face and look like the pro she wasn't.

"We'll have four California rolls, four futo-maki, and some temaki," she skilfully ordered, smiling up at Aoi and handing her the menu.

Guess I'll have what she's having, whatever that is.

Aoi discreetly nodded and padded up to the sushi bar, order in hand.

Sitting erect and rolling her water glass between her hands, Abi didn't quite know what the protocol was for lunching. "So how did you start at Hubris?" she ventured, remembering what her father had said about getting people to talk about themselves.

"Oh, I answered an ad in the paper, actually. I was in school, working toward my degree in theatre arts, waiting for my big break, and starving in the process. Figured I needed some sort of income and that I'd be able to juggle both," she explained.

"Really? You're an actress? I had no idea." Cool. A sister in arms.

"Yeah. Or at least I was before Hubris. Hubris has quickly become my life, and I had to give up school and my fifteen minutes. Just don't let that happen to you, my friend," she advised, wiping invisible tears in mock sorrow.

It better not. "Don't worry, I won't. You'll be the first to receive an invite to my debut book launch." Unlike Cass, Abi knew that this latest turn of events wouldn't affect her forging ahead with her dreams.

Aoi returned, meekly setting a large, black, octagonal platter between them. Ten neatly rolled concoctions lay nestled in the centre, cut on the bias to reveal the decorative layering of sticky rice, avocado, cucumber, and fish. A small, pinky rose of pickled ginger with a dollop of wasabi sat patiently off to one side. Staring at the plate, Abi couldn't believe that such a meal would prove to be satiating. At least it didn't have any MSG.

Unsleeving her chopsticks and pouring some soy into the side dish, Cass delicately selected one of the mystery rolls and dipped it in the tiny cup of black liquid. Abi tried to do the same. Picking up a roll, she clumsily dropped it in the soy. Plop. Crap. There goes my career as a geisha.

"So do you ever think you'll return to acting?" Abi asked, trying to deflect attention and fishing out her roll.

"Well, I don't know. It depends on if and when Hubris IPOs. If we go public soon, then yeah, I'll go back to school. Otherwise I've got to hang in there — I've got too much vested right now," Cass explained, suavely popping the roll into her mouth.

Okay. So you *do* eat it in one fell swoop. "I hope for your sake that we do. And I guess now for mine," Abi chortled, shoving the plump, soy-laden ball into her tiny mouth. Uh, oh. Way too much sushi for this novice to handle. Chewing furiously to compensate for the sudden overload, Abi tried to discreetly hamster some of the overflow into her cheek. Unable to speak, she daftly grinned at Cass, who was already on her second roll. Man, at this rate I'll never eat lunch in this town again.

An hour later, Abi glanced at her watch. "Man, it's getting late. Shouldn't we be getting back soon?" she asked, the panic rising in her voice. She didn't want to get in shit her first official day.

"Yeah, probably," Cass concurred, obviously nonplussed. "Don't worry, though. Josh knew that I was taking you out. In fact, he suggested it."

Phew. Knowing that she had Josh's blessing, Abi relaxed back and, with only slightly more confidence, moved in for another attempt. Please don't let me drop it, please don't let me drop it.

"Aoi?" Cass called, flagging the waitress over. "Could we have the bill, please?"

Aoi nodded and quietly walked over to the register. "Well, I hope you'll like it at Hubris," Cass stated, pulling out her company card and placing it on the table.

"I already do," Abi confirmed, munching away on a final roll.

"Man, these things are quite deceiving. I think I'm actually stuffed." Who knew?

"I know," Cass giggled. "And you won't be hungry in a half hour, either."

Aoi returned and placed their bill in front of Cass. "Whenever you're ready," Aoi said.

Abi snuck a quick peek. Christ. Thirty bucks for that? Thank God it's on the company's tab.

"Actually, we should get running. If you could just put it on my card," Cass replied, setting the card on top of the bill and handing it back to Aoi.

"Certainly."

Cass was just too cool.

"Well, I guess it's back to the grind," Cass said resignedly.

"Yup. Another day, another dollar. Thanks for lunch, by the way," Abi proffered, pulling her jacket back on and laying her mittens on the table.

Aoi returned and presented Cass with the bill and a slim, cloisonné pen.

"You're very welcome, Abi," she responded, signing the slip and handing it back to Aoi.

Gathering their respective bags, they took a collective deep breath and faced the music. Abi had to admit that she felt pretty damn suave.

Filing the day's courier slips, Abi looked over at the clock. 6 p.m. Man, am I tuckered. They had covered everything from travel procedures to the new CRM to catering orders to how to handle Josh. All Abi could think was that assistantships are simple in theory, but totally nightmarish in practice. You'd have to be a master organizer to keep all this shit in line, and Abi was concerned. On top of all the logistical junk, she'd have to brush up on the industry and Hubris herself. How the hell did Cassandra do it all? Shoving one of the sales kits into her bag, she decided to call it a day. She had her homework cut out for her, and she wanted to get cracking. Slinging her bag over her shoulder, she began to go through the closing procedure. Fuck. There are still so many people here. Noticing that Josh's light was still on, Abi back-tracked to his office. He'd know what to do.

Knocking shyly on his door, she gently pushed it open. "Hi, Josh. I'm going to head home for the night. Is that okay?" She hoped he wasn't mad.

"No, that's fine. How was your first official day?"

God, I wish they'd stop saying that. "It was great. Cassandra's been fantastic at showing me the ropes." She didn't know what else to say. "Um. She had walked me through the closing procedure, but there seems to be an awful lot of people still left. Do I have to wait until they're gone?" She sure hoped not.

"Oh God, no. There'll be people here till at least ten o'clock. Scoot home, someone else will close up."

Man, ten o'clock? Better you than me. "If you say so," Abi responded hesitantly. She supposed she had been dispatched for the evening.

The heavens were already sparkling in the pristine night air, and Abi shuttled quickly past the dealer's post at Queen and Sherbourne. Women, obviously not waiting for the streetcar, stood around, their dilapidated faux fur jackets tightly wrapped around their emaciated waists in a feeble attempt to ward off the night's chill. Best not to stick around this neighbourhood too long. Bearing north on Sherbourne, Abi pulled her own jacket tight and empathized with the women, knowing that but for the grace of God there went she. Glimpsing in the ragtag rumble shops, she reflected on her day with certain misgivings. While she had appreciated her sushi lunch, she couldn't help but feel self-conscious of her financial situation and began to wonder how well she would actually fit in. They all seemed so with it, so together — financially and otherwise. Between shopping for funky wardrobes, lunching like socialites, and boogying until dawn, they packed in a ten- or twelve-hour workday, always going above and beyond the call of duty. And the scary part was that most of them were younger than Abi. Powerwalking up Sherbourne, Abi suddenly felt beset with stress. How had they achieved so much in such a short period of time? What if she didn't measure up to their expectations? She certainly couldn't let Josh or Cass down. Dodging pedestrians, Abi tried to calm herself down by repeating the *Serenity Prayer.* Baby steps, honey, baby steps. Stopping at Sherbourne and Wellesley, Abi glanced down at her worn-out getup. One thing was certain — she'd have to work on her wardrobe. *That* she did have the power to change.

chapter ten

Abi was in a great mood, having just deposited her final paycheque from ACME. She had a full wallet and a full roll of film, both of which she was going to blow at a jaunt to Kensington Market. Needing to face the day with a twelve-ounce double-double, Abi sauntered into Donut Hut, a casual look finally on her face. Only a couple of other patrons had cared to join Abi at the "office" this morning, all of whom appeared to be homeless. Sitting back in her usual chair, Abi was relieved by the dearth of raving teenagers. Geez. One little ol' shooting, and they scatter like E in a bust. At least she could think now. Scanning the room for some grist, Abi focused on the man directly to her left, who was methodically tearing up a plastic lid and placing the pieces delicately onto the table. He was in his own little world, focusing intently on his imaginary puzzle.

She had seen him before but had never sat near him. And now she knew why she had given him such a wide berth. He was clearly unwashed, and his aroma filled her little corner of heaven. The stench of urine and nicotine was almost unbearable, and Abi discreetly covered her mouth. How the hell am I supposed to consume my caffeine? She wondered how long he had been there and how long he would be able to stay within the warm, comfortable confines of the shop undisturbed. She wondered if he had a family — kids, a wife, a mother, a father. Her interest piqued, Abi began searching his table for clues to his identity, his past. A Thomas Wolfe novel lay beside him. Hmm. Good choice. He was obviously well educated and well read. Sensing that he was one of the people she had encountered at the Rosedale Library during working hours, she wondered what his deal was. How could he have fallen through the cracks? He was definitely a hard nut to crack. Setting down her coffee, Abi delved into her Harriet-like hobby of detailing those around her.

Between scribbles, Abi tried to glance out the window, despite what purported to be a chunk of cruller smeared directly across her line of sight, inhibiting her view of her world. Shit. Ever hear of Windex? Shuddering, Abi was disgusted. They were always so filthy. It was so dark that Abi could no longer make out if it was still snowing or not. The last of the Vomit Comets sped by, carrying rumbled revellers affordably home to their snug beds.

"Excuse me, Miss," an almost inaudible voice echoed from behind her. Looking over her shoulder, a young, bedraggled woman was standing timidly next to her table. Deep, dark circles surrounded her otherwise angelic eyes, straggly dirty blonde hair framing her delicate features. She looked as if she hadn't slept in weeks, and she probably hadn't. "I really have to pee, and the man won't let us *homeless* people use the bathroom," she said, barely whispering and indicating the shop owner. "Could you do me a favour and ask to go to the washroom? We just wanna see if it's actually outta order like he says it is," the girl said, gesturing to her cohort, a darker-haired, heavier-set girl.

Hmm, a little experiment in humanity. "Sure, not a problem. Sometimes it is out of order," Abi said, trying to give the guy the benefit of the doubt. Gathering her belongings, Abi trouped up to the counter and asked to use the washroom. The man buzzed her in, smiling warmly at her.

Opening the bathroom door, Abi couldn't believe that he was letting her go but not the other girls. For once nature wasn't calling, and Abi set her bags down, waiting for a reasonable amount of time to pass and covering her nose with her sleeve. The stench was a cross between a urinal puck and a load of manure.

This bathroom was positively putrid. Graffiti on the walls. A broken soap dispenser. God knows what on the toilet seat. Rusty stains in the bowl. It was like *Trainspotting.* Actually screw the worst WC in Scotland, this one was worse. Geez. Wonder what their kitchen's like. Shuddering at the thought, Abi slung her bag back over her shoulder. Thank God she was toting some trusty Purell with her. Flushing the phantom BM with her foot, Abi could hear loud voices from the coffee shop.

"I can't believe you let her go and not us. We're paying customers, too, ya know. Just 'cause we're homeless." The voice trailed off, uncertain as to how to finish effectively.

Returning to her seat, Abi set her bag down triumphantly. The guinea pig had fallen for it. The man was now standing defiantly in front of the donut racks, purveyor of all the doughy goodness he surveyed. What a bastard.

Ever so quietly, the girl rejoined Abi, sitting down at the table next to hers. "Thank you so much for doing that. I've had to go for hours, and he won't let us use it. She finally went outside and peed in the snowbank next door," she said, pointing to her friend. "I should reach over and steal all his damn donuts," she continued, fuming.

"Nah, you'll just get a really bad high from all that sugar," Abi advised, trying to diffuse the tension.

"Yeah, but at least it'd be a high," the girl retorted.

Pushing her chair out a bit, Abi tried to resume her writing. The light was transitioning from an inky black to a greyish pink, unsheathing the silhouettes of the towers above. 7:45 a.m. Abi wanted to get scooting, but with blood pressures so clearly elevated she had to park herself there a bit longer. As long as she was there, she knew the girls weren't going to exacerbate the situation any more. Participating in their little empirical exercise, Abi was clearly involved, and, feeling responsible for the safety of both the girls and the owner, there was no escaping now. Be the buffer, baby. May as well check out the *Globe*, she figured, picking up the paper and pulling out an extra smoke.

The girls continued their conversation, trading tips on what drop-in shelters were open, which ones weren't, and gossiping about their circle of friends. Abi pretended to read the paper, discreetly studying them through the corner of her eye. Their voices were calmer now; the sparks in their guarded eyes had dimmed significantly. Had they not been showing the effects of weeks or months on the streets, the pair would've passed as happy-go-lucky teens. That was the depressing part. Closing her eyes, Abi realized their dialogue could've been plucked from a twisted episode of *90210* or *Dawson's Creek*. Same shit, very different pile. Listening intently, Abi empathized with their indignation, rage, defiance. Being forced to pee in a snowbank was the ultimate humiliation, one that no one should have to endure. And God knows what other more dire abuses they had suffered at the hands of strangers on the streets or, worse, at the hands of their parents on the homestead. For these girls, the incredible sense of pride and dignity cloaked in callousness was a means to an end, a question of survival. Setting down her *Globe*, Abi felt petty as hell for whining about not being able to purchase a new pair of shoes for New Year's. What would they do to ring in the new year? What kind of resolutions could they make in the face of despair? Quit smoking? Lose five pounds? Keep warm? Not get raped? Abi pulled out another smoke, ruminating. Fuck. They should be happy-go-lucky teens.

Suppressing the urge to groan, Abi picked up the paper and continued her charade. Ugh. Worst part was that she really *did* need to pee now. And her feet were freezing. Fuck. Why do I always do this? God, I wish they would leave already. Then I'd be free to go. Crossing her legs tightly, Abi bided her time listening to the indignant chatter of the girls and reviewing the TV listings. Altruism sucks. Tapping her foot impatiently, Abi flipped through the pages. At least there was a decent double feature on PBS tonight.

The juice fountains were pumping their concentrated concoctions over the sides of the container, taunting Abi's bladder with their slight but very noticeable swooshing sound. Christ, this is like water torture.

Finally the blonde girl got up to search for her boyfriend. "Miss, do you have an extra cigarette?" she asked, pulling a worn camo jacket over her thin frame.

"Sure," Abi said, relieved that she would soon be relieved. Pulling a few smokes from her pack, Abi smiled and handed the stash to her.

"Thank you so much. Have a wonderful day," the girl gushed, walking out the front door with her friend.

Waiting till the coast was clear, Abi gathered her belongings and hoofed it to the john. "Sorry! Two jumbos will do that to ya!" she exclaimed to the suspicious owner. She didn't give a wit about how disgusting the bathroom was now. That's what quadriceps were for.

Heading down College to Augusta, Abi rushed to get to the market. It had been way too long, and she was chomping at the bit. Since arriving in Toronto, she had frequented Kensington as often as her bank balance would permit, and each excursion had proved titillating and rewarding. With its sidewalk bins brimming with colours, textures, scents, and sounds, the market evoked a European sensibility and joie de vivre. For Abi it was far more rewarding to select a handful of speckled farm-fresh eggs from the hodgepodge of shops as opposed to thoughtlessly tossing homogeneously packaged and portioned groceries into a glistening, sterile cart. She had to work it here without the convenience; Abi took pride in knowing which vendors stocked the best cheeses or punchiest chilis. Here she was the truffle hunter, strolling from specialty shop to specialty shop, in control but never knowing precisely what she would discover. There was just something so individualistic about sniffing out single items that weren't shrink-wrapped, processed, or cosmetically enhanced. No muzak, no fluorescent sky, no nuclear green coleslaw. Just a cacophony of musical tastes, bristling breezes, and pasty green-as-God-intended cabbage.

Abi rounded the corner and was transported to an older world. She grinned, pulling out her camera and lilting down the sidewalk. Despite the fact that it was -5°C, everyone was in a jovial mood. Vendors were setting up their wooden stands and pulling out their awnings, deliverymen dropped off wholesale sides of beef, early morning risers were savouring cups of coffee, freshly ground at the corner shop. Kensington Market on a Saturday morning — in her mind, there was nothing better.

Bending down, Abi picked up her camera and shot a lime that had fallen into the gutter. For once she was happy that she had loaded it up with colour film. It would capture the juxtaposition of the neon green on black perfectly. She was in The Zone. God, it feels great to afford film again. After taking several shots, Abi leaned over and picked the lime up, depositing it in the garbage on her way to the fruit and vegetable stand. What should I make tonight? Stir-fry? Yawn. She had had enough stir-fried veggies recently to feed all of China. Wandering through the bins, Abi considered what fare she would dine on. It had been so long since she had had money to cook that she was coming up dry. Um. What about fresh pasta with a sundried tomato sauce? In such a cool climate, it sounded hearty and wonderful. Thank God for comfort food. Gripped with culinary inspiration, Abi began selecting tomatoes, red and green peppers, and anything else she figured would be an appropriate accompaniment.

Lugging her goodies into her apartment, Abi was feeling the pain of rising so damn early. She really ought to sleep in once in a while. And indulge in the streetcar. She was tired but had a sense of accomplishment; she'd spent the entire day at the market and had snapped two rolls of film. Looking longingly at her couch, Abi began putting away her groceries. Unpack first, then nap. Bell peppers, fresh pasta, cheese, a little vino. Man, I'm going to feast tonight. It had been so long since she had even thought of buying such treats, and she couldn't wait to get started. Why sleep when you can eat?

"À la carte is the only way to go," she muttered, retrieving her one and only pot from the stove drawer. Time to work some magic. Dicing up the veggies and measuring out a modest amount of pasta, Abi was mindful not to overdo it, her mind meandering back to the plump woman scarfing back a cinnamon bun the size of an infant at the coffee shop. She considered how today's trend leaned toward a farmhand's supper for a chair dweller's day, the proportions not only undeserved but also perversely inverse. While portion sizes were up, dress sizes were down. What sick puppy thought that up? "Who needs a sixty-four-ounce gulp, anyway?" she asked Paw, who was busily purring at her ankles. The timer finally went off, and, plating her pasta, Abi stood back and admired her home-cooked creation. Mama would be proud.

chapter eleven

Subject:

```
Abi, thanks for your response; good
stuff.
I expect the soft copy will arrive in the
next few days.
Just a reminder, I need a package of
Hubris collateral materail .
50 sets probably a good start.
Also, if any promo tiems are avail, such
as tshirts, hats, etc, would appreciate a
supply.
adonis
```

God, and these guys are corresponding with the public? "Christ, are we in trouble," Abi muttered, typing a reply that, compared to his e-mail, read like Dickens.

Subject: Sales Information Kits and Collateral

Adonis,
You're welcome for the information.
Regarding the sales kits, I intend to make more kits this week and will forward them on to you as soon as they are complete. As for the promotional items, we currently only have T-shirts and wallets available, and I will send these along with the kits. I hope that this is okay.
Please do not hesitate to contact me should you require any additional materials.
Best regards,
Abigail Somerhaze

Composing her response to Adonis, Abi didn't think that she had actually conversed mano a mano with a single individual yet this morning. She was in e-country now. She had been constantly interceding, intercepting, interconnecting, but not actually interacting. The only voices she had heard and verbal imprints she had left had been via voice mail or mobile, the only written correspondence traded via ethernet, her messages bouncing off satellites and pulsing through underground cabling, the distinct packets of info converging on their destination simultaneously. In many ways, it should have been easier for Abi this way, appealing to her shy, timid nature. Electronic interaction was efficient, and no one had to look into her eyes and know what she was actually thinking of them and their directives. And she could go about her business at her own pace, not being impeded by social graces and protocol.

However, these shy, stealthy exchanges parlayed themselves into obstacles for Abi, and for the most part she didn't like it. The immediacy of the correspondence had caused her to stumble more than once, and she found it difficult to assimilate to the new form of communication. When she had first started to use it, she had celebrated e-mail as a time saver. But the e-mails simply came too frequently, and it was so distracting to see that little envelope appear in the corner of her screen. Her inbox now served as a conduit for Top Ten lists, inundated with the proliferation of mediocre, corporate humour. As far as Abi could figure, e-mail only served to provide a platform for spammers, verbose jesters, and pontificators. They seemed to come every few minutes, and, being a curious Pavlovian creature, Abi couldn't help but check her inbox whenever she was cued. It was too tempting not to check, and she was beginning to bemoan its distracting nature. And she resented the amount of time she had to sacrifice in order to separate the valid e-mails from the flood of lists, jokes, and anecdotes that backlogged her system. After all, the five minutes she spent downloading an uncompressed, lewd Tetris game were five minutes that she had lost forever.

For Abi, e-mail was a staccato form of communication, fostering quicker, less-thought-out messages. Being a stickler for grammar and minutiae, Abi found it difficult to maintain pace, preferring to compose traditionally formatted letters and detailed responses. All of this contemplation and proofing took time and care, and she couldn't help but admonish herself if it took her more than a few minutes to reply to an e-mail. She simply couldn't adhere to the new rules of engagement, to the modern way of interacting with a two-line, improperly punctuated, acronym-filled paragraph lacking salutary and signatory lines forwarded by a bunch of BSCs.

Completing her reply to Adonis's e-mail, Abi hit "Send," lamenting the transition to rapid-fire exchanges, the demise of formally written letters. They totally cramped her style. Not only was her wry humour lost in the terse tonality of e-mail, but also their humour was lost on her. Did they really mean "great job," or were they being sarcastic? Was the use of ALL CAPS a scathing indictment? Something always seems to get lost in the electronic translation. It was so easy to offend with a flip comment, there was no recourse once "Send" was selected, and Abi was too sensitive and naïve not to have been stung by its curt expediency. Still, it was a decent trade-off. The bottom line was that she could now say that she had e-mail.

Abi immediately went to drag her message to its proper pigeonhole. Christ. Three hundred and ninety-six sent e-mails. How many of the damn things do I have to save? Minimizing her Outlook, Abi decided to stick her head in the virtual sand. Better to wait until day's end to organize all of her pithy letters.

"Morning, Abi," a startling voice boomed from behind her, breaking the blissful silence.

Dropping her Bic, Abi felt like swearing but bit her tongue instead. "Morning Josh," she muttered.

"Listen, how would you like to start joining our weekly production meetings? They would be very educational for you, and I'd like for you to start participating in them."

Being invited to a meeting, how cool is that? Smiling, Abi was definitely intrigued. "That sounds fabulous," Abi responded, not even bothering to disguise her exuberance.

"Great. I'll add you to the list of attendees in the scheduler,"

Josh said, turning toward his office. "Oh. And can you take over the ordering of lunches? Nothing that involved — just arranging for sandwiches and salads through the caterer. I think Cass has all the information on them. See you at two, then." Josh disappeared behind the cubicle wall.

Abi frowned. Nicely done. Inflate the ego and then pop it with an unexpected barb.

So this is what happens behind closed doors. An engaging conversation over what vertical Hubris should tackle was rolling along on its own special tangent. For the most part, all the members appeared nonplussed, as if they not only expected to squander so much of their workday but also actually enjoyed it. They had embarked on the production meeting an hour before, and virtually nothing had been accomplished yet, at least nothing that was on the agenda. Circular logic was ruling the roost. Abi sat quietly observing the tableau, a bemused smile on her face. She was a dilettante in their very serious arena. Abi glanced at the meeting agenda and at her watch. One hour, one action item. Yawn. Abi looked to Joshua, the supposed moderator-cum-circus leader. He was sitting back, chomping openly on a fashionable vegetarian wrap. A few sprouts had migrated onto his lapel, and Abi suppressed the urge to giggle. He was only encouraging the debacle. So what had been revealed aside from that everyone had his or her own agenda? Didn't anyone want something productive to come from this "production" meeting? Couldn't they take their damn shopping tips offline? Focus, people, focus. Abi took another bite of her brownie and almost audibly moaned with pleasure. At least the food was good.

2:45 p.m. God, this is excruciating. All Abi wanted to do was bolt. Taking her eyes off her lunch plate, Abi scanned the room, studying each attendee one by one, and wondered if they were as mind-numbed as she was. Frank was so obviously doodling that it was laughable. Steve was silent, staring at the speakerphone in the centre of the boardroom table. Tim was typing away on his laptop, composing a salacious letter to his wife, for all anyone knew. Talk about unilateral decision making. Josh was the only one talking and, it appeared, the only one listening. He was his most attentive audience.

"I really believe that penetration into these markets would be highly lucrative," he stated confidently. Penetration. He, he, he. He said penetration. "Well, any questions?" Silence speaks volumes. "Well, I guess that's it, then." Josh looked around the room, the anointed suddenly jumping to attention, their heads bobbing in sycophantic concurrence.

"Well, that was as useful as a fart in a space suit," Abi said to herself, beginning to gather up the dirty dishes and lunch trays. Welcome to the wonderful world of futility. Christ, it was like herding cats. Gathering up the empty pop cans and half-eaten sandwiches, Abi began to feel more like a maid than an executive assistant. So much for glamour.

"Oh, Abi," Josh called, reentering the conference room. Startled, Abi looked up, nearly dropping the tray of remnants. "Sorry about that."

"It's okay. Just a little zoned out, I guess," Abi replied, bending down to retrieve an errant pop can, her eyes belying her words. She was definitely perturbed.

"Would you be able to send out the action items from the meeting? Just send them on to the sales team when you're done," he instructed.

"Sure, I — ," she began to respond, glancing up to nothing. Dropping the pop can once again, Abi was aghast. Josh had already moved on up. Before she had even accepted his tedious mission. "Bastard," Abi muttered bitterly, continuing to clean. "So much for democracy." You can take the boy out of the club but not the club out of the boy.

Stomping into the kitchen, Abi was about ready to scream. The joint was a complete disaster. Dishes were piled in the sink, and half-consumed pop cans cluttered the counter. People were simply walking away from their garbage, knowing that either Cassandra or Abi would pick up after them. Abi was beginning to feel like an overwhelmed teenage matriarch. "I swear some of these pigs have never used a dishwasher before," Abi bitterly mumbled to herself, arranging glasses on the top rack.

"Ask Abi, she'll know," a voice echoed from the hallway.

Abi paused in order to eavesdrop better. How cool. People actually think I know what I'm doing. Continuing her domestic duty, Abi was filled with pride. Cass had taught her how to navigate the company, and Abi had become a walking, talking Hubris reference repository, a feat of which she was extremely proud. Now, if she could only adopt Cass's directness and strength, she'd really be in business. Abi finished up the dishes and, grabbing a DC from the fridge, headed back to her desk for some real work.

Abi looked over at the clock on her monitor. Shit! It was almost 6:45. She was supposed to be at the church by 7 p.m. "Christ. And I'm not even close to finishing my work." She exhaled and slumped back in her chair. Maybe she could scoot over before the dinner was cleaned up, do her social stint, and come back to the office. No. Better yet, I'll just take some work home with me and do it after the program. Shutting off her computer, Abi couldn't believe that she had lapsed like that. It was so unher. Maybe volunteering wasn't such a good idea anymore. It had served its purpose when she was unemployed and needed company, a set place to be on a regular basis, but now it was becoming bothersome. As much as she tried, she simply couldn't do it all. Something had to give, and it obviously couldn't be Hubris.

"See you tomorrow, Cass." Cassandra looked surprised. "You going home?"

"Nah. If it's Tuesday, it must be the mission thing," Abi joked.

"You're such a little socialite," Cassandra laughed.

Yeah. An impoverished socialite, Abi thought as she continued out the door.

Hitting King Street, she checked the time again. Guess it'll have to be TTC. It was the only way to make it to the church on time. Screw it. Take a cab. Just this once. A cab went whizzing by her just as she was about to flag it. Damn. She looked down King. Hundreds of cars, none of which was taking paying passengers. Murphy's fucking law. Way off in the distance, Abi could make out a light, like some sort of life-saving beacon. She began flailing wildly, knowing this was her last chance, or she'd be rocketing it for sure. The cab pulled over, and she hopped in, desperate to get to her destination. There was one thing she couldn't tolerate, and that was tardiness.

Arriving at the church, she rushed in the side door and frantically began searching for Sam. Barging into the kitchen, she saw he was in the throes of preparing the evening's dessert — apple cobbler doled out in cheap disposable bowls. "Sam, I am so sorry I'm late. Work was nuts, and time just got away from me," she cried, pulling off her jacket and putting on an apron.

"Don't sweat it, these things happen. All I ask is that you help me clear the tables so I can bring the dessert out — the troops are still hungry," he responded patiently.

Abi was relieved. He was such a great guy. "It's the least I can do, man." Abi hit the door with her ass and swung into the dining room.

Clearing the tables, Abi studied the room. How come I've never noticed the smell before? The place was pretty naff. Del was right. It was all so depressing and overwhelming. Could she really make a difference? Gus waltzed up to her, patting her on the back. "Hey, sugar! How're you doin' tonight? I didn't think you were gonna make it."

Abi looked up and tried in vain not to look irked. She was way too tired to play nice. "Yeah. I know," she responded curtly. "Work was an absolute nightmare today," she haughtily explained with a Ms. Shit air of "Of course, *you* wouldn't understand that."

He leaned over and put his hand on her shoulder. Abi debated shying away but thought better of it. He was a nice guy, and the last thing she wanted to do was offend him. Picking up the last of the supper dishes, she glanced at the clock. 7:45 p.m. And she still had the movie to sit through. Too bad she couldn't do her work while they took in the flick. But no, I'm here to socialize, dammit. Let's get this party started. Abi decided to speed things along a bit.

"Hey, Sam! Where's the video? Is the VCR set up yet?" Abi could barely disguise her impatience. Didn't they realize she had work to do? Practically rushing back to the kitchen, she pushed open the swinging door, almost slamming into Sam. God, I can be such a moron at times.

"Hey! Where's the fire?" Sam exclaimed, an injured look on his face.

"Sorry about that — too much caffeine today, I guess." Abi instantly felt sheepish. "Let me help you with that," she said, grabbing the leftovers and putting them on the opposite counter. "Did you want me to throw the movie on? It's almost eight."

"Sure, why not?"

A wave of relief swept over Abi. At least she'd be out of there at a semidecent hour.

Making her way through the guests, Abi grabbed the flick and slid it into the VCR. As if on cue, Sam dimmed the lights. "'Kay, guys," she said, clapping her hands to get the room's attention. "Tonight, for your cinematic enjoyment, we have *Dirty Dancing*," she announced, spotting Gus at the rear of the room and noting his disdain.

"So, um, enjoy," she said, hitting the play button and moving back toward Gus. Man, I was such a bitch. Sitting down next to him, Abi smiled apologetically. "Sorry if I was such a grouch before, Gus," she started, hoping she'd be able to make amends.

Gus snorted. Uh, oh. Then smiled. Thank you, Lord.

"It's okay. Had one of those days myself," he conceded, shuffling a pack of cards.

"Really? What happened?" Abi sympathized, indicating that she was all ears.

"Nothing much. Just my daughter wanted me to come visit her in Owen Sound, and I don't think I can swing it. It's her birthday tomorrow. She'll be twenty-seven," he explained, choking up and staring down at the cards.

Crap. If she had had a million dollars. And she had been wah-wahing about her day. "It's okay, Gus. I'm sure she understands," she said, trying to console him but immediately feeling trite and unhelpful.

Gus nodded slowly and closed his eyes, his head tilted toward the wall. "It's just tough not being able to provide for her the way I used to. I mean, I used to throw the biggest bashes for my little girl. But not anymore, not since my bar went belly-up," he said, hanging his head and discreetly wiping his eye. "I should be worrying about her, not the other way around. I just don't want to be a burden is all."

Man, this economy sucked. "You're not a burden, Gus, and you never will be. You're way too proud and hard working for that. You've got a job, you'll be getting a place soon. You'll be back on your feet in no time, you'll see," she encouraged, bending her head toward his and trying to make eye contact. She was going to cheer him up if it was the last thing she did.

"I know, Abi. Sometimes I'm just tired of the struggle," he

managed, finally looking up at her. With a sudden burst of energy, he sat erect and stretched his neck out, rolling his head from side to side. "But I guess tomorrow is another day. Made it this far, haven't I?" he quipped, breaking into a selfless grin and patting Abi's shoulder with one of his large, gentle hands.

"There you go," Abi smiled. "Now how about watching a little *Dirty Dancing*? I know it's one of your faves," she joked, placing her hand on his. Pretending to focus on the movie, Abi couldn't believe how honest and strong this man was. He screamed integrity and stamina. One thing was for certain, she'd be crying like a baby if she had had to endure all that he had in his lifetime. He was definitely one who knew how to suck it up and be a real man.

Phew. Adjusting her thermostat, Abi shuddered and slumped onto her sofa. 20°C and 9:57 p.m. Ain't life great? It was late, and it was a school night, and the place was freezing. Abi lugged the space heater out from under the sink, set it to "High" and plunked down, crouching frigidly in front of it. It felt great to be home, to have some peace, to have no demands on her time. She looked over at the phone and didn't even think of checking her messages. She was too tuckered for that. Christ. I have no energy. Sprawling out on the floor, Abi closed her lids and began to doze in the warmth. Whatever she had to do for Hubris, it'd have to wait until tomorrow. Paw crept over, sensing her anxiety, and she pulled him close and gave him a big kiss on the nose. Hey. It's Tuesday. Great PBS night. Leaping up with a bolt of energy, Abi turned off the heater and ran into the bedroom. She had only a few minutes before the fun began. Getting changed into her jammies, setting the alarm, making the tea, grabbing the comforter, and hitting the couch, Abi looked at the VCR. 10:04 p.m. Record time. Turning the TV on and switching to WNED, Abi hunkered down and promptly fell asleep.

chapter twelve

The world is fully wired. Tech stocks are hot and getting hotter. Traditional companies are so '80s. Why mortar when you can smoulder? Millionaires cruise the streets of San Mateo and San Jose on their Harleys, in their Boxters. At twenty-something, they own the means of production. It's their world now. Everyone has a vision. Everyone has the latest enterprise solution. Everyone is scalable. Everyone has angles. Everyone wants to be the next Bill, the next Jeff, the next Larry. It all starts with a concept, germinates with a modest loan from the parents, and flourishes in a concrete-floored home office. They are growing exponentially. First it was the programmers, then the sales team, then the finance guys, then the marketers, then the admins. The back office moves to a larger space. Then a larger space still. The larger space needs renovating. Must maintain the company identity. Screw the bottom line. Nothing ventured, nothing capitalized. It's all about image, after all. Pool tables installed, espresso bars put in, dowdy drop ceilings ripped out. Hiring continues. Revenues trickle in, profits are unrealized. We need money in order to sustain growth. We must look toward going public. Put on the suit. Get the hair cut. Spit-shine the shoes. Venture to their world. Walk the Corridors of Power. Sit in their marble reception areas. Drink their coffee. Ogle their receptionists. Hope for a catered lunch. Meet with the investment bankers. Say! Looks to be the same age as your dad. Give our spiel, fingers crossed behind our backs. God, our product's flaky. That's strange — it's never crashed like that before. Good recovery. Sweaty-palmed shake. Slaps on the back. Knots released. Leave elated.

Everyone wants to fund the little companies that could. The NASDAQ is booming, and millionaires are being made overnight, at least on paper. It starts with a few investments, selected higgledy-piggledy, and receives enormous dividends. The balance sheets grow, and the angels swoop. Deep pockets troll the streets, peering like vultures at the lofts inhabited by start-ups.

The rich always want to get richer. Gotta get a piece of the action. Who would be the next amazon.com? The next boo.com? Must do due diligence. Venture to their world. Meet with the board. Meet with the CEO. Say! Looks to be the same age as your son. Watch their Power Point presentations. Study their pipelines and forecasts. Eat their catered lunches. Ogle their receptionists. Don't sweat the demo — we understand how temperamental technology can be. We've studied the kids, now throw them a bone and see how they perform. Nothing ventured, nothing gained.

The pas de deux between start-up and venture capitalist is meant to be. They both see dollar signs; it's just a matter of sealing the deal. NDAS are executed, licence agreements signed, and the discussions begin fervently. Negotiations are conducted clandestinely, the only indications being that the CEO is requesting yet another tutorial and that the finance guy is in yet another suit. And thirty-page agreements from the lawyer keep jamming the fax. The parade of suits invading their territory makes everyone jumpy. Rumours fly and are only put to rest by the smug smile on the CEO's face. The Cristal is purchased by the pert assistant, secretly waiting to christen the latest deal and counting her options as she calls the kids.

Lo and behold, the injection occurs, and the company-wide e-mail goes out. Press releases are drawn up, and the Web site is updated. Take the money and run! Time to rock 'n' roll! The booze flows, and the staff room suddenly seems small. Need a change of venue. Take the company out on the other guy's tab. We've got the dough now. Someplace nice, no more cheap and cheerful. Martini bar? Tapas? Sushi? Who cares about accountability? We're allowed to do this just this once. Besides, we're a real company now. Someone believes in us. Rent the whole fucking restaurant, invite the brokers, bring the wives, and open the bar. Let's live a little. Let's party like it's 1999.

We need a new space — a new look or a new feel at least. This place is so tired. Gotta be fresh. The designers are interviewed, selected, and dispatched with strict orders to buy the best and find the funkiest. It's got to be cutting edge. Think *Wallpaper*. Tyler Brûlé is the cat's pajamas. Construction begins, more dropped ceilings destroyed. Exposed pipes and industrial chic. Open concept creates communication and creativity. Or at least the studies show. The new furniture arrives, and the new cappuccino machine is installed. It's bliss. What a difference a mezzanine will make. That's a person's salary? Gotta spend money to make money, after all. Brand management and corporate identity are important, you know. We need new equipment. We need new servers, new cell phones, new laptops. We need Palms, photocopiers, printers. We need office supplies, marketing materials, business cards, software, a CRM, new hires, programmers, support guys, account managers, marketers. We need warm bodies. We need evangelism. We need to keep up with demand. Money's getting tight? Take the new hire's salary out of the admin budget. It's all about creative financing.

chapter thirteen

"You're going to London again?" Once again Josh needed yet more travel changes. "You were just there. Oh. Actually this is a good thing. I just read about a new hotel there in *Wallpaper*. It's called My Hotel, and it's all the rage. You simply must stay there," Abi dictated.

She had no idea what she was talking about, but at least she sounded like she did. Of course, it was four hundred dollars a night, but Abi didn't feel the need to elaborate. In her parasitic way, she wanted to subvert the system and live vicariously through Josh. And it was only slightly disingenuous. Since she had started at Hubris, she had been drawn to the freewheeling, loose-purse-strings joie de vivre. It was an ultrahip attitude where anything was possible. A pristine image where there wasn't any tarnish a little dough couldn't buffer. It was cosmopolitans at Canoe. It was furniture from Up Country. It was weekends in St. Barts. So much squandering, so much waste, so much damn fun. She was learning decadence from the best of them, and she was loving it. No franchised, side-of-the-turnpike motels for these folk. She just couldn't wait until she sat prissily on the other side of the glass.

"I think it's an Ian Schrager," Abi continued flirtatiously.

"A Schrager? You know I can't pass up a Schrager. Sounds fabulous. Try to get me in there. Oh. And don't forget to call the car, either."

Finance is really going to freak now. Screw it. It isn't my buck. "Not a problem. I'll e-mail you the e-ticket. Ciao for now." Abi hung up and smiled.

Picking up the phone to call the travel agency, she was on top.

It was so glamorous, so empowering, so sexy to be revelling in other people's money. She was falling head over heels for Hubris. "Hi Sherry. It's Abi. Yes, I know he's travelling *again*." Despite the fact that Sherry couldn't see Abi all the way from her cube in North York, Abi rolled her eyes in mock disdain just for effect. She loved the way she sounded. Being a Leo, she was a star-fucker at heart. She figured even if she played only a small part in the action, she was part of the action nevertheless. In another life, she probably would've been a stalker or, worse, paparazzi. "He needs to leave for London tonight. No. Just overnight. I know. It is crazy, isn't it? Oh. And see if you can get him into My Hotel. No, no. Not *my* hotel. My Hotel." Abi again rolled her eyes, this time in true disgust. God, it's so difficult to get good help these days. "It's a new hotel in London. Don't you read *Wallpaper*? Oh. You ought to. It's really great. Anyway, see if you can get him in there. I think it's an Ian Schrager, and he loves his boutique hotels. Ian Schrager." God, this girl really is clueless. She should go south of Sheppard every once in a while. "Schrager hotels are renowned — the best," Abi stated knowledgeably, rubbing her temples. "Oh. I've got another call coming in. E-mail me the details when you're done. Ciao." Abi glanced at the clock on her computer. Time is money, and money is beautiful.

Getting up to fax the driver, Abi noted that Hubris was like no other place she had ever worked. Frugality had reigned over all of her other employers, but Hubris was different. Here opulence was not only expected, but also revered. Everything from furnishings to catering to accommodation was top of the line. No scrimping here, man. And after several tedious months of returning beer bottles for toilet paper, Abi was relishing the permissive and gluttonous environment.

Floating by Cass's desk, Abi decided to stop for a breather. "Whatcha workin' on?" she asked, peering over at Cass's screen.

Cass was on eBay, a site that Abi had heard so much about but had never deigned to hit.

"I'm on my 'lunch break,'" Cassandra replied, making little quotation marks with her fingers. A look of concern was on her face. "There's a vase that I really want, but I have to wait another couple of hours before I find out if my bid wins or not. God, I hope some bastard doesn't come in higher than me." Cassandra slumped back in her chair in complete anguish. "Nice vase, huh?" Cassandra pointed to the thumbnail on the screen. It looked pretty much like any other vase, but to each his own.

"Wow. I've never checked it out before. What all do they have on there? I mean, besides funky vases." God I sound like such a neophyte.

"I don't know. Everything and anything. All I know is that it's very, very dangerous. My boyfriend's going to shit if I get the vase."

Everything, eh? Abi's imagination was sparked. "Do you think they have Weebles?" Abi asked, trying not to sound too desperate and geeky.

"Sure, probably. They've got everything else," Cass chuckled.

"Man, I'd love to get my hands on some Weebles. You can't find them anywhere, ya know," Abi stated matter-of-factly.

"Well, then, you have found your Mecca," Cass responded.

Abi scooted back to her desk. Fuck the fax, man, I'm on a mission. A mission for Weebles. She did a rolling stop at her desk and brought up Netscape. Come on, come on. Time is money. Looking about her guiltily, she felt like such a slacker for doing this at work. Screw it, everyone else does, so why not me? And, with a rebel yell, she typed in the URL. "Okay. Toys and hobbies. Let's try there," Abi said aloud. Tons of toys popped up, all of which were tempting and taunting her. Barbie, Hello Kitty, Fisher Price People. They were all there, displayed like whores in a red-light district, and she didn't know which flavour she wanted more.

All of them preyed on her predilection for nostalgia. It was overwhelming. "Jesus. I could buy the whole site up." Focus, girl, focus. Weebles. Ah. Here they are. Abi began to get giddy. Clicking her way back to childhood, she had finally arrived at what appeared to be her destination. With a slight amount of hesitation, she selected the link. Abi closed her eyes and prayed that she had hit pay dirt. Almost a hundred Weebles and Weeble accessories sprang up. A cornucopia of wobbly, '70s plastic toys that were guaranteed not to fall down. The tree house, the Disney rides, the bus. It was all there. "I'm in heaven," Abi muttered.

Suddenly Abi sensed a presence behind her, and instinctively she tensed up. She was so caught. Abi closed her eyes again and prayed that it wasn't Josh. Slowly she turned around, ready to minimize at any second. Phew. It's Pat. Thank God it's Pat.

"You bidding on anything?" he asked.

"Nope. Just window-shopping. For now," she tittered. She knew she couldn't afford to purchase anything, but she figured she might as well sound as if she could. Fake it till you make it. Abi casually slumped back in her seat, as if she had just finished having lunch at the popular kid's table. "I've been searching all over hell's half acre for Weebles, and check this out — there are *tons* here. It's incredible, it really is." Abi was bobbing her head and gesturing at the screen. She was completely consumed. "I mean, look at this. The Weeble tree house. In pristine condition. Just incredible." Her voice had risen, and she realized that she sounded like she had just located Atlantis. She was in awe.

"I remember Weebles. That's awesome. I'm sensing someone's going to buy something," Pat responded in a singsong, coquettish way.

"I'm thinking I'm going to have to. Who knows if this will appear again," Abi concurred. It was like reefer madness. Everybody's doing it. Besides, she should splurge on herself. Just this once.

Sipping her wine, Abi was grateful that she actually had some time to reflect on the day and take in some television. Hmm. What to watch, what to watch? So many channels, so little time. "Better educate myself, kitty," Abi declared, grabbing the TV listings and flipping through the contents.

The phone rang, startling Abi. Thank God for diversions. Maybe it's a boy. "Hello," Abi cooed in a come-hither tenor.

"Hi, sweetheart."

Crap. Always a bridesmaid.

"Expecting someone? You answered mighty quickly," Edith prodded.

"Oh, hey, Mom. Nope. Not expecting anyone. Just hoping you might be a caller of the male sort," Abi joked. "How's it going?" she asked suspiciously. Her mother never phoned on her own unless there was something seriously up.

"Fine. Just phoning to see how you were doing and to make sure you weren't working too hard," her mom replied.

Ugh. Once a baby, always a baby. "Oh, I'm doing okay, Mom. Work's going all right, I guess," Abi deflected. No need to bore her with the details. "It's been pretty busy. Ya know, same old, same old. I still can't believe how helpless some people are. I mean, what? They can't call their own cabs?" She laughed, knowing her mother would fully understand. God knows how many times she saved my ass in a pinch.

"Don't I know it. You should have seen the paces my old boss put me through. Sometimes I used to think he wouldn't have been able to function without me," her mother chuckled.

"I know, and the pay sucks, too. That's the worst part about it," Abi concurred.

"Tell me about it. I was so infuriated when I discovered that the *two* women who replaced me were each receiving a higher salary than I had been. Made me feel just slightly unappreciated,"

Edith sympathized.

"I mean, what do they expect? Us to do all their dirty work for a pat on the back? We're the ones who keep the damn organization running," Abi exclaimed in defiance, diggin' the "I am admin, hear me roar" tenor of their conversation. "It'd be nice to be remunerated enough to actually enjoy life, too. And I'm not asking for the moon, just enough to actually feel like I'm getting ahead, for God's sake. Right now my only solace is meandering down Bloor West, casually glancing in the beautifully dressed windows and pretending as if I could afford to shop there," Abi dramatically confessed.

"I used to do the same thing," her mother giggled. "Yup, sometimes the bus would be full, so the girls and I would walk all the way home, past Holt's and all the wonderful shops and boutiques."

Ah. Dreaming of shopping at Holt's. The true bond of sisterhood. "Right now I just feel like I'm never going to be able to afford anything nice. Everyone at work has got such nice clothes and things, and I just feel so shabby next to them. And I was at Cass's apartment the other day. Mom, you would love it. It was so beautifully put together — everything was coordinated, from the bedding to the bathroom to the living room to the kitchen. She even had those little neat-smelling soaps and guest towels in the powder room. . . ." Abi trailed off, staring at the particleboard coffee table and mismatched chairs, resisting the sudden urge to cry. So much for feeling bootylicious and independent.

"It'll come, sweetheart. God knows your father and I struggled, and look where we are now," Edith reminded her.

Nostalgia does wonders to soften the edges, man. "I know it will. But it just seems so slow. It's *sooo* incredibly frustrating," Abi lamented, hearing a bell go off in the background.

"Oh, honey, I'm sorry to cut this off, but that's the plumber.

The toilet's been backed up all day, and we've got to get the darn thing fixed," her mom moaned.

"Ah, that's all right. I gotta pee, anyway. And I should probably do something really wacky, like get ready for my day tomorrow," Abi laughed, shifting off the pity pot. Man, I've forgotten how uncomfortable the damn thing is.

"Okay, sweetheart. Now you be patient and keep your chin up. You'll make it soon enough, I know you will," her mother soothed as only mothers can do.

Hanging up the phone and racing to the john, Abi laughed. Yup. I can always count on my admin sisters for support.

chapter fourteen

Abi was practically skipping home from work. She felt like she was infatuated, like she had just gotten laid. But she had said when, she had said how much. She adored the fact that promptly at midnight several hundred dollars had been magically transplanted into her bare bank account. Her debts were almost completely paid off, and she was back in the black — for now. She had been stone-broke for so long that simply drawing money from the bank machine and having bills in her wallet made a difference in her demeanour. There was only eighty dollars in her purse, but it may as well have been eight thousand. It had been so long since she had had disposable income, and she was relishing every moment.

The streets were jammed with fellow consumers, the milder weather reducing the snowbanks to slush and elevating the spirits to spring. Walking down Yonge Street, Abi felt like money for the first time in months. Watching the throngs of shoppers as she waited for the light to turn, she was no longer an us but finally a them. Maybe this work thing isn't so bad after all, she thought. She was exhausted and giddy. She had had a fantastic day. She had just dumped a shitload of money — all of it frivolous, all of it necessary. A journey to the grocery store to stock up on the necessities — baguette, cheese, pop, toilet paper, and smokes. It felt great to buy three-ply. She had even splurged on some pâté but made a mental note not to have too much of it. Everything in moderation. On her journey home, Abi had even ventured off the beaten path to the LCBO and the video store. Sauntering by HMV, she had been tempted to buy a CD but decided that that would be just a little too rich, even for her, even today. A jaunt to the drugstore was the last thing on Abi's to-do list. On a glorious day like today, she had to do something zany like buy some luxurious lipstick and eye shadow and perhaps even shaving cream.

Entering Shopper's Drug Mart, Abi walked by the magazine rack and picked up an *Architectural Digest*, flipping through pages and pages of slick, taunting advertisements. "Why not?" She threw it in the cart. Perusing the shelves, Abi was transfixed. Hmmm. *Wired* or *Industry Standard*? Why not get both? After all, she needed something fun and something educational. She popped a wheelie and headed to the makeup aisle. What to buy, what to buy? She felt like snatching up the entire store, but she knew that some gloss and gel would suffice. Taking a detour down aisle ten, Abi selected one lipstick, an eyeliner, and some new blush — all in flattering shades of the new spring season. She felt pretty and confident for the first time in ages. A new her, so to speak. Strolling along, Abi looked down at her cart and tabulated the value of its contents. I must have forty or fifty dollars' worth here. Better cash out now before the damage gets any worse.

Rounding the corner of aisle nine, she noticed the massive lineup at the cash. All her joy was erased, a grimace suddenly spreading across her face. What the fuck is going on? There must be seven or eight people ahead of me. Great. Now I'm going to get home late, she thought, angrily shoving the cart up to the line. Through the crowd of customers, Abi could now see what the intolerable holdup was — a damn new person is being trained. Abi slumped over and rested her forearms on the buggy handle, her arrogance and impatience clearly showing. Moving at a snail's pace, Abi finally came to the head of the line. Before the person ahead of her had even completed his transaction, she began to unload the contents of her cart, hoping to be done with the dirty business as quickly as possible. With stilted actions, the trainee rang up her purchases slowly, one by one. Come on, hurry up.

"Oops. The code doesn't work on this one," the new girl cried, panic in her voice.

"That's okay, just punch in the code manually. Yes. That's right. You're doing well," the manager said encouragingly.

Yeah, well, "well" doesn't cut it, Abi thought. She was now standing haughty and erect. She looked away, not wanting to disguise her intolerance for their ineptitude.

"Ma'am?"

Ma'am? Abi swirled around to face the clerk. Hello! How old do I look?

"That'll be $47.53."

Reaching into her pocket for her wallet, Abi was relieved that the whole travesty had finally come to an end. With a sigh, she took her change and mumbled a thank-you. Onwards and upwards.

Still put off by the drugstore debacle, Abi made her way down Isabella. She lugged her treasures almost violently, the handles of the plastic bags slicing into her hands and cutting off the circulation to her fingers. She felt like punching someone. Maybe she would punch somebody. Setting her bags down for a rest, she rubbed her hands and took a deep breath. Looking up at the lights of her apartment building, she knew she didn't have much farther to go. Eye of the tiger. Half a block more to go. Abi bent down and bore on. God, the evening has turned into a bitch. She felt different; she used to be able to keep her cool and never let little things like that get to her, but these days her mood could go from deliriously happy to pure rage in a heartbeat. Man, I'm slowly becoming a candidate for the Twinkie Defence, she thought as she entered the apartment building.

Wrestling with her keys, Abigail opened up her mailbox, dreading the number of bills that had piled up. She hadn't checked her mail in days for fear of the inevitable truth. At least she was somewhat liquid now. Pulling out a wad of envelopes, she noticed the plain envelope with a Scarborough postmark. Could it be? She quickly squished the envelope up and down, noticing that it was stiff in the middle. Practically in one fluid movement, she pulled off her mitt with her teeth and tore the present open with her one bare hand. It was. Her first American Express card. Credit. She was officially an adult. With a sigh of relief, she fell back against the postboxes. She could buy clothes again. Membership has its privileges.

Abi ran upstairs to activate the card, hoping that it would take effect that night. Bursting into her apartment, she practically tripped over a purring Paw on the way to the phone. "Sorry, kitty, but this is for the both of us." She picked up the receiver and dialled the number on the card, trying to make amends with Paw simultaneously. Abi had to smile. It was nice to come home to such unconditional love. To her delight, the call was completely automated — quick and painless, and, yes, she could use the card immediately. 7:30. She still had time to run to the Duchess's Den for a desperately needed haircut.

Putting her jacket back on, she headed down to the street and beelined for Yonge Street. Thank God for the Duchess's Den. Where else can you walk in and get a whacked-out stylist accompanied by blaring music for thirty bucks, tip included? It was at times like this she loved Toronto. She had never actually set foot inside the joint and didn't really know what to expect. Many times she had passed the wacky cat-in-the-hat woman on her way to run errands, even taking her coupons once in a while, but she was still a Duchess's Den virgin. She opened the door, and the place met all of her expectations — gritty, loud, and real. She just hoped they wouldn't try to dye her hair fuchsia or something.

Abi took solace in the fact that she only needed her hair cut into a bob. Straight lines, easy peasy, nothing much to screw up. She hoped. Abi sauntered up to the counter, trying not to look too out of place.

chapter fifteen

"Hey! Nice hair. How Mary!" For a Tuesday, Cassandra was certainly in a chipper mood.

"Thanks. Got the ol' Amex in the mail last night. Decided to treat myself to a cut. I'm only going to use it for emergencies, though." Abi set her bag down and turned on her task light.

"Yeah, right. That's what I said, too. Just wait, honey, just wait."

She shot Cassandra a look. Nice. Talk about encouraging. Right then and there, Abi made a vow to use the card only in emergencies. She'd prove Cassandra wrong. Abi shrugged it off and leaned down to boot up her computer.

"So where'd you get it done? Frou Frou?" Cass inquired between bites of her bagel smothered in low-fat cream cheese. "I've been going there for years. Heddie is simply the *best* stylist. You must go there," she continued with authority.

Rising from below her desk, Abi banged her head on her desktop. "Fuck. No. Uh, I actually went to the Duchess's Den." Now that was a showstopper.

"Really?" Cass giggled. "That weird woman actually enticed you in? What's it like in there? Christ, I'm surprised you didn't come out with a green mohawk."

Abi shuffled the papers on her desk, wiping the crumbs from Cassandra's breakfast off the only patch of free space. Mental note — don't tell people where I got my hair done.

"Yeah, well, I figured it was an easy enough cut, so why slap down a load of cash for it?" Abi was transported back to junior high in a cheap pair of jeans.

"Yeah. I guess you're right. If you want Heddie's number, let me know, and I'll fix you up. I've referred so many people here to her that she should be paying me." She headed off to finish her breakfast at her own desk.

Abi sat down, staring at her to-do list, dashed and preoccupied with the Den. She reached into her backpack and pulled out her compact. Holding it up to her face, all she could see was imperfection. The left side was slightly shorter than the right, and the bangs were trimmed just a bit too short. She did look like a pauper in a new pair of K-Mart capris. God, I feel so uncool. How could I have been such a frugal geek? Maybe I don't belong here after all, she pondered. She was definitely going to have to get Heddie's number from Cass. Conscious of her appearance, Abi shoved the compact back into her bag and stood up. Just put a brave face on, have a cup of coffee, and it will be all right. She could get away with it this once. Abi just prayed that Cass wouldn't betray her and rat her out. God forbid anyone else should discover her faux pas.

Heading to the kitchen, mug in hand, Abi spotted the candy dish on Travis's desk. "Where'd that come from?" She pointed toward the dish. No response. She moved in to take a closer look. Yum. Chocolate macaroons and rosebuds. Oh. And bridge mix. Noticing the Wonderland Post-it that invitingly proclaimed "yes," Abi cordially obliged and delved in, grabbing a fistful. Who cares if it is before nine? She didn't have breakfast, after all. Taking a second handful, she headed back to her desk fully armed and deposited her stash. Munching away, she couldn't believe how good it felt to be so bad. She had been deprived of chocolates for so long, and she was savouring the decadence. Fuck once on the lips, forever on the hips. She was going to live a little and love a little for once. The chocolate melted in her mouth, and she was in heaven. It was better than sex. Same sensation, no risk. Picking up her mug, she took another mouthful of chocolatey goodness and went back to fetch her morning fix.

Returning to her desk, Abi was overwhelmed by the amount of information being thrown at her. It was either the sugar or the pressure, but suddenly she felt like freaking out. Tensing up, Abi glanced at the stack of papers that had accumulated on her typically neat desk. She needed to read the paper, peruse the e-mail alerts, research competitors on Hoovers, and study *Wired, Industry Standard,* and *Fast Company* for all the news that's fit to print. Rolling her eyes and neck in an attempt to mitigate her stress, she couldn't resist feeling frustrated. So far her diligence hadn't paid off. Abi felt no more ahead than the day she had started at Hubris. She felt as if she was caught in some sick game of duck, duck, goose and was dreading the day her head would be tapped. Maximizing her Outlook, she could stay up twenty-four hours a day and still not manage to stay on top of it all. Competitors, prospects, clients — not to mention current events and topics that actually engaged her. It was all too much. Peering over at Josh's office, she didn't know how he did it all. How anyone did it all, for that matter. Yawning, Abi shook her head in an attempt to rise to the occasion. Do they just not need eight hours? Something's gotta give; it might as well be sleep. She could get by on five to six, she calculated.

Leaning back in her chair wearily, Abi reviewed her to-do list and looked at her watch. There was no way she was going to make the shelter that night. She had come to this conclusion earlier but had put off making the call until she was absolutely certain. The truth was, it encroached on her time too much, and she knew she had to give it up. The way she looked at it, it wasn't paying her rent, Hubris was. And that was where her allegiance must rest. Opening her day-timer, she dialled Sam's number, hoping that she'd get his voice mail.

"Hello?"

No such luck. "Hi, Sam, it's Abi. Listen. I hate to do this over the phone, but I'm afraid I'm not going to be able to continue with the program. I simply don't have the bandwidth anymore." God. I can't believe I just said that. "It's just with the hours on the new job and all. . . ." Abi allowed herself to trail off, recognizing her tone of *I've got more important things to do* and hoping the pause would lessen the effect.

Thankfully, Sam jumped in. "I understand, Abi, don't worry about it. It's just too bad you can't come in for one more night to say good-bye. I know what it would mean to Gus and the rest of the regulars. They'll — we'll — miss you, you know. Promise me you'll come in one last night?"

This was so hard. "Sure, Sam. I promise I will. Say hi to the gang for me, and thanks for understanding." Abi hung up, knowing that she'd never see or speak to Sam or Gus again. She turned back to her computer and continued composing an e-mail. There was always next year.

spring

chapter sixteen

End of the workday. Light still. What time is it? Peer through blinds. Billowing grey clouds. Blustery rain. Where's the umbrella? Back to computer. Check meteorological site. More rain. Flash floods in the 'burbs. Sun tomorrow. Grey skies are gonna clear up. At least it's on the plus side. Shut down for the day. Throw on shoes. Where's the new slicker? Call elevator. Crap. Forgot keys. Back to desk. Grab keys. Call elevator. Exit street level. Trepidation. Umbrella won't open. Too much precipitation. Bite bullet. Chiens et chats. Grass waterlogged and shit green. Trees slick and shit brown. Buds making their debut. Worms drowning. Squirrels scampering. Birds fussing. Streets void of bipeds. Thank God. Step in puddle. Runners soaked. Umbrella still won't open. To the bone already. Cars splash. No streetcar. Run to subway. Down the hatch. Stand and dry. Platform in pissy mood. Soggy briefcases. Soggy overcoats. Soggy newspapers. Soggy moods. Hotter than Hades. Light at end of tunnel. Finally. Jockey for position. Enter car. Pools on floor. Smell wet dog. See wet dog. Almost slip. Steady, steady. Nowhere to sit. Hang tight. Next stop wonderland. Train stops. No movement. Experiencing technical difficulties at next station. Train jerks alive. Finally reach cruising speed. Train stops. Step off. Fresh air. Still light. Still inclement. Umbrella opens. Streets packed. Vie for umbrella space. Almost peg pedestrian in eye. Almost get pegged in eye. Homeless barefoot. Sure sign of spring. Mobile awning overhead. Pigeon hops to higher ground. Gutters spew. Shoes sodden. Enter lobby. Try to close umbrella. Almost give up. Take deep breath and try again.

Hoyden Drip, drip, drip. Cross marble floor. Delicate manoeuvre. Shoes squish. Avoid eye contact. Elevator actually arrives. Second floor. Doors open. Doors shut. Stare at numbers. Third floor. Doors open. Doors shut. Total milk run. Fourth floor. Thank God. Doors open. Apartment ahead. Unlock door. Open umbrella. Peel off shoes. Peel off raincoat. Peel off pants. Peel off jumper. Down to gitch. Head to bathroom. Dry hair. Don jammies. Paper towel hallway. Turn on news. The evening has begun.

chapter seventeen

www.rescuethelazy.com. Smiling, Abigail typed the URL and hit "Enter." The Web site popped up, and she felt free. It felt so great to do this. She could now afford to buy groceries online. Well, not really afford, per se, but she did have a grand left on her Amex. Kind of a buy now, pay later type of thing. No more slogging home, kitty litter in hand, apples rolling down the street, no more bruised bananas or broken eggs. No more lineups and incompetent clerks. And all wrapped in a cool user interface.

"You use rescuethelazy too?"

Abigail looked up at Josh with a knowing grin. She was now one of the cool kids in school and she deserved it.

"Watch out, though, it's addictive. It has made my life so much easier. I simply can't live without it now."

Instant acceptance. Instant gratification. Hyperlinking her way to a full pantry, Abigail navigated through the site. Cauliflower was $2.39 — not bad, not bad. Six bucks for a ten-kilogram bag of kitty litter? Definitely not bad, especially considering that she wouldn't have to lug it five blocks. She pointed and clicked, tossing anything that seemed remotely appetizing into her virtual cart. No more annoying old people blocking the aisles. No more motorized carts playing bumper cars with her buggy. She selected her list to see where the tally stood. She had to ensure that she had met the minimum amount of fifty bucks. Nope. Need another ten. Fifty dollars was certainly difficult for a single girl to attain. She had already stocked up on enough pantry items to make a doomsayer proud, and she was at a loss. "Guess there's always fresh fruit and veg," she muttered. Abi linked back to the produce section and grabbed whatever she could find, regardless of whether it would wind up wilting in the crisper or not. To her the fifty-dollar minimum plus the six-dollar delivery fee was cost-effective. After all, she was too busy to bother with such mundane tasks as running errands, too delicate to expose herself to such hardships. Checking the list again, she had finally met it. Time to cash out and arrange for delivery. Quick and dirty.

Collating sales kits for the next big trade show, Abi couldn't wait to get home to greet the rescuethelazy.com delivery van. It had been so easy, so effortless. Completely lost in her own little food fantasy, Abi didn't even hear Josh come in.

"Earth to Abi, earth to Abi."

Abi stood up erect, shaking her head. "Sorry about that. Was in my own little world. The hum of the copier will do that to you," she joked.

"Could you do me a favour and courier these for me?" Josh handed her a couple of envelopes, smiled pleasantly, and walked away.

Wham. And back to earth she certainly was.

Rushing up to her intersection, Abi espied the golden delivery van rumbling down the street, rescuethelazy prominently emblazoned on its side and front, its wholesome deliveryboy image conjuring up nostalgia for a more customer-centric era. Disregarding the gentle rain and narrowly averting becoming a pedestrian casualty, Abi ran across to her building, hoping that the grocery fairy was there to pay her a visit. All afternoon she had been distracted by visions of a full pantry, a stocked fridge, and a clean, fragrant litter box. Waltzing into her building, she felt so unencumbered. She was barely in her apartment when the buzzer went. Yeah, they're here. "Yes?" she asked expectantly.

"Rescuethelazy here for Abigail Somerhaze," the voice replied.

"Yes, that's me. Apartment 421," she responded politely, releasing the intercom button and doing a little dance of joy. Seemingly seconds later, there was a knock at the door. Abi ran to the door, throwing it open with the exuberance of greeting a paramour. A man wearing an untucked gold golf shirt nipped in, out of breath, and unceremoniously slid a large plastic crate into her apartment. Hey, he doesn't have a bow tie.

"Where would you like these?" the man asked, attempting to catch his breath and turning to retrieve a second container.

"Um, right here is fine," Abi indicated, trying to get out of the road. Certainly are rushed, aren't they? "Busy tonight?" Abi asked in a calm tone, hoping to slow the cowboy down.

"Yeah," he said, dragging the final bin in. Standing in her hallway, he wiped his brow, obviously having had quite a time of it. Poor guy. "What a night. Got chased by a dog at the last place," he explained, looking rather out of sorts but calming down. "Big German shepherd. Scared the daylights out of me."

Envisioning Rin-Tin-Tin racing after containers chock full of brie, endives, and filet mignon, Abi quelled her instinct to giggle. Poor guy. "Well, you don't have to worry about that here. All I've got is a twenty-year-old kitty," she replied, gesturing toward Paw who was asleep on the sofa. "This is about as excited as he gets."

Pulling out his clipboard, Delivery Dave looked relieved beyond belief. "Too many dogs on this job. One of the hazards of home delivery," he laughed, taking her credit card and swiping it in his handheld device. He wasn't such a bad guy after all.

"I've definitely been converted," Abi said gleefully, signing her receipt and ushering him back to the hallway. "And watch out for those dogs," she called, watching him round the corner toward the elevators.

Putting away the last of the produce, Abi opened the Lean Cuisine and popped it into the microwave. The plastic container was spinning round and round, radioactive particles blasting it to the correct temperature. Watching and waiting for dinner to be nuked, Abi was growing impatient. Maybe she should've ordered in. "It'd be so cool if I had one of those new speedy Avantiums, eh, Paw?" She looked down at the feline, who was busy spreading cat dander all over her black pant leg. "Then I could have a tasty, home-cooked supper. None of this frozen stuff." She indicated the prepackaged meal that was being attacked by atoms as it spun innocently round and round. She opened up the fridge and grabbed a brick of old cheddar. Just one slice. Okay. Maybe two.

The microwave timer and the phone rang simultaneously. Abi was torn. "Guess I should get the phone," she said to Paw, who was anxiously awaiting his soft cat-food treat. She set down the knife and cheese and reached for the phone. "Hello?"

It was Del, of course. "Hey you! Listen, I've been invited to the opening of Tangerine," Del gushed with excitement. "You know, the new department store. Did you want to come with me? It's Thursday night, and it'll be fun . . . ," she tempted.

"What? That's awesome. I think I overheard Josh say he was going, too," Abi clapped. That would be too much fun to show up at the same event that Josh was attending. He would be so taken aback that little ol' her had actually been invited to the ball. "I am so there. But I have absolutely nothing to wear," Abi confessed, trying to sound blasé but not being very successful. "Did you want to go shopping with me tomorrow after work? We could charge our way to heaven, dahling," she dripped with mock snobbery.

"Sure, doll. How about tomorrow, 6:30, at Club Monaco? They have the cutest pantsuits there that'll suit you perfectly," Del replied, infected by Abi's giddiness.

"Sounds good. See you there. Ciao bella." Abi hung up the phone, pleased as punch. She knew she could count on Del for a good spree. Satisfied, she returned to the kitchen to reheat her frozen dinner.

chapter eighteen

Thursdays. Gotta love 'em. The weekend starts today. Abi sauntered into the lobby, barely missing a young woman. "Hi, can I help you?" Abi asked pointedly, trying not to sound defensive. Another PYT. Competition.

"Yes, um, today is my first day. I think I'm supposed to ask for Cassandra?" the girl-woman responded tentatively and timidly. First day? Cassandra? Why haven't I heard anything about this?

"Oh, sure. Hi, I'm Abigail. I'm Josh's assistant," Abi responded, now attempting not to sound too confused. "Why don't you have a seat, and I'll see if Cassandra is here yet." Her cordial manner belied her sentiment of imagined betrayal. Walking back to the kitchen, Abi was pissed. Sabotage and ill communication. Why am I always the last to know? Being out of the loop sucks. Abi adopted the cherubic face of the undaunted. For every action, there's an equal and opposite reaction. Rounding the corner, she spotted Cassandra in the kitchen.

"Hey, Cass. There's a new girl here to see you. What's up with that?" Abi queried, a note of defiance-cum-cattiness in her voice.

Picking up her mug, Cassandra smiled, completely negating Abi's posturing. "Oh. Marisa's here? I thought I told you. The powers that be finally realized that admin support is worth spending money on. Looks like we've finally got some help around here," she stated nonchalantly.

Suddenly Abi felt like a complete ass. Nothing like eating crow for breakies. "That's great. I was just surprised is all," Abi smiled. I really ought to get a hold of my paranoid assumptions.

Sitting down on one of the kitchen stools, Abi watched

Cassandra as she made her way to the front of the office. Great. Just as she had adjusted to the topography, it was shifting again. The more the merrier, my ass. Hmm. And neither she nor Cassandra had been boosted to a supervisory role. Surprise, surprise. Not only were the self-professed Old Guard Busters trying to create the administrative equivalent of a cockfight, but they were also taking the egal out of egalitarian and constructing their own special hegemony. The management monsters all seemed to be moving up, propelled by the recent corporatization. But God forbid the lowly admins be given a piece of the action, Abi thought bitterly. Recalling *The Art of War*, she grinned. Competition will keep her honest. "Gotta give action to get action," Abi muttered, moving around the counter to unload the dishwasher. Practically slamming the coffee mugs in the cupboard, Abi was attempting to process the new information and calm herself down. "Boys will be boys," Abi smirked.

Marisa quietly wandered into the kitchen, looking a little lost and superfluous. "Is there anything I can do to help?" she asked shyly, reaching over to grab the last of the silverware from the dishwasher.

"Oh, no. I think I've got it. Thanks, though," Abi pleasantly replied, mindful not to seem defensive. Gotta be sunshine and roses for the new girl. Gotta be the company gal. Looking over at Marisa, all Abi could see was green.

Marisa was flipping through a Hubris brochure, her eyes bright and radiating an enviable, innocent, cherubic smile. Coifed and glossed, and geared up in new duds care of Mom and Dad, she was spit-shined to a perfect sheen. Obviously an eager beaver. And far be it for Abi to spoil it for her, especially on her first day. Hubris would do a pretty good job of that on its own.

"Are you sure? I'm feeling a little useless right now," Marisa explained, tucking her spanking new blouse into her spanking new skirt.

"Sure, it's fine. Besides, I know how overwhelming the first day here can be. You'll have enough on your plate soon enough," Abi replied, conscious of the maternal tone in her voice.

"Okay," Marisa laughed, sitting down on one of the stools, a look of relief in her eyes. "So Hubris seems amazing. I still can't believe I got the job here. Everyone just seems so friendly, so ready to help. I mean, it just seems like such a family. No power trips, no obvious hierarchy, just everyone working together. . . ." Marisa trailed off, still smiling a contented smile.

Out of the mouths of babes. "Just you wait," Abi joked, sounding eerily like Cassandra. Gotta give her some warning, man. "You're right, though. It is a pretty neat place to work," she quickly added, trying to offset any negativity. "And who knows, maybe we'll be one of those dot-com millionaires," Abi continued, hoping the girl would buy into all of the IPO bullshit. Gotta give her the sell, after all.

"I know," Marisa giggled. "Wouldn't that be great?"

So young, so naïve, so like me when I started. God, how long have I been here already? "Yup. Sure would," Abi concurred, pushing the kitchen door open. "Welcome aboard."

"Hey, Abi. Do you gotta sec?" Josh called from his office.

Nice grammar, buddy. Maybe there's a reason why I handle your correspondence. "Sure, Josh," Abi replied, walking up to the doorway. "What's up?"

"Come on in," he replied, gesturing for her to take a seat. "I need to talk to you about your MBOs. HR needs me to approve and submit them by week's end," he explained, handing her a very bureaucratic form to fill out.

MBOs? What the hell are MBOs? Abi was mystified. Sounded like some sort of genetically modified food. "Sorry, Josh, but at the risk of sounding like a complete idiot I'm not quite sure what an

MBO is," Abi mumbled, trying not to sound too stupid and unprofessional.

"Management by Objective. Basically goals that you set for yourself that are above and beyond your job description, and your achievement of them is tied directly to your bonus," he stated in a paternal way.

Hmm, more moula. Boy, does he know when to strike with the dollar signs. Cass always swore he knew when they were disgruntled.

"They're intended to not only benefit the department and company as a whole but to also assist you in your career growth here at Hubris. Kind of an opportunity to utilize a different skill set or to interact with a different department. Obviously yours will have to align with mine, so here's a copy of my MBOs for Q2," he went on, sliding another sheet of paper across his desk.

"Okay, I get it. Did you need this by day's end?" Abi asked, flushed with excitement over the new challenge.

"That would be great, Abi. This is a wonderful opportunity for you to grow with the company and really show your stuff. They may not seem significant, but they're actually incredibly useful as stepping stones within an organization. Oh, and at some point we should sit down and talk about your career path at Hubris. You've got amazing potential here, and we need to really start tapping into it," Josh advised, giving her a friendly wink.

"Thanks, Josh. Will do," Abi gushed, blushing like a schoolgirl. Grabbing the papers and rising to leave his office, Abi had to admit that Josh's timing was impeccable. Just as she'd begun to get crispy on the outside, things were moving again. Grinning as she walked back to her desk, she thought of the possible goals she could set. Bonuses. MBOs. Career paths. God, it's all so flattering. Maybe the new girl is bang-on after all. Maybe you can move up here.

Hoyden Staring distractedly into space, Abi was like a kid at Christmas. She couldn't wait for 6 p.m. Tangerine. The stark logo adorned the cover of the invitation-cum-catalogue, commanding the privileged holder to salivate over its contents. Obediently Abi cracked it open, smiling broadly. In a way, she had to laugh. She remembered Tangerine before it was Tangerine. It had been a stodgy department store frequented by grandmothers and pensioners. No one with any fashion sense would have ever deigned to peruse its polyester racks and cheap cascades. Having repelled Chapter Eleven, it had resurrected and positioned itself to rise with the new funicular, its little insignia and attitude even adopting the look and feel of the new vernacular. Like so many of its contemporaries, it was ebbing with the movement toward celebrating status and materialism. For those with any sense of history, Tangerine was so blatantly catering to the new class of DINKS that it had become more of a caricature than before. Fortunately for them, the well-heeled have fleeting memories and permanent credit. As long as they have decent trunk shows, who cares what they offered before? It's all about the now. Studying the wide array of luxury items, Abi was impressed. They had done an incredible job of reinventing themselves, proving that market research can be a lucrative investment. Just snatch that money before the bubble bursts, baby. Slapping the brochure closed, Abi couldn't wait to be inducted into the upper echelon. And there would be so many eligible men there, too. Thank God Del convinced me to buy that sexy new pantsuit.

Tangerine was so *Town and Country*. It was $200 jean jackets, $20 eyeliner, $95 T-shirts. It was ridiculously sublime, and Abi adored it. She couldn't afford anything there and normally would have balked at entering such an establishment, but now that she was there, at its opening, for God's sake, she was feeling as much the part as any poser there. She was experiencing how the other half lived, and it was decadent. Abi had never attended a function with an open bar, and she was slurping it up.

"This is amazing, Del," she said, moving closer to the bar and signalling the bartender. She desperately wanted in to this impeccably appointed world. At least they weren't serving Pellman Estates.

"I know, just check out the scenery," Del quipped, drawn to some young stable boy in the corner.

Sipping her glass of Wolf Blass, she began to speculate, scheme, and plot as to how she could possibly be initiated into The Club. How much would it take? Not much, probably. An hors d'oeuvre platter made its way within arm's length, and she took advantage. Never refuse what's put in front of you, Abi figured, being the ever dutiful and easily influenced guest.

An hour later, Abi swigged back her fifth glass of Shiraz, immediately wanting more. Setting the empty glass down on a display case, Abi wandered out to the sidewalk to indulge in a cancer stick instead. The joint was packed with suits and money, and everything was eligible and delectable. She took in the scene, lighting a cigarette and deeply inhaling. Life is indeed good. Indulge, baby, indulge. She had to be at work at eight the next morning, but she knew the night was far from over. Screw it. She was young. She could handle it. More importantly, she had gotten away with it thus far, so why stop now? Opening her wallet, she glanced at her last twenty. Shit. And the cheap bastards are going to be converting to a cash bar soon. Hmm. Spotting Josh through the large picture window, Abi waved cordially, a plastic smile across her face. She could always hit her boss up for some free booze. Yeah, that'll work. Josh will totally treat me; he'll probably expense it, after all. Extinguishing her cigarette with her brand-new boot heel, Abi grinned contentedly. Alcohol had a way of making her complacent, of loving life when she really didn't. So much for in vino es veritas.

"Bacchus, take me away," she muttered to herself, pulling the chrome and glass door open and rejoining the scene.

Manoeuvring her way through the reams of plastic and silicon, she felt important just being there, even if it was through Del. They didn't have to know that. Only she and Del did, and Del certainly wasn't going to give her up.

"Having fun? Have you *seen* the Prada section yet?" Del came trotting over to the bar like a kid at Christmas. She was such a nerd. A very cute nerd, but a nerd nonetheless. Brandishing a sherry and a couple of crisp Tangerine bags, she had obviously already raided the bar and plundered their Grand Opening "sales." Sometimes Del had more money than sense. "Oh, darling! You must meet Billy! He's a photographer, and I've already bragged to him all about you and your photo genius. And you are such a minx — he's going to love you!" Del, gripping her sherry in one hand and the side of the bar in the other, was surrounded by a gaggle of admiring suitors.

Wanting to get extremely intoxicated, comme d'habitude, Abi cautiously sauntered up to the bar. "Jesus, Del. What the hell did you tell him, anyway? I mean, I haven't even picked up a camera in months." Lapping up her vino, Abi savoured its warm embrace and invited it into her bloodstream. Although she was dressed to kill, she didn't want to deal with the advances of some young frat boy or some old bar fly. Abi immediately regretted her choice of attire.

"Once a photographer, always a photographer," Del quipped, raising her glass to her.

Josh appeared out of the deep, orange sea, holding the arm of some young bimbette. Saved by the boss. "Abi! I'm so surprised to see you here," he said, a look of disbelief in his eyes.

Yes, boss, I can and do run in the same circles as you. "Oh, well. I heard about the opening and just had to be here," Abi responded with a shit-eating grin.

"Abi, this is Mia. Mia, Abi," he introduced, gazing lustfully into his fawn's vacuous, hazel eyes.

"Pleased to meet you," Abi replied, attempting to shake Mia's petite paw. Gross. The limp-fish shake. You can tell a lot about a girl by her grip.

"Likewise," Mia breathlessly cooed, leaning her head on Josh's shoulder.

Come on, girl, your head can't be that heavy.

"Well, it's quite a party, isn't it?" Josh asked, raising his glass and gesturing around the room.

"It sure is," Abi replied, already bored. Now where is Billy?

"Oh, listen. I've got a proposition for you."

I'm all ears, boss.

"I know how hip you are and how plugged in to the scene you are." Plugged in to the scene? Vomit. "And that, if anyone has their finger on the beat of T.O.'s underground scene, it's you." Enough with the buttering up, man. "What I was wondering is if you could be my private ears." Private ears? That's a new one.

"Um, sure. But what exactly are private ears?" Abi asked, one eyebrow raised and a glass paused at her lips.

"Oh, well, private ears are all the rage. Everyone has them these days. A little assistant who helps to suss out cool music for super-busy people who don't have the time to do it themselves. You know, help select music for soirées, events, even soundtracks," Josh explained. Now she had heard of everything. "And Mia and I are planning a little wine tasting two weeks from now, and I was wondering if you could help us set the mood. Something elegant but edgy. Maybe a little acid jazz or something," he continued, reaching his arm around Mia's narrow frame and stroking her shoulder.

"Ooooh. Acid jazz. I hadn't even thought of that," Mia murmured.

What nerve. And she knew she wouldn't even be invited. "Oh,

sounds, um, neat. I could probably hook you up," Abi responded, nodding her head with some scepticism.

"Time to meet Billy," Del instructed, tugging at Abi's arm.

"Sorry, Josh. I'll talk to you tomorrow. It was nice to meet you, Mia," Abi giggled, grateful for being led away. Private ears. Sure, whatever you say, boss. I am your Girl Friday.

"Oh, shit. I'm out of chits. You okay to get home on your own?" Del slurred, almost stumbling into the gutter.

"Oh, sure. It's a gorgeous night — I'll just walk home," Abi replied, not wanting to let on that she couldn't even afford TTC.

"If you say so. I'm going to catch this one here." Del indicated to a taxi that had just pulled up in front of the store.

Well, this is rich, Abi thought, as Del's chariot pulled a U-turn. The irony that she had just attended one of the premier chi-chi events, that her photo may even wind up in tomorrow's gossip columns, while she couldn't even scrape together five bucks for a cab was not lost on her. She was so annoyed for allowing herself to be swept away like that. She wasn't one of them and probably never would be. She turned and staggered her way up Yonge Street.

Her head was killing her. "Fuck. What time is it?" Peeling up her eyeshade, she instantly knew that it was way late 'cause it was so light in her bedroom. She tried to leap out of bed, but her heavy head slowed her progress. She had so much work to do, both for Hubris and for herself. Why the fuck did I drink so much last night? Why is Del always able to coax me to have more than a couple of drinks? She truly needed to get a backbone. And some Advil. Standing in front of the bathroom mirror, she looked old. And she had the turtle eyes that only came from too much booze and too little sleep. A pimple was appearing on her chin. She was getting a canker in the corner of her mouth. Simply put, she looked like crap.

Closing her eyes as she brushed her teeth, she tried to conjure up energy. It wasn't coming. Whom could she pray to? She was willing to make a thousand promises she'd never keep. What did she do last night? Other than make an ass out of herself? What was she going to wear? Would breakfast help or hinder her? Fuzzy-headed, Abi turned off the taps and began to shuffle back to the bedroom. Realizing that her next step was actually to take a shower, she turned back slowly and shuffled back to the bathroom. Shower. Gotta shower. She couldn't decide which would benefit her more at this juncture — a cool shower or a warm shower. Warm shower always wins. Fiddling with the temperature, Abi carefully undressed and took the plunge. "God, I hope this wakes me up."

Facing the nozzle, Abi tried to rinse away the pain. Fridays were such hell lately. Whoever said that the weekend starts on Thursday was wrong. Or retired. Why did Del have the ability to twist her rubber arm? Why did Abi let her do that? Abi always set out on these excursions with a firm personal commitment to remain relatively sober, to put her foot politely down, but it never quite turned out that way. She always succumbed to either someone else's demons or her own. Whichever way you cut it, it wasn't healthy. Hell, at this rate I don't even need a toxic twin. She was debauching without any assistance. Getting out of the shower, Abi made her ritualistic Friday-morning vow to never drink again or at least never drink on a Thursday night again. This has got to stop. Her mind was a total lint ball, her body bloated, and her esteem trampled.

Getting dressed, she couldn't decide if she would be revived or repulsed by a cigarette. God. I smoked way too much last night. Hmm. Suppose I should sport my new Armani jacket, she thought. Caressing the buttery sleeve, Abi couldn't believe Del had talked her into buying it last night. Christ, give a girl some vino and some credit, and she'll do the darndest things. Still, at least she could say she owned an Armani. And at forty percent off, it really had been a good deal, she had to admit. Putting her blazer on, she shrugged. "Nothing succeeds like excess." The little Wilde quote had become her mantra. She threw her keys in her bag and gingerly opened the door. Good morning, sunshine. Hello, sunglasses.

chapter nineteen

Reclining in the beige leather chair, Abi couldn't remember the last time she was so relaxed. Closing her eyes and relishing her near-vertical position, she could feel her shoulders relax as she drifted off, the voices around becoming more and more distant. Mmmm. Muzak. To lounge, to lounge, to lounge. If only she could squander every morning like this.

"Hi Abi. I've got your X-rays here," a tenor boomed from behind, jolting Abi out of her near-catatonic state.

Opening her eyes, Abi found herself staring directly into the examining light above, its beam stabbing at her retinas and eradicating any sleep from her eyes. Fuck. Couldn't he have at least knocked? "Oh. Uh, great," she said, pulling herself up and wiping the drool from the side of her mouth. God. I hope I wasn't out for long.

"And they show exactly what I had been suspecting . . . ," her dentist trailed off in suspense, snapping the film on the light box on the wall.

What? Did aliens implant a transistor in my molar?

"You're grinding your teeth," he said, finally announcing the verdict.

Como? When the hell do I grind my teeth? She had never done that in her life. If anything she was a slack-jawed, happy-go-lucky fool. "Pardon me?" Abi laughed in surprise, the tension returning to her narrow shoulders and neck.

"That's right. You're grinding and/or clenching your teeth. Probably at night, though, and that's why you're not aware of it. That's why you're experiencing the sensitivity in that front tooth

— it's begun to wear down, exposing the nerves," Dr. Death explained, sitting down in the chair next to her. "What I suggest is a dental appliance to be worn at night. It'll significantly reduce the wear on your teeth and will probably even reduce any headaches and jaw aches you may have been experiencing, too."

Crap. Nothing like a sexy mouth guard to lure those lovers. At least she had one hundred percent dental. "Oh. Okay. Man, I had no idea I was even doing that. I mean, I've never ground my teeth before. Speaks volumes about work, man," Abi managed in disbelief. She had no idea Hubris had even begun to encroach on her maxiofacial health. "Maybe I should start yoga or something." Yeah. Like I could meditate after six cups of coffee.

"Oh, don't worry about it. So many people have this problem — it's a fact of life. The appliance will help substantially, I promise," he sympathized, reaching for some industrial floss.

Yeah. I know an appliance that could help substantially.

"But first if you could open wide," he instructed, wrapping a piece of floss around each forefinger.

Abi obeyed with the zeal of a Pavlovian chick.

"When *was* the last time you flossed, anyway?" he quipped, reaching into her gaping mouth and giving her a knowing glance.

They always know, man. They always know. "Ezvenaawhal," Abi tried to sheepishly reply, giving a gaping grin. Closing her eyes, she tried to recoup some sense of tranquillity, but it was futile. There was something about his chubby fingers running string between her teeth that was disturbing her chi. Oh, well. May as well suck it up and start gearing up for work.

10 a.m. It felt so good to saunter in late. Cass wandered by, waving at Abi as she went. "Oh, hey, Cass. I was wondering if I could get the number of your shiatsu therapist. My neck's been killing

me lately," Abi called down the hall, trying to catch up with her.

Reaching her desk, Cassandra turned around and set her purse down. "Sure, not a problem. He's great. Shiatsu is *totally* addictive," she affirmed. "He's not totally covered by benefits, though," she warned.

"That's okay. That's what the trusty Amex is for," Abi smiled.

"And I thought you were only going to use that in emergencies," Cassie chided, knowing full well how the story read.

"Yeah, well, gotta live somehow," Abi retorted.

Walking into the kitchen, Abi was aghast. Can't she just do her fucking job? The kitchen was a complete mess. Why the hell didn't Marisa empty the dishwasher? Then again, the poor girl didn't know any better. Abi opened the dishwasher and began unloading it.

Cass came in, ready for café numero duo. "What are you doing? That's not your job anymore — you've got *way* too much to do," Cass scolded, pouring herself some coffee.

"I know, I know," Abi conceded, tossing mug after mug into the cupboard. "Just trying to help the poor kid out. She's not supervised, and I figure it's better to lead by example." She closed the dishwasher and wiped down the counter. "Besides, I've been acting like the jealous big sister lately, taking out all of my frustrations on her. When I saw all this, I was tempted to send a scathing tell-all e-mail to HR, but I just couldn't be that petty."

"It's not petty, it's called paying dues," Cassandra pointed out in that cynical way of hers.

"I know. And sometimes I get so frustrated by the fact that Marisa has it so easy compared to the way we had it. Truth is, I'm pretty resentful that Marisa's coasting up the ladder where we had crawled. None of it's her fault, though. She's fairly hard-working and ambitious. A little young but a good seed," Abi admitted, trying to see the best in Marisa.

"Yeah, but that doesn't mean doing her work for her. If you keep doing this, she'll never know what she's not doing." Cass was taking the tough-love approach.

"True, but I remember how patient you were with me, how many times you saved my butt, and I figured I may as well try to help her out a bit. You know, I just think she needs a mentor is all," Abi said, grabbing herself a coffee. "And anyway there's enough time yet to bestow a little admin angst on the young Miss Marisa."

"You're a better woman than me," Cass said, opening the door for Abi and following her out.

Sitting down at her cubicle, Abi was pleased with herself. It was kind of cool thinking that maybe she could mentor someone the way Cass had mentored her. Sort of like passing the torch. And Marisa was a total project, that was for certain. And in a maternal sorta way, she'd do her damnedest to ensure that Hubris didn't get to Marisa like it had begun to get to her.

chapter twenty

Polished granite. Chrome appointments. Gentle pot lights strategically highlighting the impeccable heads of impeccable folks, their reflections refracted in an abundance of mirrors. Manicured men and manicured women strolling from washing station to stylist chair, sipping herbal tea, and politely laughing with the witty wash girl. Frou Frou people in Frou Frou Salon.

Opening the salon door, Abi felt immediately at ease, the sounds and smells of Yonge Street diminishing and melding with the lilting jazz and hinting aromatherapy. Ah. Pampered bliss.

Bottles of way-too-expensive products lined glass shelves, displayed more like china and crystal than glycerine and goo. Hmm. This place looks a tad cher. Thank God for American Express.

Following Cassandra up to the reception desk, Abi decided to let Cass take the lead. It was her haunt, after all. "This is so worth it," Cass chirped, her eyes filled with glee. "Wait till you meet Heddie. Not only is she an amazing stylist, but she's adorable and just a treat as well," Cass continued, eyeing the berets and baubles in the display case.

"Hey there!" a voice called from the back of the shop. "I thought I heard you, Cass," the little blonde dynamo said, approaching the front. "And you must be Abi — I've heard so much about you from Cass. I'm Heddie."

Christ. The woman's got a grip stronger than mine. "Likewise. Cass has been singing your praises for ages — it's so nice to finally meet you," Abi reciprocated, discreetly massaging her right hand.

"Well. Let's get started. Cass, since you're both in today, I was thinking you could go for your manicure while I started on Abi's hair," Heddie said, taking Abi's arm and leading her to the back.

"Sure thing," Cass replied, heading down the stairs to the aesthetics area. "Have fun, Abi," she called, disappearing from sight.

Following Heddie past the ladies who lunch, Abi began to feel like a lumbering, not-so-chi-chi idiot. Catching a glimpse of her jeans and frayed shirt in a mirror, she wished she had put a little bit more effort into her wardrobe. Mental note — must go shopping.

"So what are we thinking about doing today?" Heddie asked as Abi took a seat in the chair.

"Well, I was kinda thinking of something more sophisticated, more sassy. Kind of more Princess Di," Abi responded, studying herself in the mirror and running one hand through her mousy hair.

"Sounds good. How about some colour? Some blonde highlights would give it a kick, too. And it's *so* in this season," Heddie prompted, taking Abi's cue and running her hands through Abi's mop. "Where do you usually go?" Heddie asked.

Uh, oh. She hated that question. "Um. Well. I'm fairly new here, so last time I just went to the Duchess's Den down the street," Abi quickly mumbled, shyly looking up at Heddie to gauge her reaction. No smirk. No wisecracks. Thank God for non-judgemental people.

"Okay. Well, I think some highlights would work really well," Heddie continued, focusing on the task at hand.

"I was thinking the same thing," Abi said, suddenly excited about the whole process. New do, new attitude.

"Why don't you get changed and meet me back at the washing station?" Heddie said, leading her to the change room and handing Abi a black linen robe.

"Sure thing," Abi said, grinning and entering the change room. Man. Why didn't I do this sooner?

Walking out of the change room, Abi glanced over at the window. The huge-ass picture window showcased the world like an aquarium. On her corner, people were going about their Saturday business. Waiting for the bus, getting the Saturday paper, walking a yappy Pekinese. She couldn't help but feel like a sloth for not appearing as productive as they were. Que sera. Productivity would have to wait. Today she was going to be pampered.

"Well, you look great," Cass commented, sipping her coffee and reaching for her smokes. "Heddie did an amazing job."

Abi grinned, knowing that Cassandra was right. She did look fabulous, the best she had looked in years. "Thanks. She really did do a great job, didn't she?" she said, gently playing with her fringe. Her hair even felt amazing. So clean. So cut. So healthy. Astounding what $120 could do. "I just hope I can keep it up, though," Abi said, taking a gulp of her double-double. "I certainly couldn't afford to do this once a month. I mean, how do you do it?"

"Credit, hon," Cass laughed, lighting another smoke and looking around the coffee shop.

Following her gaze, Abi was disgusted and embarrassed. The Puzzle Man continued to snooze at the table next to theirs, snoring and snorting occasionally. Christ, can't he find somewhere else to do that?

"So this is my joint. The place where I write," Abi said with mock pride, broadly gesturing like she was queen of all she surveyed. Man, I hope Cass isn't too grossed out. I really ought to find new digs.

"Nice. At least you've got some characters here," Cass replied, indicating Puzzle Man. "How are the johns here?"

Fuck. Of all the questions. "Um, you really don't want to know," Abi warned. "If you gotta go, we should blow this pop stand. Shall we venture to Queen West or Bloor West?" she asked, knowing full well what the answer would be.

"Queen West is too full of teeny-boppers and trend-mongers," Cass replied, finishing her own coffee and enjoying one last haul.

Deciding Bloor West was best, they collected their belongings and donned their jackets. Opening the door, Abi knew why the owners were so indignant about the indigent. If *she* could be driven away by their presence, anyone could.

The sex shops, tacky tourist traps, and dollar stores were prepping for the day, the less than patient owners rolling their wares onto the sidewalk and rousing and shooing the sleepy-eyed street kids from their transient pads on their stoops. A group of kids, having already been ousted, stood and squatted at Yonge and Bloor, laying out their ball caps and filling their buckets, preparing for their own day's work. Folks were lined up at the coffee shops, reviewing the sports page and selecting their sugary morning breakfast. A few anxious *Mortal Kombat* junkies were staked out by the arcade, ready to convert their pocket change into highest scores. The longest street was blowing off its hangover and steeling for the day.

Abi and Cass, feeling glam from their royal treatment, transgressed poverty to Bloor West, leaving the filth of Yonge in their wake. At Bay tailors waited outside couture boutiques, sipping their lattes and elegantly smoking their foreign cigarettes. Diligent supers rinsed the sidewalks of the sparse litter and smattering of noxious chewing gum. Petite French-looking women gently placed crown jewels in marble and bevelled-glass showcases, reminding yuppie couples that a rock was forever. Yorkville was rising and shining.

"God, I love this city," Abi said, happy that they had decided to make a move. "Sometimes I walk along here after work, pretending like I could actually afford to waltz into one of these joints," she continued dreamily, pausing in front of Cartier and gazing into the bulletproof window.

"How Audrey Hepburn of you," Cass cajoled, tugging at Abi's sleeve. "Come on, Holly. And wipe that drool off your chin. We've got credit to burn."

"Oops. Sorry about that. I get distracted by bright shiny things," Abi laughed, following Cass's lead down Bloor.

Reaching Avenue, Abi and Cass were surrounded by well-heeled tourists piling out of the Four Seasons and the Park Hyatt. The Volvo set, 2.2 kids in tow, were milling about in front of the ROM, chatting with each other and doling out juice boxes, anxious to educate their kids on Edo and Ur. Overachieving tweens rushed into the Royal Conservatory, toting their violins and dragging their cellos. A handful of U of T students who weren't hung over purposefully strode toward Robarts, bolstering themselves for eight hours of studying. Closer to Spadina, cyclists peddled toward Chinatown and Kensington, grocery lists in hand, vying for the yellow jacket and dodging traffic. As Abi and Cass passed The Brunnie, the bohemian types of the Annex wheeled their grannie carts to Mom and Pop shops, radiating patchouli and clutching their hemp purses. Man, Toronto sure runs the spectrum.

"Oh, this is one of my favourite shops," Cass exclaimed. "They take American Express," she whispered, nipping in the door.

Neat and narrow, it was one of those stores that Abi would never have entered on her own. Delicate cases proffered delicate anklets and delicate barrettes, delicately constructed by a delicate jeweller. With no pegboard in sight, dryclean-only pants, and cashmere sweater sets hung cleanly from chic stainless steel racks, Abi wasn't sure about the prices. A polished broad stood quietly behind the register, perched on a distressed stool and flipping through *W*. "I don't know, Cass. If you have to ask, you can't afford," Abi shyly whispered.

"Pshaw. That's why we've got plastic," Cass retorted, beelining for the pyramid of angora jumpers. "These would be perfect for you. It's sassy and *so* this season," Cass encouraged, holding one up. "Look — it's even got a little beading along the neckline," she tempted, demonstrating the garment's attributes and reeling Abi in.

"Man, is that a hard sell or what? You'd put Del to shame," Abi laughed, gingerly handling the sweater and bending over to inspect the detailing. "Well, it *is* gorgeous."

"And it's on *sale*," Cass added, pushing Abi toward the change room.

"Okay, okay. I'll try it on. But that's it," Abi conceded. Maybe just this once.

Finding herself behind the taupe canvas, Abi set down her bag and pulled off her top. The angora mock looked and felt luxurious. Who knew a rabbit could produce something other than droppings? Abi pulled it over her head and, studying herself in the gilt-framed mirror, knew that she had to have it. Just this once. Suddenly a pair of slim charcoal pants appeared from the other side.

"These would go perfectly with that sweater." Cass's disembodied voice adopted the aura of The Wizard.

"Oh, I don't know. I think that would be too much."

"Come on. At least humour me," Cass pleaded.

"Okay. Okay." Christ, I am so weak sometimes. Obediently donning the pants, Abi had to smile. Weightless and forgiving in all the right places, they felt like butter. Cass sure has an eye.

"How's it going in there?"

Abi was teetering. "Um, okay. Great, I mean," Abi replied.

"Well, come on. Let's have a look."

This would be the clincher. Taking a deep breath, Abi pulled the curtain across and paraded out into the shop. Strangely confident and feeling beautiful, she didn't even care that a few other shoppers were giving her the once-over with eyes of approval.

"That looks fabulous," Cass cried.

"It does, doesn't it?" Abi replied, modest but proud. "I think I'm going to go for it," she giggled, covering her mouth like a badass schoolgirl who'd just admitted to a crush.

"Good for you. You deserve it."

"I better get changed before I change my mind," Abi joked. "I think I'm going to have to wear it out, in fact. Now I just have to find the footwear to match." Heading back into the change room, Abi couldn't help but feel elated and empowered.

"I know just the place," Cass replied.

Ah. The power of plastic.

Bloor West was buzzing. People were everywhere — laughing, smiling, shopping, and kissing. It was worlds away from Yonge Street. People here were happy. Settling on the patio of Futures, Abi was extremely satisfied with her choice. Couples were sprinkled about the tables, and there was a healthy peppering of healthy writers and sketch artists. The clientele was coffeehouse as opposed to Donut Hut. The place had a fab vantage point, and access by the panhandlers was limited. It was the best of both worlds. To top it off, she looked like she belonged. From her funky new coif — chi-chi short and toxic blonde — to her funky top — mock, sleeveless turtle — to her funky pants — charcoal capris — to her funky footwear — Chinese-inspired, platform thongs — she looked fabulous. All she was lacking was some cool eyewear. Maybe she could pick up a pair around here. Cass must know of a joint.

"Cappuccino or latte?" Cass asked.

Scanning the menu, Abi realized that her new office would cost her a bit more, but she knew it would be worth it. "Nonfat latte for me." It was time she moved up to the west side.

chapter twenty-one

Abi had had an incredible week. Shopping, shiatsu, salons — this is what the good life's about, man. No wonder she felt so terrific. The weather had started to warm up, and Abi could walk home after work again. The advantage? Getting some much-needed exercise. The downside? It gave her time to think about her life, which was never good. As soon as she started thinking about things too much, she could only imagine what would go wrong.

To her, Café Society was a strange combination of culture and money, wealth and power, reality and delusion. She could not decide if she were simply an outsider, an anthropologist, a spy, or actually belonged to this strange clan. She knew that her present financial situation negated her from actively participating in their whirlwind series of gallery openings and society galas, but she also recognized that her breeding and her inheritance secured her a place on the Social Register. The real question was, did she want to be a part of the elite? Like anyone who has ever been excluded, she resisted the idea of becoming a member of their foolish society, choosing instead to poke fun at their rigid rules and frivolous concerns. But also like an outsider, she desperately wanted nothing else but to be a part of it.

These sentiments ping-ponged through her mind as she met Del to crash an open house for a new condo development. Adorned with black-and-white photos of svelte female figures in formal wear, the open house ad had boasted private elevators, valet parking, and exclusive amenities — all for the princely sum of $500K to a mil. Not bad, not bad at all. If you're a millionaire, that is.

A pert young woman in a tailored suit greeted them at the door, ushering them into the upper echelons of voyeurism. As construction had not yet begun, Abi, Del, and the other crashers were forced to imagine the high-rise luxury from a first-floor mock-up. It certainly was beautifully appointed. Marble bathtubs, granite countertops, mahogany panelling. Opulence at its best.

Abi closed her eyes and pictured herself as the quintessential socialite. She was beckoning the maid and bedecked in a regal gown. Her GQ husband, dapper in his tails, would casually saunter in and give her a peck on the cheek. They were congratulating themselves on what a good deed they were about to embark on, how they cared about the community and the welfare of others. The charity auction would raise tens of thousands of dollars and only at the cost of five hundred dollars a head. Yes, they were good, caring folk.

"Earth to Abi, earth to Abi."

Abi tore herself away from her daydream to find Del standing in front of her. Suddenly the room was filled with onlookers, and she wondered how long she had been gone for. "Sorry, just a little tuckered, I guess," Abi mumbled, looking and feeling rather sheepish.

"You certainly looked like you were a thousand miles away," Del said.

More like light-years away, Abi thought. A different galaxy altogether.

"Isn't this positively *gorgeous*?" Del was practically drooling.

Easy tiger, it's only a showroom. To Abi it was futile to engage in such activities as The Drool. The grandeur of Rosedale was off-limits to Abi, and her paltry paycheque-to-paycheque world, and there was no sense in taunting herself. It all seemed a little too much for her anyway. Deciding to keep her thoughts to herself, Abi muttered in concurrence. Besides, feeling the texture of the smooth, granite kitchen countertops, she was beginning to waver again.

"What's up? You look upset all of a sudden," Del asked, pulling Abi aside.

"Oh, nothing much. It's just, oh, I don't know," she tried to reply, her eyes bandying about the well-heeled clientele.

"Something's wrong. Tell me," Del encouraged.

"It's just that I feel like I don't belong here, I don't belong at Hubris, I certainly don't belong in Rosedale," she confided, staring at her feet.

"That's nonsense. What are you talking about?" Del said, trying to make eye contact with her.

"I so don't, Del. I mean, you totally do, but I don't," Abi stated. "I just feel so inadequate, like such a phoney around these people." A Miu-Miu couple pranced by, ga-gaing the stainless steel grill.

"Pshaw. You're as good if not better than any of these people, Abi. So you may not make as much money or live in Rosedale or take cruises in the Bahamas, but who cares? You've got to stop comparing yourself to others all the time. It's not healthy. Be proud of what you've got and what you've accomplished."

"You're right, I've been so ashamed and stressed over what I don't have, and I'm so tired of it. I guess I've just been trying too hard," Abi admitted, knowing full well that her friend was right. "I guess part of it, too, is that I'm not being true to myself, that I'm not really pursuing my writing and shit anymore. I mean, if I could only find a gig where I was proud of what I do, where I could come home with some sort of sense of accomplishment, I'd be a lot happier," she quickly added, figuring she may as well lay all her cards out on the table.

"One step at a time, baby. Focus on Hubris and settling in

there, and the rest will fall into place," Del instructed. If only it were that easy.

Making her way back to her own humble abode, Abi could hear the ruckus as she approached the building. "Good evening to you, too," she muttered, nonplussed. Peering through the glass doors reluctantly, she hesitated, not particularly relishing the idea of becoming embroiled in the altercation. Still, it was the only way into the apartment building, aside from the stinky door by the garbage bins at the rear. Taking a deep breath, she made her entrance, trying to appear as confident as possible.

The super was standing between the elevators and the entrance to the stairwell, the vein in his head pulsing rapidly. His hand rested on his trusty Hoover, ready to strike and sweep at any second. The homeless kid from before had staked out his territory near the ancient lobby couches, his belongings strewn across the floor. It was a tenement standoff. Neither man was about to budge.

"Get the hell outta here! I don't care if you have nowhere else to go. I'll call the cops again and have you forcibly removed," the super shouted, his voice cracking with emotion. Still no movement. The boy looked as if he was going to cry. "There are shelters you can go to, so don't give me any sob stories," the super continued, sensing the kid's vulnerability. Either out of shame or anger, the super's countenance was growing redder and redder. He looked like he was going to spontaneously combust.

Abi froze near the office door, shrinking slightly and attempting to be as invisible as possible. Crap. She was trapped. Abi moved into the super's office, figuring that if she needed to dial 911 she could use his phone. Standing in the doorway, Abi did what any self-respecting doe would do — she stood there gawking. Man, I wish they'd hurry up. Her nicotine level was dangerously low, and she desperately needed another smoke.

Suddenly and silently, the boy gruffly picked up his knapsack and sleeping bag, violently slinging them over his shoulder. She couldn't tell if he was going to deck the super or not. The super flinched and moved toward him. Getting close enough to spit in his face, the boy quietly responded to the super's tirade. "Fucking asshole," he muttered defiantly, heading out the door.

The super followed him quickly, and, knowing that the window for violence had closed, he threw his fist up in the air. "Don't fucking come back here, ya punk."

Ya. Like that'll learn 'em. Sheepishly making eye contact with Abi, the super scooted back to the utility room. Phew. Crisis averted. At last she could have dinner.

Opening the door to her apartment, Abi couldn't help but feel disenchanted with her surroundings. After the Rosedale open house, her humble abode was just that — humble. She hated it. Oh, to win the 649. Just imagine. Then she could have a decent pad, a place where she'd be proud to entertain. Maybe then she'd actually have people over.

Abi plunked herself down on the couch, reaching for the phone and dialling for dinner. She was pooched. She turned on the TV and searched for something mediocre to lull and dull her senses. God, I love cable. Flip, flip, flip. Seventy channels of nothing. She paused on an infomercial. Those were always entertaining. Relaxation gimmicks. Hmm. Maybe there is something to that New Age for the New Economy shit. Mental note: buy wind chimes for super.

Waiting for the pizza guy to arrive, Abi remembered that she still had a few Heinekens stashed in her fridge. Mmmm. Beer. Why not indulge? One beer can't hurt none. Now for some musical accompaniment. CJRT. Cool, crazy cat. Nothing like a little jazz to sass up the evening. Grabbing the bottle opener and cracking open a cool one, Abi headed to the balcony, journal in hand. Sitting down at the table, Abi lit a smoke and gave a contented sigh. A perfect spring evening. Peering over the banister, Abi checked out the 'hood. Trucks rumbled by, anxious to deposit their wares. Children giggled and played in the alley, laughing about nothing. Couples joked and murmured sweet nothings from the balconies across, aiming to score. Twilight was just making her fabulous entrance. And a light, hazy, violet, and palpable smog hung over the skyline. Abi reclined in the chair, crossing her ankles. There was something so sexy about pollution. It makes you aware of your body, of your surroundings, of your being. Switching her gaze to her Heineken on the table, Abi had to admire it. Gentle beads of sweat trickled slowly down the cool neck, pooling at the base of the frosted bottle, the light refracting through the condensation and tempting taste. Icy-cold perfection. Nectar of the gods. The damn thing had to be captured for posterity.

Buuuuzzzzzzz. Fuck. Don't they realize that you just have to hold it for a second? Abi raced to the intercom, knowing that the thirty minutes were up. At last. Sustenance. Paying the pizza guy, Abi was famished. Time to grab a fresh one and have some din-dins.

Abi cut off a substantial wedge, opened her second beer, and headed to the balcony for some late-evening entertainment. God, life was good. Munching on a massive bite, Abi began scribbling in her journal, careful not to get any sauce on the pages. Now this was what it was all about. Pizza. Beer. And writing. All the stress of recent days dissipated, evaporating into the sax and cornets. There was something so relaxing about hanging by her lonesome. Something so relieving. So liberating. Evoking. And thought-provoking. Too bad I can't do this every night. Her belly full, Abi leaned back and smiled. She hadn't been this mellow in a long, long while. Why hadn't she done this before? Time for a little Cowboy Junkies.

Rising as quickly as she could with a tummy full of carbs, Abi wandered over to the stereo. Lying down on the parquet, Abi made her musical selections for the evening. A little Junkies. A little Ella. A little Metallica. Hell, why not throw in some show tunes, as well? Anything with a strong vocal that she could belt her heart out to. Throwing on a disc and rolling onto her back, Abi took a substantial, savouring haul on her smoke. Picking up her bottle, Abi went to take a sip. Crap. Have I finished my second one already? Pushing herself ever so slowly up, Abi trotted over to the fridge. Why not have a third? It's going well so far. Sitting back down in front of the stereo, Abi began to let 'er rip. Oh, yeah. That's the stuff. She had a good voice when she wanted to. Too bad she couldn't perform this well at karaoke.

Racing to feed the cat, Abi stopped dead in her tracks to yell at the radio. "It's *Hungry Like the Wolf,* you morons!" Apparently caller number two didn't hear her either. Shit. Do I have time to call in? She checked the time on CP24 (on mute, as it should be). Nope. Her fifteen minutes would have to wait for another time; she had to get to work. Still, she listened, keeping her fingers crossed for Steve, the fifth "first-time caller, longtime listener." Tick, tick, tick. Yes! Jumping up as if she had just won the two passes to a banal blockbuster, she was finally put out of her misery. "Time for Time Saver Traffic, folks," the morning lackey announced. Time Saver Traffic. What a joke. Like people actually save time commuting in from Guelph and Barrie.

"Listen, Abi, I was thinking you should go on the strategic-selling course. I think Cass's going in a couple of days to the one in Chicago. Would you be interested?"

Interested? I'm ecstatic, man. Finally all her hard work was paying off. And maybe this would give her the boost she needed to overcome the admin stigma. Dream, dream, dream. "Sure,

Josh. That sounds fabulous. I'll liaise with Cass about it today." She was tempted to kiss the receiver, but despite the fact that he'd never know she figured it was still inappropriate. Hanging up, Abi couldn't believe her luck. She *was* having a good day after all. And she had been losing faith in Josh, in Hubris. Silly girl. She got up from her desk to tell Cass the good news. Windy City, here we come.

"Hey, Cass. Guess what? Josh asked me to go on the strategic-selling course with you," she proudly exclaimed, giving Cass a girly-girl embrace.

"No kidding? That's awesome," Cass giggled.

"I'm so excited. I mean, it finally feels like we're being appreciated around here," Abi added. "Like we might be actually getting somewhere in this damn company."

Cass wrinkled her nose, still smiling. "Now don't get too far ahead of yourself, there," she laughed, trying to curb Abi's exuberance.

"I know, but maybe they'll start trusting us to do more than travel arrangements and fucking lunch menus," Abi mused.

"We can only hope," Cass cajoled.

"At any rate, could you e-mail me your itinerary? I'll need to book my travel pronto. Congratulations, partner," Abi squealed, giddy at the prospect of her first official business trip and giving Cass a high five. She could finally use trial-size shampoo and conditioner.

chapter twenty-two

Abi was on Cassandra's mobile trying to track down the driver. Where the hell is he? Abi looked at the growing traffic on King and checked her watch. Great. Afternoon rush hour. They'd never get to the airport at this rate. "I've got my advance on me — we should just catch a cab," Abi said, cupping her hand over the mouthpiece.

"You're probably right — the flight's in an hour and a half," Cassandra said.

Still on the call, Abi trotted over to King and started scanning for a cab. Any cab, it didn't matter at this point, as long as it could get them to the terminal on time. "Hel — yeah, I'm still here. Listen, don't worry about sending another driver, we're just going to hop in a taxi. No, no. Don't worry about it. No sweat. These things happen. Bye now." Seeing a cab, Abi began to wave furiously, grabbing her roll-on and lumbering toward the street. Cassandra joined in, and they got their game. "We're in business now!" Abi said, opening the passenger-side door. "Pearson Airport, please." With a silent nod of affirmation from the driver, they settled in for the journey.

As they edged onto the Gardiner, traffic was a nightmare. How do people cope with this shit day in and day out? Abi couldn't believe the gridlock. It was so severe people were riding the shoulder as if it was a fourth lane. This city was sprawling way too much, and its infrastructure obviously couldn't handle the load. It was like a middle- aged man shoving his Molson Muscle into thirty-two-inch-waist pants. Yeah. You've got the same waist size you did in high school. "No wonder there's road rage, man. I'd have a wee pent-up anger if I had to spend half my life in a mind-numbing commute like this," Abi said.

Cassandra nodded, already on her cell, tying up some loose ends before they embarked on the adventure known as the sales-training course.

Figuring she may as well do likewise, Abi plucked her mobile out of her carry-on and called Josh. Hitting speed dial, she felt so suave.

"Hi. This is Josh. I'm in meetings all day today, but please leave a message or, if it is urgent, press pound and have trendy-fire track me down."

Crap. She hated trendy-fire. Beep.

"Hi, I'm trendy-fire. Josh asked me to cover the phones for him," a sassy 999-automated voice cooed. Fucking trendy-fire. Only Josh. "Please state your full name."

"Abigail Somerhaze," Abi complied, enunciating carefully.

"Is this call urgent? Yes or no?"

"Yes," Abi responded.

"All right, then. Let's see if I can find him," she crooned.

You go do that, honey. Tapping her foot, Abi listened to the rings as trendy-fire tried to track down her elusive boss. Beep. Beep. Beep. Strange, he normally has the phone forwarded wherever he is.

"I'm sorry. I couldn't seem to find Josh. Would you like to leave a message? Yes or no?"

Man, this is like twenty questions from one of the Stepford Wives. "Yes," Abi stated impatiently. The final beep finally sounded. At last. "Hi, Josh. Abi here. Just wanted to let you know that you've got a 9 a.m. con call tomorrow with Hal from Goliath Pix. He said he'd call you on your cell. I'm on my way to the airport right now, so if you need anything call me on my cell. See you when I get back."

Leaning back and watching the suburban world go by, Abi

tried to relax. While she wasn't exactly over the moon about the specific course they were going on, Abi was excited about going on her first business trip. It felt cool to be able to say "Sorry, I can't hang that night. I'm going to be in Chicago on business." Wild. She never would have thought a year ago she'd be saying that. She felt so cosmopolitan and grown up. She was followin' in Dale's footsteps, and it was wonderful. Plus the whole thing sounded so trite, so Mitch & Murray, that she had to laugh. It was definitely going to be an interesting experience.

Like salmon on a spawning spree, they took twenty-five minutes just to make it to the 427. Thankfully it was moving fast, and they were able to make up some lost time. Snaking their way through the Pearson labyrinth, Abi was getting jittery. She shouldn't have had all that sugar. There was a very real possibility that they would miss their flight. Great goin'. Screw up your first business trip. Stupendous. Pulling up to the terminal, they had forty minutes to spare. Man, we'll have to hustle. Thank God for express check-in.

Finally retrieving their boarding passes from the more than personable kiosk — it even said thank you — they made their way into the Immigration area, brandishing their passports and papers. A break. There was virtually no lineup. Wheeling luggage and lugging laptops, they breezed through and did an O.J. for the gate. Panting, Cassandra and Abi stared at the pixel board above their gate. Delayed twenty minutes. Great. No wonder there's air rage, Abi thought. Sweating like banshees, they set their bags down and joined the ranks of the disconcerted. And all Abi wanted was a smoke.

The plane was packed. Some jerk was taking his own sweet time situating himself in his seat, plugging up the entire aisle behind him and pissing off a whole lot of peons. Ready for a first-class diatribe, Abi was already feeling claustrophobic. Trapped in a metal fuselage with all these freaks and nerds droning on for hours, invading her personal space and boring her with the details of their banal existence, and spreading their germs throughout the recycled ventilation. She caught the eye of the woman in the opposite aisle and smiled one of her *I really don't want to smile, but social etiquette dictates that I must* smiles. I really ought to work on my issues with tolerance. Abi found her seat and put her stuff in the overhead compartment. Economy. She despised it.

Trying to shove her knapsack under the seat, Abi already wanted to disembark. She had never been able to relax in economy. People are too squashed together, and she loathed being shunted to the back with the rest of the disadvantaged. The worst was that walk of shame through the front of the plane. Skulking to the back, Abi made it a policy to avert all eye contact with the complimentary-drink-sipping fat cats. She just hoped they remembered what it was like to be in her shoes. Sitting back, Abi wondered what her meal would be. Gruel, probably. Christ. She wished she could be trusted with real china. But noooo. As a lowly coach — sorry, *hospitality* — passenger, she had utensils hermetically sealed in plastic, fresh from the decontamination treatment. Geez. It's inhumane. No tablecloths, no cup holders, no personal television set, no nifty toiletry bag. Completely barbaric. Abi leaned back her seat and waited for the stewardess to order it up.

As the jetway pulled back and they began to taxi, Abi looked around the cabin, her gaze settling on a young businessman practically hugging his laptop. She couldn't help but think about how ironic and unnecessary all of this was. They were supposed to be living in this virtual global village where e-commerce was king and wireless was queen. Supposedly. Studying the mystery man, Abi almost felt like giggling. It was so ridiculous that in this day and age, this stage of the New Economy, people were commuting more and more and farther and farther. Despite all of the inroads in technology, face time was still a necessary evil. And with the increased demands on time, minions were being forced to scurry across the globe at a moment's notice. They were being forced to move at the speed of business, which seemed to be careening out of control. Employees were now viewed as commodities that could be shuttled to a client site faster than a zip file. If you can submit the proposal by e-mail or courier by end of the business day, then you should be available to shake hands on the deal by the end of the week. Racking up frequent flyer points and reaping the benefits of repeat-stay memberships meant you had bragging rights. The more time zones you crossed in the shortest amount of time meant you had boasting privileges. It was ludicrous. There was something to be said for latitude after all.

"Abi?" Cass asked, jolting Abi out of her internal diatribe.

Man, how long was I gone for? "Yeah?" Abi said, slowly turning away from the window.

"Do you want a drink?"

Abi looked up at the smiling, middle-aged flight attendant, accepting the minute package of pretzels from her hand. "Um, sure. Can I have a Diet Pepsi, please?" Abi asked, hoping they didn't have just Diet Coke.

"Certainly," the woman said, grabbing a shot glass-sized plastic cup and filling it with ice. Crap. I forgot to tell her no ice. Mama FA handed her the fizzing glass, still smiling and pushing her cart along to the next row.

"Listen, Abi," Cass whispered.

"What? I can't hear you very well," Abi replied loudly, indicating the massive turbines churning under her window.

"Sorry," Cass said a louder but still hushed tone. "Listen, I've got something to tell you, but you can't tell a soul. At least not yet."

Holy suspense. Did she kill someone or something? "Okay. Pinky swear," Abi vowed.

"I've decided to go back to acting — full time," she managed.

"That's awesome," Abi exclaimed, slapping her hand down on her table and nearly spilling her teaspoon of caffeine. "I'm so proud of you. You've been wanting to get back to it for so long. Good for you."

"I know. I just finally decided that it was do-or-die time. I mean, I'm not getting any younger or anything," Cass giggled.

"Well, I think it's stupendous," Abi concurred, beaming for her friend and raising her cup.

"So I'm going to be leaving in the fall. I just wanted you to be the first to know. Please don't tell anyone, though. No one else knows about this, and it's still a few months before I'll be leaving," Cass reiterated.

"Sure, not a problem. Won't tell a soul," Abi swore, making a sign of the cross.

Cass grinned and put her headphones back on, looking content and relieved.

Abi turned back to the window, a dark cloud passing over her. She had never even thought of Cass leaving Hubris. It hadn't even been one of the possibilities. What was she going to do without her? Cass was her anchor, the one who made her laugh, the one who kept her from strangling Josh. More importantly, what was Hubris going to do without Cass? She had helped to build the place from the ground up. She *was* Hubris. It would be bizarre without her. Catching glimpses of the countryside below, Abi tried to reconcile her feelings. She was truly happy for Cass. Really, she was. But she was also saddened by the tremendous void she'd leave behind and more than a bit envious of the fact that Cass would be getting out and pursuing her dreams. She had the courage to leave. What if Abi didn't? Putting her own headphones on, Abi tried to relax to the muzak and not think about it. The seatbelt sign came on, and they prepared for their return to terra firma. At least one of them was getting out.

Prancing off the jetway, Abi was only half listening to Cass's chatter. This place was far too interesting to negate with business. Pulling her carry-on through the crowds, Abi couldn't help but feel as if she were running the gauntlet. At the gate, some welcome wagons were waving signs and peering down the jetway, anxious to wrap their Midwestern arms around their weary traveller. Scanning the faces and scrutinizing their body language, Abi was having a field day. An elderly man was standing in front of the floor-to-ceiling window, holding up a toddler and pointing out the planes. They began to wave as if the passengers could actually see them. A young woman was standing by a pillar, gussied up in a new dress from Target and waiting not so patiently for her beau, having endured a heart-wrenching weeklong absence, Abi imagined. She looked as nervous as a filly. Had it really only been seven days? Following Cass, Abi looked back at her, wishing she could see the reunion that had been days in the making. If she could only hang long enough to see his reaction, she would be satiated. The reaction would be the denouement, after all. Would he be happy? Would he be tentative? Would he have remembered to put his wedding ring back on? Realizing that she was lagging way behind Cass now, Abi hurried to catch up. Airport motel, here we come.

Over an hour late, Cassandra and Abi finally arrived at their destination — the O'Hare Marriott, a perfect picture of glamour and exoticism. The building was a product of the '70s, replete with concrete balconies and garish attempts at regal appointments. Leafing through one of the brochures from the tourist info rack, Abi giggled with nostalgia. "Hey, Cass! They even have one of those indoor/outdoor pools. Man, I remember those. I used to love swimming through the little hole into the great outdoors when we were on family road trips down to Florida," she squealed, the kid in her returning. The gentle rumble of jetliners overhead simply added to the homogeneously refined atmosphere of the foyer. Abi wandered over to the massive portrait of Mr. J. Willard Marriott displayed along the side wall. Abi had to chuckle. Hanging over a high, cherry wood table, it even had a lit candle underneath. Thing looks like a bloody shrine to Corporate America. Studying the faux bronze etching beneath, Abi read about how this decent man and fine entrepreneur had built the worldwide chain from the ground up, using the simple philosophy that the same was better. Standing back, Abi shuddered at the tribute to mediocrity. It was going to be a long three days.

Checking in to room 216 (which was identical to room 218), Abi found that the room wasn't all that bad. Sure, the view left something to be desired, but beyond that it afforded all the amenities that she required and therefore cared about. A coffeemaker, a television with cable, and a bathroom with one of those heat lamps. What more can a girl ask for? She turned the set to HBO and began to unpack. Cool. A documentary on strippers. Salacious television: there's nothing like it.

Laying out her outfit for the next day — standard black pants with standard conservative twin set — Abi was so nervous about the course. What if they grilled her on Hubris? She felt so uninformed about the company, and the last thing that she wanted was to be a poor ambassador. And what if she made an ass of herself in front of Cassandra? She couldn't handle that kind of setback at this juncture of her stint. Buggy-eyed, Abi stared at the papers sitting on the faux colonial desk. She and Cassandra had barely had time to review the business opportunity that they were supposed to present. Fuck. What a debacle. Abi got into bed and tried to assuage the anxiety. Too bad the bar is closed.

chapter twenty-three

The sun was shining through the glass dome of the pool area, indirectly lighting the hotel's restaurant. Finishing up her breakfast, Abi proudly folded her WSJ. She sat up erect and surveyed the room like a queen before her court. Businessmen and -women sat silently munching their bagels or croissants and reading papers, wiping cream cheese from their chins, and anxiously preparing for the day's events. Others, obviously waylaid at the hotel, were in their vacation attire, sneaking that extra large repast that they would never get away with at home. They were the only ones with gleeful glints in their eyes. Maybe it was her new sweater or the three cups of coffee she had swigged back, but she felt strangely refreshed, ready and raring to go. The waitress, a young woman with a British accent, brought Abi her bill. A grand total of $5.38. She suavely signed her name and room number to the tab and collected her belongings. Rising, she bid her wayward travellers a silent adieu and made her way to the seminar. 7:38 a.m. She had managed to work out, eat breakfast, *and* peruse the paper with twenty-two minutes to spare. She felt professional and on the ball.

Abi made her way through the lobby toward the conference room area. The carpets, once plush and luxurious, had been pounded paper-thin by years of travellers and traffic. People were everywhere, rushing to check out, stacking luggage on carts, and greeting comrades-in-arms. Now where is that seminar? Ah. Salon A. Right next to the Baltimore Room. What a picture of elegance. A flip chart stand barely supporting a piece of bristol board indicated that she was indeed in the right place. Abi grabbed her name tag from the table, surprised by how slapshot the deal was. She figured that in this day and age they would have aimed for a more professional image. Branding was everything, after all. No swanky name cards printed in Futura font here. No expensive signage emblazoned with logos to be seen. No corporate-stamped power points to speak of. It was all quite rudimentary, as if content was king or something.

Selecting a spot close to the front, Abi detected the distinct rumble of a jet in takeoff, the clattering of carts from the service corridor behind the drywall, and the voices from the neighbouring Baltimore Room. Outdated floral wall coverings, stackable banquet-style chairs in desperate need of reupholstering, stained ceiling tiles, and equally soiled tablecloths. Splendour it was not. Taking her seat, Abi didn't know what to do with herself. She knew that she should socialize and make nice, but it was too early in the morning for that, and she was too shy. The room was filling up fast, and there was still no sign of Cassandra. Where the fuck is she? All the other company teams were present; Abi was the only loner, and she felt like a sore thumb. One thing that Abi couldn't tolerate was tardiness. I may as well look busy. Abi reached over and grabbed a blank name plate and neatly printed "Cassandra" on it.

"Hey! Sorry I'm late. I made the mistake of checking my voice mail. BIG mistake." Cassandra slipped down into her seat, as confident as always.

Abi felt bookish and self-conscious. "No problem. There's coffee and muffins over there," she said, gesturing to the table at the back of the room.

"Mmmm. Yum. Stale baked goods. Think I'll pass. So how are you this morning? Sleep well? I always sleep well in hotels. Gotta love a king-size bed." Cassandra was exuberant, and Abi hated her for it. And *she* was accused of being too perky in the a.m.

Todd, their instructor, rose to address the congregation. The moment of truth. They were about to be initiated and anointed. "Hi. I'm Todd, and I'm going to be your instructor for the next three days. I should probably begin by telling you a little about myself, my background, and how I came to be involved with strategic selling."

Sure, go for it, Todd, we're all ears. Abi pretended to listen intently, taking the opportunity to study the room full of sales types. Thirty-two other individuals inhabited the room, all looking as bored as she was. After a quick head count, Abi determined that the group was comprised of seventy-seven percent males, none of whom was ripe for the picking. The majority of the men appeared to be middle age, all sporting modest wedding bands and appearing obedient and intent, as if they had been shuttled here by a dictum from above. The few women were much younger, hanging on every word and ardent not only to hold their own but also to climb the ranks of the fraternal order. Shifting her gaze to the back of the conference room, Abi reviewed the list of companies that were attending. No competitors, that's good. She had been concerned about that and had even come armed with a phoney opportunity to throw them off the trail. Abi was intrigued by the mix of traditional companies and software firms. Should make for an interesting combination. Abi sat back and took a sip from her fourth coffee, drinking in the scene and only half paying attention to Todd's rambling soliloquy.

"For most of you, this course will serve as a reiteration of what you've already learned, either through previous course work or actual experience."

Blah, blah, blah. Preaching to the proselytized, Todd had obviously picked up on the fact these men had been around the cubicle more than a couple of times.

"The agenda's pretty straightforward. We'll begin at 8 a.m. and go until approximately 6 p.m., with morning and afternoon breaks. As I realize that business doesn't stop just because you're at a course, you'll get an hour for lunch to catch up with the office and deal with pressing matters."

"This is certainly going to be a trial. It's going to be sit and eat, eat and sit," Abi whispered to Cass, rolling her eyes and silently chuckling.

"And being cooped up in a windowless room for more than eight hours a day is worse than being back in school," Cass concurred.

"At least you don't have to pay attention to all this now," Abi pointed out enviously. Too bad she wasn't in the same boat. Glancing about, at least it was fabulous grist for the mill. And being among strangers in a new environ, she could attempt to resurrect Super Temp. Abi was completely lost in observation and began to relax and enjoy herself.

"So let's go around the room and introduce ourselves, and then we can go on a bio break. Why don't we start at this end?"

Abi swiftly landed back in Salon A and came to attention. Todd was indicating the opposite side of the horseshoe from her, and Abi was at once relieved and disappointed. She would have time to compose her autobiography, but her bladder was filling up fast. Those three coffees sure zipped through her. She didn't know if she could hold out until last, but she didn't have much of a choice. She was trapped. All she could think of now was that holding it led to incontinence later in life. Great. She'd wind up in Depends because of this. Her only solace was that it was a great anthropological discourse on career people. She was tempted to take notes on their vignettes, but she knew that would be too obvious and rude. Beginning to tap her foot, Abi wondered how long these people would drone on for. God, do they have to recount their entire life stories?

The conch had been passed yet again, and the orations rounded the final corner. It was Don's turn at the mike. Suddenly Abi was all ears. Don appeared to be close to retirement, years of hard selling etched into the kind curves of his face. Don had definitely endured a battle or two during his lifetime. Now here was a character she could really sink her teeth into. Abi picked her poison and decided on the spot to sketch this guy out. At least it would give her something interesting to do.

"Mornin'. My name's Don, and I've worked for Industrial Lubricant for over twenty years. I've pretty much seen it all, but we're going through a restructuring now, and management wants us to attend these courses."

His tone was evident. He was one unhappy camper. At least he has the courage to demonstrate his disdain, Abi observed. She tried to gauge the reaction of the audience, but everyone's eyes were on the table or on each other. No one dared to look at Don, for fear of fraternizing with the enemy.

Sensing the discomfort he had created, Don tried to make amends. "Still, I'm sure I can learn a lot from you folks, and I'm looking forward to the next couple of days." His voice was cracking, and his facial expression belied his words. He resumed his place of honour, and the baton was passed yet again.

It was almost her turn, and it couldn't come soon enough. All of her attention was focused on one thing — her bladder. It was stretched to the size of Texas. Shooting Cass a look of desperation, Abi seriously thought she was going to pee her pants. That would make a great impression. Just when she thought she couldn't hold it any longer, it was her time to shine. In her discomfort, she had totally forgotten what she was going to say. She stood up to address the room, praying to God that the floodgates wouldn't open right then and there. Look around, make eye contact, don't say "um." All the hours spent in Toastmasters were now paying off.

"Good morning," her voice echoed cheerily. "My name's Abigail Somerhaze, and I work for Hubris, a software company headquartered in Toronto, Canada." Normally she would've just said Toronto and left it at that, but she was in Marlboro country now, and she always felt she needed to enlighten the ethnocentric Americans to the geography north of the border. "I've been with Hubris for four months now, and my role is in sales support." It felt great to rattle off a title that didn't include administrative or assistant in it, even if it wasn't totally accurate. "This is the first such course that I've attended, and I'm looking very forward to learning as much as possible. And, um, I guess that's about it." Good ambassador, good ambassador. She would give herself an eight. Her score would've been higher, but she kind of faltered at the end, and she had to dock herself points for that. That "um" was at least one demerit. Abi shrugged her shoulders and glanced at Todd, searching for a lifeline, for some sort of closure.

Todd looked at his watch and made the announcement Abi had been waiting a very long fifteen minutes for. "Why don't we take a bio break and meet back here in fifteen minutes. Bathrooms are at the end of the hall, to the right. See you in fifteen."

Recess. Abi grabbed her bag and, without even looking at Cassandra, bolted for the door.

Back in Room 216, Abi readied for dinner and collected her thoughts. Not bad, not bad at all. The first day had gone much better than she had expected. She had contributed several times, surprising even herself and bolstering her confidence substantially. And she had been extremely impressed by Cassandra. Cass had been the darling of the day. She had spoken so eloquently and knowledgeably about Hubris. Abi shouldn't have been so surprised — Cass was brilliant and affable — but it was just that Cass was typically so self-deprecating. She was constantly lowering people's expectations of her and shifting the blame for any incompetence onto her own narrow shoulders. On any given day, Cassandra could be heard differentiating herself from the management types and executives, claiming she'd never know what it'd be like to be one of them, as if she could never be one of them. From what Abi had seen so far, Cassandra had been fooling herself. She had it in her, she just didn't *believe* she had it in her. Brushing her teeth, Abi took comfort in the fact that Cassandra wasn't all brazen and full of bravado. She was as self-conscious and insecure as Abi was. "At least I'm not the only one," Abi told the mirror, shaking the water off her toothbrush and placing it in the little glass next to the sink.

Anthropologically, Abi was content and satiated. During the course of the first day, the personalities had begun to round out, and she had absorbed a fair amount. Her only disappointment was that everyone had gone separate ways to complete the evening's assignment and to enjoy dinner with fellow employees. When she had arrived here, Abi had envisioned supping in the core of the Windy City, a camplike atmosphere where booze bonded the motley crew under the guise of their unlikely circumstance. This obviously was not the case, and Abi couldn't help but feel shafted out of a true people-watching opportunity. Besides scant smoke breaks with fellow addicts (who says smoking isn't social?), how else could she get under their skins and into their minds? "Where there's a will, there's a way," she said, checking her makeup in the mirror. Abi slipped on her loafers, turned off the news, and grabbed her key card. Guess it's dinner and drinks with Cassandra tonight. It was probably for the best. They had to prepare for the next day's events, after all, and she'd rather be refreshed. There's always tomorrow. She closed her door and headed for the stairwell.

The next morning, sitting down to breakfast, she caught the eye of Don and decided to take advantage of the situation. Barbara Walters time. She stood up and moved in for the kill. "Hi Don. Mind if I join you?"

Don looked up, smiling. "Sure, go right ahead," he said, indicating the spot across from his. He was certainly pleasant enough one on one.

Abi sat at the table for two next to his. "Cassandra's probably coming down any minute now," she explained, a little sheepish for not taking a seat at his table. She didn't want to get *too* friendly with the man. Folding her napkin across her lap, Abi started her interrogation slowly and purposefully. "So how was your night last night? Did you make it downtown?" She tilted her face sideways to face him, her eyebrow half cocked expectantly.

Don masticated loudly. "Nah. Was too tired for that. So what do you think of this course, of Todd?" He put his napkin down on the table defiantly.

She was about to respond when he continued on course, thrusting his fork violently in the air. Holy Anger Management, Batman. Here it comes. Instinctively Abi wanted to duck and dodge the wrath she knew Don was about to unfurl. She decided to let him have his tirade uninterrupted.

"I just think it's hokey. I mean, come on. None of this is new. And Todd — how boring can you get? You know the story about the sacrificial lamb Jerry mentioned yesterday?" Abi nodded, listening intently. "Well, that was me. *I* was the sacrificial lamb." Abi was all ears and prayed that Cassandra wouldn't come down now and disturb the silent trust that had just been brokered. "We were in the midst of this damn restructuring, and they wanted me out, but they knew with me being so close to retirement — that's the only reason I'm still with the damn company, by the way — they knew that it would cost 'em too much in severance to give me the golden handshake. So they set it up so I wouldn't get the promotion I was next in line for, hoping that I'd quit on my own. New young guy got the job. He's the one who sent us on this course. Damn fool. It's bullshit." Embarrassed and defensive, Don was getting red in the face just recounting the gory details.

Can't teach an old salesman new tactics. Abi was struck by the poignancy of his tale and thought of The Machine. God, it would suck to be put out to pasture like that. Delving into dangerous personal territory, Abi didn't know how to react to what Don had just said. She knew that there was nothing she could proffer to console him or at least nothing that wouldn't come out trite and insincere. The man had probably heard it all, and any such advice coming from a stranger would do more harm than good. She decided not to jeopardize their newly formed confidence and changed the topic, nodding in tentative concurrence. "Have you seen the waitress? I'm starved."

Like a true gentleman, Don got up and flagged a server as she passed a nearby table. The service here certainly isn't stellar, Abi noted. The waitress, the same young British woman from the previous day, was jotting down Abi's order when Cass finally joined them. An expression of relief crept across Abi's face.

"Hi, guys! How're you doing this morning?" Cass swung her bag across the back of her chair, sat down, and scooted toward the table.

Uh, oh. Don't ask the man that. Abi glanced over at Don, hoping that he wouldn't erupt again.

"Fine," he responded curtly.

Phew.

"So, Don, how are you enjoying the course so far?"

Uh, oh. Don't ask the man that. Again Abi glanced over at Don.

"Not too bad. Nothing I haven't heard before, of course."

Phew. Reprieve number two.

"Well, it's nothing I haven't heard before either, but I think as a reiteration it's very helpful. I mean, it may *seem* like common sense to the seasoned salesperson, but it's critical to have these things hammered home once in a while." Cass sat back impressed with herself.

"Yeah, but what's the point in sending us all out on some expensive course when we won't even use the shit?" Don waved his butter knife in the air, and for a split second Abi thought they were going to spar. "It's not going to change our sales strategy one iota. I mean, they say they want to implement change, but it's never going to happen. They've got their set agendas, and they don't have any interest in what happens to us small fry," Don continued bitterly.

Suddenly Cass was caught in the headlights, and Abi wondered what her next move would be. Feeling the heat, Cass settled on the same tactic that Abi had. "What's good to eat here? That looks healthy." Cass was studying Abi's fruit platter that had finally arrived. "I think I'll have that. Where's the waitress?"

Uh, oh. Don't ask us that.

Two days down, one more to go. And it's only a half-day, thank God. Back in her room to change, Abi had to give herself a pat on the back. She'd done good, as her father would say. The course was actually pretty interesting, and she had gleaned quite a bit from it. A major in Cold War history, Abi found herself surpassingly intrigued by the course's use of military terms and strategy. In a Sun Tzu sort of way, the program liberally plagiarized verbs such as flanking and frontal attack from the military community and translated them into civilian usage. And better yet, the course was succinctly compartmentalized, broken down into fill-in-the-blank scenarios and tactics. These were concepts and practices that she could relate to, that she could grasp. She felt comfortable with its lingo and confident in her endeavours. As a result, she had been throwing her two cents in at every opportunity, to the point where she'd had to edit herself so as not to hog the platform. Cassandra had even commented on what a brown noser she was being, but Abi didn't care. She wasn't trying to impress anyone but herself.

It was intriguing, too, to observe all of the posturing that was occurring, especially among those who were accompanying their obvious superiors. They were the keeners, the ones who eagerly waved their hands to answer the instructor's queries. It was quite repulsive, actually, and Abi had to laugh. She'd like to think that she was above ingratiating herself like that, that she would never kow-tow for the sake of a paycheque. But who would she be kidding? She knew she'd be right there with them if she had gone with Josh. At least she wouldn't be so blatant about it.

Lighting up a smoke, Abi turned her thoughts back to Don. The man certainly was a piece of work and with good reason. He had given his whole damn life to his company and for what? A demotion, for all intents and purposes. It certainly hadn't been quid pro quo. She couldn't help feeling sorry for the man. Much like the seasons, her own career was just blossoming, and his was fading into the August twilight. He had achieved all that he would achieve. He was without hope, and Abi could tell he was begging to be put out of his misery. Fuck. Why *not* start fly-fishing now? It wasn't as if they would afford him any additional accolades. Rolling onto her back, Abi took a long haul and wished she knew Don well enough to tell him what she really thought. "Carpe diem, Don, carpe fuckin' diem. Screw them and get your joy back," she said aloud, staring at the ceiling. It was yellow verging on brown from years of nicotine. "Disgusting, man," she choked, rolling back over and stamping her cigarette out in the ashtray. She reluctantly got up and headed to the hotel lounge.

The ambience was typical lounge. Dark, heavy panelling, burgundy leather seats studded along the arms and back, brass railings and coat hooks. For some reason, it had adopted a nautical theme, which struck Abi as strange as they were in the middle of the landlocked Midwest. Ours is not to wonder why. There was sailing on Lake Michigan, but she couldn't envision a body of water all the way out by O'Hare. Nonetheless, Abi found its darkness cosy and inviting; she just hoped they had a decent house wine. She was the first one there and, being the first, took the liberty of staking their spot in the corner of the room. She always favoured the corner seat as it afforded the best vantage point from which to survey the room's inhabitants. A couple of guys sporting name tags parked at the table next to hers. Crouching down in her seat, she hoped they wouldn't talk to her. Checking her position, she inadvertently made eye contact with one of them. Damn. Too late.

"Hi there. How're you doin' tonight?" the one on the left slurred. According to his name tag, he would be Dave.

"Fine," Abi responded curtly.

"We're here for a retirement party," he continued.

A retirement party here? In an airport motel? How depressing. "That's nice. Who's retiring?"

The one on the right, Tom, tried sitting up. "Jack. Good guy. Had to take early retirement due to a merger. He's a trooper, though. He'll survive," Tom explained.

Hmm. Another one who gave up the prime of his life for the greater good. I should introduce him to Don.

"Hey there!" Cassandra sauntered over and plunked herself in the seat across from Abi. Saved by the bell. "This place isn't half bad, eh? For an airport hotel, I mean."

"My sentiments exactly," Abi responded. "Cass, meet Dave and Tom," Abi pointed to the pair, who were puzzled as to how she knew their names. "You're wearing name tags. Let's go to the bar — I need a drink," she whispered to Cass, pulling on her arm.

The others had begun to arrive, and it looked like they might actually have a good turnout. Drinks in and dorks out, Abi was beginning to have a good time. She felt proprietary, but alcohol was such an effective social lubricant, and Abi couldn't wait to see what the evening might hold. Finally it was her chance to study these people outside Salon A and in a more social context. They certainly looked better, having been removed from the room and taken out from under the glare of fluorescent lights.

"Hey, whatcha thinking?" Cassandra jostled her arm and handed her a glass of red wine.

"Nothing. Just people watching. How are you holding up?" Abi only half listened to Cassandra's response. She was too busy watching Don and one of the other attendees talk. Abi wanted to move closer to hear what they were saying but figured that would be too obvious. Best to wait for them to come to you.

Over jug wine and bottled beer, the seminar quickly broke down along gender lines. The dim lighting and illuminating spirits invited confidence, and the women got together to talk shop. They began to deconstruct the conference, and discussion rapidly turned toward how male-dominated the course was, how the verbiage and tactics were antiquated and inherently patriarchal. There was nothing blatantly misogynistic, per se, but the tone was there, they concurred. The Old Boys Club still reigned. The male attendees were naturally oblivious to this female impression; they were too busy enthralling each other with tales of the last great deals they had signed. The men were intent on networking and showing their plumage. Only the women had bothered to pay attention to their nuances.

Suddenly Abi began feeling drunk. Damn. The Chex Mix hadn't held its own. "Well, I think this girl is going to bed," Abi stated, rising somewhat steadily from her seat. "Bye, guys," she called, walking out of the lounge. Don't want to be hung on the last day, after all.

Packing her carry-on, Abi just couldn't shake Don, and she knew that something other than alcohol and PMS was at play. Like her, he had believed in the system, had played the game. The fact that his life had been picked apart and left as so much corporate carrion was what was haunting her. Abi could be him in twenty-five years. What had been portrayed by her father as a concrete path, what he had toted as a fantastic corporate truism, seemed like such a lie now. Companies don't care. Companies don't feed the soul and nurture the spirit. Sure, you can act the company man, but they'll devour you for their bottom line and feed you to the change management monsters. Bitterly, Abi gathered her dirty laundry off the floor. "What if they do that to me?" Abi mumbled, shoving yesterday's pair of gitch into the outer zippered pocket. Suddenly she felt very vulnerable — and not because her dirty panties were in such an accessible spot.

The plane lurching northward over the city, Abi leaned over and attempted to trace the Mother Road. Where the hell is it? Smiling, Abi struggled to sneak a peek at the famous highway. Gotta love the Route, man. When things got particularly rough, Abigail could count on Route 66 to cheer herself up. Some day she'd drive it, she had vowed long ago. Life on that road is different. The Route was slower than the seventy-five miles per hour of the interstates, following the contours of the earth on its two-lane path to freedom and documenting the ups and downs of the nation and illuminating the soul. Along this solitary belt, stories seeped from the general stores and motels, history saturating the towns that dotted the westward way. The cycles of economy bore down hard on this place, the umbilical cord of transportation and tourism having all but dried up and shrivelled away in many of the tiny towns and hamlets. Those rooted along its soft shoulders lived there with a dream of prosperity, of providing an honest, independent life for themselves and their families. Route 66 was real life. And the diner food *had* to be great.

Straining to pinpoint the minuscule highway, Abi was giving

up. No sign of the Route, just a maze of turn lanes and overpasses. The fields that had been tilled for generations, the land that had escaped the grip of the almighty dollar, and the homesteads that had been passed from great-grandfather to grandfather to father were now being dissected, split, and penned out a million different ways so that all could rape and leech the riches from the soil. Heredity be damned. The land was now worth more than gold, more than the family legacy. The solitary countryman had sold out to the interests of the bankers and developers, having long ago been squeezed out by the agro of the multinational agronomists and the rising price of pesticide and the lagging price of produce. It wasn't a question of pride; it was a question of survival.

"So I guess you didn't have to absorb all that bullshit, eh?" Abi chortled, tiring of the view and turning her attention back to reality.

"Pretty sweet, huh?" Cass gloated, obviously content with her decision.

"So how about that Don guy?" Abi asked, still not able to get the man out of her head.

"I know. Holy bitter man," Cass replied, flipping through the inflight magazine.

"Yeah, but with good reason. I just couldn't help feeling sorry for the guy," Abi commented, reaching for her own copy from the pouch in front of her. "I mean, he gave up the best years of his life for his company and got completely shafted in return. Talk about reciprocity."

"Yeah, but that's the nature of the beast. No one asked him to do it. It was his choice to stay."

Man, she can be harsh sometimes. Harsh but one hundred percent accurate and honest. She really ought to be a rehab counsellor or something.

"True enough, but maybe he didn't feel as if he did. Some people are programmed to believe that they're doing what they're supposed to be doing and just never question it. Call it blind faith, but I guess he just believed in the system," Abi retorted, giving Don the benefit of the doubt. He was a smart man. "Besides, he couldn't have just shifted gears with a couple of kids, a wife, and a mortgage. It's not so easy to go out on a limb then," she quickly added, satisfied that she had made her point.

"Yeah, I guess you're right," Cass conceded, now reviewing the safety instructions.

"Could it be any drier in here?" Abi asked, trying to change the subject. Damn recycled air. Reaching down to grab her bag, Abi was definitely relieved she was homeward bound. Crap. I can't get to my hand lotion. Damn. Could there be any less space in economy? Only forty-five minutes into the flight, and the lack of space to properly situate herself was beginning to piss her off already. Peering over the seat to the first class section, Abi grunted. Bastards are probably up there ballroom dancing and sucking on oysters. Tugging at her purse, Abi was getting frustrated. Life at thirty-five thousand feet was certainly harsh. The purse dislodged, and Abi smiled. Ah, freedom at last. When she opened the tube, a stream of cream shot out, almost hitting Cass in the face. Thank you, pressure.

Looking back out the window, Abi tried to relax. As they were finally reaching cruising altitude, the clouds were growing thicker, appearing like downy dunes and shrouding the towns below. Mmmm. Marshmallow topping. The clouds diffused, and the horizon edged into black infinity. The wings of the plane, now bathed in a bloody red, sliced through the layers, revealing the orangey lights of their destination in the distance. Sensing the ailerons lifting and the plane changing course, Abi closed her eyes. She could have a cigarette soon.

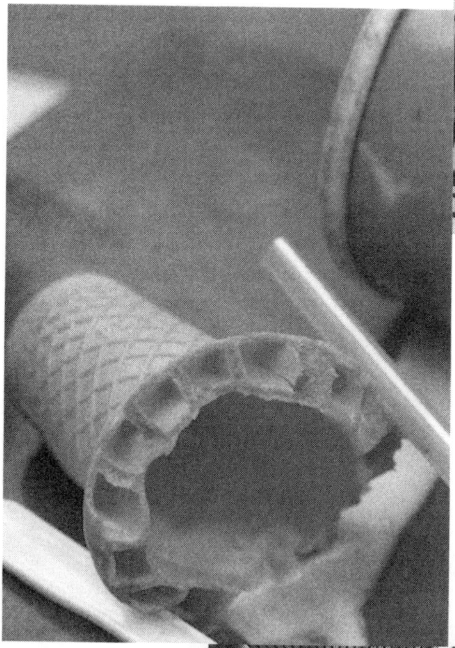

summer

chapter twenty-four

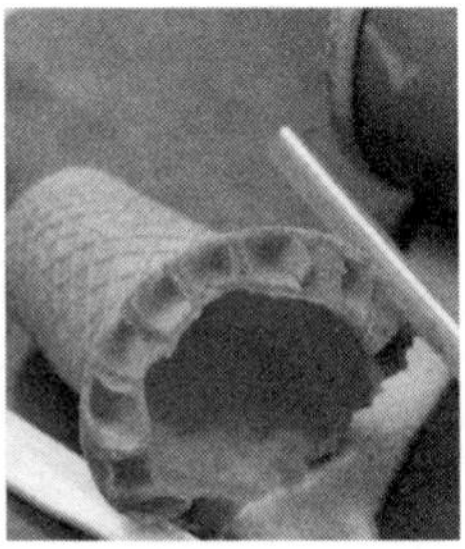

Hunger pains. What time is it? Look at clock. High noon. Air chills. Rub hands. Pull cardigan tight. What temperature is it? Finish e-mail. Pull on runners. Grab purse. Don't forget wallet. Time for noonday jaunt. Beeline for 'vators. Reach street level. Sunlight. Beeline for heat. Cascade on to street. Light smoke. Relish warmth. For one second. Damp. Humid. Too hot. No shadows. Head to market. Sidewalks packed. Heatwaves shimmer. Dodge kids. Dodge parents. Dodge tourists. Smile and nod. Must be a good ambassador. Dodge suits. Dodge homeless. Deadpan. Must be street smart. Where to go? What to eat? Spot wiener cart. Espy ice cream truck. Soft serve wins. Grab cone. Grab side of DC. Cone drips. Soda sweats. Juggle without losing a drop. Smile. Head to park. Jostle admins. Fight for market share. Find bench in shade. Green canopy overhead. Oxygen pumps. Almost sit in bird shit. Too good to be true. Find new bench in sun. Almost drop pop. Chocolate down arm. Crap. Only wore this once. Dab not wipe. Pit stains start. Brow perspiring. Thank God for short hair. Feet swell. Loosen shoes. Look as if you're enjoying the sun. Feel the burn. Wish for SPF 30. Slurp last of cone. Lick fingers. Look at clock tower. Shit! How'd it get so late? Pick up purse. Deposit refuse responsibly. Trip over blader. Curse the city. Head onto street. Miss the light. Suffocating heat. Smog. Heat waves and tar. Garbage. Urine. Vomit. Horns honk. Tensions rise. Crowd at lights. Avoid contact with hot body. BO. Stifling. Ever hear of deodorant? Light changes. Off the mark. Lose the crowd. See building. AC in sight. Revolving door. Beautiful release. Savour the moment. Wipe perspiration. Cool marble. Elevators. Onwards and upwards. Doors open. Chill sets in. Climate-controlled be damned. Head to watercooler. Pour a tall cool one. Hold to cheek. Take sip. Lick lips. Sigh of relief. Mop brow. Look at watch. Sigh of disdain. Return to cubicle. Pull on cardigan. Put on pumps. Apply the gloss. Check the voice-mail. Check the e-mail. The afternoon has begun.

chapter twenty-five

Abi was downloading three songs while playing a fourth. She had just delved into Napster. She had been a virgin; she had been so good for so long, so chaste, so pure. Now she was a hypocrite. Normally she would've felt as if she should have an N tattooed on her chest, but she was enjoying herself way too much to feel guilty. It was a phenomenon that she had resisted participating in for several months, agreeing with the RIAA that it violated rights management and ripped off musicians. No more. She was sucked in. Screw the musicians and their whining. She had herself to think about. All of it was frivolous stuff she would never buy anyway. Oh. Old Blue Eyes, baby. Come on, give me some of that "Lady Luck." Clicking on "Search," Abi typed in the name. It was musical six degrees of separation. As soon as she'd think of an artist or a song, she'd think of ten more that she wanted to download. Her thoughts turned to burning CDs and expanding her music collection. For someone as broke as her, music had been a luxury that she couldn't indulge in for so long and she felt exhilarated by the ease with which she could access any songs — favoured or mediocre. Press a button, wait for the download, and voilà. Instant music library. Now she wasn't bound by her five CDs. All you need is 'Net access and patience, she thought, waiting for "New York, New York" to download. Five more minutes to go. Veni, vidi, vici, man.

The blast of reggae from the kitchen jolted Abi out of her Pentium-induced trance. She had completely forgotten about the afternoon company shindig. Sliding her headphones off and shutting down Winamp, Abi decided if she couldn't beat 'em, she'd join 'em. Everyone was milling about the kitchen, drinking wine and beer and nibbling on the cheese platter. People from all departments were chattering over the stereo, obviously more interested in the free booze than in the reason behind the gathering. Abi manoeuvred her way through the programmers toward the impromptu bar that had been set up next to the microwave. Screw-top wine. Domestic beer. Screw-top wine. Domestic beer. Domestic beer wins. Popping open a cold one, Abi scanned the room for someone, *anyone,* whom she knew. Christ. She used to know everyone in the joint. Spotting Cass and Joe over in the far corner, she headed over to them.

"So what's up with this?" she asked, taking a long-deserved swig.

"Oh, some sort of announcement by our esteemed leader," Cass responded, savouring a plastic glass of the screw-top white. "Probably just another rally for the troops. You know, get us plied with alcohol and tell us how great we are. Fuck. I think this was bottled yesterday," she chuckled, wrinkling her button nose.

"Yup, booze is love, after all. At least it's free," Abi laughed, shrugging her shoulders.

"Shit, I hardly know any of these people. I mean, where the hell did they all come from?" Joe asked.

"I was just wondering the same thing. I used to know everyone at Hubris. Not anymore, man. I mean, I barely recognize half these people," Abi concurred.

"Kind of bites that we've gotten so big," Joe lamented, shoving another chunk o' cheddar into his mouth.

Studying the sea of faces, Abi had to agree. Developers, alliance managers, HR types. They all seemed to have cropped up out of nowhere. She'd be hard pressed to name one of them, let alone list his or her role within the organization. Christ. I haven't even gotten loaded with any of them.

"It was so much more fun when Hubris was a little family, when everyone knew everyone, and we all jived together," Abi commented. "I mean, I haven't been here as long as you guys have, but I remember when the stereo was always playing, dogs were running around sniffing butts, and shit was getting done. And there were people here all the time. It was a good two months before I turned on the alarm in the office because there was always someone here. There just used to be such a buzz, man. Now it's just nine-to-five bullshit. Come in and punch the clock. All the passion's been sucked out of the joint. It's just one disjointed mass of people now, man."

"I know. Today I had to fill out a PO for file folders. Fucking ridiculous. It was so much better before we had a CFO," Cass concurred, biting hard on some crudité and looking more and more pissed off.

"Let's just hope it doesn't all go to hell in a handbasket," said Joe. "Although I fear it might be. Who knows, maybe we're being bought or some shit."

"Come off it, like big ol' Parks Bigg and his hefty ego would let that happen," Cass sniggered.

"Here's to the joint going down the shitter," Abi remarked, raising her beer absentmindedly and nearly smacking the CEO, Parks Bigg. Oops. His ears must've been burning. At least she hadn't spilled anything on his Holt's jacket. "Sorry about that, Parks. I'm heading for a drink. Can I get you anything?" she asked respectfully but not deferentially. Never let them see you sweat.

"No thanks, Abi. Maybe after the presentation," Parks replied, moving behind the podium that had been set up in the corner.

"Well, I guess it's show time," Cass quipped, setting down her drink and crossing her arms in expectation. This had better be good.

"Ahem." Parks cleared his throat, looking nervously out at his masses. Not a flinch.

Gotta try harder than that, Parks. Most people don't even recognize you now. Besides, they're more interested in the free booze.

"Um. Hi there, folks," he continued. A few people looked up attentively, but they were mostly the ass kissers whom he dealt with on a daily basis. "Folks," he continued more assertively. Eyes up front, peeps.

"The reason we're all here today is because Hubris turned a significant corner yesterday," he announced, garnering a wink and a nod from Bob the CFO. "And we wanted to thank all of you for helping us get to this stage."

Finally the din had dimmed, those assembled having decided they could take a break from drinking for at least five. A little fireside about dinero will do that.

"I'm sure that most of you have read the press release, but in case you haven't yesterday Hubris signed its largest client to date, Goliath Pix, to a deal totalling over a million dollars. Highly referenceable and well connected, Goliath will assist us in ushering in a new era of prosperity," he continued, beaming with the realization that he finally had everyone's attention.

Everyone was smiling at each other, a glint of satisfaction and excitement in their eyes. We're in the money. The sales guys were huddled together, slapping each other on the back and raising their glasses collegially as if they alone had created the company.

"Right now I'd like to bring up Josh Nesatis. Josh, could you come up here for a minute?" Josh, puffed up like a proud papa, moved toward the podium. "For those of you who don't know, Josh Nesatis is our EVP of Sales here at Hubris and has become my right-hand man since my arrival here. Suffice it to say, it was primarily due to his diligence over the past few weeks and months that we succeeded in closing the Goliath deal. Right now I'd like to present Josh with a little token of our appreciation. Marisa, could you come up here?"

Grabbing a giant baby-blue Birks bag, Marisa rushed up to the makeshift stage and, smiling broadly, handed it over to Parks. What a demo dolly.

"Josh, congratulations. I hope there will be many more deals to come," Parks laughed.

How schmarmy. Opening the bag, Josh looked like a kid at Christmas. Oh, the anticipation. Digging through the mounds of tissue paper, Josh pulled out a large oval silver platter. How useful. Grinning appreciatively at Parks, Josh held it up high over his head, as if he had just mastered the centre court. From her vantage point, Abi could myopically make out the "Goliath Pictures — $1,279,599 USD — July 21st 1999" proudly etched along its edges. A polite amount of applause broke out. Clap for the winner, folks.

"Thank you, Parks. This is a wonderful surprise," Josh fakely stammered. Come on. At least *try* to look surprised. "But of course I didn't do this on my own." No shit. It wasn't like I scheduled all of your meetings or anything. "I'd like to thank all those that worked with me behind the scenes — legal, finance, and all of the support team." Yadda, yadda, yadda. Thanks for thinking of us little people. "It's been a long road, I know, but well worth it in the end. All I can say is let's kick some butt," he said with all the vigour and poise that an EVP can muster.

"Thank you, Josh. Let's raise our glasses to Josh, Goliath, and to maybe IPOing in the fall," Parks toasted.

"IPO?" Abi asked, stunned.

"Yeah, but don't get your panties in a twist. He says that every few months," Cass noted.

Only slightly bemused, a few people raised their glasses, but most began shuffling their feet and switching their gaze toward the bar. Sorry, man. It's the age of ADHD.

Sensing the growing impatience, Parks stepped back behind the mike and wrapped up the paltry presentation. "That's about it, folks, so sit back and enjoy. Congratulations. Good job, everyone." Parks stood back and slapped his hand on Josh's shoulder.

Fraternitas es eternitas. Now that was well worth losing an hour's worth of work.

The din returned, and people began milling about once again, a look of relief and satisfaction in their eyes. "For once I wish they'd announce something we didn't know," Cass asserted cynically. "What a waste of time. And on a Friday afternoon, too." The crowd began to thin, people filtering back to their desks.

"And we've still got to drop code tonight," Joe remarked. "So much for having a Friday night."

"Come on, guys. It's not all that bad. At least we finally signed a deal. I think it's pretty cool, actually," Abi chimed, trying to be gung-ho and play the company gal.

"Yeah, I guess you're right, Abi. But then again you haven't been here long enough to be jaded," Cass snickered, giving Abi a playful wink. "In the meantime, it's back to the grind."

"Yup. Time to wrap it up. Another week, another dollar," Abi chirped.

Staring at the monitor, Abi smiled weakly. Despite her earlier cynicism, Abi had to admit that this was big time. Finally there was something in the pipeline. Pretty zany. Sitting back, Abi reviewed the press release. After an insane sales cycle, they had finally landed the big one. Forwarding the release to Dale, Abi knew he was going to be ecstatic. The office had taken on a festive atmosphere, and she decided to get while the gettin' was good and knock off early: 5 p.m. A reasonable time to depart, she thought. She hoped Josh wouldn't disagree. Fuck it. She had logged in so much unpaid overtime that one or two hours off couldn't lodge a black mark against her name, at least not an indelible one. Besides, it was the least he could do for all her "behind the scenes" work.

Shutting off her computer and packing her bag in a frenzy, Abi made a mental list of what she had left undone. Meeting info in scheduler, filing, caterers to confirm. Nah. Nothing that couldn't wait until Monday. Slinging her backpack over her shoulder, she marched into the kitchen and tapped Josh on the shoulder.

"Josh — hey, yeah, how's it goin'? Congratulations, by the way. Listen, I'm going to knock off early," she stated confidently, searching his eyes for a response. "If that's okay with you," she quickly deferred. Man, I hate kow-towing like a kitten. "It's just I've got a ton of errands to run, and. . . ." Why do I always feel like justifying my actions to him? "And I need to get home at a decent hour tonight." She scanned his face, checking every movement of every facial muscle, attempting to gauge his reaction. He smiled. Thank God, he smiled. It was probably a few too many domestics.

"Sure. Looks like we're not going to get much work done this aft anyway. Sure you don't want to stay for a drink? It's on Hubris."

Abi smiled back, tempted. "Nah. I really have to get going. If I don't leave now, I'll wind up staggering home at midnight. Thanks anyway, though. See ya on Monday." Abi made her way through the hangers-on and headed toward the lobby. Just as she approached the elevators, the doors opened and she gingerly stepped on. Kismet. She had exited Hubris before 6 p.m. for the first time in months. What a happy day.

The sun was still out, and the evening was full of promise. Ah. How glorious it is to leave work at a humane hour. Waltzing north up Sherbourne, Abi grinned, the magnitude of what had just transpired finally settling on her. Goliath Pix. And IPO. Initial public offering. Now *that* will really get Dale going. Waiting for the light to change, Abi felt richer already. Taking their product to market. Divulging their financials. Opening their kimono. It was their ultimate goal as a start-up, and the prospect was somewhat titillating to her. Watching gentlemen enter the mission for their warm supper, Abi furrowed her brow. IPO also meant being accountable to the shareholders and not to the employees. Going public would bind them and shackle the option-laden developers, the hopeful single-mother secretaries, and drive the Greedy Gretchen SVPs, CFOs, COOs, and CEOs. The stock ticker would become their carrot, their raison d'être, and not the concepts themselves.

People, cars, and trucks filled the avenue, beelining for the weekend. A couple of girls dressed in thigh-highs and halter-tops worked their regular corner, attempting to get enough for their next hit. Watching the coked-up working girls on the corner, Abi knew that, if and when it went public, Hubris would never be the funky collective it once was. Under corporatization it was already dissipating into a larger-than-life, dysfunctional family. The flexible specs that had been hastily traced on cocktail napkins and had come to fruition in a tiny basement apartment had morphed into hard, recirculated pipelines. Employees, once dubbed with friendly monikers, were now known as numbers. Personal had been replaced by personnel. And as they stoked their dream, Hubris became less about the greater good and more about the bottom line. Studying the girls hawking their wares, Abi shrugged. Maybe Cass was right. Maybe it won't be for a while.

Following the flow of traffic and hoofing it at full speed, Abi tried to figure out where she stood on all of it. It was all so bittersweet. After years of capitalist grooming, deep down she knew that this was what they had been working so hard for, that this metamorphosis was a necessary evil.

Stopped at a light, Abi weighed the impact of the day's

announcement. While the transition appealed to her fiscally responsible side, she lamented the impact of corporatization and the recent swelling of the ranks. The company, once staffed by bright-eyed visionaries, had swiftly moved from adolescence to adulthood, skipping the carefree university days and landing them smack in mortgagedom. They were once renegades blazing new trails and conquering new territories. The light changed. Now it was all about underwriters and analyst reports, all in the name of surviving, competing, and prevailing.

A ladder truck screamed by, parting traffic and likely heading for a false alarm at a towering, nondescript high-rise. Traffic was getting heavier, the city unloading and transforming itself for the evening that lay ahead. Walking past a minivan headed to cottage country, Abi tried to reconcile her feelings, which was hard because it had been her cosy, frenzied, surrogate family. But the family was on the move, and her more sensitive alter ego felt like an ungrateful, recalcitrant prepubescent reacting to news of that transfer, her emotions running from betrayal and victimization to support and empowerment. A homeless man screamed obscenities as she gingerly wandered by.

Abi knew she wasn't alone. Many of the longtimers, the true entrepreneurs, were crying foul, lamenting the changes and hearkening back to more collegial times. People like Joe, who had sought out the start-up as misfits who did not wish to conform to their parents' image to begin with. They had signed on to prove themselves, to develop the New Economy, to show the world that geeks are people, too. They had wanted to set their own hours and create their own work environments, proving to the world, the naysayers, and the high school bullies that they too could succeed, and succeed on their own terms. They were the sheriffs of this town. Or at least they had been. Money had been important, sure, but seeing a product crystallize right before their eyes had meant more. They had owned it, and their personal reputations had been at stake. Back in the day, the drive had come from within, not from above.

Taking a left across Sherbourne, a careening car narrowly missed Abi, its driver leaning on the horn as if she had done something wrong. Abi was beginning to get pissed off. She recognized that people like Joe and Cass had put their all into this company and that their work ethic had been lionized. The hours had been long, and start-up widows lined their roadway to success. Twelve- to fourteen-hour days spent in the shadowy, open-concept loft (medium lit to reduce monitor glare) had been accepted as the norm. And they had been happy to do it. It had been a simple concept — get the shrink-wrapped product out with no bugs had been the only goal. That and piss off as few customers as possible. Find the void, fill that niche, and pay off your student loan in the process.

The light changed again, and, after her brush with death, Abi decided to obey it. It was startling how quickly things had changed. The CFO had been hired, the HR director brought in, and salary banding implemented. Managers now demanded status reports. Finance calculated billable hours, and high-maintenance clients clogged the support line. Yes, Abi could definitely empathize with Joe and Cass. They had created this baby, and it had morphed into a monster. Mary Shelley would be proud.

Absentmindedly, Abi started into the intersection just as it was her turn to go. A horn honked, bursting Abi out of her little bubble and bringing her back to Sherbourne and Carlton. Fucking red-light runners. Giving the offending driver the finger, Abi began to feel some relief. Still somewhat of an outsider, she knew what an amazing experience this was to observe firsthand. She could really use this shit. Almost at her building, Abi chuckled, thinking of her coworkers and their reactions to events of late. The sales people must be positively creaming themselves. Yup. They're probably feeling pretty great about themselves about now, she thought. From here on in, it was all going to be Power Point presentations, revenue projections, and personal commitments. All about zeroing in and targeting that account. Flooding that pipeline and ensuring it gushes. The company was now on parade, indulging in pomp and circumstance, in arrogance and evangelism. And from what better point of view to watch the majorettes than her innocuous EA desk? Opening the lobby door, Abi was amazed to see an elevator door at her beck and call. Wonders never cease. Abi selected her floor and set down her bag, thinking the situation at Hubris could be worse. At least with her options agreement, she could afford dinner at Canoe. Maybe.

Ring. Ring. Ring. Fuck. Struggling to locate her keys in her bag, Abi knew who was calling. It was almost certainly Del calling for her to come out and play. And she had been hoping for a healthy Friday and an even healthier Saturday morn. Finally managing to open the door, Abi dumped her belongings and picked up the receiver just in time. "Hello?" she said, panting. This better be good.

"Abi? Thank God you're home." It was Del but not the upbeat, go-get-'em Del she knew and loved. Something was up, and it obviously wasn't good.

"Hey, hon. What's up?" Abi asked, calming down her breathing and her tone.

"Well. Um. I don't know how to say this, so I'm just going to come out with it. . . ." Del trailed off, obviously under the influence.

Well, then. Come out with it. "I'm all ears, babe," Abi encouraged, mindful not to rush her. Del hated that.

"I lost my job today."

"What? What are you *talking* about?" Abi cried. Holy neutron bomb. "What are you going to do?" Del *was* her work. She lived and breathed the shopping channel. "I mean, what happened?" Abi quickly changed her line of questioning. Asking a freshly canned person what her future plans are is not the most supportive thing to do, after all.

"I don't know. I went in today like normal. And it was going to be such a good day, too, 'cause I was supposed to debut a new line of *to-die-for* jewellery. And I got called in to the producer's office just before air. It's all such a blur. I mean, they just started rattling on about production costs and falling ratings and the new merger with Titan and downsizing. Then they escorted me to my desk, banker's box in hand."

Wow. "I can't believe that. You're the best they had. I mean, if they could do this to you, they could do it to anyone. Total bullshit. You gave them your heart and soul," Abi said furiously. And it was true. How could they look at someone like Del as just a number? It had to be political, or else it didn't make sense.

"I know, Abi. But a lot of others got laid off, too. They cut twenty-five percent of the workforce so it wasn't just me. It's just the nature of the beast, I guess," Del sighed.

It was a beast all right. "I can't believe you're taking this so well, Del. Did they at least give you a decent severance package and stuff?" Abi hoped for Del's sake they had. Del would shrivel and die if she couldn't shop at Tangerine and dine at Bar Italia.

"Yeah, they did. Only two months, though, so I figure I'll start temping to boost my savings and to keep busy."

Wow. Del temping again? Abi was horrified that Del had been reduced to this. Del was so far beyond temping in the working world that it was ridiculous. Still, at least they could clip coupons together now.

"It just seems so bizarre knowing that I don't have a job to go to tomorrow. I was going to order rescuethelazy this afternoon and then realized that I had all the time in the world to pick up fresh produce. Hell, I could even go to Brazil for coffee if I really wanted to," she laughed, obviously trying to keep up a brave face.

"I know, that must be so strange. You were at Convenient for three years. At least you have a shot at a new routine," Abi consoled, trying to highlight the faint silver lining.

"I just can't help but think that I didn't measure up. That I'm just a fuck-up and that's why they let *me* go," Del cried, the tears finally emerging.

"Del, that is so not true. How could you think that about yourself? You were the best damned host they had. God knows you worked like a dog, always going above and beyond the call of duty for those assholes. Remember the time you sold Christmas ornaments for fourteen hours straight? By yourself? And it was August, for God's sake. Besides, you said yourself that it was a massive layoff. No one in their right mind would single you out. Don't let it get to you, babe. Don't let *them* get to you." Abi was pissed off beyond belief that her closest friend had been reduced to thinking that about herself. Don't they realize the human toll of their decisions?

"I know, I know," Del sniffed. "It's just that's all. In this city, you are what you do, and now what am I?" she asked, clearly taking a long sip of her vino.

Isn't that the truth. "One sassy, hard-workin', badass gal," Abi replied, trying to lighten the tone. "And don't you ever forget it, man."

"You're awesome, Abi. What would I do without you?" Del said, giggling again. "Just don't tell anyone about this yet — it's too embarrassing."

"Don't worry, your secret's safe with me," Abi vowed. Damn. How sad it is that the bottom line always wins.

chapter twenty-six

It was her first day off in months, and Abi had gotten up at 4:30 a.m. to shoot the commencement of the morning rush hour. She loved rising with the sun. It was the only positive lesson that she had gleaned from years of insomnia. There was something so sacred about observing and partaking in the onset of a new day, of being a part of its transformation. The day starts slowly and quietly. There are no horns, no sirens, no screeching of tires. Dawn holds so much promise, and Abi felt blessed that she was up while the rest of the city was hittin' snooze. Yonge Street was empty and silent as she made her way to the subway station. She had decided to go to the Mecca of commuters: Union Station. Having encountered only one other individual in her travels, Abi took pleasure in her solitude. The city seemed so different, so curious and inviting when it wasn't writhing and teeming.

Meandering onto the street and depositing three quarters into the paper box, Abi pulled on the door. Not even a budge. Damn thing just swallowed my change. She yanked again, and the grey box rattled but refused to give it up for seventy-five cents. Nada. What the? She looked around, tempted to wail and cry but, noticing a fellow insomniac, thought the better of it. Got to at least appear sane. Abi heaved on the door, praying that the third time would be the charm. Yawning open, the box finally released its worthy content. Grabbing all the news that was deemed fit to read, Abi triumphantly continued on her way. The paper, and the day, were hers.

Paper in hand, Abi made her way to the first stop on her field trip, marvelling at the empty avenue. Aside from a handful of overnight shift workers, the streets were deserted. Not a raver was stirring, not even a louse. She loved Hogtown this way, and, savouring the solitude, she was cognizant that it was such momentary blips as this one that kept her in the city. A lone street sweeper hoovered stealthily up Yonge, picking up Styrofoam cups and half-eaten Big Macs, Listerine bottles, and pizza slices. Wearing massive headphones and a brilliant orange jumpsuit, the man behind the wheel danced along to music only he could hear, intent on sucking the rotting marrow from the gutters and wiping the slate clean. Abi cordially nodded at the young man as he zipped by and, hanging a right, entered the silent subway station.

Paying her pittance, Abi wound through the turnstile, very conscious of the racket it made in the tomb. Arriving on the platform, Abi looked about. The rebirth had not yet begun. Camera and steno pad in hand, she was incognito, a veritable Harriet the Spy. She wondered about her fellow commuters. Why were they here at this hour? Conscious not to overstep the yellow line, Abi made her way down the concrete expanse. She noticed a haggard-looking woman fighting off sleep on a hard plastic bench. Hmm. Take on the risers or the retirees? I wonder who will win the parry? Abi pondered. She decided to attack the fatigued ones first. Have they been partying till dawn, or are they just getting off the night's janitorial gig? Were they up all night fighting with a partner or caring for a sick child? Abi turned to the more refreshed commuters. Is this their first day on the job? Are they beating the boss in an attempt to get that promotion, the promotion that will give them the raise, the raise that will put the pool in the backyard next spring? Are any of these people happy? Where do they find joy in their lives?

The first train pulled into the station, and, unlike the clamour that would occur later, everyone boarded the car calmly and quietly. As Abi sat down, she looked through the window at the train on the opposite track. A passenger was snoozing, her ponytailed head resting gently against her buxom chest. "Must've had a hard night, the poor thing," Abi said to herself. With a lurch, the train jolted alive, and they were on the move. At each stop passengers trickled in, wiping the sleep from their eyes and trying to read the paper. Or at least trying to *look* as if they were reading the paper. Generally people seemed content, but maybe that was because at this hour they were guaranteed a seat for the duration.

The car followed the curve of the track, metal wheels screeching loudly in protest against resistant metal tracks. It rounded the final bend and came to rest at Union Station. Like cattle at a stockyard, a bevy of people lined the platform, waiting to board and start their day. These were the people from the 'burbs, that behemoth known as the Greater Toronto Area. The mortgaged mothers and fathers from Oakville, Mississauga, and Markham, all of whom were on the final leg of a long trek. Abi disembarked and wondered where she should park herself. What would be the ultimate vantage point? She headed up toward the cavernous lobby, figuring she would see the most action there.

As she ascended the graceful staircase, the main terminal, the locus of the station, was eerily quiet. There was barely a soul there. Its granite floors didn't yet absorb the impact of hundreds of feet; its large columns and sweeping arched ceiling didn't yet echo and reverberate with the sounds of thousands of commuters. It was a stunning sepulchre, a monument to transportation that had yet to be consecrated for another day. For this portion of the station, the pilgrimage had not yet begun. After waiting a few minutes, Abi decided the better of it and headed back down to the GO part of the station.

Suppressing her agoraphobia and supplanting it with journalistic drive, Abi knew she had made the right decision in coming down here. Commuters were streaming in from all directions, and the place was happenin'. Pay dirt, baby. She quickly sat down and pulled out her camera, mindful not to be seen by anyone. She wanted to capture the rush hour candidly and didn't want to offend some unsuspecting person with the camera's presence or her own. The last thing she needed was to be punched by some angry secretary or feel the wrath of some embittered and embattled exec. Abi rested the camera innocuously on her backpack, the lens ready to capture the unfolding panorama. She figured she'd wait until the joint filled up a wee bit more, and then she'd leave the shutter open to catch all the action.

Art in motion. It was incredible to observe everyone in various states of consciousness. Shooting a secretary here and a janitor there, Abi grinned. Some were bright-eyed, expectant, and ready to take on the day. Others were only half awake, more reluctant, and indicating that they did not see this hour on a regular basis. They were the ones who appeared confused and stunned, anxious to arrive at their destination but too tired to hurry. They were the ones who were waiting to wake up.

Shifting her attention to the business that prospered under the rush, Abi had to smile at the predictability of it all. Lineups had formed at the coffee shops and breakfast bars, extending past the magazine racks and ticket booths. The lottery kiosk located in the terminal was doing a brisk business. It was Thursday morning, and commuters were checking the 649 numbers to see if they still had to show up at the office. It was only 6:50 a.m., and already twenty or so hopefuls had gone to its counters. Watching a man buy fifty dollars' worth of tickets, Abi was struck by how telling it was about their lives, how insightful it was about their longing to escape the drudgery of the workaday world. By scoring the winning ticket, these people could rise two to three hours later, pay off the house, yank the kids out of daycare, and get their dignity back.

If only, they say. But for them, it was yet another day of work to live, live to work.

Wondering which ones were the Dons and Dels, Abi decided to partake with the masses and got up to indulge in another cup of coffee. Lining up, for the first time in a long while Abi felt like an outsider looking in. There was something almost depressing about the throngs of people. They are like sheep, for God's sake. They were the ones upon whose backs the city had been built and upon whose backs the city would continue to balloon. They had sacrificed their own aspirations to make the conquests of others come to fruition. And they had never once considered the awful prices that they were paying. They didn't realize that they indeed had a choice in the matter. On the one hand, it was noble that they relinquished their individuality and the essence of their beings in order for the world to turn. The disheartening part was that they were all toiling in the fields of their own making and paying the price per bushel.

Sitting back down, coffee in hand, Abi began scribbling in her journal, attempting to distil the flurry of activity and emotions surrounding her. A recent admin course grad, perhaps twenty-one or twenty-two, flitted past, fake leather briefcase and gift bag-disguised lunch in hand. The woman, humming to soft rock on her headphones and barely conscious of the world around her, had a look of satisfaction and purpose about her and was focused solely on getting to work. Abi felt like shaking her. There was something so sad about watching the secretaries, assistants, and executives converging on the station. Spotting three or four more seemingly identical females, Abi began to notice subtle differences in their demeanours. Some were focused intently on beating their colleagues to the cooler. They were the eager and enterprising ones who were always on the make. Others, typically the older and more worn admins, were obviously on autopilot, already dreaming of 4 p.m. when they could reverse their steps. They were not driven by ambition or exigency but by instalment plans and car loans. Writing furiously in her journal, Abi noted that they were all connected by a collective sense of duty, compelled out of necessity or at least the illusion of necessity. They had no clue how dispensable their dreams were.

Footsteps clattered, and cell phones bleated, reverberating throughout the station and bringing Abi back to reality. Picking up her camera once again, Abi tried to freeze the onslaught. The call to arms had truly begun. Leading the charge, the power brokers who pay the salaries of so many shunted past with intensity marked by greed. A suit nipped by, disregarding her personal space and practically kicking her camera bag, clearly oblivious to her presence. Harder, faster, better. He knew that the markets hadn't slept. The Nikkei's been up for hours. Beating the boss wasn't his goal de jour — greeting the overnight crew on their way home was. It was for him, one of these chosen few, that his single, surrogate mother secretary had relinquished her life and subjugated her worth in the name of fetching his dry cleaning and coordinating his ludicrous schedule.

Her eyes following the Golden Son as he continued his pilgrimage to prosperity, Abi tried to dissect the pinstripe element. Testosterone enveloped in the best silks, wools, and cottons, Abi could detect delicate distinctions among the Old Boys, illustrations of integrity as faint and varying as the hues of blue of their suits. A few were cognizant of their fortune and proved compassionate. Many more were oblivious and unconcerned. They were too intent on completing the next deal, of garnering more praise, of cornering the market and spreading their gospel. They were not driven by the diamond baubles or Boxsters; they were in hot pursuit of power and recognition, in a never-ending race to feed their egos. To be the best. Abi snorted in disdain. Greed and ego were why these self-professed power brokers neglected their wives and husbands, missed school plays, and drank a wee too much on weekends. Self-medication was the rule, not the exception. The possibility of going down in the annals of corporate history, to have one more accolade in their obits, was worth it to them.

Flanking their generals, the younger ones filed by, still fresh-faced and wet behind the ears. They were still filled with hope, sycophants in the making. Smiling their "drink milk, love life" smiles, they were perhaps mooning over their fiancés or may actually have believed that they'd escape and move above the masses. The slippery rungs didn't intimidate them. They were aiming for the middle anyway. They were proud of their newfound independence, of moving out of their parents' homes, of buying their first suits with their own hard-earned dough. They simply wanted security and stability. Enough for a downpayment and to put the future kid through university. They aspired to be middle managers but would never dream of being president and CEO. They were content with their current courses and asked not for what they could attain but how little they would have to pay for it.

Abi looked at her watch. 7:30 a.m. Most of the worker bees had arrived by now, she figured. Packing her belongings and slinging her bag across her shoulder, Abi decided to make a move back to her abode. Time to do some reading and writing. Glancing back at the flow of people marching to cubicles and offices, Abi had to gloat. So long, poor sods. Have a great day at work. Exiting Union Station and fighting the pedestrian traffic north on Yonge, Abi couldn't help but feel lucky to finally have the day off, to finally have the opportunity to collect her thoughts and observe the world around her. To think is to live, after all.

A sprightly woman sat on the sidewalk, barely out of the fray. A blackened bomber jacket slung over her shoulders for warmth, she was holding out her baseball cap and hoping to cash in on the rush. Rummaging through her bag for some spare change, Abi came up empty-handed and, gingerly walking by the woman, continued her course north. Pausing in front of the Tangerine window, she practically gagged at the sight of the seven-hundred dollar ensembles and impractical couture. Moving on, Abi couldn't believe what a difference a few steps back made. Union Station had been brimming with dozens of Dons and Dels, hundreds of people clamouring for unattainable wealth and fulfilment. And had it not been her Happy Day Off, she would've been one of them. What the hell am I doing with my life anyway? How much longer can I prostitute myself? Rushing home, she wanted to retreat from the street, from her life. She definitely needed a change of pace.

What to wear, what to wear, what to wear? Jeans. Jeans. Ratty old work pants. Ill-fitting lil' black dress. Fuck. Totally bereft of style and substance. Abi dialled Del's digits; this was a crisis. "Del? I am having a total fashion emergency. What are you wearing tonight?" Abi frantically demanded, pulling every article of clothing out of her closet. "I mean, I've got nada."

"Sssh. Calm down, honey. I know you'll look fabulous — you always do," Del cooed encouragingly. "Okay. Let me think. Um. Fuchsia sweater?"

"Check."

"Low-rise black jeans?"

"Check."

"Sassy gitch?" Giggle.

"Check."

"Black high-heeled boots?"

"Check."

"Okay, girl. You've got it goin' on. You are going to knock 'em dead tooo-night."

"You are a fashion angel, a maven of mode, my dear," Abi exclaimed, ecstatic once again. "How did you do it? You know my wardrobe better than I do." She was impressed that, even in her unemployed despair, Del had it together.

"'Cause I'm your closest friend, and it's my job, Abi. And my only job," Del laughed, taking a rare poke at herself. "Now hurry up and get over here. I'm on my second glass of Chardonnay, and it's going down smooth as silk," she instructed.

"Will do, I'll see you in a jiffy. Ciao, bella," Abi said, setting down the receiver and setting out her wardrobe for the evening. Thank God for Del and her easy attitude. If she could be excited about the evening, then so could Abi. Fuck Hubris. Fuck layoffs. Fuck stress. Fuck being single. She was going to look and act sexy tonight, even if it killed her.

Heading over to Del's apartment, Abi couldn't help but think of Don, Del, and the day's carnage. Companies can be such bullshit. Man, I feel so cheated. How could I have been so blind? It was all like Don had said — they just use and abuse and only care about the bottom line. Pouring your heart and soul into an organization doesn't matter a wit. For the health of the company, my ass, Abi thought, waiting for the concierge to buzz her in to Del's building. "Damn Fat Cats," she mumbled bitterly, stunned that she had uttered it out loud. Abi quickly glanced around, trying to see if anyone had caught her talking to herself. Phew. Nobody had. Or at least nobody was letting on that they had. Gotta work on that. Studying herself in the mirrored elevator, Abi grinned. She was the bomb tonight. Picking up the pace, she felt empowered and ready to take on the night. I am woman, man. One thing was for certain, Hubris wasn't going to own her and define her. Not anymore it wouldn't. She had played the party line, given Hubris her best, but no more Mister Nice Guy. Hubris could own her apartment, her clothes — hell it could own her mouthguard — but it couldn't own her soul. No company could.

Opening her apartment door, Del swayed, spilling a few drops of what appeared to be her third or fourth glass.

Hmm. Laying it on a little thick, eh? Que sera. She was still in a very delicate place. "Heya," Abi squealed, giving Del a quick hug.

"So are you ready to partee?" Del giggled, handing Abi an already poured glass.

"Mmm. This is good. What is it?" Abi asked, savouring and swilling the vino around her mouth.

"It's actually a cheap local wine. Who knew?" Del replied, full of satisfaction and holding out her bottled bargain find.

Local wine? At least she was learning to curtail. Moving into the living room, Abi couldn't help but note how relaxed and content Del looked. She certainly was putting on a brave and beautiful face. "You're looking so good, babe," she commented. "So calm and together." Sitting down on the pristine sofa, Del smiled tranquilly. "So how's the temping? It sure looks like it's treating you well."

Gently rolling her baby blues, Del kind of wrinkled her nose in mock disdain. "It's getting kind of stale, but at least it's paying *some* of the bills," she quipped. "But it's getting so hard to go out on auditions. I mean, whose call do I take — my talent agency's or my placement agency's? Get back in the game or afford groceries?"

"Ah. One of life's age-old conundrums," Abi joked, trying to keep the mood light but at the same time sympathizing with Del. She had forgotten what a frustrating purgatory temping could be. Despite the façade, Abi knew that both Del's pocketbook and pride must be hurting. And the worst part was that temping never seemed to have an end in sight. "Well, don't sweat it, sweetie. It's not going to last forever," Abi consoled.

"Hellooo? Like I don't know that?" Del responded defensively.

"I know you know that, Del. But sometimes it helps to be

reminded is all," Abi retorted, suddenly feeling like their roles had been reversed. Freaky Friday, man.

"You're right, Abi," Del conceded, getting up to apply her umpteenth coat of lipstick.

"Just hang in there. You've already landed on your feet, and it's only a matter of time before you're back in front of the camera. Did you want your copy of *What Colour Is Your Parachute?* back?" she cajoled, checking her own glossy pout in her trusty compact.

"Ha, ha. I just may," Del smiled, draining her cut glass and setting it on the cherry wood coffee table. "Hopefully it is just a matter of time, but I'll worry about that tomorrow. Right now we gotta get going, or else we're going to be late for the big soiree."

Abi rose quickly and grabbed her matching Vuitton bag. Enviously studying Del's stunning ensemble, Abi realized Del was way too well dressed to be a temp. Abi placed her half-finished wine on the breakfast bar.

"Hey, now. You can't leave that," Del ordered, swooping it up and swallowing it in one gulp.

Way to self-medicate. Maybe work at Hubris isn't so bad after all.

Fake desks. Fake pictures of the fam. Fake computers. Fake files. Fake stairs and doorways leading to nowhere. Peering into one of the cubicles, Abi could've sworn she was back at the office. Man, this is weird. They certainly hadn't forgotten any details. What a neat idea to have a fund-raiser at a TV show set. "Hey, Del. Let's see what's in the desks," Abi said, pulling open one of the drawers and revealing a stack of papers. Shit. They even thought to squirrel stuff away here.

"Babe, I need a drink. Let's head back to the bar and mingle," Del responded, tugging at Abi's sleeve.

Sheesh. She can be such a spoilsport sometimes. Abi headed back to the "lobby" of the "law firm," continuing to admire the television show's set.

"You can be such a star-fucker, man," Del joked, laughing.

Yeah, but at least I have fun, Abi thought. Standing at the bar set up by the reception desk, Del and Abi drank in the view. Hmm. Definitely superb scenery. An hors d'oeuvre plate passed under their noses, and they both gestured "no" as if they had just been offered dog meat.

"If we don't watch our figures, no one else will," Abi quipped, taking a swig from her third glass of wine.

"Right you are, my dear," Del said, raising her glass.

Scanning the room, Abi was happy. It was so nice to be out, especially after the reclusive day she had had. Of course, the wine helped, but so did the high proportion of eligible men. Deciding to be proactive, Abi slipped away to chat with an intellectual type standing near the stairs to the second-floor offices.

"Fascinating, isn't it?" she asked coyly.

"Yes, it is," the tall, dark, and handsome stranger responded.

"I'm Abi," she stated, thrusting out her hand in an oh-so-subtle feminist way.

"Paul. Nice to meet you. Say, great handshake," Paul said, releasing his paw from her grip and caressing his hand.

Hmm. No wedding ring. Very promising. "I bet you say that to all the girls," she answered coquettishly.

He laughed.

Hmm. What to say next? "So what do you do, Paul?" God, that's such a dumb question.

"I'm a researcher at U of T." Looks *and* brains. "What do you do?"

Time for her well-rehearsed spiel. Can't let on I'm only a lowly admin, after all. The trick was to stun them with lots of verbage and pray that they didn't ask too many questions. "I work for a software company. I've been there for several months, and it's been incredible. We're probably about to IPO, so it's definitely been a zany ride," she said, barely stopping to take a breath. Not bad.

"Now that's fascinating. Did you study computers in school?"

Wow. He almost appears enraptured. "Oh, no. I was a history major actually. Hubris more or less found me as opposed to vice versa," she responded casually. The key was also to act coolly confident. That way they assume you know what you're talking about. Looking down at her drink, she was getting dangerously close to requiring a refill. "Listen, I'm going to the bar for a top-up. Do you want anything?" she asked, indicating her half-full glass.

"No, but I can come with you if you'd like," Paul said.

Yup. Things are definitely going well.

An hour later, Del came sauntering up, practically dragging her purse behind her. Uh, oh. Time to cut her off.

"I hate to break up the little love fest, but Abi I really need to get going."

No shit. "Oh, okay. Listen, why don't I meet you over by the coat check. I just want to say good-bye to Paul," Abi said, adopting her big-sister voice.

"Sounds good. I'm Del, by the way," Del slurred, waltzing right past Paul and heading to the front of the set.

"Sorry about that. She had a really harsh day," Abi said, turning to Paul and setting her glass on the bar. She was slurring herself. Thank God I didn't have that sixth glass of vino. Pulling out her wallet, Abi retrieved one of her cards and handed it to Paul. Shit. It said admin assistant on it. Fuck. "I'd love to get together for drinks sometime. Why don't you e-mail me, and we can hook up," she said, completely expecting the gesture to be reciprocated.

"Oh, sure. I'd enjoy that, too. Unfortunately I don't have e-mail, so is a call okay?" Paul joked.

"You don't have e-mail? You must be some sort of social pariah in this day and age," Abi giggled, her statement sounding much more harsh and condescending than she had intended.

Stepping back, Paul looked like he had just been slapped or, at the very least, betrayed. "Yeah, something like that. Why don't I just call you?" he said curtly. She deserved that.

"Sounds good. It was very nice meeting you, Paul. Call me, okay?" Abi said, leaning to give him a chi-chi kiss on the cheek. At least she could always get 'em with sex.

Swaggering through the glitterati over to the coat check, Del was on a mission to get home. Maybe she had finally realized that she had had enough for one night. Either that or her recent budget restrictions were cutting into her fun. Abi was attempting to catch up to her, zigging in and out of the partygoers. Man, she moves fast for a drunk person. Penetrating a thicket of suits, Abi ran smack into a broad chest. What the? Stopping dead in her tracks and peering slowly up the sternum to the face, Abi began to stutter her apology. "Oh, I'm so sorry," she stammered, feeling like an ass.

"Oh my God! Abi, is that you? Abi Somerhaze?" the gent exclaimed.

Stepping back in surprise and carefully studying his face, Abi recognized him, too.

"Steve? H-o-l-y-s-h-i-t! How long has it been? Three, four years?" she asked, blown away. Man, does he look good.

"Yeah, I think that it has," he laughed, infected with her enthusiasm.

"So what are you doing here? What are you up to these days?" Abi prattled.

"Oh, I'm working at a new magazine. You know, personal interest stuff, a little celebrity profiling. That kind of shit. I'm actually covering this for work. Not a bad job if you can get it," he remarked, holding up a flute of bubbly.

"That's for sure," Abi chirped, raising her brow in good-natured disbelief.

"So what are you up to?"

Uh, oh. The dreaded question again. Crap. Too bad Steve hadn't caught her spiel earlier. She had pulled it off flawlessly. "Oh, I, uh, work for a software company," she replied dismissively, shuffling her feet and averting her eyes.

"Still doing the writing and photos, though, I hope," he commented.

Man, that's even worse. Totally busted. "Um, well, the photo and writing thing has kind of taken a back seat. What with work and all. . . ." Abi trailed off, obviously embarrassed. What a lamo excuse.

Suddenly feeling the need to escape, Abi started to look about for Del. Del was standing — barely — near the coat check, struggling with the weight of their summer jackets.

"Listen, if you're interested, we're looking for freelance writers and photographers right now. Nothing permanent yet, but you never know. At the very least, it'd be a great way to pad your portfolio and get a couple of bylines under your belt," Steve proffered.

"Really? That'd be great," Abi beamed. "It could just be the impetus I need."

"Cool. Well, here's my card. Give me a call, and we can talk a little bit more about it," he explained, reaching into his wallet and handing her his card.

"I'll definitely call you. It was great seeing you again, Steve. I feel so bad for doing this, but my friend is about to fall on her face," she said, pointing to Del swaying at the coat check.

"No sweat. Great to see you, too," Steve concurred, leaning over and giving Abi a peck on the cheek.

Continuing over to Del, Abi glanced discreetly down at Steve's card. Cool. My first real lead on a job in journalism. Maybe there is hope yet.

chapter twenty-seven

Rushing down the stairwell, Abi could hear the hoovering. Christ, the super is already up and at 'em. Grasping the railing, she checked her watch. 7:13 a.m. Not too bad. She could make it in at a reasonable time if she really booked it. Fuck. If I wasn't so damn tired. Bursting through the door, she nearly tripped over the vacuum cord.

"Well, someone's late," the super called over the loud hum.

She hated it when people commented on her comings and goings. He was over by the elevators, steeling himself for the day and looking as tired and harried as Abi did.

"Um, not late, just busy," Abi responded curtly, moving toward the door as quickly as possible. Don't people realize that driving yourself is so much sweeter than being driven by The Man? Glancing back at the kind, ageing man, she was immediately sorry for her abruptness. Waving quickly, she tried to buffer her abruptness and atone for her tone. "Have a good one," she called as cheerily as she could muster.

Storming out onto the street, Abi almost didn't see the thick cables snaking their way to the film truck. Almost tripping and dumping her bag, she cursed the fact that she lived in Hollywood North. "Goddamn film crews," she muttered. They were such an annoyance. She almost wished she was in tourist or suburban mode. At least she'd enjoy their presence then. She was sick and tired of them parking their asses on *her* street for a couple of weeks running. Abi hadn't even caught a glimpse of a B-list starlet, much less an L.A. power broker. Stomping past the caravans, she threw a silent hex on them. "Be gone, unionized vermin. Be gone." The

Hollywood magic had definitely worn off.

She was so angry. As soon as she had decided to rededicate herself to writing and photography, some massive fucking project always came up. Always. Josh wanted her to compile hours' worth of research for a document that she knew none of the sales people would read. She'd never get anywhere in journalism at this rate. She wanted to rage, kick her computer, and blow up the joint. She wanted to pull a Jerry Maguire, grab her fish, and go. She looked at the display on her phone. 5:57 p.m. She had dozens of e-mails, and her hunk of junk had frozen up again. "Fucking piece of shit." She swore the damn thing was powered by gerbils. Slamming an innocent file folder against her desk, Abigail leaned down and rebooted. "When are they going to get me a real machine?" She honestly felt like crying. Sure, none of it was that big a deal, she just felt so trapped, so tired, so controlled, so owned, and *so* ready to bolt. She could clean out her desk, get really drunk, and forget this place ever happened. She felt like screaming.

Time for a little Metallica. Tossing the CD in the drive, she opened Outlook — again — and began to send the last of her e-mails. *Hero of the Day*, baby. Lately it was taking every ounce of her being to suppress her true emotions — her rage, her resentment, her resignation. It had been a doozie of a day. It had started off great. First it had been "How would you like to go to a trade show in Amsterdam this September?" Ten days in Amsterdam for a convention? Oh, like *that* would be torture. She had been ecstatic, thinking perhaps that Josh was taking her seriously now and that all her hard work was paying off. Then, in almost the same sentence, Josh had asked the unbelievable. "Do you mind covering reception over lunch?" Like she even had a choice in the matter. It was like being asked to the prom but as a designated driver. All the elation and empowerment she had experienced seconds before evaporated. Almost a year of back-breaking work trying to gain distance between herself and that fucking desk, and it had all been for naught. And now she was tasked with this make-work project. Matching her to-do list with her calendar, she was going to be spread thin. Between the research, prepping for the trade show, and her stellar reception assignment, she was going to be slaving twelve- to thirteen-hour days just to meet her deadlines. No time for working out, no time for socializing, and certainly no time for writing or photography. She should have told them all to shove it, but Hubris clearly had her by the financial balls. Hopping onto the 'Net to begin her research, Abi knew she could kiss her freelance career good-bye.

A little envelope appeared in her mailbox. Great. Probably more work. It was a quick and dirty e-mail from Cass. Just "Wanna go for a drink?" in the subject line. Thank God.

"You are the angel of mercy. I thought you were going to be Josh asking me to take out the garbage or something," Abi quickly typed, hitting send. Abi sat back and waited for Cass's response. Bing. Thank God for fast servers.

"How about swinging by my desk in five minutes?"

"Sounds good to me," Abi punched. Closing her e-mail, Abi began cleaning up her desk. Fuck. She had so much work to do. Enough that it would have to wait until tomorrow. She threw her wallet into her purse and hit the road, not even bothering to shut down her computer.

A typical summer weeknight, and the Jason George was packed. Maybe it was the nice weather, but everyone seemed to have converged on their joint. Sitting on the patio, Abi tried to unwind, but it wasn't working. She was way too pissed off, and there were way too many strangers crowding their haunt. Some assholes were even meeting at *their* table. "They just don't get it, do they? I mean, how can they not realize that we deserve recognition?" Abi implored, swigging back her beer. She lit another cigarette, drawing heavily. Come on, nicotine.

"Nope. And they never will. Why would they?" Cass countered, swirling the wine in her glass.

True enough. Abi slumped back in her chair and watched the traffic go by. "But Hubris seemed like a place where sex didn't matter, where normal gender rules didn't apply. It used to be that you could move up in this joint. Clearly that isn't the case anymore. It's just droves of old boys now trolling the halls, spewing their attitudes like so much contagion," she commented bitterly. "They don't have a modicum of decency when it comes to equality. The discrepancies in pay, bonuses, allowances, and tasks are inexcusable. They don't care if I'm doing it all on my own on an iniquitous salary. They don't care that I've sacrificed the past year just to be plunked right back where I started. To them we're just tits that fax. That's all. Just tits that fax," she continued, her raised voice and her less than ladylike reference to breasts catching the attention of the folks at the neighbouring table. "I thought I could beat them at their own game but apparently not," she quipped, taking another drag of her smoke. Cass listened silently. "I just keep thinking about Don. Remember Don from the course? He had it right, man. You can't buck and fuck the system from the inside out." The sixty-something Tilley woman at the next table raised her eyebrow at Abi in disdain. Sorry for the slip. That's what you get for mistaking this place for a tourist trap, lady. Abi lowered her voice and her head in embarrassment.

"Look, honey. If you want to move up, you're gonna have to move out. Hubris just isn't structured that way. Not anymore," Cass advised, snatching a cigarette from Abi's pack.

"Easy for you to say. You're already leaving," Abi replied.

"Hey, you could be, too," Cass reminded her.

A fire engine from the nearby station screamed down Front street, providing Abi with somewhat of an escape chute. "So how're your plans going, anyway?" Abi asked, trying to deflect attention away from herself.

"Nice segue," Cass laughed, catching her ploy. "Actually they're going really well. I've got two auditions the day after I leave. Not bad, eh?" Cass proudly proclaimed.

"Really? That's amazing. Man, I really admire you, Cass. I wish I had your guts," Abi said, suddenly feeling washed up and pithy.

"You do, Abi. You just have to follow your heart is all. I know you haven't been happy at Hubris for a long time. Sometimes I feel bad for bringing you in there. Truly I do. But you can't let it get to you. If there's something else you want or need to be doing, go for it. You only go around once."

Abi gestured to the waiter to bring another round. "You're right, you're right. I have to say that your leaving has spurred me on, got me thinking about my writing and photography again," she mumbled tentatively, unsure of how much she should reveal. She didn't want to burn any bridges at Hubris, after all.

"That's great. So what are you working on?"

A Heineken and a glass of wine quietly appeared in front of them. Gotta love great service.

"Well, I've been thinking about writing this piece on the homeless," she answered vaguely, trailing off. Ah, fuck it. What has Hubris done for me lately? May as well spill all the beans. "To be honest, I ran into an old friend at that fund-raiser Del and I went to. Turns out he works for a magazine, and he said they may have some work for me. Freelance at first, but you never know where it may lead," she elaborated excitedly.

"That's wonderful, Abi! Why didn't you say anything sooner? It sounds like this could be your big break!" Cass encouraged.

"I know," Abi chortled. It felt good not to have her dreams

shot down. "And I'm even thinking about driving across the States. Maybe hitting Route 66 or something. You know, just me, the road, and my camera. Fucking beautiful way to boost my portfolio. All I need is a car, and then I'm set," she joked, taking another sip of her beer.

"Hey, where there's a will, there's a way. Well, cheers to hittin' the road," Cass congratulated, raising her glass and tapping Abi's bottle.

"Cheers to getting the fuck out of Hubris some day," Abi concurred, smiling at Cass.

Several hefty bills tumbled out of her mail hole. Fucking great. Abi bent down to pick up the treats, ruing the day she had applied for a credit card. She had been tempted, lured, and tranquillized into a false sense of security. And for what? She hadn't achieved anything but substantial debt. She was sick, literally, of giving in to every craving. She had the pounds and debt to prove it. Leafing through the envelopes, Abi leaned back against the mailboxes. How had she gotten herself into this mess? Abi quickly tallied the events of the months prior. A haircut here, a book there, a binge here, a dinner there. I was just living life, man. Still, she needed to start equating loving herself with exercising discipline, saying "no" to herself more often than not. That's what *treating* herself was about — everything in moderation. Jesus, and I used to live by *Walden*. "Just because I can doesn't mean that I should," Abi quipped, sounding eerily like her mother. It had been fun while it had lasted.

chapter twenty-eight

Beep. Beep. Beep. Slam. Raising her eyeshade, Abi couldn't believe that it was already 6 a.m. How could it be 6 a.m.? She had only just gone to sleep. Fuck, I'm tired. Barely rolling over, Abi turned off the alarm and tried to get up. One. Two. Three. Okay. One. Two. Three. This isn't working. Paw traipsed over to her pillow, purring and sniffing her face. "Howdy, Paw," Abi managed, giving the feline a pat on the head. "Mommy's gotta get up," she said, still lying flat on her back. "At least Mommy *should* be getting up."

Slowly pulling off her comforter, Abi felt as if she hadn't slept in days. Complete and utter fatigue. Zero zeal. Finally upright, she knew getting ready was going to be a very long process indeed. Turning on her bedroom light, Abi squinted through the Venetian blinds, hoping for some ray of light. No energizing Vitamin D here. Grey. Mist. No impetus. Leaning on her bureau, Abi tried to conjure up some energy, some drive. I think I can. I think I can. I think I can.

Abi began stumbling to the bathroom, feeling light-headed and dizzy with fatigue. Must shower. Standing before the mirror and studying her saggy, lacklustre countenance, she couldn't believe how shitty she looked. Teeth clenched. Glands swollen. Throat sore. Sinuses filled. Glint gone. Total pallor. Man, the light of day is harsh. Resting on the side of the tub and picturing her morning routine of primping and walking, Abi barely had the energy to review it, much less execute it. She knew it was futile. Attempting to wipe the sleep from her eyes, Abi knew what she had to do. She had to succumb.

Picking up the receiver and deliberately not clearing her throat, Abi dialled Josh's direct line. Looking at the clock on the VCR, at least she could be assured that he wasn't in yet. "Hi Josh, it's Abi," she croaked. "I'm really not feeling well, and I wanted to let you know that I won't be coming in today," she said as pathetically as possible, praying for the sympathy vote. "I think you have my home number, so if you need to reach me don't hesitate to call. Hopefully see you tomorrow." Leaning back against the wall, Abi smiled, instantly feeling better. Hmm, that wasn't so hard. Getting up to take her shower, Abi could feel the tension release from her neck. Nothing like a little truancy to brighten your day.

Riveted to *Rosie,* Abi felt so relaxed, the best she had in months. Hooky was way more fun than she thought it would be. Comfort food, a little personal TLC, actually reading the paper. She felt like such a rebel. Screw Dad and his "I never called in sick in thirty years" bullshit. Abi wanted to *live* her life. Besides, it was a Belgian day. Drizzly, foggy, depressing, forlorn. All this but in a comforting way. Days like these are meant for cocooning — curling up with her coffee, her cat, and *Breakfast at Tiffany's.* It's a day that is designed for solitude and reflection. Abi guessed that it was the pale, overcast lighting and the heaviness of the air. It gave her licence to listen to "Black Coffee," "Fever," and "The Beast" and to gaze out the window wondrously and wonderfully as in some cheesy cappuccino commercial. Black turtleneck and an even blacker cuppa joe. It made her feel like a hep cat, a beatnik with a reason to be disillusioned with the world and all that it doesn't have to offer. Whatever it was, it fit her mood and aura at that moment just dandy. The ferns, birds, and trees, laden with moisture and dampness, seemed to agree and commiserate with her. All the dreariness was not without hope, though. Life was shitty and cold right now, but it was a means to an end. The sun would come out tomorrow.

Turning off the TV, Abi wandered out to the balcony to check the temperature. Hmm. Not too bad. Fall's certainly approaching. Leaning on the railing, chin in her hand, Abi studied the environment around her and inhaled the atmosphere of the rainy Thursday. So apart was she from the frenetic dealings of the day that she felt as if she were watching it reel past her like in an old 35mm movie. Total *Rear Window*. Abi glanced at the cars rushing past her apartment, the occupants probably meeting or mall bound. Abi couldn't help but wonder what their lives were like. Are they happy, or are they just getting by like me? Are they on a mission to purchase a romantic offering for a loved one, or are they simply attempting to placate their depression with an impulse buy of lipstick and lingerie?

Moving over to the end of the balcony, Abi felt surprisingly at peace. Suddenly it dawned on her that she should put the brakes on her obsession with public perception and her public scrutiny. Who the hell cares what everyone else's mundane existence is like? She had her own life, and she had to start dealing with it. Her self-esteem was definitely at an all-time low, but the problem was elevating it. Self-empowerment seemed to be an elusive concept that the junk psychologists had invented exclusively for lost souls such as her. God, they must make a killing from their infomercials, tapes, seminars, and workbooks. Spanking your inner child has become a lucrative business with little thought as to whether or not their quickie solutions and exercises actually produce results. She should know because, care of Del, she'd tried them all. What it came down to is that she couldn't find peace in a CD, DVD, or book. And she certainly wouldn't find it buried in her work. No self-professed psych-guru could aid her or sweatshop placate her. Abi would have to find it in her reflection in the mirror. Not that it was that simple. It wasn't. She still didn't know if she'd ever find inner peace, but she knew she would never find it at Hubris. She knew that it was up to her to discover some sort of contentment with the world, or at least a tolerance of it, that it was up to her to find her own way. She knew she had to write. Staring up at the sky, Abi caught sight of a tiny Cessna scooting across the skyline and trailing a banner behind it. Squinting, Abi could barely make out what it was toting. "Monster.ca. There's a better gig for you," it proclaimed. Of all the fucking banners. How rich.

Traipsing over to her former office, Abi couldn't recall the last time she had produced anything aside from pigeon scratch in her journal. God, it's been ages since I've been here, Abi thought guiltily, marching toward the door to Donut Hut. Approaching the counter, she adopted that we're-not-in-Kansas-anymore look. Neatly printed and stylized signs hawked confections, and glistening new racks displayed them. Sturdy new matching countertops. And they even splurged on new napkins, for God's sake. Eyes darting around the shop, she was amazed. Shit. It *had* been a long time since she had been there. The joint had been completely transformed into an updated and sanitized version of what had been a forlorn and neglected coffee shop. The place was now a slick, franchised replica of an older, disenfranchised, less pretentious time. Banished were the antiquated register and the cracked tile floor. No more gross grout, no more faded colours, no more decrepit holiday decorations dangling from the ceiling. The only items that appeared to have survived unscathed were the wobbly chairs and tables, the cream dispenser, and the tripartite juice fountain. And for them it appeared to be only a matter of time. Abi was shocked and more than a little disgusted. It had been her final bastion against modernization, improvement, homogeneity. It was tantamount to making mac and cheese with Emmentaler. Christ, even *this* place isn't sacred, she thought. The dirt had kinda worked for the joint, adding a certain je ne sais quoi and illustrating character and time similar to striations in a geological formation. Waiting for the proprietress to emerge from the back, Abi noted that they had even managed to dislodge the cruller from the picture window. Man, and I was saving that for later.

The large back wall was in the process of being painted, the final stage in the shop's evolution. A huge drop cloth constructed out of heavy, stiff plastic was draped from the ceiling over all the chairs in the rear, scrunching all the patrons to the front and forcing the Jets to meld with the Sharks. No such thing as nonsmoking, now, suckers.

The woman finally emerged from the kitchen, her old uniform of golf shirt and pants having been replaced by a neat button-down, ball cap, and apron, all sporting "Donut Hut" tidily across them.

If they serve espresso now, I will scream, Abi thought as she was about to order. "Double-double, please," Abi said, scanning the back wall for any signs of an obtrusive Italian machine. Nope. No nonfat frothing here. Thank God.

Comforted by the absence of a cappuccino maker, Abi grabbed her fix and moved toward her spot. At least they couldn't pilfer *that* away from her. The Puzzle Man was back, testing his cognitive abilities, an Oscar Wilde book to his side. Testing the sturdiness of her chair, Abi contemplated how the new spit shine would affect the calibre of clientele, recognizing that this was a clear attempt to eradicate the more unsavoury characters and capitalize literally on the recently well-heeled. There goes the neighbourhood. Satisfied with the chair, Abi sat down sighing. So much for the freak show. Lighting up a smoke, Abi pondered how long it would take before offended Petruchian noses prevented her from this indulgence. Vowing never to return should her office go nonsmoking, Abi took a long haul and began outlining her piece on the homeless.

"Hi Dad. How's it going?" It was the typical call with the parentals.

"Fine, honey. How are you? How was your week?"

Think, Abi, think. Hmm. Better not mention that I skipped work that day. There's gotta be something interesting that happened.

"Okay, I guess. Oh, wait! I almost forgot to tell you guys," Abi said, excited more about the fact she had something new to report than about the sound byte itself. "I might be going to a trade show in Amsterdam," she gloated, leaving out the little detail that she now had to cover reception. What a schmuck. Why do I always do this? I am so one-dimensional, man. She had begun to detest Hubris, but it was always the first topic of conversation for her, her lame little party trick. And with her parents, she was even worse. Work was her connection to them, her source of pride and accomplishment and acceptance. It was too easy to boast about Hubris, to show that she had taken the safe route and touted the traditional line. Too bad she didn't feel as confident about her writing and photography.

"That's fantastic, honey," Dale exclaimed. "You must be doing something right if they're even considering you. Hey, Edith. Abi might be going to Amsterdam for Hubris," he called, obviously cupping his hand over the receiver. "Your mother says congrats. She's in the bath right now, or else she'd get on the phone," he beamed.

Feeling their pride over the phone, Abi had to smile. She had done good. "Oh, and I'm starting a new piece on homelessness, too," she added, figuring she may as well tap into the excitement of her captive audience. "I ran into an old friend who might be able to throw me some freelance work, and the research I've been doing on the homeless would be right up his alley. Pretty cool, eh?" she paused, waiting for his reaction.

"Sure, honey. That sounds good. Just remember not to extend yourself too much. You don't want to burn yourself out or anything, especially if you've got a trade show coming up. I know you tend to take on too much at once."

Crap. Why can't he be just as happy about this? Why does he have to taint this with common sense? She knew that he wasn't discounting her work, that he was being supportive and only wanted the best for his daughter. While she was grateful for his pragmatic advice — it had saved her skin more than once — for once she wished he would buy into her vision, her enthusiasm, and her dream. Couldn't he just appease her? Being an adult sucked.

"Dad, I'm not going to burn myself out. It's just that I've got to start working on my writing again. I mean, I'll never establish myself if I don't get out there and give it my all. I'm trying to be smart about this by working *and* doing the journalism thing," she continued passionately, trying to placate his practical side while emoting her sense of urgency.

"I know, honey, and I admire you for it. It's just that I get concerned about you taking it all on at once. Just one step at a time, honey."

Well, he did have a point. She did have a tendency to flit off willy-nilly. She loathed hearing the voice of reason sometimes.

"I gotta run now, Dad. Tell Mom I love her, and I love you, too," she said, suddenly dying to get off the phone.

"Love you, too, Abi. Don't work too hard," Dale said.

Hanging up the phone, Abi burst into tears. Why was everyone so keen on Hubris and not on her writing and photography? All she ever heard from people were words of caution when it came to pursuing journalism. "It's a tough field to break into."

"Only the best make it, you know." "Make sure you get the rent paid." From Del to her parents, it was always about taking the safe, responsible route and, in the process, dismissing the passion that lay beneath. Sure, she had to make sure that she could eat, and she had to proceed logically, but didn't they take her dream seriously? Didn't they think that she could do it? Didn't they believe that she had the talent?

Walking into the bathroom and turning on the taps for a bath, Abi knew that she had to believe in herself and prove to the world that she could do it, that she wouldn't be another Don and relinquish her dreams for someone else's. She was not going to be another cog in the Machine. She was going to make it even if she died trying. She was Mary Richards.

The phone rang again, pissing Abi off to no end. Why did it always have to ring when she least wanted it to? This better be good, man. "Hello?" Abi said curtly, clearly perturbed. Dabbing her eyes, she hoped that her voice didn't give away her current state. She just didn't want to get into it.

"Abi?" a feeble voice cracked.

"Del? Is that you?" Abi asked, putting her own emotions aside.

"Yes," Del barely managed, beginning to sob.

"Sweetie, what's wrong?" Abi said, incredulous, a rising concern in her voice. This had to be something massive. Del *never* lost it. Hell, she barely wavered after being canned. Of the two of them, she was supposed to be the rock. "Where are you?" Abi gently asked, turning off the taps and attempting to obtain the basics.

More weeping. Verging on hysterical, Del sounded like crap. "Um. I'm at St. Mike's."

What? "St. Mike's? What are you doing there? Are you hurt? Are you alone? Do you need me to come down?" Abi rattled off the questions in rapid-fire succession, every horrible scenario racing through her mind. Car accident? Death of a family member? Hangnail?

"I'm okay. Or at least I think I'm going to be," Del sniffled, gaining some composure.

"Well, what happened?" Abi cried, impatience and alarm evident in her tone.

"I, uh, God, this is so embarrassing," Del bawled, quickly unravelling.

Fuck. This is getting frustrating. Patience, baby, patience. "Shh," Abi consoled. "Take your time. Take your time. It can't be all that bad," Abi encouraged. Intermittent sobs. "Why don't I come down there, and you can explain everything to me then? If you want to talk about it, that is. Whatever you want," Abi said, leaning over and gathering her wallet and keys on the coffee table, knowing that some things are just easier to explain in person.

"I'd like that. God, Abi, I'm such a fool. . . ." Del trailed off, obviously embarrassed and beginning to cry again.

"Del, the absolute last thing you are is a fool. Sit tight and don't worry about anything. I'll be there in a jiffy. Are you in emerg?" Abi gently asked, pulling on her jacket.

"Yeah," Del croaked feebly.

"I'll be there before you know it," Abi assured, hanging up the phone and quickly shaking her head in disbelief. Racing out the door, Abi was totally confused and completely weirded out. Dependable Del was in dire straits. For the first time, Abi was the one doing the saving and consoling. What a bizarre role reversal. Reaching street level and hailing a taxi, Abi hoped that she could be the selfless and sagacious amie that Del had been to her. Hopping into the first chariot, Abi was grateful she had enough money to take a cab.

Whoosh. The doors slid open, audibly breaking the hermetic seal. Her eyes frantically scanning the waiting room, Abi detected the distinct odours of death and disinfectant. Humming fluorescent lights illuminated the sanitized, stackable, green plastic chairs, reflecting off the mint gloss walls and grey waxed floors, casting a shadowy, sickly pallor over the countenances of the patients and highlighting their pain and grief. Racks of medical literature hung disorderly on the walls, the clear plastic holders clouded with age. From *Chatelaine* to *Reader's Digest*, antiquated magazines and periodicals were strewn about the coffee tables, offering bored and desperate souls a momentary reprieve. A Styrofoam cup lay on its side, with old, cold coffee oozing from its lip. In a dim corner, a middle-aged woman gripped the frail hand of an octogenarian slumped over in a hospital wheelchair, her face drawn and stricken and searching her elder's eyes for some glint of hope. Across the room, a young woman sat quietly next to her beau, her head resting lightly on his shoulder, and gently favoured her right, swollen wrist. A few seats over, a concerned father cradled his feverish son, feeling the chubby toddler's temple with the back of his hand and silently signalling to his wife that the worst was over. Not a word was being spoken.

Closing her nostrils and winding through the chairs and low tables, Abi manoeuvred her way to the reception desk and rang the bell. A stout woman, replete in standard greens, appeared from behind the row of grey metal filing cabinets. She obviously did not want to be there. "Yes," Nurse Nonchalant inquired with disdain.

"Yes, a friend of mine is supposed to be here. Del Lopeil?" Abi responded in a calm tone, attempting to placate the marm. Kill her with kindness. Perfunctorily punching at her keyboard, Nurse Nonchalant remained reticent. Come on. What's the verdict?

"Yup, she's here," she finally instructed, pointing to the seating area.

"Um. Is there any way I can see her?" Abi practically pleaded. "She called me, and she's very upset."

"One moment," Nurse Nonchalant sighed, rising from her seat and giving Abi the evil eye.

Closing her eyes and yawning, Abi just wanted to know what the hell was going on, that Del was okay. Returning to the desk, Nurse Nonchalant motioned for Abi to follow her. Quietly opening the door, Abi was somewhat relieved. Momentarily she'd have the facts. Her shoes squeaking on the linoleum, Abi forced herself to slow down and keep pace with the plodding nurse. Slow and steady. Empty gurneys and IV stands eerily littered the hallway. Stocked medical trays stood ready for any emergency. Hushed voices lilted from one of the curtained examining areas. Stopping abruptly in front of it, Nurse Nonchalant discreetly pulled one side across and peeked in. "There's a visitor here for Del Lopeil," she said.

"Okay. Let them in," a male voice practically boomed.

Pulling her head back out, Nurse Nonchalant stepped aside and let Abi move into the examining area.

"Thank you," Abi said, but Nurse Nonchalant was already gonzo.

Del was propped upright, a paper-thin, washcloth-sized blankie covering her slender legs and barely revealing her strappy sandals. Her manicured hands neatly folded on her lap, she looked more like she was calmly enduring her annual as opposed to some life-threatening crisis. Her mascara barely smudged, she smiled weakly at Abi, her years of being on camera having trained her to keep up appearances. Christ. Even in her moment of grief, she looks stunning.

"Hey there," Abi comforted, moving around the equipment and reaching for her hand. "How're you doin'?"

Fluttering her lashes, Del fought to respond. "Okay," she murmured sleepily, rolling her head over on the standard-issue foam pillow. "I'm a little cold, though," she mumbled, tugging weakly at the flannel.

"So what happened?" Abi implored, helping to pull the blanket farther up her chest.

A tear rolled down Del's cheek. "I OD'd on Midol," she answered, closing her eyes and laughing out of embarrassment.

What? Who the fuck tries to commit suicide on over-the-counter PMS medication?

"What? Why?" Abi asked, beside herself. "What happened?"

"Oh, it was so awful, Abi. I went to pick up the most darling satchel in Holt's. Oh. You should have seen it," she recounted dreamily. "It was the prettiest pink and matched my Versace dress perfectly. I just wanted something nice. I mean, something to pick me up. But I didn't have the cash for it," she babbled.

What? She OD'd on PMS medication over the failure to accessorize properly? "Okay. Go on," Abi encouraged, trying not to look too shocked.

"And so I —" sniff. "And so I —" sniff. Come on. Spit it out. "And so I tried to put it on my Holt's card," she blubbered, suddenly racked with sobs. "And they cut up my card. Right in front of me. Right in front of *everybody*," she bawled. Oh my. "It was so embarrassing, Abi. I wanted to disappear. Right in front of *everybody*. And I know people recognized me, too. I just wanted to die," she cried helplessly, gripping Abi's arm and searching Abi's eyes for some understanding and assurance. "I mean, here I am, this, this arbiter of style who's supposed to tempt and convince housewives that they too can have beautiful things for just nickels a day, and I can't even afford to buy a fucking handbag," Del stuttered in a low voice, conscious of the doctor's presence and eyeing him suspiciously.

Yeah. It was pretty ironic. "Who cares what they think, Del?" Abi implored, knowing full well that a Momism was not going to wash. It was going to take way more to mollify her.

Lying back on the gurney in a fragile little heap, Del was beginning to look pale and puffy in a striking sort of way. Sitting on the edge of the bed, Abi had never had to feel sympathy for Del before. But this was different. For Abi, being denied credit was a fact of daily life, something to sheepishly laugh about and discount. But not for Del. Del had never known strife. She had never known struggle. She had never known rejection. And Abi knew that this was the worst thing that had ever happened to her. At least Abi could use such experiences and unabashedly ply them into life stories. But Del had no such use for grist. In Del's world of four easy payments, the price tag for such an indignity was dejection and despair. Del was now a faltering fashionista, someone to be pitied and ostracized, knocked off the A-list and isolated for fear of spreading the dreaded fever and contaminating the cappuccino. The poor and unaccessorized cannot be trusted, after all. And it would be the not-so-subtle whispers of judgement in the salons of society that would be the toughest aspect to endure for Del. She had never been betrayed and banished before.

"Shhh. It's going to be okay. You're all right," Abi hushed, patting Del's forearm. "We're going to get through this."

The doctor silently leaned over and placed a blood pressure cuff on Del's arm, pumping and monitoring the gauge.

"Oh, Abi. I don't know how you do it. I mean, you're so focused. I've always been so envious of your strength," she said, looking wide-eyed and fragile.

Envious? Of me? "Pshaw. You're the one with strength and focus. I mean, who's the one who has dusted me off time and again? The one who got me off my ass and encouraged me?" Abi insisted, trying to provoke a smile from her friend. "Fuck, you're my personal Laker Girl."

Removing the cuff from Del's arm, the doc shot Abi a look. Mental note — do not utter expletives in the presence of medical professionals. Fucking Curse Police.

"Dr. Harris to Trauma. Dr. Harris to Trauma."

"Excuse me," the doctor stated unapologetically, fixing his stethoscope and placing the cuff on the metal table. He speaks. The doc disappeared behind the curtain, shooting Abi another look for good measure on his way out.

"Thank God he's gone," Del sighed, obviously very relieved. "I mean, what if he leaks this to the press?" she whispered suspiciously.

Some people will never learn. "He can't. Doctor-patient privilege," Abi reminded her.

"Anyway, what I was trying to say is that you've got so much passion, Abi. Such a raison d'être. Nothing stops you. And me? I fucking breakdown at the sight of split ends," she continued.

"Unstoppable? If anyone is unstoppable, it's you, Del," Abi replied, incredulous. This is turning into quite the mutual masturbation session.

"What are you talking about? You're the one with brains and ambition, Abi. Not me. I am so jealous of that," Del confessed, wiping a tear from her cheek.

Abi was in shock. She had had no idea that Del viewed her that way. "What? You of all people don't have a reason to be jealous of me. I look up to you for everything," Abi said. "Besides, I couldn't have done anything without you, Del. Anyone who has put up with my whining and has gotten me to read umpteen self-help books deserves a medal," she exaggerated, maternally tucking the hair behind one of Del's delicate ears. What's a little white lie to placate a friend? Besides, it was mostly true. Sure, Del could be annoying and cloying in her quest to proselytize and assist Abi, but it wasn't her fault, and it certainly wasn't done out of malice. She just didn't know of any other way. And despite their disparate approaches to life, Del had indeed been a good friend who had helped her. God knows she had certainly provided a stellar example of gumption and guts. But now it was Abi's turn to be the rock, her opportunity to impart her knowledge and wisdom. Of course, Abi couldn't think of anything sagacious to say, but she'd give it her all. She owed Del at least that.

"You're a good person, Del. On *and* off the camera. No matter what happens or what anyone says about you, always remember that," Abi counselled, sounding more and more maternal. Del's eyes began to fill with tears, and she turned her face to the wall. Way to go. Make her cry even more, man. "You're strong, you're beautiful, and who gives a shit if you can't buy the latest handbag? Kate Spade is way overrated anyway," she comforted, trying to quell the tears. Silence punctuated by sniffling. Man, I suck at this. "Look, you're going to be okay. I'll help you get through this — I promise. It's not the end of the world." God, how trite do I sound? Sniffling heaved into sobs. Great going, Abi. Crisis intervention was clearly not her forte. "But in the meantime, are we going to sit here all night while you try to finagle Clooney's number, or are we going to get you to bed, where you belong?" Abi asked, trying to elicit a more positive response. When in doubt, try humour.

"Ha, ha. Maybe if I were fifty years old and blind. The man's repulsive," Del smiled weakly, her tears slowing and the colour finally beginning to return to her cheeks. At least she still had her faculties.

Suddenly the curtain pulled all the way across, and Doctor Harris stomped in. What? Were his ears burning or something? "Miss Lopeil," he began, holding his clipboard across his chest as if he were Moses holding the Commandments.

"It's Ms., actually," Del corrected, suddenly sitting primly upright.

Yup. She still has fire. The gal is going to be fine.

"Excuse me. *Ms.* Lopeil, we'd like to keep you here for observation purposes. Is that okay? You'll be able to rest comfortably, and you'll be released by the afternoon," he continued, pulling a wheelchair up to the gurney and indicating for her to sit down.

Sounds more like an order than a request.

"Um. Okay, I guess," Del responded, looking relieved at the prospect of finally catching some Zs.

"Fine, then. We'll take you over to Admitting and get your paperwork filled out."

Man, he has to work on his bedside manner. "Ha, ha. You have to eat hospital food," Abi taunted, helping Del down into the chair. "That'll learn you for scaring the shit out of me," she said. Another look o' death from Doctor Harris. Crap. Now she'd really have to wash her mouth out.

"Thanks for the support, Abi," Del retorted wearily. Sitting patiently in the wheelchair, Del was resigned. The institutional lighting was casting shadows under her eyes and bleaching out her golden tresses. She looked so timid and weak, so unlike Del.

Watching Del wheel out into Admitting, Abi tried to absorb and duly process what had just transpired. Holy weirdorama. Who'd have guessed that she'd ever wind up consoling Del? Walking back past the waiting area, Abi felt strangely content about it all. In an ugly, startling way, this had been a good thing. The Midol Incident had been one amazing revelation, and any petty envy she had harboured against Del had disappeared as a result. As much as she hated to admit it, Abi was relieved to know that Del, unshakeable, unflappable, and pedantic Del, was not above reproach, that her über friend suffered from the same anxieties and shortcomings that she did. For so long, she had lusted after Del's life, using her own as a harsh measuring stick, but now Abi knew that the grass was not so verdant and charmed on the other side of the tax bracket. All of her own worries and jealousies had been for naught. She was not an incompetent, bankrupt freak after all.

More importantly, their little mutual admiration fest had been incredibly enlightening. Abi had never realized that Del held her in such high regard, that, just as she viewed Del as a glowing, unattainable example, Del had put her on her own pedestal. Seeing her now, Abi realized that Del was a good egg who just wanted to help. She hadn't meant any harm by her pestering and cautionary words, and she hadn't tried to rub her good fortune in Abi's face, as Abi had mistakenly suspected. She was just a good friend who recognized and respected Abi's work.

Hailing a cab, Abi felt at peace and empowered, as if she had just begun to unravel one of the mysteries of the universe. Not only had she begun to finally figure out Del, but she had also received a tiny confirmation that she was indeed on the right path. Thank you, Midol.

fall

chapter twenty-nine

Autumn air. Lingering dew. Glistening sidewalks. Verdant lawns. Turning leaves. Sparrows chirp. Pigeons strut. Sit on park bench. May as well take five. Sip coffee. Peruse paper. Smile as summer clings on. Check watch. Won't be long before all the green is gone. Time for work. Weave through parents and strollers. Crying toddlers. Not quite ready for daycare. Doting mothers. Not quite ready to let go. Wade through bus stop. Giddy gaggle. First day of school. Brand new backpacks. Mint outfit. Spanking white sneaks. Friends gossip. Siblings tease. Bullies posture. Girls flirt. Boys pretend not to notice. Toss the sack lunch. Play monkey-in-the-middle. Hide-and-go-seek. Walk on by. Smile and reminisce. Head down street. Drift by elementary school. Stand and pause. Schoolyard full. Jungle gym swarmed. Tetherballs fly. Screams and yells. Reunions and riots. Basketball and tag. Peek in classroom. Tabula rasa. Teacher's up front. Anxious for a fresh start. Crisply marked desks. Name tags all set. Hope they're ready for their ABCs. Blackboards and bulletin boards. Erasers and chalk. Paste and art supplies. Mobiles and games. Innocence and bliss. Oh, to be in school again. New notebooks. New pencil cases. New pens. New highlighters. New lockers. New projects. New uniforms. Time to knuckle down. Homeroom. PE. Recess. Show and tell. What did you do for summer vacation? Hall monitors and principals. Lunch ladies and milk money. Mystery meat Mondays. Taco Tuesdays. Macaroni Wednesdays. Grilled cheese Thursdays. Fish stick Fridays. Trade ya these carrots for that Twinkie. Afternoons are a drag. No more nap times. Just social studies and math. Can't wait to be released at 3 p.m. Homework assignments and try-outs. Band practice and play rehearsals. Anything is possible. School bell rings. Damn. So much promise. So many possibilities. I'm going to be a doctor. I want to be a fireman. I want to be a teacher. Does anybody want to be an admin? Start walking again. Summer is over. A new year has begun.

chapter thirty

The world had been completely wired, but now it was short-circuiting. The money flowed freely at first. Farmers were everywhere, spreading seed and watching their profits grow. But the NASDAQ stalled; a few start-ups failed, analysts balked, and bankers were canned. The purse strings tightened, and the days of living high and dry were definitely over. It was boo.com that started it all off. Spent some $120 million of other people's money and still wasn't able to make anyone afraid enough to buy. No one was buying it anymore, especially the workers who had made it all possible.

The mass exodus had begun. Those with any ounce of entrepreneurship and a mind of their own had packed their bags and begun to hit the road. They simply didn't believe in the material anymore. The product had begun to be managed and had been transformed from their baby into some sort of corporate tagline. And the endless spin and spiel had become so tiresome. Don't piss on my leg and call it rain, man. The company wasn't half as good as it used to be; at least from an innovative standpoint it wasn't. At this point, they actually began to return calls from the smarmy headhunters, who had been annoying butts of jokes only a few short months before. They knew that they didn't need to take the shit being doled out to them. They knew that they could waltz through the lobby and within twenty-four hours have negotiated a far more lucrative deal with far more lucrative perks. There had to be a better life on the outside. Besides, it was only a matter of time before they were gobbled up.

chapter thirty-one

Rounding the corner of her office building, Abi was about to coax the heavy glass doors open when she noticed him. An elderly man, obviously trying to ward off the crisp back-to-school air, had nestled himself in the warmth of the vestibule. A soiled rucksack and an empty Listerine bottle appeared to be his only possessions. She had seen him before, staggering and babbling incoherently on the sidewalk outside the office building. What his story was, she did not know. Gently opening the door so as not to wake him, she was overwhelmed by the stench of urine and body odour. The Listerine obviously wasn't for hygienic purposes. Abi was at once repulsed and sympathetic. "God, I hate this city," she said, tiptoeing by him. Pressing the elevator button, she was perspiring and already close to tears. Clearly today would be no different from the hundreds that had preceded it. "I can't do this anymore," she gasped under her breath.

As the elevator approached the 14th floor, Abi seriously debated heading straight back home to bed. Feeling another tantrum coming on, Abi beelined for the ladies', bursting into tears as soon as she reached its safety. Throwing down her bag on the counter and sobbing, Abi hadn't even thought to check for evidence of any other occupants. Sliding her back down the wall, Abi clenched her teeth and gave in to it all, weeping uncontrollably.

"Abi? Is that you?"

Shit. Why now? Why today?

"Um, yes," she said, reaching up to the dispenser and quickly dabbing her eyes with some raspy paper towel. Looking down at the bag next to the door, she knew it was Cass.

The toilet flushed and the stall door swung open, and, continuing to cry, Abi braced herself for the inevitable. "Oh, my God. Are you okay?" Cass rushed over to where Abi was sitting, kneeling down to eye level.

"Oh, Cass. Thank God it's you and not someone from HR. They'd probably have me call the EAP line or something crazy like that. It's just . . . I can't do this anymore, Cass. It's not me," she blurted, beginning to sob violently. Cass, always the good listener, patiently waited for Abi to regain some modicum of composure. "And now that you're leaving, who am I going to rail with? Who am I going to vent to about reception duties, bad salaries, and catering to The Man? At least you understand what I'm going through.

"I mean, we're like a bunch of Okies, like sharecroppers of this, this, this fucking New Economy. Working for The Man and all disgruntled and shit. We've got this support system going on, ya know, this kinda union. Us admins versus the, the, the pundits of power and privilege," Abi stammered, flailing her hands in despair. "Swapping job-site tips, agency names, scathing e-mails. It was the only thing that was keeping me semistable here, and now it's gonna be gone. What am I going to do now?" she pleaded, praying that Cass would have some magical response.

"I just don't know what to do. I have to leave, I know I do, but I can't let everyone down like that," she bawled. "I mean, what would Josh say — hell, what would my parents say — if I said I was quitting? I mean, I have nothing to fall back on, nothing to go to. All I know is that I want to travel, to write, to do my photo thing. God, how pathetic is that?" The tears were coming more slowly now, and rational thinking was beginning to take root. Abi sniffled.

"Look, you've got to do what you need to do. Do you think these guys are this loyal to *you*? You have to follow your heart. And if that means hitting the road, then fine. Just take care of you first," Cass said, handing Abi another wad of Kleenex.

"Yeah, you're right," Abi said, sniffling slightly. "It's just going to be tough telling Dale and Edith," Abi blurted, finally cracking a smile. Cass laughed and gave her a you're-gonna-be-okay-kid kind of slap on the back.

Getting up, Abi was feeling better. It's amazing what a good cry can do for the soul. "Oh, I can cover reception today," Abi said, dabbing her nose and trying to cover the puffy red blotches on her face. "The show must go on. Those meetings are such a bore anyway. It's just a room full of egos and futile, circular debates. I'd rather surf the 'Net. Guess having tits that fax does have its advantages. Thanks for listening, Cass."

Leaning over, Cass gave her a quick squeeze on the shoulder. "Anytime, Abi. Just take care of you," Cassie repeated, heading out the door.

Red Dawn. HR and Goliath suits everywhere. Abi was in shock. Sure, the water cooler gab had focused on the impending acquisition, but no one, not even her, had believed that it would actually come to this. It had all seemed like a surreal game, like some reality TV show, with everyone pitching conspiracy theories and positing strategies, creating key alliances and burning bad bridges. Would Hubris IPO? Would it get more financing? Would it be bought? Any and all closed doors brought a new wave of suspicion, tipping off endless debates over drinks. Naturally she had been booking Josh's meetings with Goliath and knew how dire things were, but she could never let on, knowing how sensitive the deal was. She was too much of an NDA scaredy-cat for that, and, more importantly, she would never betray Josh's confidence. Instead, Abi had simply revelled in the drama of it, giggling and playing along as if they were discussing a prime-time soap. Like everyone else, she had been hoping for her snow day, gleefully anticipating that school closure bulletin, but she had never thought that the blizzard would actually hit or what course the storm would take. It had all seemed like harmless gossip, nothing worth even mentioning outside the office, but she had obviously been way off base.

Abi sat back, a strange sense of betrayal settling over her. Goliath Pix had bought Hubris. Those bastards. Parks had actually caved. All those evenings and weekends. Constantly pushing the envelope. All that work for naught. Abi looked around at the programmers. They must be feeling even worse. They had all been slaving 'round the clock to build the company, carving their niche, buying into the bullshit that if they acted big time they'd actually become big time. And for what? To be swallowed up like a dinky guppy. They hadn't meant shit after all. "I want my time back," she felt like screeching.

"Abi, can I talk to you?" Josh tapped her on the shoulder, sending a wave of fear through her core.

"Um, sure, Josh," she responded, fixing her collar and figuring that her neck was on the line. May as well make the job as easy for them as possible. A hush had fallen over the office; not a word was being spoken. Josh was marching ahead of her, refusing to look her squarely in the eye. Fuck. It's coming. Don't let the door hit ya where the good Lord split ya. Following him into his office, Abi instinctively closed the door. Do not cry. Do not cry. Take it like a man, babycakes. It's going to be okay. They're just a bunch of twats anyway.

Abi stood at the door expectantly, waiting for Josh to say something, anything. This is just too much, man. Josh sat down and indicated for her to do the same. Slumped in his chair, he was ashen and dishevelled and looked like he hadn't slept in weeks. No wonder he had been so reserved lately.

"Well, Abi, I'm sure you're aware that Goliath's management is in this morning, and I just wanted to discuss it with you and go over any questions you may have," he calmly said, a look of legitimate concern in his eyes. Man, why does he have to go all paternal and nice? Tears began to well up once again, and Josh leaned over and handed her a box of tissues. "As you know, the merger with Goliath has been in the works for months, and late last evening we succeeded in inking the deal. Considering the resulting redundancies and the fact that they already have a Toronto office, this unfortunately includes restructuring." Restructuring? Nice. There goes rent. "As a result, we will be laying off a large number of individuals today. I know that this will be very difficult for you, and I wanted to give you a head's up," Josh continued. Great. Here it comes. Time to dodge the HR peeps. "As for myself, considering the fact that the Goliath sales team, especially at the senior level, is already mobilized and has considerably more experience in our target markets, I will be remaining on during the transition, and, once everything has been handed off, I will be resigning," he explained hoarsely, clearing his throat in a manly sort of way and wearily leaning his forearms on his desk.

She'd never survive the interregnum. This was just way too much. Abi grabbed some tissues, wadding them up and dabbing her eyes and cheeks. Damn sandpaper. Couldn't they have sprung for the shit with lotion in it?

"Before you panic, I have made the recommendation that you remain on board — if you wish to, that is — as part of the Goliath sales support team. The offices would remain right here, so there'd be no relocation involved. There's a place for you at Goliath if you want it, Abi. Goliath is a huge company, and you could go far in it. This could be a massive opportunity for you if you wish to take it," he reasoned, leaning back and attempting to gauge her reaction.

Super. So I can work for some monolithic corporation. Yeah. Getting lost in the bureaucracy could be a *really* fun ride.

"Of course, if you choose not to stay, there'd be a buyout package offered. Not much, but at least a month or two's salary. I tried to get you more, but unfortunately Goliath is very stringent about these things. They have to offer the same packages across the board, you realize. And, of course, if you ever need a letter of reference, I'd be more than happy to provide one," he said, fighting hard to maintain his own façade and looking sincere.

Studying his hollow cheeks and dark circles, Abi realized that this was just as hard on him. In fact, probably harder. He had built the sales team, after all, and had made Hubris pretty enough to be purchased. That could not be a warm, fuzzy feeling. No wonder he looked like shit. Thank God I never made it to management.

She nodded in understanding, giving her nose an almighty honk. Great. So now I have a decision to make. Abi had thought that she would be ecstatic about having her snow day, her reprieve. But it was all so bittersweet, like praying for flurries and receiving a debilitating six feet of snow. The company that had nearly given her a nervous breakdown was now gone. Poof. Gonzo. No weather warnings, just a cursory mention of precip. Abi sat back, taking a deep, cleansing breath. "Um, okay. I guess I'll have to think about it. I mean, I wasn't really anticipating all this. Is it okay if I sleep on it?" she asked meekly.

"Of course, Abi. No one expects you to make such a huge decision on the spot. Take all the time you need," Josh replied. "Talk to your parents, talk to me, talk to your friends. Do whatever you need to do. Just consider it carefully, and do what's right for you," he encouraged.

Aw, crap. Why did he have to go and mention Dale and Edith? Her parents would be over the moon about Goliath. They would be so incredibly proud to have her slave for such a sexy beast.

Abi pushed her chair back, attempting to process all the info and reconcile her feelings. "So what are you going to do?" she asked, still dumbfounded that Josh was actually leaving. Josh bail-ing on Hubris was tantamount to some ugly-ass rock star ditching a supermodel. What the hell is he going to do with all that time on his hands, with any time on his hands? Paint decoys? Maybe take up a little macramé? Picturing Josh delving into the world of taxidermy, Abi laughed silently to herself.

"Well, I've got a few prospects lined up, but other than that I'm just going to take it easy. It's been a pretty wild couple of years. Looking forward to getting some R & R," he said, reclining back and finally smiling. "Mia and I are probably heading down to Azores for a time, maybe even do a little trekking in Africa."

Abi could see the tension drain from his face and shoulders. Spotting the Frommer's guide peeking out from his laptop case, Abi flushed with envy. Lucky bastard. With his options and package, he could afford to ponder his next move.

Ruminating in the lobby of doom, Abi couldn't help but engage in a little self-appraisal. She couldn't believe that she had been crying about leaving just that morning, but she hadn't thought a decision would come so soon. Now that she had been given a choice of freedom, she didn't know what to do. Should she stay or should she go? Reflecting over the past year, she knew she was a fake, a phoney. Truth was, she deserved Goliath less than Goliath deserved her. She had been rendered completely ineffectual, rarely having so much as a brain fart, much less a brain dump. She was constantly stressed out, constantly feeling on the verge of a meltdown, constantly feeling like the race had been rigged. She detested how she now lashed out at her innocent coworkers and became violent with that uncooperative mouse at her fingertips. Being bitchy didn't suit her, and she was so tired of apologizing and justifying her behaviour. Super Temp was long gone, that was for certain. She had officially become a loose cannon. She was in the wrong line of work.

Compulsively pressing the elevator button over and over again,

Abi just wanted to leave it all behind. She was tired of not feeling good enough, like she had so much to learn, like she had missed the starting gun. She had been bombarded with so much information that her thinking processes were completely garbled. Newspapers, industry magazines, *Ahead of the Curve*, Gartner reports, press releases. There were too many cattle in the pen. But boot camp had done its duty. She had no idea who she was anymore. All she knew was that she had become completely one-dimensional, devoid of all identity. She had eradicated everything that made her her. Had erased all that truly mattered and supplanted it with superficial shit. The last thing that she wanted to talk about was work, yet it was all she found herself discussing with friends and family. She loathed hearing herself speak. She sounded so damned pretentious and overbearing. The elevator finally arrived, and Abi got on, relieved that she was going down. She had actually believed that, if she had acted the part, she'd become the part. See and be it. But she was a dilettante, and she couldn't do it anymore. She was too fucking exhausted. Crossing the street, Abi knew that, whatever Hubris had started, Goliath would certainly finish.

Stomping up Sherbourne to Queen, Abi realized that Cass was totally right. It's my life, dammit. For so long, she had let Hubris own it, steal it, abuse it, take it for its own. But no fucking more. She could sidle in and play charades at Goliath or get the fuck out of Dodge and reclaim her life. It was completely up to her. Sure, she could get really drunk and wallow like she had for the past year. Or she could take control and right her wrongs by writing her ass off. Write her own ticket, literally and figuratively. She controlled her life, and she wouldn't let Hubris or Goliath or any company get the better of her anymore. Abi began strolling confidently up Sherbourne, chin up, shoulders back, and grin on her face. Yup. I might just make it after all.

chapter thirty-two

Walking down King West, Abi came to the intersection and waited for the light to change. She looked across and saw it — The Trough. For the first time in nearly a decade, she was setting foot in it. She remembered The Trough as the place where they served underagers. She recalled a joint where pickled eggs stood proudly on the bar, a watering hole where veterans and bums parlayed their pensions into beer and rye. Welfare cheques and pitchers of beer, snaggle-toothed gents trying to get a grope and whores slapping their hands away in a coquettish faux defence, war heroes and real men. A jukebox and a few tattered pool tables and weathered wooden benches. Abi chuckled, recalling the time that Roy, the toothless sixty-something bus"boy," had tried to get her and Del to dirty dance with him like he was their Fabio or something. Luckily they had been underage and way too drunk to be seriously offended by his advances. And even more fortunately, they had come away from the experience without so much as a topical rash. Ah, to be young and foolish again.

When Del had told her about its grand reopening, Abi had jumped at the chance to try to revisit her youth. Scurrying up to the door in anticipation, she wondered if it had stood the test of time. A bouncer was cordially welcoming customers, as long as they had invitations. Abi reached into her pocket, produced her ticket to ride and was less than graciously permitted entrance. As soon as she heaved the door open, she wished that she hadn't.

Déjà vu. First her office, now her former haunt. The new and improved Trough. What a crock. She was incredulous at the transformation. The seedy hole in the wall had been morphed into a trendy dive, refurbished and reopened as so-called shabby chic. The ageing hookers and cads were long gone, having been replaced with new rakes and social X-rays. Coasters and napkins adorned the polished bar. And they were actually being used. Imports were displayed proudly, showcased like relics between mirrors and glass. Glossy tables and sleek, black decor. Industrial chic. No peanuts or stale pretzels here, only Japanese mix and canapés. The staff all looked young, rested, and healthy. All of them had a full set of cosmetically straightened teeth. No true drunks, just frat boys out to score. You can never go back, and it's best if you don't try, Abi thought.

Abi scoped the crowd, hoping to spot Del. Man, it's just past midnight, and the place is packed. Craning her head over the herd of coifs, she bet The Trough hadn't seen this much business in the last year, let alone the last quarter. Media and advertising types were three deep at the bar, their petite, fake-baked girlfriends waiting patiently at the cosy tables that lined the rear of the bar. A shooter girl in a Hooter's-style halter waltzed by Abi toward a group of hotties to Abi's immediate left. A shooter girl? Jesus, I never thought I'd see a jiggly, giggly young 'un hawking her wares here. How pitiful yet poignant. Oh well. May as well get a free drink. She devised her game plan and made a run for it.

"*Abigail!* I was wondering where you were. Have you gotten a drink yet?" Del popped beside her, looking puzzled at her empty hand. Naturally she had a drink already. She had certainly recovered from her Midol Rebellion quickly.

How the hell does she always manage to get served so fast? Must be the five inches she had on Abi. Easy visibility is always a plus.

"Sorry, I was running a bit late. I *tried* to get a beer earlier, but it is every man for himself in there," Abi said, indicating the bar.

"I figured I'd wait until the bimbo came round again and order from her. I can't believe this place, man," Abi said, still stunned.

"Yeah, I know. Great, isn't it?" Del replied.

Man, she doesn't have a clue. Abi began to explain what The Trough had been, what it meant to her, but, realizing that it would all be lost on Del, she stopped herself. It wasn't worth it. Not here, not now. Besides, the jazz was way too loud.

Del held her hands up in front of her face, framing Abi with her fingers. "I see the Prada window, darling."

Abi smiled knowingly. What a knob. She was wearing one of her mother's hand-me-downs. Thank God Mom took care of her clothes. "Actually, it's Jaeger, darling," she retorted.

"Well, you mustn't *tell* people that — it looks like Chanel. Speaking of which, have you popped by Tangerine recently? Their fall collection is to *die* for."

Abi shook her head. Some things never change. "Nope. Haven't had an opportunity yet. Suppose there's always *next* season." Abi looked longingly at the bar, trying to think of something more intelligent than wardrobe to discuss. Nope. Zero. Zilch. Nada.

"Oh, hey. There's Frankie. You must meet Frankie." She pulled Abi over to a young woman who was standing near the bar.

Abi didn't care who Frankie was, just as long as Frankie could produce a beverage. The service was crap. Christ, I almost miss that toothless busboy.

"Abigail, this is Frankie. Frankie, Abigail. Frankie is the proprietor of this wonderful establishment," Del stated with enthusiasm, spreading her arms out as if she were the mistress of all she surveyed.

Really? Maybe she can get me a fucking drink. "Really? That's wonderful," Abi said, pumping Frankie's hand with her infamous vise grip. "The place looks great," she said, motioning her hands around the room. "I remember coming here in my university days, and, well, um, it doesn't look a thing like it used to." Shit. Abi hoped that she didn't give away her disdain. The last thing she wanted to do was offend the woman who controlled *all* the booze in the joint.

"Uh, thanks." Frankie did the shoe glance and looked back up at the room, avoiding any eye contact. "Yeah, well, I figured it was time to spruce the place up a bit. Ya know, engage in a little 'keep up with the restaurateurs.' My dad wasn't too crazy about it, but, hey, you gotta roll with the times in this town. Change or die." Frankie did the glass glance, as if studying the swirling contents. "I keep telling him he would be a lot more disappointed if the place languished into extinction. But no, he's a stubborn old fool. Thinks that some things never go out of fashion." Frankie's eyes flitted about the room, finally settling back on Abi and Del. She took a deep breath, as if lost in thought. "Oh, geez. Do you want a drink? For a bar owner, I can be such a shitty hostess."

Abi smiled and nodded. "That'd be great. Red wine. Cabernet sauvignon, if you have it," Abi cordially replied. Well, it's about time. She felt better knowing that she'd have un peu du vin in un moment.

As Frankie made her way behind the bar, Abi followed her with her gaze. She couldn't help but wonder what Frankie's deal was. She couldn't be much older than Abi, obviously successful and attractive. And all of this was hers, too. The girl had it goin' on. Yet here, on the night of her brilliantly attended grand opening, she seemed defensive and looked as if she were about to cry. Weird, man. Just plain weird. Catching sight of a *NOW* magazine photog, Abi inconspicuously checked out his equipment. Christ, if I could switch places with Frankie, I'd be right in there, lapping up all the media attention I could muster. Abi tried to cut her some slack. Maybe the girl's just camera shy.

Frankie rejoined their enclave, much-anticipated glasses in hand. Abi assumed the role of investigative journalist. "So tell me, how'd you wind up running this place?" Christ. Abi sounded as if she was interrogating her. Backpedal, backpedal. "Um. It's just that you seem so young to be a restaurateur." Abi looked at Frankie, who was now smiling sweetly, as if remembering a lost lover. That seemed to suffice.

"It's a family business, actually."

Abi's interest was piqued. Family business, eh? Family business like the mob family business? Or family business like a Mom and Pop family business?

Frankie continued, as if detecting Abi's silent questions. "My grandfather built it in the '30s, and it's been a neighbourhood fixture ever since. After his death in 1970, my dad ran it until a couple of years ago. He's got heart trouble and decided to pass the reins over to me early."

Okay. So Mom and Pop kind of family business. Cool. At least some ethnocentric multinational didn't own a piece of the pie. Abi took another lap of vino. She was all ears now. "That's awesome. So weren't you terrified to take this place over? I mean, it's got so much history encapsulated within its walls. The responsibility must be tremendous." Uh, oh. Must've said the wrong thing. Frankie's face had clouded over, the sweet smile having been replaced with pursed, tense lips. Crap. She hated it when she stuck her foot in her yap. Jump in any time, Del. Really. Any time.

"But the mantle couldn't have rested on more capable and perfectly structured shoulders. You've made such a tremendous success of it, darling," Del cooed, giving Frankie a delicate, chi-chi peck on the cheek.

Thank you, Del. Nice touch about the shoulders, by the way. Abi was relieved until she noticed Del's comment hadn't quite placated Frankie.

"I'm sorry," Frankie said, taking a giant swig. "It's just that Dad hasn't shown up yet."

What the hell do you say to that?

"I'm sure he's just caught in traffic or something," Del assured.

Great. Steal my words of comfort, why don't you?

Suddenly a head thrust itself between them, as if disjointed from its owner. This could not be good. All Abi could make out in the darkness was a heaving, hacking head of hair with horrible roots. The spastically offending noggin, apparently belonging to a young woman, opened its spastically offending mouth to pour its contents over the newly polished parquet. What a twisted game of show and tell, Abi thought. Why dontcha eat something next time?

"Jesus," Frankie exclaimed. "I am so sorry. Gus, can we get this girl out of here? And she's cut off, way off, by the way."

Frankie ran to the bar to grab a J-cloth, leaving Del and Abi to view the intoxicated rack being supported by two other racks, her furry little arms wrapping easily around their petite, bony wing-backs. Abi wanted to thank her for breaking up their lil' tête à tête but thought better of it.

The young woman who had projected so much only moments before was now practically lying on the floor, barely being supported by her equally drunk cohorts. One was using the sleeve of her jet-black Holt's jacket to mop up her pouty, pale lips. Abi felt nauseous just watching them. As she calmly inspected the spray on her shoes, she felt a bump from behind. Fuck. Not another vomit comet. Abi looked up, about to yell. At first all she saw was a clean uniform and thin build. Some young buck pumped up on 'roids. Her eyes moved up the chest, past the tidy collar, and finally rested on the face. She immediately turned albino. Gus had arrived to haul the girl away. Gus. Gus from the shelter. Geez. Of all the joints, of all the drunken altercations, Gus had to walk into this one. He looked so different here, away from the unflatteringly lit

Sunday School room and in a freshly pressed uniform. He looked proud and filled with purpose. Instantly Abi knew that facing her past wasn't going to be fun.

"Gus! How're you doing?" Abi shuffled her feet and prayed he wouldn't be too pissed at her for not dropping by the shelter for a final good-bye.

"A little busy here. But I guess you know all about that." He looked ticked, but she knew deep down that he wouldn't hold it against her. His eyes and kind countenance were too forgiving for that. Besides, they had spent too many hours piecing together dull puzzles such as their lives to let something like this come between them. Time to bite the bullet and recite the mea culpa.

"Look, Gus, I'm really sorry about just ditching you guys like that, but you know how it is. Time got away from me, and before I knew it the program was over for the season. I had no idea how to track you down. If I had known you worked here, I woulda dropped by sooner, you know that," Abi said, pleading to his sensibilities.

Gus regained his grip on the girl, who had begun to slump farther to the floor. A pack of Exports fell out of his breast pocket, and Abi picked them up and handed them over.

"I only mentioned The Trough a few dozen times," he responded. Man, no such thing as getting off easy. "But I guess what I spouted about wasn't important enough to you."

Check. I deserved that. So much for being a keen and observant journalist. The purger was slumping farther, and Gus leaned down and threw her arm up over his shoulder. Raising his torso up, he lifted her clear off the floor. Now that's leverage.

"I can't discuss this now," he yelled over the music, shifting the limp body over his other shoulder. "But you know where to find me." He hesitated and then moved toward her, as if to give her a hug. Abi, remembering who accompanied him, stepped back, almost straight into a gaggle of girls. Gus got the gist and hauled out, pretending that he had never intended to invade her personal space. He disappeared into the crowd, rakes clattering behind, and Abi's gaze followed him as he made his way back through the crowd toward the front of the bar, toward the fresh air. She felt as if she had just been slapped.

"You *know* that guy? Who was he?" Del inquired, as if asking if Abi had been infected by the plague.

Abi shook her head in betrayal, realizing that she was still in a busy bar. The incident seemed to have occurred in a void, a surreal shot sequence. "Oh, no one. Just someone I knew from before," Abi quietly responded. Nice response, Judas.

Del handed her a smoke and lit it for her.

"Ah. He's just a bouncer," she said, waving Gus off. "For a second there, I thought he was actually going to *hug* you. You know I would have had to step in at that point." Abi shot her a look, and, sensing that she had overstepped her boundaries, Del now had to do a little spinning. "What you need, my girl, is another drink." Del grasped her hand and led her to the taps.

Abi didn't protest and followed her obediently. She knew Del wouldn't understand. It was better to just play along with her. God, I feel like such an asshole. When in Rome.

"Hey, isn't that your friend Justin?" Del asked, swaying a little bit and wagging her finger across the bar.

Abi looked over, squinting in the general direction of Del's index finger. Damn dim lighting. "Holy shit, it *is* Justin," Abi shrieked, flinging her hands up and spilling her wine all over the back of some jacket. Abi froze, waiting for the gent's response. Nada. Not so much as a twitch. Ah, what he doesn't know won't hurt him. Abi handed her glass to Del and shoved her way through the crowd to Justin.

"Of all the places, my man," she guffawed, tugging his sleeve and impulsively giving him a smooch on the cheek.

"Abi, how the hell are you doing? I just got in this evening, and these guys dragged me out here," he said, indicating his two very manly-in-a-GQ-kinda-way friends. Hmm. They look pretty ripe for the picking, she thought. "I was going to call you tomorrow, see if you wanted to get together for brunch or something," Justin explained, putting his arm around her. It felt good to be held by a man, even if he was just a friend.

"Oh, that's okay. That's just fine. I know you don't have much time for lil' ol' moi," Abi gibed, realizing that she was actually grinning for the first time that day.

"Ha, ha, little Miss Guilt Trip. Seriously, though, how have you been doing? What's new? Between both our schedules, I barely know what's going on in your world these days," he asked, peering down at her face.

"Oh, well, you know. Life's comme ci, comme ça," she responded, shaking her paw in front of him. "Suffice it to say I no longer work at Hubris," she continued with glee. Man, this is so good. She wasn't going to have to drink and dial tonight. She could drop the bomb on him right here, right now, while she was still slightly sober.

"What do you mean? What happened? What are you going to do?" Justin interrogated, standing back in surprise.

"Justin, please don't grill me about this, not here anyway," Abi implored, praying that he wouldn't give her the third degree. The DJ had started up again, and the music was pumping at full tilt. "Hubris was bought by Goliath," she shouted.

"What?"

Fuck. "Hubris was bought by Goliath!" she repeated, trying desperately to compete with the bass. "They offered me a job, but I've decided not to take it. I've decided to go back to writing," she yelled, hoping she wouldn't have to repeat her spiel.

"Well, I guess that's great news, then," Justin's voice boomed over the bass. Thank God. She knew he'd understand. "Listen, you want to blow this pop stand?" Justin asked, setting down his drink on the speaker next to him.

"Sure, I could use some fresh air," Abi said, taking another puff of her smoke. "Let me just find Del, and we'll be outta here." Abi began walking back toward Del, who was deeply ensconced in a profound conversation with a fellow fashionista.

"Oh, you must check out the new line from Isaac. Positively *to die for*," Del drawled.

Hmm. This looks pretty serious. Maybe I should come back later. Screw it. She talked pret à porter in her sleep. "Um, Del? Justin and I," Abi began, trying to get Del's undivided attention. "Del?" she repeated loudly, tugging at Del's smooth-as-a-baby's-butt arm. Del pulled her arm away, obviously under the impression that it was an unwelcome suitor. "Del, Justin and I are heading out for some fresh air," she yelled.

Del, finally realizing that the person next to her was actually someone she wanted to speak to, turned slightly to face Abi. "Hi, sweetie. This is Tish. Tish, Abi," she introduced.

"Hi Tish, nice to meet you." This was getting ridiculous. "Del, listen. Justin and I are going to bail. You know, catch some fresh air and catch up on things," Abi explained, praying that she would be released soon.

"Someone's going to get laid," Del taunted, draping a congratulatory arm across Abi's shoulders.

"You know it's not like that with Justin," Abi quickly corrected, smiling nevertheless. "Are you going to be okay here by yourself?" Dumb question but one a good friend always has to ask.

"Sure, honey. Call me tomorrow, and don't do anything I would do," Del joked.

"I won't, promise. Nice meeting you, Tish." Yeah, like Tish

even said two words. "I'll call you in the morning."

"Not too early," Del called after her.

Walking back to Justin, Abi spotted Gus. "Gus," she yelled, busting through the crowd. She had to apologize to him for everything. She had been acting like such a dink for a few months, and she really owed it to him. Shit! She could make him the subject of her piece, a sort of tribute to his integrity and honesty. If anyone deserved to be featured, it was Gus. Her mind was suddenly whirling with possibilities for the treatise — his life as a small-business owner, his love for his kids, his life on the streets, his struggle to survive. It was all so incredible, all so poignant and illuminating. She knew she had to get his story out there. It was the only way people would understand the trials of the human condition. "Gus!" she cried, struggling for her voice to be heard over the stereo. Fuckin' loud-ass Top Forty crap. "Gus! Hold on a sec."

Abi raced over, trying to catch him before he nipped into the stock room. "Gus, listen. I've got to apologize. I am so sorry for everything. I wasn't paying attention. I admit it. But you gotta know that I wasn't being myself, that I'm not normally like this. Please take my word for it," she begged, scanning his face for some sort of reaction and hoping that his judgement wouldn't be that harsh. Gus stood there, silent. Say something, anything. Man, he's a hard man to win back over. "Look, if you just give me another shot. I'm not some prissy-ass chick from the 'burbs, I promise," she continued, giving her best Girl Scout salute.

Gus leaned back and smiled. Success at last. "I know you're not, Abi. Just hurt is all. Thought we were pals, and then you ditched me. And God knows I've had way too many people bail on me in my lifetime," he replied.

"Thank you, Gus. I hoped you'd understand. Listen, if you don't mind, I'm writing a piece on people who have been homeless, and I'd like you to be my first subject. You've led such an amazing life, have overcome so much, and I'd love the chance for people to hear your story," she said.

Gus cocked his head to one side, stunned and giving it a good think. Please don't say no. "Well, Abi, I'd really have to think about it."

Damn, it's going to be a long road back for me. "I completely understand. Can I call you? Maybe we could grab lunch or something? You got a piece of paper?" she asked, looking around for something to write on.

Grabbing a book of matches, Gus jotted down his number and handed it to her. "Give me a call on Monday, and we'll talk."

She was thrilled. She knew she'd have to work hard to gain his trust, but he was so worth it. She was finally getting back to her.

"You're going to adore this place. Best eggs in town. Consider this an early brunch," Justin joked, practically pushing her toward the door. Justin, ever the escort, had convinced her that what she needed was not her bed but a good, decent start to the day. The breakfast of champions.

As she opened the door, the din of diners and the sizzle of artery-hardening bacon made Abi dream of Route 66 again. She immediately fell in love with the joint. Now *this* is a true diner. A diner with well-heeled, chi-chi, drunk patrons but a true diner nonetheless. Low counter dividing the dining area from the open-air kitchen, stainless steel back splashes and buffed Formica as far as the eye could see. Christ, they don't even produce this linoleum anymore. The smell was amazing, and Abi, thoroughly intoxicated, couldn't wait to get her hands on a trucker's breakfast. She wanted the whole deal — fried eggs, buttered toast, bacon, and sausage. Calories don't count here.

It was well past two, and the place was packed, almost as packed as The Garden. This was way better than Chinese, though.

Justin whisked by her, darting directly for the back. Drunkenly obedient, she trotted behind him like some sort of Boss groupie. They fell into a booth for two, sliding across the padded, plastic seats.

Immediately on their heels was their gracious waitress, Mandy. "Just so you know, you can't smoke back here," Mandy stated deadpan. Okay. So I'll save another chunk of my lungs. Justin and Abi stared blankly and shrugged in submission. "You want menus, then?" They nodded. Mandy reached down to her belt, whipped out a tattered, moist J-cloth, and gruffly glanced at the table, slapping down two laminated menus when she was satisfied with a job well done. She stalked away, not even considering to offer the pair water. Abi half expected her to belt out "Kiss my grits!" and she began to giggle.

Abi looked over at the line cooks, who were slaving away behind the modest counter. She was gripped with the need to create a culinary delight. After spending so much time eating at greasy spoons, she wanted to cook at one. At least once in her life. Courage in a bottle, man. Mandy returned, and Abi tried to be as sweet as pie, knowing that with Mandy in her corner she'd succeed in getting in front of that griddle. Work it, girl, work it. "Mandy — it is Mandy, isn't it?" Mandy stood back, street smart and sceptical. "I was wondering if I could fry my own egg," Abi stated, gesturing to the open kitchen. "I mean, just one little egg. I'll pay extra. It's just that I've *always* wanted to cook at a proper griddle — it would be a dream come true, really, " Abi pleaded.

Mandy sighed, and Justin tried not to look embarrassed. "I can't let you do that. You'll have to talk to the owner."

Abi was steadfast. "Where can I find him or her?"

Mandy indicated the front of the restaurant, pointing to a diminutive woman standing behind the register.

Abi was fully bolstered. The proprietress looked like Mom.

Easy peasy. Like swiping candy from a baby.

Parlaying her strength into politeness, Abi sauntered and swayed up to the front. She was on a mission and would not concede defeat. "Hi. My name's Abi," she said shyly, with an expression she knew could not be denied. "I was wondering if I could fry my own egg — you'd be making a childhood dream come true," she continued, firmly but softly playing to the woman's maternal instincts. Her slightly slurred speech was barely audible above the clatter and chatter. She looked coquettishly down at her feet and then back up, making eye contact with the owner. "I'll buy my own egg," she quickly and more adamantly added.

The woman was shaking her head. "I'm sorry, I just can't let you do that."

Okay. So she hasn't gotten my point. "Please, please, *pleeaasse.* This really means a lot to me," Abi begged, almost stomping her foot down in protest.

Sensing her despair and realizing that this was one drunk who wouldn't relinquish, the woman gave in to Abi's request. "Okay, but just one egg. And you have to pay extra for it. Follow me. I'll have Travis give you a lesson," she replied, smiling and shaking her head.

Abi had prevailed. Tonight she was the victor.

The owner flung open the hinged counter and set Abi free behind the bar. Woohoo! She was behind the bar! Abi did a little victory dance and traipsed up to Travis, awaiting her introduction. "Travis, this is Abi. Could you show her how to fry an egg on the griddle?" Travis, put off by the interruption in his beat, glared at her like she was one spun, condescending chick. Abi simply grinned back at him, hoping to alleviate his fears.

"Don't worry, I'm a quick study. I'll be outta your hair in no time." Abi pulled on an apron and anxiously awaited her tutorial.

Abi scanned the room, attempting to get Justin's attention. He finally glanced up from the menu, and she followed his gaze from the washroom doors to the griddle. His eyes finally resting on Abi, he looked as if he had just seen the Virgin Mary in a piece of French toast. He was incredulous and obviously impressed. Abi gave him the big thumbs up. She contemplated sticking her tongue out, but she figured she better not push her luck. She rubbed her hands together, as if preparing for the challenge of a lifetime. Come on, come on. Let's get this show on the road, baby.

After completing a grand slam, Travis turned his attention to Abi, looking like a seventeen-year-old who's just been asked to mind his bratty little sis.

"Okay, Master. Show me how the big boys do it," Abi cooed. Abi detected a faint blush, and her lesson commenced. Flattery will get you everywhere.

Grabbing an egg from the dozens perched on the shelf, he handed it to her and began to guide her through the process. Suddenly Abi was gripped with performance anxiety. She sucked at breakfast food — what if I fuck up after all this fanfare? I'd look like a right twat then. Deep breath. Travis handed her a bowl, and she took the leap of faith, whacking the little white shell against the rim. No wussy-tapping for this gal. Like a surgeon, Abi accepted the fork into the palm of her hand and began her delicate operation. Shit. A bit of shell. Oh, well, it won't hurt none. Julia Childs she was not.

Whisking away, she realized that all eyes were on her. Smile and nod. Just pretend like I do this all the time. Satisfied that the crap was beaten out of the egg, Abi stopped and wondered where Travis had gone. He was down at the end of the kitchen, unwrapping some fresh bacon. Work with me, Travis. "Uh. Travis? I need some help here."

Travis rushed back, fearing that she would deign to take on the griddle solo. "Okay. So here's what you do," Travis instructed, demonstrating how to pour the egg onto the griddle.

The yellowy-white goo screamed in protest as she poured it onto the searing surface. She diligently followed his instructions, and, voilà, she was frying her egg. She was the Iron Chef. One more thing to cross off life's to-do list.

Plating up her din-dins, Abi sidled over to their booth, looking like the cat that had just eaten the canary. "Nice cookin', Tex," Justin laughed, reaching for a napkin and wiping some egg off his lip. "So tell me about this piece you're writing. It sounds fascinating."

"Well, I'm kinda keeping it under wraps for right now, but I can say that it's about the homeless in T.O. I guess I just want to give a face to it all, you know. Create portraits of some of the men and women I've met through the program, really demonstrate to people that just 'cause someone's on the street or in a rough spot doesn't mean that they belong there, that they deserve to be there," Abi replied, snapping off a cold piece of toast. "I mean, everyone has this perception that the street kids and homeless are all on drugs or are drunks, that they're irresponsible wastes. Guess I just want to help dispel that," she elucidated.

"Well, I have no doubt that it'll be a smashing success. I'm so proud of you for making this decision, Abi. I know that it couldn't have been easy to make," Justin lauded, raising his glass of pop up in a toast. "Just promise me that I'll be the first to read it, kay?"

What a guy. "Of course," Abi promised, clinking her glass against his. Now if only she could get him to tell her parents.

Satiated, Justin and Abi exited the diner triumphant. Justin's lactose intolerance appeared to have held off, and Abi had managed to burn herself only once. Their stomachs full, they had sobered up to the point of being semicoherent and intelligible.

Fatigue was descending. It was now 2:45 a.m., and the witching hour was drawing near. "Listen, I'm going to a friend's place down the street. You okay to get home on your own?" Justin inquired, his slur barely noticeable now.

"Pffft. You know me, I'll be a-okay," Abi responded, her own slur slightly more pronounced.

"Call you tomorrow. You go, girl," Justin smiled and waved and staggered west down the avenue.

Alone on the sidewalk, Abi couldn't help but feel empty. Sure, she was self-sufficient, but she was tired of not having someone to escort her home. Fuck it. She was fine on her own. Abi looked right, then left, hoping to see a taxi. A few stragglers whizzed down College but not a single sign of a suitable chariot. Finally a solitary light appeared on the horizon. Hope. Abi stepped up to the curb and, with a commanding gesture befitting a gung-ho trooper, hailed her ride. The green and orange sedan quickly pulled up; slightly grazing the curb as it docked in front of her. Toronto, we have lift off.

Relaxing in the somewhat comfortable confines of the cab, Abi laid her hand on her belly, rubbing it gently. Christ, I'm full. She'd definitely have to stop at Rabba for some R-E-L-I-E-F. Justin had been right, though, the eggs were amazing. Coasting down College, the cab hit the streetcar rails and lurched sideways. Christ. Where do these guys get their licences? She leaned forward to try to read the taxi info in the plastic holder on the headrest in front. Curse myopia, man. The car lurched again, and she fell back into her seat. This guy was definitely trying to kill her. May as well take the hint, though, and sit back and enjoy the ride.

She looked out the window and began to succumb to the nocturne. The streetscape whirled by, partially due to speed but primarily due to alcohol. Reviewing the evening, she was relieved and pleased that it had all ended so well. The night had started off so poorly — revisiting The Trough and initially encountering Gus. She had feared the entire evening would be doomed. But then she had hooked up with Justin. Man, I had a blast with him. And making it behind the diner counter was definitely a notch in her bedpost. But the real coup, the true root of her relief, was making amends with Gus. She was just so glad he had forgiven her and over the moon that he was willing to chat with her. Thinking about her piece, Abi couldn't wait to get started on it.

The cab screeched to a halt, tapping the bumper of the car in front. "I should have taken the streetcar," Abi muttered to herself. Slumping back, Abi continued her critique. The Trough had changed so much. She couldn't help but wonder if gentrification always felt this horrible to those in the know. On the one hand, it was a fabulous opportunity to salvage a treasure. But on the other, it meant compromise, and compromise usually entailed selling out. Sell yourself to save your soul. Is gentrification a pursuit of preservation or a derivation of greed? Abi mused. It was all so Darwinian, really. Evolve or die. As they continued past storefront after storefront, all Abi could think was that it sucked royally. In a world governed by revenues and profits, history was not revered or construed as sacred.

The cab hung a wide left onto Yonge, and her bag rolled off the seat, a victim of the cabbie's erratic driving. The car barely slowed to correct itself, and Abi noticed a solitary panhandler near the entrance to the College Street station. Her digestion continued. Why had she been such a schmuck about Gus? About the mission? She was so ashamed that she hadn't reached out to Gus earlier, that she hadn't stood up for herself and her beliefs when confronted by Del. She had sheepishly conformed and to what end? In order to maintain her faux glam image? To be accepted as one of them? She reeled at her own lack of integrity and selfishness. "Mental note — be yourself *always,*" she mumbled to herself as she reached for her purse, spilling its contents on the grimy floor.

Practically kneeling on the floor, Abi reached under the front seat to retrieve a toonie. Holding the coin, Abi thought again of Frankie. Now she understood why Frankie had been so queer and self-conscious. Frankie had sold out. Abi couldn't help but feel sorry for her for being torn between her duty to herself, to her business, and to her father. Frankie had been forced into an unenviable position by the changing times, and Abi related to her all too well. After all, if you try to please all people all the time, you wind up pleasing no one none of the time. The important thing was to be true to yourself and your goals and to attempt not to compromise both. At least I'm not the only vanquished one out there, Abi thought. And at least I can try to write my wrongs.

Nearing home, Abi was filled with a sense of relief. In recognizing her own failings, Abi was suddenly able to place the entire evening into context. Getting her wallet ready for the payout, she was able to put her finger on it. It wasn't the grease in her stomach that was making her queasy. It wasn't her encounters with Frankie, The Trough, and Gus that had marred the night and left her with an unsettled aversion to life in the city. It was her own stupidity and carelessness that was giving her heartburn. Like a Whit Stillman, an Altman, or, worse, a John Hughes, the shot sequence had been a parable for the manner in which she was presently conducting her life. She had sold out. In her pursuit of power and privilege, she had been foolishly tilting at windmills. She had corrupted herself to the point of being unrecognizable. She had come to this city with honest intentions and under the guise that her personal and professional lives should be integrated, that there shouldn't be such a strict differentiation between them, and that one should be empowered by passion, not pecuniary advance and obligation. Every time she had entered Hubris, every time she had engaged in polite conversation at a cocktail party, every time she had longed for those to-die-for Steve Madden shoes on Bloor West, her judgement had been eclipsed and her compass jammed. The events of the past year melded together into a kooky kaleidoscope, fracturing her soul and distorting her view of the world and its pleasures. How could she have deviated so much? How could she have permitted it to happen? She wanted to hurl. Grasping the holy shit bar over the door, she steeled herself and vowed to regain her composure. She needed to reconcile her beliefs and values with her past, present, and future and purge herself of all her misconceptions and misguided notions. She must recommit herself and give photojournalism all she had. In the morning, that is. Right now she had to focus on getting smokes, Diet Pepsi, and some alcohol-induced sleep.

The cab turned the corner onto Isabella, barely missing a pedestrian. The driver was going just a tad too fast for Abi's liking. Abi was about to command him to let her off outside Rabba, as was her custom, when the swirling red lights near the end of her street caught her eye.

"What the hell is going on down there?" Abi uttered aloud.

"I don't know, miss."

That was a rhetorical question, ya dumb ass. "Take me down there. It looks like it's my building."

Now the cabbie couldn't go fast enough. Come on, come on. He attempted to snake through the traffic but came to a dead end. She could see the police lines draped straight across to the intersection of Sherbourne and Isabella. One. Two. Three. Four squad cars and an ambulance. Shit, this must be big.

"The street's blocked, miss. I can't go any further."

Fine. "I can walk the rest of the way." Abi looked at the damage. Ten bucks? What a rip. She handed the driver twelve and hopped out of the car as quickly as she could. God, I'm such an ambulance chaser. Why does this always have to happen when I don't have my camera on me?

A crowd had gathered along the yellow tape, and Abi struggled to get through, craning her neck to catch some of the action. She couldn't tell, but it looked as if they were in her lobby. She began to push more forcefully. "Excuse me, pardon me." Goddamn rubberneckers. I need to get in there, dammit. Okay. Enough with the niceties.

Abi shoved past a woman in her housecoat. "Sorry, but I live in that building," she called back apologetically. Cool carte blanche. Abi marched up to the entrance, traipsing defiantly by several officers. One caught her by the arm, and she swung around.

"Ma'am, you can't go in there — it's a crime scene."

Abi yanked her arm back. Ma'am? God, I hate that. "Yeah, but I live here. How am I supposed to get into my apartment?" She smiled sweetly at him, praying that her feminine wiles would work their magic.

"Sorry, you'll have to wait at least another hour. By then you'll probably be able to use the back entrance."

Shit. May as well play nice. At this point, it was 3 a.m., and she was too tired to put up a fuss.

"So what happened anyway?" Abi looked up at the cop, hoping to at least get the inside scoop.

The officer shrugged, as if this kind of thing happened all the time. "Superintendent killed some homeless kid. Nearly tore his head clean off with a shovel. That's why we're keeping everyone at such a distance. It's a very disturbing scene. No motive yet. The perp just keeps muttering about how he should have stayed in Guelph."

What? Abi couldn't believe what she had just heard. She had figured it was some vice takedown that had gone wrong. Junkies or prostitutes or something. But that nice old man? The chipper man who gave her little presents each and every holiday? The man who had helped her move her fridge? She couldn't believe that such a kind, caring man could be capable of such violence. She couldn't believe that he was now a perp.

Abi had to try to see how he was doing. She moved away from the clump of blue toward the other side of the building. Climbing over the railing of the yard, she wove through her fellow residents and closed in on the entrance. Looking through the lobby windows, Abi saw the boy's body, congealed pools of deep purple spreading from the hood of his jacket across the floor. Abi thought she was going to vomit. Last time she would drink tequila and visit a homicide scene. A member of the 51 Division spotted her and ushered her back, trying to shield her view.

Abi moved silently back toward the squad cars. In the darkness, she focused on the one with the most activity around it. There he was. The super was sitting in the back of the cruiser, handcuffed and broken, his wife sobbing by his side. Even in the darkness, she could see the blood splattered across his shirt and speckled on his cheek. His hair was tousled, and the vein in his forehead was pulsing furiously. She could see that he was trying to sit proudly as his wife burrowed her head into his lap, but it was clear how overwrought and remorseful he was. An officer, the tall one she had spoken with, opened the driver's-side door and gestured to the others. It was time to haul the super away. Put the animal behind bars, where he belongs. The engine started, and the sick, loud parade began its descent downtown. As the squad car pulled away, siren blaring, all Abi could see was a grief-stricken and fragile man and his hysterical wife. Sirens wailing in the distance, Abi attempted to absorb everything. God, I have to get out of this town. But she knew she never would. It was a part of her now. Besides, nobody had a good first year in the city.

Watching the crowd disperse, Abi scrutinized the bizarre tableau and mentally tried to capture it, knowing that all the quirks and quarks of her environment only supplemented her existence. Perfection is predictable and such a bore. Lighting a smoke, she headed down Isabella to her old office for her morning fix.

Entering the coffee shop and heading straight for the phones, Abi knew she had one call to make before picking up that jolt of heaven. Picking up the scuffed receiver, Abi carefully wiped it with her sleeve. God knows where it's been. Digging through her purse for a quarter, Abi was coming up blind. Shit. Abi looked out at the street, watching the stream of cabs cruise by. Fuck. I must've dumped *all* of my change back in the damn cab. Standing in front of the pay phone, Abi peered out into the darkness in the direction of her building, at a loss as to what to do. She couldn't go back there. Not yet anyway. Gotta wait until the ME declares death. Knowing public servants, God knows when that would be. Glancing over at the woman behind the counter, she debated asking the server for some change but thought the better of it. She looked way too pissed off, tired, and disgruntled to be charitable. Abi set her bag down and stared at the phone, tapping indecisively on the metal box. Checking her watch, she confirmed it was way late. Her parents would not be impressed. But she knew she had to make the call. If there was a time for a little 1-800-COLLECT, it was certainly now. She had to come clean and tell them her plans. Taking a deep breath, Abi hit the metal hang-up and took the plunge. Pressing zero, Abi hung her head, knowing that it was going to be one helluva 911 for Dale and Edith. Waiting for the pickup, she just hoped they'd understand.

A Toronto-based writer and photographer, Pamela Westoby was raised abroad by corporate gypsies and lured back to Canada by the smell of poutine and a scholarship to the University of Western Ontario. A Girl Friday by day and student of pop culture by night, Pamela has sought to capture the glitz, glam, and grit of the metropolis and to truthfully document the kitsch and camp of Americana. A lover of Heineken and all things Hello Kitty, purveyor of pageants and pizza, Pamela aspires to become a pageant judge and professional bowler.